S.E.NETHERY

HEAVY
LOAD

To all those Australians who served
during the Vietnam War

and

In memory of my cousin Fiona

Chapter 1

Yowie Bay, Sydney, 2005

IT WAS DAWN when I was woken by the shrill laugh of a kookaburra on my deck. Its cries echoed around Yowie Bay and soon it was joined by an answering chorus of its mates across the water.

It was my favourite way to wake up. Probably always will be.

I still remember that Friday in 2005 like it was yesterday, just like I can still recall what I was doing the day John Lennon died. I had no earthly reason to believe that day would be different from any other, but it was. That was the day I met Tim Finnegan.

As a recovering alcoholic myself, Tim wasn't the first person I had tried to help overcome their drinking problem, and I can tell you he certainly won't be the last. Tim reminded me so much of myself at the worst of my boozing: aggressive, confused, broken and very lonely. Ultimately, it was me sharing my life story with him that sowed the seed in his mind as to the real problem behind his boozing, and more importantly, how to solve it, how to heal it, and how to get his life in order.

Although, in the years since we met, I have often told Tim that he helped me more than I helped him.

As things worked out, meeting Tim was the catalyst I needed to overcome the death of my wife. Karen had died on Valentine's Day of that year and her death had affected me deeply. In the months that followed her passing, I had gone into such a deep depression that I thought I was never going to come out of it.

A number of times I had driven to work only to turn around and come back home because the thought of facing my staff was too much for me to handle. Karen was my world. If it hadn't been for Tim, I just don't know if I would have made it.

In bed on that Friday morning, listening to the kookaburras, I stared at Karen's photo, deep in thought about the great times that we shared. The photo sat on my bedside table and was taken on our wedding day. She looked absolutely beautiful with her long, flowing brown hair and stunning dress, and as I stared into her piercing brown eyes I felt a sense of gratitude that our paths had even crossed at all.

I reflected on that happy day when we exchanged our wedding vows. Karen's words came back to me as her father, Joe, handed her over to me at the altar. "You look very handsome, Ed," Karen said with a smile, as she looked me up and down in my wedding suit.

A huge grin had come over my face and Karen touched me on the nose with her finger as was her custom when she showed me affection. Such a small gesture can leave a huge imprint on one's life, and I buried my head into my pillow, overcome with a fresh wave of feeling.

The sharp pangs of grief that I had been experiencing since her death stabbed at my side and I took the photo in my hands and kissed her on the forehead. "Keep safe, my love. We'll catch up down the track."

I put the photo back on the bedside table and looked out of my window. As I sat up, I could see my feathered friend clearly in the early morning light. The kookaburra had been visiting me every morning for the previous few months and I looked forward to his visits. Karen loved nature, and kookaburras in particular. She had a favourite quote which she would often say to me:

The kiss of the sun for pardon,
The song of birds for mirth,
One is nearer to God in the garden;
Than anywhere else on earth.

Beyond the kookaburra, I could see water lapping against the pontoon at the front of my dwelling and heard a light ripple of wind as it blew across the turquoise waters of Yowie Bay. In the distance, on the other side of the Port Hacking River, the green canopy of the Royal National Park was slowly starting to become clear as the early morning sun shone its first rays upon the trees. It was only a matter of time before the screech of the sulphur-crested cockatoos would be heard. Every morning they made their daily pilgrimage from their homes in the eucalyptus trees over the river to disturb the peace of Sutherland Shire in the south of Sydney.

I got out of bed and made my way to the kitchen where I threw on the kettle. I rubbed the sleep from my eyes while the kettle did its thing. When I blinked, they settled on a nearby photo of four generations of my family taken when I was a little tacker. The photo was black and white and very formal. All the men were wearing suits, including five-year-old me in a coat and tie and short pants. We all stood there with our proud smiles; great-grandfather Paddy, grandfather Jack, my father, Ray, and myself, sitting on my father's knee. The inscription under the photograph read:

Four generations of Costigans: Paddy, Jack, Ray & Ed
Taken at 'Coorigil' Eumungerie, 1951

It brought back memories that photo. I looked at the photo next to it—probably one of my favourites. It was of my grandfather: Jack 'Stumpy' Costigan. He was dressed in his army uniform and looking very dashing. The photo had been taken in front of the pyramids in Egypt in 1915. Stumpy had given me the photo 37 years earlier, just as I was about to embark on my tour of Vietnam. On the back of the photo he had written a blessing for Irish soldiers which had been handed down through the Costigan family for generations:

God bless and keep who fought and lived.
God bless who fought and died.
For where and when the Irish fight, our God is on our side.

Grandpa Stumpy, as we all used to call him, was my childhood hero. As a boy, I wanted nothing more than to emulate his deeds on the battlefield when my time came. He had been my mentor, and ours was an especially close bond as my father had died in a tractor accident on the family farm at Coorigil when I was just ten years old. Stumpy basically brought our family up in his absence. He lived in the original homestead adjoining our property, which his father Paddy had built shortly after purchasing the farm in 1890. The homestead had wide verandahs halfway around the dwelling and inside were four bedrooms and five fireplaces. A brightly coloured garden adorned the front and one side of the homestead. It was a great old place.

Stumpy was a wise old owl who imparted much wisdom to me as I was growing up. Although he liked a drink, he never let it rule him. It was on this point he taught me to use my head and to respect alcohol, as he had seen it bring many men undone. Turns out I wasn't such a good listener on that score. Stumpy used to regularly tell me a story about a mate of his in his platoon named Dwyer. They were in France and were on leave from the front line when Dwyer went into the DTs after being on a rum bender all weekend. He tried to shoot an MP and then he shot up an estaminet in the small village where they were billeted. Stumpy and a few others managed to tie him up and sort it all out. I guess Stumpy's point was that alcohol leads you to make stupid decisions, but all I heard was a ripping yarn about a fellow soldier. I loved Stumpy's stories as they were always filled with adventure. They fired my spirit.

Grandpa received his nickname as a young boy. Against his father's wishes, he tried to chop the head off a chook for dinner one night and missed it by a wide margin. The axe did its work and lopped the top off his little finger on his left hand instead, leaving a distinctive stump. From then on most people just called him 'Stumpy'.

Stumpy was a legend throughout the district. He was as tough as nails, but he was well-liked by everyone and a wise man with a generous heart. He fought at Gallipoli and truly thought he'd seen the worst of warfare until he reached the Western Front. Poziers, in southern France, was one such place. In July 1916, the true horror of the Great War hit home, but in the heat of battle, Stumpy became one of the immortals. Armed with a Lewis gun, he took out three German machine gun posts. He killed seven of the enemy single-handed and took a dozen prisoners before moving behind German lines and capturing more prisoners. For this action he was awarded the Victoria Cross. He was a hero, but he was always modest about his wartime exploits. So much so that he kept his medals in an old cigar box at the bottom of the linen press. He only ever got them out on ANZAC Day. Although Stumpy told us kids stories about the war, he was always reluctant to talk about the action that led to him being awarded the Victoria Cross. I had to really press him to hear the story. I never really understood why until I saw action myself.

I smiled at the photo of old Stumpy and made myself a small pot of Earl Grey tea. I wandered onto the front decking where my feathered friend, whom I had christened 'Jatz' because of his fondness for the cracker biscuit of the same name, flew to where I sat and perched on the table in front of me. I hadn't forgotten to bring a couple of biscuits outside with me and when I sat down, I crushed them in my hand and placed them on the table where Jatz devoured them.

I took a deep breath and when I inhaled, my senses were overwhelmed by the organic scent of the lavender bush not far from where I was sitting. When the weather was nice, Karen loved nothing more than to sit outside and have her morning cup of tea while breathing in the lavender.

"Lavender. It's great for headaches, Ed," she would often say to me.

Karen, being a nurse and all, was always talking about the medicinal qualities of herbs and plants, and lavender was one of her favourites.

"Smell this, Ed," she would say, holding purple plumes to my nose.

"Mmm, that's beautiful, Kaz," I would reply.

My little dwelling by the water was really a two-bedroom cottage which had been named *Shiloh*. I only learned when I moved in that 'shiloh' is a Hebrew word which means 'peace'. *Shiloh* had indeed brought me much peace in the years I had lived there. She was surrounded by a paved and landscaped area full of Australian natives, and had a pontoon out the front where my little putt-putt boat was moored.

After breakfast, I got ready for work. It was only a half day on that particular Friday as I was to attend a Christmas lunch at nearby Watson's Bay. As I picked up my watch, running my fingers over the words that Karen had gotten engraved as a present for my 50th birthday (my full name—*Edward John Costigan*), I stared at an envelope sitting on my dresser.

I carefully picked it up and placed it in my back pocket. A weight had come off my shoulders with that letter. It had arrived a couple of days earlier and its contents had truly blown me away. In fact, it had started to heal much of the pain that had been with me for many, many years. It was as though the years of guilt surrounding the accident—that horrible, horrible accident—had fallen off me like a tree shedding its leaves in autumn.

I took a quick peek in the mirror and then made my way out of *Shiloh*. I was walking across the deck when I saw my brown kelpie, Foo, lying under a tree. I could see the sadness in his eyes and I knew it was because he missed Karen. He used to love greeting her first thing in the morning as she gave him a bowl of warm milk. "Come on, Foo-boy, it's time for your morning milk," Karen would say, then gently pat him on the head.

We had owned him since he was a pup, and although I was his master, Karen was his soulmate and he missed her terribly. In fact, one of the few arguments we ever had was over Foo. She insisted that Foo live in the house. I was off the land and with the way I was brought up, working dogs always lived outside.

"Come on, Ed! Foo thinks he's human, and it's cruel keeping him outside," she would say, peering at me with her innocent big brown eyes.

"He's a dog, not a human and dogs live outside!" I would say, laying down the law.

"But Ed, Foo is like our child!"

"Child be buggered, Kaz! Dogs are dogs, not humans!" I would always reply, before walking away exasperated.

But Karen being Karen was able to get her way and a compromise was met where Foo was allowed to stay in the house, but had to sleep in his kennel outside at night. Although I grew to like having Foo in the house, the boy from the bush on the inside had a conflicting view. It wasn't until years later that I realised how important Foo was to Karen, as our inability to have children meant that he filled a huge void in her life.

After Karen's death, all my protesting seemed so trivial.

These days, I gladly enjoyed his company in the house, especially at night where he slept at the end of my bed. However, on this particular occasion he'd slept outside the previous night. The return of summer had led to some humid nights, so he'd pitched up under the stars.

"How are you, pooch?" I scratched the forlorn dog behind the ears. He reciprocated by licking my hand and wagging his tail. A mental picture of Karen and Foo came into my head and I could hear her saying, like she was right there, "You're such a beautiful pooch, aren't you, Fooey-boy?"

I was suddenly overcome with emotion. I dropped onto the back step and broke down in tears. It happened like this occasionally. I thought I'd be having a day where it was all under control and then *wham!* Like a right hook to the face, my eyes would be watering and that was it.

Foo buried his nose under my chin and licked my neck.

"I miss her terribly, Foo," I told the kelpie while the tears ran down my cheeks. Foo whimpered and nudged me with his nose, trying to get closer to me. "I'm so glad I've got you to remind me of her and all the good times we had together." I hugged Foo tight. "We *will* get through this, Foo-boy."

I spent a few minutes patting Foo, and composing myself. "Got to get it together, Foo," I told him, taking a few deep breaths.

Foo wagged his tail and then grabbed his favourite tennis ball and rolled it towards me with his nose.

"Ha, always up for a play, aren't you, boy?" I nudged it back to him.

Foo barked, wagged his tail, and rolled the ball towards me again.

I kicked the ball again and said, "I'd love to take you to work with me, Foo, but I'm going to a party. You'll have to mind the fort while I'm away."

Foo barked, and I patted him once more and bade him farewell.

***

Shiloh had originally been part of a larger complex that also had a double-storey brick and timber house up the top of the property. That house had a verandah which ran around the top storey on the southern side and gave stunning panoramic views of both the Port Hacking River and the Royal National Park. That dwelling was owned by Bob and Julie Rowe who lived there with their five children: Matt, Gerard, Martin, Luke and Fiona.

I first met Rowy, as people called him, in 1967 at Kapooka in Wagga Wagga where we went through recruit training as National Servicemen. We later did our tour of Vietnam together, so we've been friends for a long time. The two properties out there on Yowie Bay had been subdivided some years earlier when Karen and I had purchased *Shiloh* off the Rowe family. *Shiloh* was fully ours, but they still had access to the water, as we shared a small boat shed and a pontoon.

I made my way up the steep path to the main house from *Shiloh* via an electric carriage which ran on a set of small tracks. The *Rocket*, as it was nicknamed, was made of fibreglass and could sit two people in the front and two in the back. It was covered by a fibreglass canopy with tarpaulin sides that could be rolled up, and it had a laminated window at the front.

The trip took three-and-a-half-minutes as the *Rocket* ascended through a steep gradient of trees and landscaped little parks until it reached the top—the carpark situated at the front of the Rowe's house. I looked at Karen's red Toyota Celica. I hadn't moved it since she had passed away, and as I ran my hand over its bonnet, I muttered, "I gotta sell Karen's car someday soon, but for the life of me, I just can't bring myself to do so."

She had been absolutely hopeless when it came to basic car maintenance. A smile came over my face as I reflected on some of the situations she used to get herself into by not looking after her car. I couldn't remember the amount of times she had broken down in the middle of nowhere.

I dragged myself away and hopped into my white Toyota Hilux work ute to make my way over to Waratah Street, Kirrawee. I turned into the driveway of a large industrial yard. A large corrugated iron shed served as the headquarters of my mechanical and towing business. At the front of the shed was a large roller door and inside was enough space to park four semi-trailers, but there was also an enormous amount of space in the yard to park all kinds of gear. Just above the roller door in navy blue writing was written my company name: *Costigan's Mechanical and Heavy Towing*.

I went upstairs to the kitchen, made myself a cup of tea and grabbed a couple of Scotch Finger biscuits out of the tin before going into my office. My secretary, Barbara Chigwidden, had placed a stack of invoices on my desk the previous day which needed to be sorted before she could post them out to customers. "Bloody paperwork, it's never-ending," I muttered, staring at my desk. I took a sip of tea, munched on a biscuit and sighed. "Righto, sunshine, let's get this stuff licked before we go to lunch."

I ploughed through office work, made some phone calls, and then wandered downstairs into the workshop to inspect the output of one of my mechanics. Luke Rowe was Bob and Julie's youngest son and a good young fella. He was busy replacing a blown turbo in a Kenworth Bogie Tipper.

"Everything under control, Lukey?" I asked, peering in from the other side of the motor.

"Yeah, Ed, just about got it licked now, although a couple of these bolts were hard to get off because they were in a prick of a position," he said, inspecting a bolt in his hand.

I nodded. "Just make sure everything goes back where it came from."

"Roger dodger, Ed, reading you loud and clear."

"I've got total faith in you, son," I said with a wry smile.

"I don't doubt that." Luke flashed me a grin.

Luke was a good mechanic in his mid-twenties. His light sandy hair, height, and facial features were just like his mother's, but he had the mechanical aptitude of his dad. He had started with me as an apprentice mechanic at the age of seventeen and was quickly proving to be an asset to my business. "Anyway, I've got some office work to finish before your old man arrives."

"I've just about got this job licked, Ed."

"When you've finished, you better have a shower and get ready because your old man is picking us up at 11.00 am sharp," I told him, looking at his greasy hands. He was streaming with sweat in the hot workshop.

"And Dad hates being late. Don't worry, Ed. I'll be ready," Luke said, grinning at me through the engine.

"Correctamundo, Lukey!"

I had just gotten off the phone, about an hour later, when I heard the familiar sound of Rowy's Nissan Patrol coming up the driveway.

"Shit! 11.00 am already!" I exclaimed, looking at the state of my desk.

The familiar voice of Rowy echoed around the bowels of the workshop. "How you going Lukey-boy?"

"Alright, old man," I heard Luke reply.

"I see you're all cleaned up and ready for the shindig, now where's that bloody Costigan?"

"Upstairs in his office."

"I better go and rustle him up because I want to get cracking."

I could hear Rowy's all too familiar heavy trudging as he made his way up the stairs to my office.

"Here's the man they couldn't root, shoot or electrocute," Rowy said with a big grin, leaning against the office door.

"They tried that, plus thrown the kitchen sink at me, and I've still survived to tell the tale!" I said and laughed, leaning back in my chair.

"Ain't that the truth, Cozzy," Rowy said with a grin.

Bob Rowe was tall, lean and extremely fit. He spoke with a distinctly laconic Australian accent that identified him as being from the country straight away. Those meeting him for the first time found his quick dialogue near impossible to understand and many a person unwisely took him for an uneducated hick from the outback. Nothing could have been further from the truth—Rowy was a multi-millionaire who'd made a packet in the earthmoving game.

Bob Rowe, like so many of us Vietnam veterans, had come back from the war disturbed. He was lucky in that he had a great woman named Julie, and she had given him stability. As a result, he was able to get on with his life. There were plenty of vets like him—lucky to have the love and patience of a good woman, and be settled and happy; but on the other hand, there were also plenty like me who were deeply affected by what had happened to them and had been unable to settle.

But for all his wealth, Rowy remained unaffected. He was

essentially that same boy from the bush with all his down-to-earth charm. He was a hands-on type of man who could still be seen in his yard at 6.00 am preparing his men for another day's work. He would often say to me, "If you're not at the helm of the ship, then you're bound to capsize!"

Rowy had decided to park his car at my work that day because he planned to have a few drinks at the Christmas party. As for me, my boozing days were over. I had left a trail of destruction in my life because of my drinking and those closest to me, including family and friends, were more than happy on the day I decided to put the cork in the bottle and seek recovery from my alcoholism. It had been 21 years since my last drink, so I volunteered to drive to the Christmas lunch.

"I spied you through the lounge-room window looking at Kaz's car this morning when you were on your way to work," Rowy said, his gaze earnest.

I responded, knowing that this true friend was one person I could talk to honestly about how I was feeling. "I had one of those moments again this morning, Rowy. I was thinking about how Karen used to talk to Foo, and like a bolt of lightning, I was overcome with emotion and the next thing I know I was a mess."

"It's not hard to get emotional about Karen, Ed. She was one in a million," Rowy said with a rueful smile.

"You think you're over the worst of it, and hey presto! It hits you like a ton of bricks all over again," I told him, shrugging my shoulders.

He nodded. "We all miss her terribly. She left a huge imprint on all of our lives, Cozzy. I know Julie still has those days too, and well, Fiona hasn't really been the same."

I almost felt overwhelmed again, but I kept it together. I

cleared my throat. "She treated your family like her own, Rowy. She loved you all very much."

"I know, mate, the kids loved her and so did we."

I could read his mind, such was the bond that existed between the two of us. It was a bond forged through the anvil of experience. A friendship tested through the steaming jungles of Vietnam and the subsequent experiences we had shared together in the years that followed. He knew what I was going through. He understood.

"I haven't had a chance to say this, Rowy, but I just want to thank you, Julie, and the family for being there for me over the last few months. You've all been an incredible support and I don't know how I would have got through it without you," I told him. I got up to shake his hand.

Rowy nearly crushed mine in his. He looked a little emotional himself. "I wouldn't have expected anything less from you, Cozzy, if I was in the same situation."

We looked at each other for some time, before Rowy slapped me on the shoulder and returned to his loud and cheerful self. "Righto, old son, we better get going to this shindig before all the fun's over."

***

The Christmas party was being put on by Rowy for all his employees at Rowe Civil Contracting. Rowy's annual Christmas party was always a big affair as he had around 50 staff. It always started off with lunch at a restaurant then usually developed into a pub crawl with the end result being very messy. Rowy invited me to his Christmas party every year and Luke, being his son, also got a guernsey.

As we were driving, Rowy said, "I hope this is a good arvo,

Cozzy, but I'll have to keep my eye on some of these young chargers because it got out of hand at last year's party."

"Well a bunch of construction workers on the piss can be a recipe for disaster, Rowy," I said.

"Too fuckin' right, Cozzy. I mean, they almost destroyed that Lebanese restaurant in Surry Hills last year after the manager refused to bring out the belly dancer because they were running amok."

"That was total madness. I thought they were going to destroy the place."

"Why?" asked Luke. He'd missed the previous year's party.

"The poor young sheila was too shit-scared to come out and perform because the lads were raising the tables above their heads and catching 'em just before they hit the floor," replied Rowy.

"Lucky I'm not on the piss these days, Rowy, because I would have probably thrown the table through the window and then performed my own belly dance," I said with a grin.

He laughed. "Too bloody right, Costigan. You probably would have followed up with a strip tease as an encore."

I slapped Rowy on the shoulder and laughed.

"Was Ed really that mad on the drink, Dad?" Luke chimed in from the backseat.

"Mad, Luke? That's a bloody understatement. Costigan was a dead set lunatic when he was on the juice."

I nodded, soberly. "I remember when we got back from Vietnam we had some wild nights. The difference being you didn't let it rule your life like it did mine, Rowy."

"Too bloody right," agreed Rowy. "Gee, I sure am glad you don't drink these days, Cozzy, 'cause you were an absolute fruit loop."

"Ain't that the truth," I said with a wry smile.

"Yeah, Dad told me you did some crazy stuff in Vietnam, Ed."

"We're lucky we're still on the planet, Luke, after some of the stunts we pulled over there," I told him.

We pulled up at Doyle's restaurant at Watson's Bay, just before midday. The summer sun was shining and there was a brilliant sparkle on the water of the bay. We were greeted by the sight of Rowy's employees milling around drinking, talking and laughing.

I spent five minutes talking to various people before Rowy tapped me on the shoulder and said, "Gee, Ed, a man's not a camel. A schooner of VB would be nice."

"Leave it to me, Rowy." I made my way to the bar where I ordered a couple of drinks for Rowy and me, mine being strictly non-alcoholic. He happily took his beer and as we finished lunch and the afternoon started to flow on, so did the grog and with it the laughter. Although stone cold sober, I soon found myself the centre of attention, entertaining the gathering. I do have a way with stories and I like nothing more than hearing people laugh. It wasn't unusual to see me spinning a yarn to an audience of avid listeners and it was no different on that day.

My belly was aching from laughter. In fact, I hadn't laughed that hard since Karen's passing. The loneliness that goes with losing a loved one was never far from me, especially at night when Karen was no longer around. The party was just the medicine I needed, and I realised that despite the odd moment of intense grief, I was starting to feel like my old self again. And even though I was sober, I didn't feel like I needed the booze to enjoy myself. This amazed me, and still does now, as there was a time in my life where I would have felt like a fish out of water if not drinking while socialising.

We had been at the party for a couple of hours—Rowy was in his element, reminiscing about the early days when he started his business—when I received the call on my mobile phone that changed everything.

On the other end of the line was Father Frank Casey, who like me, was a recovering alcoholic. Frank and I had become good mates after he helped me get off the booze. His patience and encouragement helped me build the healthy habits that see me sober to this day. He had also set up a program named 'Break Through the Barriers' of which I was a part.

The program was set up to help disadvantaged youth who were either homeless, drug and alcohol dependent, or suffering from abuse, whether it be physical or psychological. Frank had initially set up a food van around the back of Woolloomooloo to feed homeless youth and it had slowly expanded to help people recover from addiction through AA and NA, and finding them employment.

I came on board a few years earlier when I helped a bloke in his late teens get a job as an apprentice carpenter with an inner city builder, and since then had helped a further 30 or so young people get back on their feet through finding them employment. Frank had about a dozen volunteers involved and by this stage, they'd helped thousands of kids get a new start. It was a worthy cause and one that I was proud to help with whenever I could. I believe in second chances. I've had a few of those myself.

Anyway, Frank had been informed by a friend of his about a young man who was in a bad way after a massive bender. He was staying in a caravan park at Kurnell, on the edge of Botany Bay.

I had always been willing to help an Alkie who was in a

bad way, and this particular afternoon was no exception, even though I was enjoying myself with Rowy and his mob.

"What about it, Ed?" asked Frank. "I hate to drag you away, but would you mind having a yarn with this young bloke?"

I gave a little laugh. "As much as I'm enjoying myself, Frank, I think these troops are going to get out of control soon and I don't want to be around to witness the carnage. Happy to help."

"Good. I know how good you are when it comes to handling some of these wild young blokes, Ed. Besides, I know from past experience there is nothing quite like getting through bereavement than helping another human being," Frank said, seeming to know only too well how I was feeling.

I shook my head. "You always know how to say the right thing at the right time, Frank."

"Well, Ed, I'm sure Karen would agree with me, knowing the sort of girl she was."

"Yeah, she was pretty good at helping other people, wasn't she?"

"She sure was, Ed. That's one of the things that made her so special," agreed Frank. "You take care with this young man."

We finished our conversation, and I strolled over to where Rowy was sitting.

"I've gotta go, Rowy," I told him, clapping him on the shoulder. "I just got a call from Frank, there's a young bloke who's been playing up," I said, giving him a wink.

"That's bad luck, Ed, you were really enjoying yourself!" Rowy exclaimed. "Are you sure you can't stick around?"

"As much as I've had a good arvo, Rowy, helping the young fellas helps me as much as it helps them, I think."

Rowy raised his glass and winked at me. "You go for it,

Cozzy. Me and Luke will catch a taxi home. Catch you tomorrow, old son."

I was about to leave when I remembered the envelope in my back pocket. I pulled it out, waved it in front of Rowy and said, "I need to read this letter to you later. Its contents will blow you away."

"What's it about?"

"It's about the accident."

"Yeah?" Rowy said, raising his eyebrows, suddenly serious.

"I'll tell you more later. You'll never believe it," I said, waving goodbye.

***

It was close on 3.00 pm when I arrived at the caravan park. When I got out of the car I was met with a refreshing north-east breeze which was blowing directly across Botany Bay. I entered the front office and although it was empty, I could hear a television on in the back room. I pressed the electric buzzer on the counter and after a minute or so, a grey-haired gentleman in his early seventies appeared from behind the door. He was neatly dressed in trousers and a short-sleeve shirt.

"Yes, can I help you, sir?" he asked.

"I'm a mate of Fr Frank Casey. I believe you've got a young bloke here in a bad way?"

"Oh, yes, you're the man that Fr Casey spoke about. How do you do, Ian Hennessy," he said, as he extended his hand. His expression carried some relief.

"Pleased to meet you, Ian, Ed Costigan's my name." I took his hand and gave it a firm shake.

"There's this young bloke in his late twenties," Ian whispered cautiously. He looked around, almost like he expected the fella to come storming into his office.

I put my hands in my pockets and listened. "Go on."

"He rented a van about a week ago, and at first he seemed okay, but then he took to the drink about three days ago. He's been in a bad way ever since." Ian looked troubled.

"How exactly?" I said. I felt like a detective quizzing a suspect. It was always best to get as much information on the state of an alcoholic before approaching them. You just never knew if you were going to get a hug or a whack to the head.

"Well, he's been yelling and screaming, and to be perfectly honest with you, he sounds as though he's been in the horrors."

"Why didn't you call the cops?" I asked him.

"The thought did cross my mind and then I thought maybe Fr Casey might be of assistance," he said, a serious expression on his face. "I know he's had a lot of success helping people on the drink, and it's probably a better option than the police if the young man can be helped first."

I nodded. This man had it right and I liked his attitude. "So, what number is he in?"

"Number 28 in the far left corner of the caravan park."

"Leave it with me, Ian, and I'll see what I can do."

"I really appreciate your help, Ed. Be careful though, he's a wild one," he said as he shook my hand again.

"Wild one?"

"Yeah, he could be a bit violent."

"Thanks, I'll watch myself," I said.

It was quite a change in mood from the relaxed lunch I'd just enjoyed. I walked down the driveway and then darted between the caravans where the long grass had not been cut in some time. Spying around, I spotted a lone caravan in the area Ian had indicated. It was old with a green and brown stripe running horizontally along its side and rust grizzling its corners. I took Ian's advice and approached the van with caution. I knew from personal experience that practising alcoholics can be unpredictable creatures.

Squaring up to the door, I took a deep breath and knocked three times. I waited a while and knocked again, but there was still no response.

"Hello, anyone there?" I called, looking for signs of life.

There was no answer. I was starting to get a bit edgy myself. "If this young bastard doesn't open the door soon, I'm getting out of here and back to the shindig," I muttered quietly.

I decided to give it one last try before I called it quits. This time I knocked a lot harder and after a brief wait, an angry voice from inside the caravan screamed out, "Who the FUCK is it?"

I was taken aback by his aggressive tone and initially did not respond while I sorted out how to approach this. "My name's Ed. I've come to have a talk with you," I said, eventually.

After a brief moment he responded, "What do ya want to talk to me about?"

"I've been told that you're in there tying on a big one, and I want to know if you want to talk about what's bothering you."

"There nothing bothering me, fuckwit, so why don't you just fuck off back where you came from!"

"For a bloke who's got no problems, you sound pretty angry," I observed.

"Listen, prick, you better fuck off real quick or I am gonna come out there and fucking clean you up!" he shouted through the door.

"Whatever you reckon, champ, but I just want you to know that if you ever want to have a talk about your drinking problem, I'll be here to have a yarn with you," I said.

That comment must have pressed his buttons because the next thing I knew, the door of the caravan came flying open, nearly breaking the hinges, and I was face to face with an enraged young man holding a metre-long length of scaffold pipe. His face was close to mine as he held the pipe tightly in his right hand. He was wearing a blue shearer's singlet and work shorts with a pair of ratty thongs on his feet. I estimated that he was no taller than 5'7" but he was a powerful looking bloke. It was like his physique was formed from years of hard toil rather than in a gym. His forearms and biceps had numerous tattoos on them including one of an Australian military unit which I couldn't quite see properly as he squared up to me, and he looked as though he hadn't shaved for a couple of days. He wasn't drunk, but it was obvious that he was coming off a huge bender.

"Look here you prick, I am sick to death of do-gooders and god-botherers like you interfering in my life," he growled at me aggressively.

"Sorry, mate, but you've read me wrong because I'm certainly no do-gooder or bible-basher," I said as I took guard, not knowing if I was going to cop the pipe over my head.

"Who sent you down here then? Was it that nosy caravan park owner?" he snarled angrily.

I tried to dial back the hostility. "Hey, mate, easy does it. Just take it nice and easy. No one needs to get hurt here," I said, trying to speak calmly.

"I knew it! It's that Ian who runs the park. The nosy old bastard! Wait till I catch up with him! I'll wrap this pipe right around his head," he shouted, turning and slamming his fist again the door jamb.

"Listen, mate, that old bloke up on the front desk is only

concerned for your wellbeing, otherwise he would have called the cops days ago," I told him, holding onto my calm.

He gave me a menacing stare but held still for a moment. "He better not call the cops or I'll shove this scaffold pipe right up his arse," he said through gritted teeth.

"Easy does it, mate. There's no need for all this aggression," I said. "I'm just here to chat."

He pushed the pipe into my stomach, testing the waters. I pushed back, trying to keep it off me. We started to jostle; me pushing the pipe away and him grabbing my shirt collar and trying to shake me. It was starting to get hairy. Back and forth we grappled, both of us trying to control the pipe.

"I can't stand bastards like you interfering in my life. I've got a good mind to clean you up," he said with a snarl, trying to shake my hand off the pipe.

"Don't even think about it, mate, or I'll knock you flying," I replied, breathing heavy. He had a look in his eye that resembled that of a mad horse just before it kicks you.

We shifted about as we struggled over the pipe, and I glanced over his shoulder into the caravan. It looked as though a bomb had hit it with filthy clothes and empty beer stubbies strewn all over the place.

I stopped dead.

Ya see, just when I was getting ready to be on the receiving end of a cracked skull, I noticed a plaque hanging on the wall of the inside of the caravan. It was made of timber and showed an insignia of a black boar's head with white tusks. Behind the boar's head were two rifles crossed over each other. The insignia was surrounded by a beautifully painted jungle that was instantly recognisable to me. It jabbed right at my heart, as I knew it as well as I knew my own face.

The words on the plaque read:

11 Battalion

Royal Australian Regiment

No guts no glory

I was also mesmerised by the painting. In fact, I was that taken aback that I stopped jostling with him and just stood there looking at the painting with my mouth open. He noticed that my attention was somewhere else and stopped jostling to stare at me. It was probably the best move I could have made, as it was unexpected and derailed his immediate violent thoughts.

"What?" he asked, a quizzical yet wary look in his eye.

"11 Battalion," I said in amazement, still staring.

"What did you say?" he said, his voice menacing, the pipe raising slightly.

"11 Battalion, Royal Australian Regiment," I said, pointing towards the painting. I was blown away by what I was seeing.

"So? What's it to you?"

"*No guts no glory.* That's 11 Battalion's motto."

"What?" he growled.

"11 Battalion RAR. *No guts no glory.*" I looked back at the kid in amazement. "That was my battalion in Vietnam."

The young man dropped the pipe. A hesitant look of surprise crossed his face. "You were in 11 Battalion?"

"Yeah, I did a tour of Vietnam in 1968," I said.

"1968?" he said with a look of wary interest. His hackles lowered a mite.

"What's your connection with 11 RAR?" I asked him, sensing that we now had common ground, and I had something to build on.

"That's my old man's battalion," he told me.

A look of astonishment came over my face. "What was his name?" I asked.

After a long pause he said, "Bill Finnegan."

I felt a tingle run up my spine. It was as though time stood still as memories of long ago raced through my head. The look on my face probably suggested I had just had a near death experience because the young man's face filled with surprise.

"You look like you've seen a ghost, mate!" he said, his aggression starting to fade.

"Finno? Bill Finnegan was in my platoon," I told him. My voice was barely more than a whisper. The letter in my pocket was burning a hole through my pants.

"You knew my old man?" He was astonished, the pipe totally forgotten.

"Your old man," I said, lowering my head and gathering my thoughts for a moment, "your old man and I share a lot of history, mate."

"You were mates with him?"

"Finno? Oh yeah, he was one of my best mates over there. Mad as a hatter, but still a good bloke." I looked at the kid, trying to see Bill in his face. "What's your name?"

He looked at me for some time before answering. "Tim."

"Well, you're a chip off the old block, Tim. Just like Finno, never telling your right hand what your left is doing. Mind you, when you got under the surface there was a really genuine bloke in there."

Tim frowned at me. "What's your name?"

"Ed Costigan." I extended my hand and he shook it. It was

a minor victory to me. "Gee, I can see a lot of Finno in you, son," I told him, looking him up and down.

"What do you mean?"

"You've got the same nose as him," I told him, looking carefully at his face.

"My nose is the same?"

"Yeah, it's shaped like an eagle's. A bit hooked."

His eyes narrowed.

"Oh, don't take offence," I said with smile. "It was just one of Finno's defining features."

Tim's hackles lowered. "What else reminds you of him?"

I looked at him with my hand on my chin. "You've got the same thickset build with the broad shoulders and..." I trailed off, knowing that I was probably going to set him off again.

Tim looked at me suspiciously. "And what?"

"Well, to be perfectly honest with you, it's obvious that you're a bit of a hothead like your old man."

He rolled his eyes and gave me a dead look.

I thought it best to move on. "I tried to catch up with your old man after I got back from Vietnam to no avail. Where is he?" I was eager to know what happened to Finno. I knew where most of my old Vietnam mates were, but he seemed to slip through the cracks.

Tim looked away, suddenly uncomfortable. "He died in a car accident."

"What!" I said, my shock apparent.

"Wiped himself out on the piss." Tim looked bitter.

"Oh, that's terrible," I said, a sudden wave of guilt claiming me. "What happened?"

He frowned. "It was in 1988. The old man had been drinking in a pub at Wee Waa after finishing up shearing one Friday night. About midnight he got into his ute, as pissed as a chook, and took off like a bat out of hell on the road towards Burren Junction. The next morning a farmer found him dead in a dry creek bed."

I stood there, stunned into silence, the hairs on the back of my neck standing upright. "I'll be buggered. I never knew he died," I said, the shock etched on my face.

Tim shrugged, his expression dismissive. "It was bound to happen sooner or later. He used to drink drive all the time."

"He was a mysterious bloke your old man," I told Tim, hoping to engage him again. He was starting to close up. Something about his dad had him shutting down. "He played his cards close to his chest and didn't give much away."

"What do you mean?"

I shrugged. "He was hard to keep track of. After Vietnam, it was like he just disappeared off the planet."

"He was usually off shearing on stations, so I didn't know what he was up to," said Tim.

I leaned up against the outside of the caravan with my arms folded, totally rattled by what Tim had told me about Finno. "I hadn't thought of your old man in ages, but all the old memories of him have come flooding back."

Tim shifted about to get a good look at me. "You say you were good mates with my dad?"

"Oh yeah, Finno and I had a very close bond," I told him.

"Why?" asked Tim, a reluctant curiosity on his face.

"He was on a machine gun and so was I," I told him. "I carried one of those heavy M60's all through the mud and jungle in Vietnam."

He stared at me. "I was on a MAG 58 in Iraq."

"A fellow machine gunner, hey?" I said, the recognition of

a fellow brother now flowing between us. I knew this was definitely my way into helping Tim. "When were you in Iraq?"

"I went in with the initial deployment in 2003." His tone went bleak.

"You had a hard time over there," I said, observing his face tighten. I also noted that he can't have been back for too long. No wonder he was all messed up.

"Yeah, lost a good mate, but I don't really want to talk about it 'cause it still spooks me a bit." He looked away, so I shifted about and looked inside the caravan again, at the painting.

"I know that work. Your old man painted that when we were in Vietnam," I told him. I still couldn't believe I was seeing it after all these years.

"I know, my mum gave it to me when he died."

"He was a talented bloke your old man. He had an artistic streak about him."

"Yeah, I know. Mum told me all about it."

I studied the painting for some time, when I suddenly remembered a photograph I had in my wallet. "I've got something that might interest you."

"What is it?" he asked with raised eyebrows.

"A photo that I think you would like to see."

"A photo?"

I took my advantage. "Yeah, but it's getting a bit hot standing out here in the afternoon sun. Do you reckon we can go inside so I can show you? Chuck on a brew?"

I could see by the look in Tim's eyes that the small amount of trust that I had built up was threatened by my request. After what seemed like an eternity he said, "You gotta be kidding, mate. I don't let any old joker come waltzing into my caravan."

"I'm hardly going to be waltzing into your caravan, mate,

and it's just a photo. You'll find it interesting. And what's a few minutes of your time? Besides, it's getting bloody hot out here," I said, wiping the sweat from my brow.

He looked me up and down again. "Alright. You can come in, but this photo better be interesting 'cause I don't normally let anybody come in here."

He motioned me into the caravan and my attention was diverted from the painting by the wreck of the place. I looked through the van down to where the double bed was and noticed that his clothes and beer bottles were more than just in the open doorway, they were strewn all over the place. I suddenly realised what a paradox it was between the painting and the scene in front of me. This bloke was a mess. I sat down at the booth-style table.

The wind suddenly caught the door and it slammed shut. This made him snap around quickly and he looked agitated. The realisation that we were together in the van made him wary and he kept glancing back at the van door with a look of apprehension on his face.

"So, where's this photo you want to show me?" he said, trying to push things along.

I took my wallet out of my back pocket and after rummaging through it I came across the photo. "I've had this buried away in my wallet for years. Totally forgot about it. Your old man took it and gave me a copy while we were on R and R in Vung Tau."

He took it and studied it carefully, a look of astonishment coming over his face.

"Your old man had one of those old box brownie cameras. He was always taking snaps of people, especially when we were on the piss back in the boozer," I told him, remembering Finno wandering around camp, making a nuisance of himself.

His head snapped up. "Did you say a box brownie camera?" His eyes were penetrating. It was rare that I'd come across such intensity in a young man.

"Yeah, that's right," I told him. "He was a pretty good photographer your old man. He took a good snap. Old Finno certainly had a keen eye," I said casually, trying to lighten the mood.

He walked down to his bed and after rummaging around for a while under the mess, he pulled out an old camera and brought it back to the table.

It was Finno's camera!

"I'll be buggered. That old camera certainly brings back memories!" I laughed.

My cheerfulness seemed to ignite his curiosity, and he relaxed a bit. "So, who are these blokes in the photo?"

I took the photo and grinned at him. I pointed at the bloke on the end. "That's Schooner Rooney and your old man. That's me in the background with the smoke and beer in my hand with Rowy, the both of us acting like a pair of smartarses. If you look carefully, you'll see our unit insignia hanging up on the wall behind us."

He studied the photo carefully, eyes straining. Eventually, a look of recognition came over him and some of the tension lifted off his face. He looked up at me and then back at the photo. "I can see the resemblance with you, but who's Schooner Rooney?"

"Schooner Rooney was from Condobolin and before you ask, Rowy was off a big property just outside Coolabah. They were in my platoon."

He went back to studying the photo, so I glanced around the inside of the caravan. I spied a magnificent colour photograph glued to the wall of the caravan. It was of an assortment of half a dozen birds flying in different directions with a wetland area as a backdrop. The colour of the flora and fauna gave you the impression that you were standing right in the middle of the scene.

"Who took that photo?" I asked, blown away by its sheer beauty.

He briefly glanced up and then back at my picture. "I took it."

I was floored. "Gee, it's a nice photo. You've got talent, mate. What type of birds are they?"

"White-necked herons, straw-necked ibises, pied honeyeaters, royal spoonbills and a host of others."

The names of the birds rolled off his tongue like he had been around them all his life.

"Where did you take the photo?"

"The Macquarie Marshes."

"I know where they are, I'm familiar with the country out that way," I told him. "It's a beautiful area, I once took my late wife there. She was mesmerised by the beauty of the birdlife. She would have loved your photo."

He didn't reply. He was quiet now, but he hadn't dropped the photo. It was time to broach the gap. There was a long pause before I spoke.

"You know, Tim, I've met your type before. Loaded with talent but around the twist."

"What do you mean?" His eyes narrowed and his fingers tightened on the photo.

"Listen, mate, I didn't come down on the last shower. You look like you're totally screwed up."

"Hey, just because you knew my old man doesn't mean

you can come in here and start telling me where my life's gone wrong," he said with cold eyes, his tone just as icy.

I kept my cool. "You might not want to believe this, but I understand where you're coming from. I've been in your position myself."

"Like how?" he asked, his voice a menacing growl.

"Like the fact that I've been to war, just like you."

"Big deal. What else?"

"I've been to hell and back, mate," I told him. "I was just like you once. My life was out of control until I got off the grog and turned things around."

"I told you before I haven't got a problem with grog, so will you knock that shit off," he snarled.

I pointed around the van. "You don't have to be Albert Einstein to figure out that you aren't firing on all cylinders."

"What's that supposed to mean?" he demanded.

"Have a look at the inside of this caravan, it's a disaster area."

"Okay, it's a bit messy, but that doesn't mean my life is off the rails."

I quickly changed the topic to keep him off guard. "You know, Tim, I would give my right arm to have the sort of talent that you have." I pointed to his photograph. "Do you want to go on living like this and risk losing the ability to take brilliant photos like this one?"

His face twisted in anger. "Listen, you come into my caravan to show me a photo and then you start preaching to me how my life is out of order. I've had enough of you. Why don't you get your photo and just get the fuck out of my van." He thrust the photo back at me, his other fist clenched.

I sat there looking at him for some time. I shook my head calmly. "You know something, Tim?"

"What?" he snarled.

"You can be told, but you can't be told much. I don't know why I'm wasting my time trying to help a smartarse like you. I've got better things to do with my time, so I won't waste anymore of yours."

I got up to leave, but a loud thud sounded on the outside wall of the caravan, stopping me in my tracks. I looked at Tim and his expression was filled with anxiety. I felt my own heart thud. Whatever scared this kid must have been serious!

"Hey, bro, are you there?" A Maori voice could be heard loud and clear from outside the caravan.

"Who is that?" I whispered.

"That's fuckin' trouble," Tim replied, with a look of apprehension. "Shit."

There were more loud thuds and then I saw the face of a large Maori man in the window of the caravan. "Hey, bro, are you in there?" His piercing dark eyes suggested that this wasn't a social call.

I noticed four thickset men gathered outside the door. "What do they want?" I whispered to Tim.

"I've been waiting for these bastards," he said quietly.

"What? What are you talking about?"

"I owe these pricks a heap of money." He looked squarely at the door.

"How much?"

"A shitload," he said.

Just then, the door of the caravan flung open and in walked four of the meanest looking Maoris I'd ever seen. They were decked out in bikie leathers and sported intimidating face and body tattoos. They were so big they barely fit in the rig.

They looked at Tim, and sized me up too, and then the

largest member of the gang, who was at least twenty stone in weight, said, "We were wondering where you were hiding, ya maggot. Who's this fucking dickhead, bro?" He pointed at me.

"Just some bloke," Tim said, shrugging his shoulders.

I kept quiet. I didn't want to provoke a confrontation if I didn't have to.

"Well, we aren't too keen on having 'some bloke' around when we've come here to talk business. When we've finished with you, we'll deal with this dickhead," he snarled.

"Who told you I was here?" Tim said.

"We'll ask the questions. Now, where is our money?"

"Look, I just need a little bit more time to get all your money together—" Tim began.

"We told you that we wanted the money three months ago and we haven't seen a cent of the cash yet," interrupted the Maori. He grabbed Tim around the throat with one hand and pulled a sawn off 410 shotgun from underneath his leather coat with the other. He pointed it at his head. "You're history if you don't pay up."

"Listen, mate, I don't want to fuck you blokes around, but I lost my job and I haven't got all the money together!" said Tim.

"That's not good enough, bro. We don't like being fucked around, especially when we had an agreement," he said, still holding the gun at Tim's head.

I said nothing. My heart was pounding and my mouth was as dry as the bottom of a cocky's cage. As I looked at the Maoris, my head was working overtime trying to figure out how I was going to get out of this situation.

The Maori holding the shotgun looked as though he was going to shoot Tim at any second when I chimed in. I knew what to do. "How much money does he owe you?"

"What?" he bellowed, glaring at me over Tim's shoulder.

"I said, how much dough does this joker owe ya?" I asked him, trying to keep calm.

"What the fuck has that got to do with you, bro?" He swung the shotgun around towards me.

I was looking down the barrel of the 410. My palms were sweaty and my mind was working overtime when I said, "Maybe I can help you out with the money."

The Maori holding the shotgun said, "Are you for real, bro?"

"Yeah, I'm fair dinkum, mate, so can you lower the shotgun please?" I asked, trying to keep it together.

The Maori looked at me for what seemed like an eternity and then lowered the gun.

I let out a sigh. "How much does he owe you?"

"Seven thousand bucks."

"Phew, that's some serious coin! What have you been doing to rack up that sort of debt?" I said to Tim.

"Pokies, bro, the scumbag's addicted to the poker machines," the big Maori said before Tim could say a thing.

"Just brilliant. You got the daily double, hey, Tim. The piss and gambling," I said with a grimace.

Tim said nothing, but he looked away, the situation obviously shaking him to the core.

I had a large amount of money in my safe at home as I had recently done mechanical work on a Lebanese demolition contractor's fleet of trucks, and he had paid me in cash. I knew that this was probably the only way that I could save both his and *my* life.

"Listen, I might fall short a bit, but will $500 see you through until I can fix up the balance?" I said to the big Maori.

"$500," he sneered. "That's chicken feed, bro."

"That's all I can manage here and now. I can fix the balance up tomorrow with cash."

The Maoris looked at each then looked back at me. "How do we know you won't fuck us around, bro?"

"Listen, mate, I don't want to get hurt, so I can guarantee you I won't fuck you around. Here's my business card with all my details on it. I'll give you $500 in cash now and the rest in cash tomorrow." I pulled one of my cards out of my chest pocket and handed it over. The big Maori snatched it out of my hand.

"See? All of my details. You can find me if something goes wrong," I told him.

He glared at me. It was like he couldn't believe I was for real. "Where will we meet you?"

"In front of Cronulla Post Office at 7.00 am tomorrow morning," I said. No way I wanted them at my business.

"You sure, bro? Because if you short change us, not only will scumbag over here cop it, but we'll come looking for you also."

"I'll give you the $500 in cash right now. It's right here." I produced five crisp one hundred dollar notes from my wallet and handed them to him.

The Maoris looked at each other and the one holding the shotgun said, "You won't frig us around with the money, hey bro, because we're not the sort of people who liked to be double-crossed."

I gave them a reassuring nod. "I give you my word. I'll fix you up with the rest of the cash tomorrow. Besides, I don't want to end up with a hole in the back of my head."

"Okay, we'll be there at 7.00 am tomorrow morning."

"No worries," I said.

The Maoris looked at each other and shrugged, as if to say

'his funeral', then turned around and disappeared out the door. Tim and I exchanged a relieved glance, but a moment later, the big bloke returned and stuck his head inside the door. "7.00 am tomorrow in front of Cronulla post office or else. Okay, bro?" He drew his finger across his throat.

"I'll be there, I've given you my word," I told him.

With that, they disappeared.

I sat in my seat, my heart beating fast at my near-death experience. The caravan was filled with a strained silence.

"Crikey, I nearly shit myself," I said, giving Tim an anxious look.

"You're not the only one," Tim replied. He looked shaky.

I felt myself fill with sarcasm. "So everything's just hunky dory in your life, hey Tim?"

He avoided my glance. "Yeah, well I have a few money problems."

"You don't say! I think you're in more trouble than Osama Bin Laden."

Tim gave me a submissive look and said, "You showed some quick thinking there."

"Someone had to or we would have both been dead," I told him, my heart still racing. "Oh shit, I can't believe that just happened!"

"Well, thanks for that," Tim said. "I thought I was a dead duck."

My head was still spinning, but I remembered what the Maori boss had said. "So you've been on the punt, have ya?"

Tim looked at the floor. "Yeah, I've been giving them a bit of a nudge."

"You got any money at all?" I asked.

"I had six grand saved, then I had a blowout at Cronulla RSL on the pokies just before I moved into the caravan."

"Blown it all, have you?"

"Yep, every last cent."

"Brilliant. You're lucky I have that cash at home or we would have both been history. I can't believe the situation I've got myself into here." I pointed my finger at Tim. I had him now. "Don't think that you're going to get away with this scot free."

"What?" he said, snapping his head up to look at me.

"No, siree. You get nothing for nothing in this world," I told him.

"Why, what are you going to do?" he asked, suddenly wary again.

"It's not what I am going to do, it's what you're going to be doing," I said. "You're going to be changing tyres, washing trucks and being a general dogsbody around my workshop until you pay every cent of that money back."

His eyes had gotten big. "What? Where?"

"In my truck mechanical business and don't think I'm a soft touch either, Tim, because I'm not. My blokes work a full day, and you will too."

Tim sat there in stunned silence. His aggressive demeanor had dissipated somewhat and I got the sense that a load had been lifted from his shoulders after the Maoris had left, and out of nowhere, he now had a new job.

"Tim, I know you're in denial of your problem, but because you're Finno's son and I usually feel a lot better after trying to help another drunk, I'm going to help you," I told him, leaving him no room to refuse me. "For what it's worth, I'm going to tell you something about myself. God only knows why, but something tells me you're worth trying to help."

Tim looked away, his face flushed.

"If something registers in that brain of yours, well and good," I told him. "If not, there's nothing more I can say or do. You'll do your hours to pay back that money and then we'll go our separate ways." I leant forward in my seat, my head in my hands as my elbows rested on the table. "You know, I really *was* like you. I was crazy when I was your age and on the piss."

Tim looked up.

I nodded. "Yeah, I ended up around the twist, although things didn't start out that way when I came down from the bush to the big smoke."

Chapter 2

January 1963, Eumungerie Central, New South Wales

WHEN I LEFT home all those years ago, I was full of hope and optimism. I was embarking on a great adventure and there was excitement in the air. Little did I know at that tender age that it was to be the start of a rocky road. In retrospect, my upbringing was stable and there was no reason why so much mischief was to befall me down the track. I didn't know at that stage of my life that once an alcoholic, always an alcoholic, and my destiny was already set.

All of my family; including Stumpy, my mother Monica, and siblings John, Margaret, Noel, Dan and Anne, had driven from our wheat and sheep farm at Kickabil Junction, 20 kilometres west of town, to the railway station at Eumungerie to see me off. I was approaching my 17th birthday and was travelling to Sydney to start an apprenticeship as a motor mechanic. I was to live with relatives in the beachside suburb of Maroubra.

It had been a stinking hot day and there was a dust storm blowing in from the west. As I stepped out of Stumpy's EK Holden station wagon, I could feel my shirt stick to my back and my white moleskin trousers felt as though they were glued to my legs. I had a huge mark on my right wrist where my elder brother, Noel, had administered a Chinese arm burn as a good luck sign for the future.

"It's part of your initiation into manhood, Ed. All us Costigan's have to go through it," he told me, trying to keep a straight face. Noel was two years older than me and good at spinning a yarn. Although we were close, he seemed to always be pulling a swifty on me.

"Be buggered, it'll make me into man, Noel!" I said with sarcasm as we approached Eumungerie.

"As God as my witness, Ed."

"I've got my doubts about that," I replied.

"Here's another one to double your luck, Ed. Take that!" Noel gave me a karate chop right between my shoulder blades. A blast of pain ran across my back, but I still managed to get a nice jab into Noel's stomach which made him stagger backwards. As a result of the horseplay, I could barely lift my bag out of the boot when we arrived at the railway station.

My beautiful sister Anne, a mere 11 years old at the time, helped me carry my bag to the train. "Mum, Noel's been hitting Ed in between the shoulder blades and he can barely hold his bag," said Anne. She looked so sweet with her shoulder length brown hair and her pretty floral dress. She always stuck up for me.

"Stop hitting Ed, Noel, he has a long trip to Sydney ahead of him," said my mother, her voice terse. She always worried about us kids.

After losing my dad in a tractor accident on the farm seven years earlier, Mum had become increasingly protective of her brood. Her Catholic faith and her family were at the very centre of her existence and she wanted nothing more than for us all to be friends and lead decent lives. Mum lived a life of simplicity, like most country women of her generation. She was a stalwart of her local CWA (Country Women's Association) branch, and her date scones and sponge cakes were legendary throughout the district. She often won ribbons at the local show for her food. She was a small woman, but her love for us was big. She had such a warm nature and rarely spoke ill of anybody. She also loved the farm and after Dad died, she stayed on to help run it with Stumpy and my brothers.

Eumungerie, a small town halfway between Dubbo and Gilgandra, had originally been named 'Coalbagge' after the inn that was situated there. It had been settled in the late 1800s due to its rich selection of timber which included ironbark, cypress and yellow box trees. The original settlers were mainly Scots, Irish and Germans, and it was around this time that my great-grandfather, Paddy Costigan, came into the area as a timber getter, eventually taking up 2000 acres of land west of the town. Paddy had named the property *Coorigil*, an Aboriginal word that means 'sign of bees'.

Paddy left the old family farm just outside the village of Callan, in County Kilkenny, Ireland, at the age of 18. He'd been looking for a better start in Australia. Debt and famine were a part of the fabric of Ireland at that time, and after a number of his siblings had departed for Australia, he followed too for the chance of a better life.

Noel was being groomed to eventually take over the property as he had the head for it, so it had been agreed by my mother and Stumpy that I should secure a trade for my future. Mum had made some calls and found an apprenticeship for me as a motor mechanic in Sydney. I had always shown a natural ability towards mechanics, so Mum approached an old army mate of my late father, a bloke named Reg Steel, to take me on in his transport business.

I was going to live with Mum's eldest brother, Uncle Kevin O'Grady, and his wife, Eunice, at their house in seaside Maroubra. I was very excited about this as I had been to Sydney just once, and it was on that trip that I had seen the beach for the first time. Coming from the landlocked farm the ocean was a real drawcard.

For me, a great part of the adventure was that I felt as though I was being set free from my upbringing. Although I loved the bush and the family farm, the allure of Sydney and new adventures really excited me. Strangely enough, as I got older and the bright lights of my youth were behind me, it was the bush and nature that gave me great solace.

Mine was a very strict Catholic upbringing. I had been badgered all my life, both at home and at boarding school, to live a moral life as the fires of hell were waiting for any small indiscretion on my account. Nana O'Grady was one of the main advocates of a strong moral life.

"Don't you be falling for that evil liquor," she would say to me when I was growing up. This was mainly due to her family being a bunch of pisspots. They were legendary around Dubbo for their antics while on the drink.

The day of my departure for Sydney, she was present in all her Irish Catholic eccentricity and she continued to pepper me with advice throughout the afternoon.

"Don't you forget your Sunday masses while you're in Sydney, Ed!" She kept at me with her strong Irish brogue. Nana O'Grady also gave me a set of rosary beads that had been blessed by the Pope and a holy card from St Jude, who is the patron saint of lost causes. Looking back now, it was a prophetic gesture considering the trouble I was to get into in the coming years.

John, my eldest brother, had cornered me during the afternoon and reminded me in his pompous manner to knuckle down and apply myself to my apprenticeship. After Dad's death, John took on the role as disciplinarian of the family. He was different from the rest of my brothers; he was an intellect and more attuned to things of a studious nature like music and the arts, rather than sports and life on the land. He had always been a remote figure to me and the fact that he was studying to become a priest made him appear more like an uncle than a brother.

In the late afternoon, I said my goodbyes to everyone, making sure that I gave Mum, Margaret and especially little Anne big hugs, and caught the Garrett steam train from Eumungerie to Dubbo with Nana and my cousin, Sean O'Grady. Sean, like me, was to tread his own perilous path on the journey that is alcoholism. Sean and I always had a natural bond. It could be said that we had a type of telepathic link where we instinctively knew what the other was thinking, such is the affinity from one alcoholic to another. Although we were to spend long periods apart during our lives, whenever we caught up with each other again it was though we had only been talking five minutes before.

For the duration of the train trip, Nana O'Grady insisted that we recite decades of the rosary and when we weren't, she told us dire stories about long lost O'Grady relatives who had fallen foul of the drink and perished in the fires of hell.

"And then was great uncle Joe O'Grady, who stopped doing

his Sunday masses and making a regular confession. His drinking spiralled out of control and he ended up living in sin with a slip of a girl from Limerick named Rosie Ahern," Nana said, with a look of terror and hellfire in her eyes. "And you know what happened to great Uncle Joe, don't you, Edward John Costigan?" Nana's terrifying gaze burned into me.

"No, Nana," I said, trying to conceal my laughter.

"He danced a merry dance with Lucifer in the eternal fires of hell," she said with a manic look in her eyes.

I averted my eyes, staring into space, trying not to laugh in case I brought the wrath of Nana down on top of me.

"So don't let that happen to you, Edward Costigan, in that city of sin, Sydney," she said, her sermon closing as she brought her fist down hard on the cushioned railway seat.

I knew only too well from past experience what Nana could be like when her hackles were up. I still remember the time she found out that I had been drawing swastikas on the front cover of my spelling book when I was in third grade. I had no idea what I was doing, nor any idea of wider context of what the sign meant. I was all of seven years old at the time.

"Don't you know that this evil symbol was the cross that Christ was crucified on, bent by the Nazi's for their wicked ways?" she had said, almost in tears. How was I to know?

"Shit a brick, I can't wait till I'm away from this crazy Irishwoman," I said to Sean while we waited at Dubbo for my Sydney-bound train.

"Don't worry, Ed, once you're in the big smoke you'll be able to undo the shackles and hey presto! It'll be party time," Sean said, a devilish look in his eye.

When the 3801 steam train eventually pulled out of Dubbo Railway Station late in the evening, I was all 'rosaried' out. I let out a huge sigh of relief. I was finally out of the web of my eccentric Nana. I was free from everything.

As the train moved swiftly through the warm night, I felt a tingle of excitement as the adventure had finally begun! From where I sat, I could smell the freshly cut Lucerne hay from the paddocks that ran adjacent to the railway line, a smell that I adored. It was one of my favourite jobs on the farm, making hay.

I was hit with a tinge of homesickness as I reminisced about life on the land. I was in that melancholic state for about half an hour before a man in his mid-thirties entered my dog box compartment, which brought me back to the present. He was a big bloke, well over six feet tall, and had a ruddy complexion with bright red cheeks. He was dressed in an old suit coat, similar to what you see many farmers wearing in the paddock.

"Howyergoen?" he asked in a laconic tone, his words running together.

"I'm a bit homesick to be honest with you," I told him with a shrug.

"That's no good. Whaddaya homesick about?"

"I'm heading to the big smoke to live, and just feeling a bit sad about leaving the family farm."

"Gee, that's no good. By the way, my name's Artie." He stuck out his hand and I shook it.

"Hi. My name's Ed."

"G'day, Ed. I've got just the thing for ya, mate."

"What's that?"

Artie opened his coat wide to display six small liquor bottles neatly placed in the inside lining of his coat. There was scotch, whiskey, rum, vodka, tequila, bourbon and sherry.

"Ta-da. Doctor Artie has just the medicine that'll fix ya up, Ed," he said with a devilish look in his eye. He selected the scotch and poured out a liberal portion into a small paper cup. "Would ya like a drink?"

"Ah... well, I'm not, ah, real sure if I should, ah," I replied nervously, the stinging words of Nana O'Grady still ringing in my ears.

"Come on, mate, don't be shy. One of these bastards won't hurt ya! Besides, it'll cure that homesickness, I guarantee it," he said with a grin as big as a Cheshire cat.

I took the cup and drank it in one long gulp.

"Crikey! I can hardly breathe," I said, almost choking, but that quickly changed. Initially, I felt as though I had inhaled fire and the inside of my cheeks burned as the scotch went down the hatch. But after the alcohol took effect, I felt as though I had been lit up like a Christmas tree. I had never experienced a feeling like it before.

It was love at first sight.

Artie was watching me with a sly look on his face. "Ya like that, Ed?"

"Yeah, bloody oath, Artie," I replied, feeling flush with good feelings.

Artie laughed. "You want another one?"

"Yeah, why not?"

It didn't take long before we were engaged in a good old fashioned drinkathon and my homesickness had miraculously disappeared, while Nana O'Grady's dire warnings had vanished into thin air. I set about having a bloody good time with my new-found friend. The booze had served its purpose and left an indelible mark on my mind, and I noted that I must call on it in the future if the need arose. There were no warning signs at that early stage as to what the grog might do to me, so I saw that first experience of alcohol as one of absolute joy.

Artie told me he worked as an engine driver on the railways and he was heading back to Lithgow where he worked. He'd been visiting his brother in Dubbo for the weekend. When he told me that he knew some of my O'Grady relatives who worked on the railways in Dubbo, our friendship was sealed.

Artie was a good at spinning a yarn. For the remainder of the trip he fired my imagination with stories of places he had travelled to around Australia. In some ways, he served as a prelude to many other interesting drinking mates I was to meet in my travels as the years progressed.

We got to Lithgow and when the train pulled up, Artie departed with a big 'cheerio!'. As he disappeared into the night, I could hear him singing Johnny O'Keefe's *Shout*.

***

Tim glared at me across the small table in his caravan.

"Thanks for saving my hide back there with the Maoris, but I fail to see how one drink turned you into a raving lunatic," he said, his arms folded tightly across his chest.

"I never said it turned me into a lunatic," I said with raised finger. "But I took special note that if I should find myself in a bind in the future then the booze could certainly bail me out."

"A bind! Oh, this is weak!" he exclaimed. "Water off a duck's back if you want my opinion."

"It was a little more than water off a duck's back. I know now that it sowed the seeds for the future," I said.

"Sounds like a fuckin' good night on the piss." Tim's fear of the Maoris was fading, and his hostility was starting to return.

"Ha, yeah, I use to think just like that," I told him, trying to keep my tone light. "That it was just a good time, until I finally realised that if I didn't put the first one down my throat, then I couldn't set the wheels of disaster in motion."

He looked at me contemptuously, but I ignored him.

"I never laid eyes on Artie ever again, but I can still see his huge frame with a grin from ear to ear, standing in the doorway of the train biding me farewell." I tapped my fingers on the table and was momentarily engrossed in my own thoughts, lost in my memory of that first drink. I snapped back to it. "Perhaps I should tell you how I nearly drowned on the day I arrived in Sydney," I said. Tim might have owed me to for saving his hide, but I didn't want him to get resentful at my presence. Maybe a story of me being in physical peril would give him some kind of perverse joy.

"Drowned?" He looked like he quite liked the idea of me drowning.

"Yeah, at Maroubra Beach."

***

The train pulled into platform one at Central Railway Station in the early hours of the morning. Uncle Kevin and Aunty Eunice were waiting for me. As soon as I stepped off the train, I pestered them about going for a surf at Maroubra Beach. I was excited about seeing the ocean again!

I loaded my bag into the back of their Simca sedan and we headed to their house overlooking the sea. I was mesmerised by the sheer size and beauty of the big blue ocean. Right from the start, the ocean had a very calming effect on me and I have always found great solace near the water.

We drove down the street to their Federation style three-bedroom brick home, where it overlooked Mistral Point. Uncle Kevin and Aunty Eunice lived there with their three children.

Robert was two years older than me and was about to start a civil engineering degree at university, Les was a year younger than me and Patricia was thirteen.

Uncle Kevin was a builder, and a no-nonsense but very likeable character. He was a wiry bloke in his early forties, and although he liked a drink or two he was as fit as a fiddle. Aunty Eunice, or Aunty, as we all called her, ran the house. She was a school teacher and both highly intelligent and very politically savvy. She didn't mind having a say and had been to a few protests in her time.

I had barely stepped foot in their house when I had my beach towel in my hands and was pestering Uncle Kevin to take me for a surf.

"Come on Uncle Kevin, I'm itching to get to get out there!" I said excitedly.

"There's no way I'm taking you down to the beach today, Ed. You'll get drowned in that surf," he said, shrugging me off.

"Aw, come on Uncle Kevin, it's my first day in Maroubra!" I pleaded.

"I said no, Ed, now scoot before I give you a kick up the behind," he said with an icy glare.

After about an hour of negotiating with Les, I was able to convince him to take me for a surf.

"Ed, if the old man finds out I've taken you down to Maroubra Beach, he'll kick my arse from here to the Sydney Cricket Ground," he said, but I could tell he wanted to go too.

"Aw, come on, Les. What are you, soft or something?" I sniggered.

"I'll show you who's soft around here, Ed," Les said, looking around to see if Uncle Kevin was in earshot. He looked like he was about to shape up, but changed his mind. "Okay, let's go, but you've got to be as quite as a church mouse because if the old man catches us..." Les drew his finger across his throat.

The O'Grady's kept a number of surfboards in their garage which were made of balsawood and were between eight foot and nine foot long. We carried those heavy planks down Marine Parade towards Maroubra Beach, and by the time I got down there I was stuffed. They were bloody heavy!

There was a ten foot swell running and it looked absolutely gnarly. Les gave me some very basic lessons in surfing that went in one ear and out the other. I was as toey as a tick to get into the surf, and I was still feeling the buzz of the previous night's drinking. Les told me to stick to the white water for the time being as the surf was too wild, but while he was still giving me instructions, I got impatient and jumped in the surf. I just wanted to be in the water! And being a country lad, I was wearing my footy shorts and an old South Sydney Rabbitohs jersey. Not exactly great surfing gear.

Les swore, but then paddled out to the back of the breakers where he waited for the sets to arrive, which left me to my own devices. I paddled out and got smashed time and time again. It felt as though I was in a washing machine. Finally, after about half an hour of trying to get control of my board, there was a break in the sets and I managed to paddle out to the back of the breakers.

Then out of the blue came the mother of all waves and I felt my short life pass before my eyes.

"Shit a brick on Sunday!" I screamed, right before the twelve foot wave crashed on top of my head and completely pulverised me deep into the ocean below.

Miraculously, I managed to hang onto my surfboard while I was tossed around like I was in a washing machine, slowly being pushed back in the direction of the shore. I swallowed a lot of water and honestly thought I was about to drown when through a stroke of luck, I surfaced. I lay on top of the surfboard while the surf thrashed me about.

While I was being washed to and fro, I somehow managed to hit a bloke on a surfboard who was coming into shore on the same wave. When I reached the beach, I was totally exhausted and coughing up salt water. When I finally managed to stand up, the bloke I had hit approached me, a look of thunder in his eyes. He was a well-built young man who appeared to be a couple of years older than me, at least six foot tall, and had blonde hair and blue eyes. I initially thought he was coming over to see if I was okay, but it took me completely by surprise when he hit me in the side of the head with a right hook that made me stagger backwards before falling to the sand.

"If I see you on this beach again, punk, I'll clean you up for good!" he shouted, before picking his surfboard up and walking away down the beach.

It was a good ten minutes before I recovered from my ordeal, but when I did I spied the bloke who had hit me just down the beach. I was by nature a fairly reserved kid, but I never liked being picked on. My hackles were up, so I picked myself up and walked down the beach towards him.

Stumpy had taught me how to box as a boy and I had carried that knowledge with me to boarding school where I had been a handy little southpaw. That's a boxer who has his right hand and right foot forward and leads with a right jab.

Forgetting my size and with my pride severely dented, I was determined to administer some justice to this joker. I was known for punching well above my weight and had sat a number of boys older than me fair on their arses. With that in mind, I approached this bloke without any fear.

As I got nearer, I noticed he was chatting up some blonde-looking bimbo while bragging about what had just happened.

"I cleaned this bloke right up, babe. He won't be surfacing for a while," he said, his chest all puffed up. I decided to interrupt his little speech.

"Hey, dickhead!" I yelled.

He turned around with a look of rage in his eyes. "What do you want, squirt?"

"I want you," I said, pointing at him menacingly.

"Why don't you piss off back to mummy before I clean you up for good, shortarse?"

"Ah, ah," I said with an icy glare, as I shook my head.

Well that just infuriated him. He charged at me, screaming, while throwing haymakers left, right and centre. It was obvious that he didn't have a clue how to fight, so I ducked under his misguided missiles with ease. As he shaped up in front of me, getting ready to land what he thought was the killer blow, I shook my head, stood on my toes and hit him with two lightening quick right jabs to the nose. I then followed with a cracking left hook to his jaw and a combination of devastating punches to his head and solar plexus which left him squirming on the beach like an octopus.

"I know who'll be crawling back to mummy bawling his eyes out now, prick!" I said triumphantly.

I picked my surfboard up and winked at the bimbo, who had a look of horror in her eyes.

"Bottom rail on top now, hey love," I said to her.

As I walked away, I noticed a girl in her mid-teens sitting on the beach not far from where the incident happened. She was attractive with strawberry blonde hair, and she wore a floral bikini and white shorts. As I was walking past her, she started clapping. She then stood up and walked over to me.

"There's a lot of us locals who have been waiting for someone like you to sort out Moose Payne for years. Congratulations," she said, and she kissed me on the cheek.

I blushed, as I wasn't used to being kissed by strange young women, especially ones as pretty as she was!

"I've never seen you around here before," she said.

"I've just come down from the country to live with my relatives," I said shyly.

"Well, you've come just at the right time because Moose Payne has been causing havoc around here for years." She stuck out her hand. "I'm Julie McCabe."

"G'day, I'm Ed Costigan."

We talked for a while and before long, Julie invited me back to her parent's house in Bona Vista Avenue for some lunch. I had no idea then, but our lives would become intertwined and Julie would eventually marry my best mate.

***

"So, you knocked out the local Maroubra Beach bully?" Tim said, a hint of worry on his face. It was always harder to threaten a man when you know he's got some boxing smarts.

"Yeah, I sorted the smartarse out," I told him, watching the change in his demeanour.

It was obvious by Tim's slightly more subservient attitude that the incident with the Maoris had shaken him to the core, and my description of my boxing prowess seemed to have hit a nerve too. I couldn't help but wonder if he thought the Maoris were going to come waltzing back through the door. Although I didn't have him eating out of my hand quite yet, he had become more receptive to what I was saying. He'd even given something like a smile as I described my near death experience.

"What about those Maoris?" he asked suddenly. "Do you reckon you could have sorted them out?"

"With that 410 shotgun in his hand?" I shook my head. "Not on your life. That's why I had to talk my way out of it."

"What about if he didn't have the shotgun?"

"I might have been in with a shot once upon a time, but definitely not all four of them together. I mean, let's face it they were a bunch of hard bastards and I'm not a spring chicken anymore. Mind you, when I was a young bloke it took a bit to stop me."

"You fancied yourself as a fighter, did you?"

"I fought pro. I could fuckin' handle myself, I shit you not... and I still can," I said, looking Tim straight in the eyes. I could see him flush, but he regained his composure quickly.

"Professional fighter, hey? Who else did you sort out?" he said, folding his arms.

"I fought plenty of good fighters in the ring, but I sorted out Moose's older brother Archie a few years after that. He was even bigger and meaner than Moose."

"What happened?"

"It wasn't long after I returned from Vietnam and I was at a party in Maroubra. I was in the backyard, drinking around the keg and talking to my girlfriend, when Archie gatecrashed the party. He was really drunk, hassling women and trying to pick fights with some of the blokes. I had just bought the Rolling Stones album, *Get Yer Ya Ya's Out,* and had the LP playing on the stereo. Mick Taylor was letting rip with a sublime guitar solo in the middle of *Sympathy for the Devil* when all the trouble started. Archie wanted to play an Elvis Presley album, so he snapped the Stones record in half."

Tim grimaced. "What did you do?"

"After Archie threatened to rearrange my head when I confronted him, I belted the living daylights out of him." I shrugged. "I was trigger-happy just after Vietnam and it didn't take much to upset me."

"So you really can fight?" Tim asked. "You're not just saying it?"

I nodded to him. "My grandfather taught me how to box when I was a kid. He won the VC in World War I and was as tough as nails."

"The VC? What did he do to win that?" he said.

"He cleaned up a bunch of Krauts at Poziers, and took some prisoners."

Tim whistled. "He must have been a hard bastard."

"He was, but as much as he was tough he was also a humble man. A good man." I gave Tim a look. "Something that you could learn a thing or two about, Tim."

He shuffled in his seat uneasily and changed the subject back to the Maoris.

"I must admit, you handled the situation pretty well with the Maoris. I mean you were pretty quick to think about the money you had at home; I honestly thought they were going to shoot me." He fidgeted for a moment. "So, you're not bullshitting me? You really fought pro?"

I gave him a reassuring smile. He was starting to lighten up. "Yeah, sure did, almost went all the way, too. It was just after I started my apprenticeship that I went to train as a boxer with one of the best in the game."

***

Shortly after the incident with Moose Payne I started my apprenticeship as a mechanic at R.G. Steel Transport, which was based in Coward Street, Mascot, not far from Sydney Airport. Reg Steel was a tough, stocky little man in his mid-forties who had served as a commando in New Guinea with my father during World War II. A good bloke and good to my family.

One of the mechanics who worked at Steel's Transport was a flaming redhead named Jimmy Fraser, who came from Newtown and rode an old Norton motorcycle. Jimmy was built like a brick shithouse and at 22 years of age was playing first grade rugby league for the Newtown Bluebags as a front row forward. He had been given the nickname 'Thumper' after his reputation as an enforcer became apparent. Thumper was a likable larrikin and a genuine hard man, but he was as loyal as they come to his mates. Thumper had a tattoo on his chest of both the Australian and Scottish flags, just like his grandfather, who was a piper on the Western Front during the Great War.

About four months after I had started at Steel's Transport, we were having smoko and Thumper was telling me a story about a local thug he had sorted out when I recounted the incident with Moose Payne.

"So, I stood on my toes and gave it to this big bastard, Thumper. I was really pissed off after he smacked me in the side of the head, so I got stuck into him and landed some great combinations which left him flat out on the beach."

Thumper broke out in a broad grin and exclaimed, "So you fancy yourself as a bit of a pug do ya, Ed?"

"Yeah, I've been boxing since my boarding school days. I can handle myself," I told him.

"Is that right? Are you interested in getting in the ring?" He looked at me appraisingly.

I grinned. "I'd love to, Thumper."

"I train with this bloke in his gym, and I kid you not, Ed, this bloke knows his stuff. If you like I can introduce you."

"Yeah, count me in, Thumper." I grinned again as he chugged me on the arm. Life in Sydney was going well.

A few days later, Thumper introduced me to Johnny Hunter. Johnny ran a boxing gym behind his house in Matraville and had a number of classy fighters training with him.

At first sight, Johnny's gym didn't look like anything special. It was an old iron shed at the rear of his dwelling that looked dilapidated, but its outside appearance didn't do justice to what really happened inside. Johnny's gym produced champions and those who entered came out a different person after they had been introduced to him.

The smell of liniment hit me when I first walked into that gym. Even today, whenever I smell the stuff it always takes me back to Johnny's ramshackle old shed. I loved Johnny's gym from the beginning. It had a type of charm about it, and it reminded me of the old converted dairy bale we used as our gym when I was at boarding school.

Johnny was in his mid-thirties at time; he had a medium build, average height and light brown hair, but he spoke in this calm manner that was just so great. There was no hint of ostentation about him which attracted me to him right from the start.

No sooner had Thumper introduced me to Johnny when he invited me to spar with him. "Did you bring your kit with you, Ed?"

"Got it all in my bag right here, Mr Hunter," I replied respectfully, tapping my bag.

"We don't go on formalities around here, Ed. Johnny's the name."

"Johnny's fine by me, Mr Hunter," I said, smiling.

I got kitted up and Johnny watched on with interest, leaning on the ropes, while Thumper helped to bandage my hands. I donned a pair of training mitts and then entered the ring.

"Righto, Ed, let's see what you can do."

Over the next five minutes, Johnny moved around the ring with ease, as I landed combinations on his mitts. The entire time he gave me instructions.

"That's the shot, Ed. Keep that guard up and move those feet."

Through the corner of my eye, I spied Thumper peering through the ropes with a grin on his face, watching me spar. We danced about for a while and eventually Johnny slapped me on shoulder, signifying we were done.

"I tell you what, Ed, I like what I see. There's some stuff we have to work on, but all in all you're as sharp as a tack."

I was chuffed. "Thanks, Johnny. I'd like you to help me get more speed with my combinations, if possible."

"We can do that and a whole lot more. I'd be more than happy if you came on board and trained with me, Ed," he told me.

A broad smile crossed my face. "I like the feel of this place, Johnny. I think I'll come back."

I heard a chuckle from the corner of the ring. "I think we may win a race with this young bastard, Johnny," called Thumper, smiling.

Over the next few months I sparred with both Johnny and

a number of the other blokes he was training. Although I was initially a little homesick after arriving in Sydney, this soon dissipated after joining his gym.

Johnny helped a lot of troubled youth in his gym and this was a real eye-opener for a country kid like me. Some of the local Aboriginal kids, especially from down Matraville way, were tough street kids who had been in a lot of trouble with the law, and as a last resort, had been brought to Johnny to see if he could straighten them out.

He was ahead of his time, that bloke. He tried to instill in them a sense of pride in themselves and by doing so, they could learn to have pride in their culture. "Don't worry where you've come from, think about where you're headed," he would tell us all. Didn't really matter where you came from, he was all about knowing yourself. Through his steady influence many of those troubled kids were able to become great boxers and turn their lives around to make something out of themselves.

Johnny taught me about positive thinking, something that he believed was essential for making a great boxer and great human beings. "Get the mind thinking right and the rest will follow," he would constantly say to me. And his favourite, "You are what you think."

In time, Johnny was to have a great influence on my life, and although I was to hit the skids down the track I never forgot the great wisdom he imparted to me.

One of the boxers who sparred at the gym was a talented Aboriginal from La Perouse named Rory Gilbert. Rory was my age and fought as a middleweight, whereas I fought as a welterweight.

He had been in a lot of trouble with law, stealing cars and

doing break and enters before the authorities brought him to Johnny to straighten him up.

It was a couple of weeks after I first came to train with Johnny that he put Rory and I in the ring together for the first time.

Rory wasn't too keen on having a talented white kid like me in the gym, as he saw himself as the top dog. He made his feelings toward me known from the start.

"So, you're Johnny's new wonder kid, hey Whitey."

I said nothing, but leaned up against the inside of the ropes, rubbing my new leather boxing gloves that Stumpy had recently bought me.

"I see you've got your new, little shiny-arse gloves on, Eddy-boy."

This automatically made me resentful, as I hated being called Eddy. Rory himself wore an old, battered pair of gloves that looked as though they had seen a lot of bouts. He punched them together.

"I'll whip your little fuckin' Whitey-soft-marshmallow-arse before you hit me with those gloves, pretty boy Eddy," he said sarcastically.

I said nothing but boiled inside. I wanted to smash the smartarse, but he was a middleweight so I needed to be wary.

Our bout got started and he was *quick*. His punches were hard and they stung, as was to be expected when sparring with a boxer from a heavier division.

"Come on, white fella! Is that all you've got?"

Rory gave me a good working out in that first month, and although I was quick on my feet and with my fists, so was he, and he managed to get through my guard frequently. His punches left me bruised on a regular basis.

Then Stumpy came to Sydney to visit. I was mighty glad to see him, but shortly after arriving he decided he wanted to go to Johnny's gym to watch me spar.

He saw the trouble I was having with Rory and that night back at the O'Grady's, he gave me a boxing tip that turned my fortunes around. "Ed, I don't want to steal Johnny's thunder because I know he's a very good trainer, but I've got a little suggestion that might help you overcome that Rory fella."

"What's that, Stumpy?" I said. "I'd take any tip if it'd help me down Rory Gilbert."

"You know how I've told you about Dwyer, who was in the war with me?"

"Oh yeah, I love your yarns about him, Stumpy."

"Well, as much as he was a crazy bugger, he was also a very good boxer," Stumpy told me. "He developed a combination of punches that proved to be very effective."

A new combo sounded pretty good! "What was it, Stumpy?"

"The best way to describe it, Ed, is like watching two pistons going up and down."

"You mean he was just using his fists and running them up and down?" I started moving my fists, trying to do what Stumpy suggested.

"Exactly, Ed," nodded Stumpy, "but with incredible speed. What Dwyer lacked in finesse, he made up in sheer speed. I saw him use it on a number of occasions with great effect."

I grinned.

It was two days after this when Rory and I faced each other again.

"You ready for another pasting again today, Eddy?"

I said nothing but gave him a steely look. I glanced at

Stumpy, who was leaning on the ring ropes, and he gave me a subtle wink.

We commenced sparring and true to form, Rory gave it to me with his customary flurry of punches. We had been sparring for a while when I sensed that Rory was about to up the tempo, and just like Stumpy had suggested, I hit Rory with a flurry of piston-like punches under his elbows that took him by surprise. Rory tried his best to move away from me, but I stuck to him like glue the whole time, hitting with a quickly executed flurry of punches that totally unnerved him.

"What you up to, Whitey?" asked Rory through gritted teeth.

I said nothing, but kept up my onslaught. Rory started to tire after a minute of this barrage of punches, and then he dropped his head. That's when I went in with my knockout punch. The right uppercut that I hit Rory with that day was one of the sweetest punches I ever threw. There have probably been more technically better punches that I'd thrown in my career, but that one punch was full of venom. Rory's head flung back with the sheer force of it and he completely lost his balance. As he was falling to the canvas, I countered with a left hook to the side of his face that finished him off. The end result was that Rory was left lying on the ground, motionless.

I stood in the ring with my hands on my hips surveying Rory lying on the deck. Stumpy stood there with a grin from ear to ear, when Johnny came walking over.

"What's going on here, Ed? You two are suppose to be sparring, not trying to kill each other," Johnny said, somewhat agitated.

"He was getting a bit too big for his boots, Johnny. Had to stand up for myself."

Johnny stepped into the ring to get Rory up. After a short time, Rory came to and sat up while Johnny supported him.

"That's enough from you two young Turks. You'll end up killing each other," Johnny said, frowning at both of us.

Rory wiped his nose, shook his head, then focused on groggily on me. "You got lucky, Whitey. Wait till the next time we meet, I'll teach you a lesson."

Although Rory continued to hit me hard when we sparred, he never did get the better of me after that day, as he was always wary of what I might have up my sleeve. As my confidence grew, so too did my skills.

Two things changed after that day. Rory found a new respect for me and he never again called me 'Eddy'. And in time, what became grudging respect turned into outright respect, and after my first bout, it developed into a friendship. He was a good man.

"From now on we will call that combination the 'Coorigil Killer'," said Stumpy after we got home from the gym.

I trained hard with Johnny over the next two months and by July of 1963, he had secured my first amateur bout on a Friday night at the Bankstown Police Citizens Youth Club. The bout was against a tough as nails Yugoslav boxer named Zelko Tomasovic who was living in the Villawood Migrant Hostel in Sydney.

The fight was scheduled as three two minute rounds, and as I waited for the bout to start, I adjusted my headgear and shorts and looked long and hard at my opponent. Zelko was a tough looking character with jet black hair, an olive complexion and a scar across the front of his chin. He had a mean look in his eye that suggested his path through life had not always been rosy. He was dressed in black shorts and black boots, and while he was sitting in his corner waiting for the fight to start, he yelled at me in a thick accent, "Hey, Aussie boy, I am not Yugoslav, I am a proud Croatian. Don't you forget that!"

As Johnny put my mouthguard in place, I instinctively knew that my first fight was to be an initiation of fire.

I had a full house of family watching the fight that night. Stumpy was there, and Noel and Sean O'Grady had caught the train down from Dubbo earlier that day. Uncle Kevin and Les O'Grady had also come from Maroubra, not wanting to miss my first bout.

Stumpy had spoken to me just before I had gone to the changeroom to prepare myself for the fight. "I can see great things in you, Ed. Not only are you a classier boxer, but you have a brain on your shoulders. Remember, Ed: think, think, think," he said, before slapping my shoulder and going to find his seat.

When the bell for the first round sounded, all my suspicions about Zelko's toughness came to fruition. The bloke came out firing, looking for the knockout blow from the start. For the best part of that first round, Zelko punched the living daylights out of me and if I hadn't been keeping my hands up near my face, I would have gone down. Towards the end of that first round he tried a cheap shot by standing on my foot and then he landed a cracking left jab right on my chin. I staggered backwards and had double vision before the bell to end the round saved me from further harm.

"He's as mad as a fuckin' hatter, Johnny," I said, panting heavily as I sat on my stool in the corner of the ring.

"I know he's crazy, that's why you have to keep your guard up," said Johnny, trying to force some water into me.

"Did you see the dirty bastard stand on my foot?" I said through gasps.

"Oh yeah, he'll have a bag full of those little dirty tricks waiting for you, Ed, but you're a classier boxer. Use those quick feet of yours, keep away from his rough stuff, wait for the opportunity and then *whammo*! You go in there and show him what you're made of," said Johnny.

Rory Gilbert was my second and as he sponged my face he said, "You'll get this bloke, Ed. He's a street fighter and sure, he's tough, but you're just as hard, plus a lot smarter than he is. Remember, you have a knockout drop in both your hands."

I looked at Rory in surprise. This newfound admiration was surprising to me at that stage, but I suppose it was one of those things where inside the gym is one thing, but two blokes from the same stable had to be united against an outsider. He smiled and winked at me before giving me a final sponge on my face.

I looked across at Stumpy where he was sitting, and he raised both his fists and gestured for me to give it to Zelko.

When the bell for round two rang, Zelko came out like a man possessed once again and attempted to punch my lights out. I was awake up to him this time and moved swiftly on my feet, managing to avoid his onslaught.

It was halfway through the second round when Zelko attempted to hit me with a right hook but I ducked and it missed me. I then countered with a beautiful right jab which landed right on his nose, followed by some nice left-right combinations to his body that stung him badly. Zelko was far from finished, as he countered with some stinging jabs to my stomach, as well as a low blow to my groin before I was able to dart away and avoid any more trouble. I wasn't happy about the cheap shot to my private parts, so towards the end of the round

I waited for him to drop his guard and hit him with a shattering right uppercut under his chin that managed to lift him off the canvas and put him flat on his back. The referee gave him the standard eight second count before he dragged himself off the canvas. Zelko was dazed, but he was one hell of a tough bastard and as he adjusted his shorts from the corner of the ring he growled, "Lucky shot. I'll fix you once and for all."

Zelko came charging for me with a demonic look in his eyes that suggested he was going to kill me. Without hesitation, I stood on my toes and gave him a straight right to his nose, followed by a left uppercut under his chin. The uppercut was delivered with pinpoint accuracy and so hard I could hear his jaw snap. This time, Zelko didn't get off the canvas.

I returned to my corner and after the referee counted Zelko out, he declared me the winner by knockout. I could hear my family cheering, and when I looked over, Stumpy pumped his fist in pride.

Johnny ruffled my hair. "Don't you forget this moment, Ed."

I grinned back with the satisfaction of a man who had just reached an important goal.

"I told you had a knockout drop in both those hands, Cozzy," said Rory with a cheeky grin. It was the first time that Rory had ever referred to me by my nickname, and I felt my chest swell with pride that my former adversary had given me a huge tick of approval.

I looked back at my entourage of supporters and sitting in the middle of them, Stumpy had a grin on his face. Through all the din of noise coming from inside the auditorium I could hear Stumpy's voice.

"You did it, Ed! Well done, you did it!"

The last I saw of Zelko was him being assisted out of the ring, barely able to walk and holding his jaw.

***

"After my first fight, my confidence soared to a new level, Tim. I didn't lose a bout for the rest of 1963. I had some close fights, but I always managed to come out on top. All the hard training and physical work at Steel's, coupled with Aunty Eunice's exceptional food filled me out. In fact, my boxing progressed so rapidly that Johnny thought I was a genuine chance for the 1964 Tokyo Olympic games."

Tim raised his eyebrows. "Really?"

I looked at Tim, smiled and shook my head. "Yeah, well, I did say it was just a chance."

"What does that mean?" Tim said.

"That's when I had an early warning sign that the booze might be a problem in my life."

Tim didn't say anything, he waited for me to elaborate.

"It all started when Nana O'Grady decided to come and live with us in Maroubra in late 1963. She reckoned she had rheumatism, so her GP in Dubbo suggested that salt water would be just the ticket she needed to get her firing on all cylinders again. And I can tell you, she was right into me from the first day she arrived." I gave a wry laugh. "'I hope you're doing your Sunday masses, Ed!' she would say, and I would respond with a pious 'Yes, Nana.' She'd come back and hound me about confession and benediction on Wednesday nights and the list would go on until I felt as though I was being tried at the Spanish Inquisition. The whole rheumatism story was a load of bullshit."

"Checking up on you, was she?" Tim snorted.

"That's all it was. Making sure the young buck didn't play

up while I was in the big smoke," I said, pointing to myself. "Yeah, she was a major thorn in my side. Nana O'Grady was as strong as a mallee bull. Besides, I never saw her saw go near the ocean in the whole time she stayed with us."

Tim gave me a wry smile.

"The reason I mentioned Nana," I said seriously, "was that I had built up a huge resentment about her being around. Like I said, she was constantly in my face, so I decided to have a night on the town with Thumper to blow the cobwebs out of my system, so to speak. I shouldn't have gone out that Friday because I was in training to gain selection for the Olympics. The temptation got the better of me though, and I went out anyway. It had disastrous consequences."

Tim fidgeted in his seat and scratched his chin. "What happened?"

"Thumper and I got on the piss in town before we ended up at Surf City, a nightclub in Kings Cross. We came out of there late and were walking down William Street when we noticed four Sharpies giving a couple of young girls a hard time."

Tim frowned. "That old gang. What happened?"

Thumper and I had a huge blue with them. We lost a bit of bark off us, but ended up belting the shit out of them."

Tim smiled. "Good result then."

I shook my head. "Not really. In the process of cleaning up the Sharpies, I fractured my right wrist giving one of them an uppercut."

The smile left Tim's face. "Oh."

"You know what that meant, right?"

He nodded. "You missed out on the Olympics."

"You betcha. The wrist never healed in time and my Olympic dreams went down the gurgler. I was devastated." I thought back to that day. It was a stupid move and I never should have been out.

"What a bummer."

"Yeah, well, Johnny said a little bit more than that when he found out I had been on the drink with Thumper. 'Are you insane, Ed? You were a genuine chance for the Olympics!' was about the best of it." I sighed. "He couldn't fathom how stupid I was to go out on the town and jeopardise my chances of Olympic glory. At the time, I couldn't figure it out either. If I only knew then what I know now, I would have stayed put." I sighed again. "The swinging sixties, Tim. I was living in Maroubra and it was sun, surf, bands, dances, parties and rock'n'roll. As much as I was dedicated to my boxing, all that stuff going on around me was like having a carrot dangled in front of my nose. On top of all that was the fact that I met Sandy McKenzie, and my world was turned upside down."

Chapter 3

March 1964, Maroubra Surf Club

THE 1960S WAS a heady time as society started to cut the loose from the shackles of a conservative past. There was prosperity in Australia, and great music, girls, booze and a carefree lifestyle that made it an exciting time to be alive. Life around Maroubra in the early sixties took on an attitude of 'put up or shut up'. There was no time for pussies in or out of the water. There were different groups that held strong allegiances to each other and you were likely to get into trouble if you overstepped the mark with a group outside of your own.

Although my surfing ability was average, I belonged to the Skegs, which was a gang who surfed and who were from Maroubra. Then there were the Bodgies who were from Maroubra but didn't surf, and their girlfriends were the Wedgies. The Sharpies were from out of the area and although they didn't surf, they liked to drink and fight.

One balmy Saturday night in March 1964, I found myself at the Maroubra Surf Club and the place was going off as Little Pattie sang *Stompin' At Maroubra*. Not long after I arrived, I met up with Julie McCabe. Although I found Julie attractive, I saw her more her like a sister. I felt comfortable in her company and able to talk to her with ease. It was nice to have a friend like her with most of my family back west.

"Hi, Ed! How have you been since your hand injury?" she asked, landing a kiss on my cheek.

"I'm okay now, but I was laid up while I recovered," I told her, giving her a grin.

"Don't worry, Ed, there will be bigger scalps for you up the track," she said with a smile.

I returned the smile. "Yeah, well I spoke to Johnny and I've decided to turn pro."

She gave me a wide smile, but just then a beautiful looking blonde girl with blue eyes walked up to Julie and gave her a big hug. "Hi, Jules! How have you been?"

"Great, Sandy," replied Julie, hugging her back. "I've just started nursing at Royal Prince Alfred Hospital and I'm enjoying it." Julie then turned to me and said, "Ed, this is a good friend of mine, Sandy McKenzie."

I was immediately taken by Sandy's beauty. With her shoulder-length blonde hair, sparkling blue eyes, gorgeous lips and high cheekbones she was a knockout, especially wearing a white blouse with a pink cardigan and a knee-length checkered skirt.

It didn't take for Julie long to notice that I had an eye for Sandy, so she excused herself and went to the bar to get some drinks so we could get acquainted alone.

"Hi," I blurted out.

Sandy gave me a broad smile and said, "You're not the Ed who sorted out Moose Payne are you?"

"Yeah, that's me," I said with a grin.

Sandy squeezed my hand and expressed her delight that I had taken out the local thug.

As we continued to talk I told her I was an apprentice mechanic and she informed me that she worked as a teller for the Commonwealth Bank in the city. Sandy was interested to find out I was brought up on a farm, and as she listened intently as I described life on the land, I found that I couldn't take my eyes off her. I was so smitten by her beauty that I was taken by surprise when a young man walked up and kissed Sandy on the cheek. He was a striking lad over six feet tall with a magnificent build and blonde hair and blue eyes.

"Hi, gorgeous, how are you?" he said to Sandy, like he owned her.

"Hello, Brian. What kept you?" Sandy asked, with a hint of suspicion.

"I was just looking at a new surfboard I was thinking of buying. Who's this bloke, Sandy?" he said, eyeing me off, his tone hostile.

"This is a friend of Julie's," she said with her hands on her hips. Sandy then turned to me and said, "Ed, this is my boyfriend Brian McGovern. Brian this is Ed. He's the guy that Julie was telling us about who knocked out Moose Payne."

"Oh yeah, I've heard all about you," Brian said, looking me up and down. "Looks like you've earned yourself a bit of a reputation after sorting out the local Maroubra Beach bully."

"He smashed me in the side of the face after a surfing mishap, so he got what he deserved." I shrugged. Les O'Grady had told me all about Brian McGovern. He was the local Maroubra surfing champion, but he was also full of himself and a real ladies man.

Brian didn't take too kindly to a total stranger talking to his girlfriend, so tried to put me in my place by belittling me right from the start.

"Heard about the mishap with your hand too. Shame about the Olympics, mate," he said with a sneer.

Well, that hit a raw nerve and brought up an instant resentment towards him. He continued to rib me about my misfortune, even alluding to the fact that my surfing ability was next to zero, and all the time talking to me in a condescending tone. I was seething inside, but could not counter any of it because I knew it was all the truth. Just when I thought I couldn't handle any more and was about to do something stupid, Julie returned from the bar.

"Hi, guys. Everyone enjoying themselves?" Julie's sudden appearance was a welcome relief as I was doing my utmost to keep a lid on my bubbling resentment.

Brian gave me a dirty look before taking Sandy by the hand and leading her to the dance floor, and as he did, Julie noticed my look of disdain towards the local surfing champion.

I know what you're thinking, Ed," Julie said, seeing where my thoughts were going. "I can't see the two of them lasting. Sandy will see through him eventually and besides, he has a reputation for fooling around with other girls."

"They say that first impressions count, Julie, and that being the case I think he's a total dickhead," I told her bitterly.

Julie could see that I was hot under the collar, so she tried to lighten the conversation.

"Did you see the way she was smiling at you, Ed? That girl likes you, that's for sure."

I gave Julie a coy smile and said, "I'd like to get to know her, Julie, but I suppose there is next to no chance while having a bloke like Brian hanging around."

"I wouldn't be so sure about that, Ed Costigan. Sandy likes decent men and you sure fit the bill."

Over the next month I thought about Sandy constantly and wondered whether there was a chance that the two of us could get together. I had never had a girlfriend before, but I instinctively knew that she liked me. Then, in late May 1964, I received a phone call from Julie one night. I could barely comprehend what she was saying, she was just that excited.

"You won't believe it, Ed, but my dad has got four tickets to the Beatles concert!"

"What?" I yelled. I was so excited for her.

"You know how my dad's the local GP at Maroubra? Well one of his patients happens to know the promoter and gave him the tickets for free, and Dad has passed them on to me."

"That's fantastic, Julie!"

"My new boyfriend Reg is just itching to go and I've decided to invite Sandy and you also."

"Sandy? And me?" I exclaimed. It was turning into a great day.

"I thought that would interest you, Ed," Julie said with a giggle.

I was suddenly struck by something. "That's unbelievable, Julie. I'd love to go, but what about Brian?"

"They broke up a couple of weeks ago."

My heart thundered in my chest. "They did? What happened?"

"Sandy got sick of him chatting up all the other girls so she told him to get packing."

She was free!

The weeks leading up to the concert felt like a real drag, but finally the day arrived. The four of us met in front of the Sydney stadium. Sandy looked beautiful in a pink dress with white buttons at the front.

"I love that blue-striped shirt of yours, Ed," she said with a beaming smile.

"Thanks Sandy, you look a knockout yourself in that dress," I told her truthfully.

Sandy laughed as she took me by the arm and I was in heaven.

After Johnny Devlin, the New Zealand rocker, had completed his set, the Beatles came on stage and the crowd erupted into a rapturous noise which I had never before experienced in my life. Sandy was screaming and then totally out of character, I also started screaming along with the thousands of other people jammed into the stadium. It was electric. Julie and Reg, who were standing beside us, were dancing like they were possessed and I started to laugh uncontrollably as they screamed with delight.

I remember John Lennon belting out *She Loves You* and Sandy and I found ourselves singing the words to *I Saw Her Standing There*. They played many of their classics that night including *I Want To Hold Your Hand*, *All My Loving* and *Can't Buy Me Love*.

To hear the Beatles that night was one of the most memorable experiences of my life. I felt as though somebody had coloured me in and I had come alive. That night truly awoke me to the swinging sixties and from then on I began to take a keen interest in many of the great bands of the time, and to embrace a period that changed our culture. I would try and get to whatever concerts I could, and between my apprenticeship, boxing, and going out, my life was full.

After the concert, the four of us went to the Silver Spade Room in the Chevron Hotel in Kings Cross. After we had been there a while, Sandy invited me up for a dance and as I held her beautiful body close to mine, she kissed me on the lips. It was like I saw the Milky Way as my mind went into outer space.

When I came back down to earth, Sandy said, "I think you're a really nice country boy, Ed."

I beamed. "Sandy, I was totally knocked over by you that first night we met at the Maroubra Surf Club."

"I liked you, too. I could see that you had a very lovely side to you," she whispered.

I kissed Sandy passionately on the lips, and as she buried her head into my chest I said, "I'd like to see you more often, Sandy."

Sandy looked up at me with her beautiful blue eyes beaming at me and said, "I'd like that too, Ed."

Over the next month, Sandy and I saw much more of each other. I felt comfortable in her company, for as well as being very beautiful, she was a very grounded girl and highly intelligent.

We would often catch up down at Maroubra Beach, the surf club, or she would visit me at the O'Grady's which was tricky with Nana living there. Nana was a constant thorn in my side; she was always sticking her nose into my personal affairs, especially my relationship with Sandy.

"Is that Sandy a Catholic?" she enquired one day.

"No, she's a Presbyterian, Nana."

"Presbyterians! They're almost as bad as Protestants."

"I don't care what religion she is, Nana. Sandy's a nice girl."

"She can be as nice as pie, Ed, but you won't be able to marry her at the altar. You'll have to exchange your vows inside the sacristy."

"Who said anything about marriage, Nana?" I said in a caustic tone.

"You know what I think of those Protestants and Presbyterians, don't you, Ed? They're a bunch of heathens. All because of that Henry VIII and the reformation, the lecherous scoundrel. I bet you he is burning in hell," she said viciously.

It was time to get out of the house as I could see that Nana was starting to wind up, and I didn't want to be on the end of one of her salvos. As I was leaving the lounge-room, she shelled one final round. "What about Julie McCabe? She's a good Catholic girl. Why don't you ask her out?"

"She's going out with Reg!" I shouted back.

"Is he a Catholic?"

"All I know is he's a carpenter and a good footy player." I grabbed my jacket and opened the door.

"Christ was a carpenter. There might be hope for him yet."

I left Nana talking to herself while I made a beeline to Sandy's home down near Maroubra Beach. It was better to just not be at home, so for the most part, I wasn't.

My wrist had totally healed and I was back training hard with Johnny the moment it was better. Since my eighteenth birthday in March of 1964, I had filled out and developed big shoulders and arms, and had moved up into the middleweight division. I had been spurred on by the fact that I missed selection for the Olympic games, and coupled with my relationship with Sandy, I was happy. I have often pondered on how a good woman can spur you on to great heights and Sandy was proof of this. Many men are distracted by a woman in their lives, but Sandy had the opposite effect on me; she helped me to focus and work hard towards my goals.

In July of 1964, I had my first professional fight at South Sydney Rugby League Club against the flamboyant redhead, Bluey O'Neil.

O'Neil, who was 20 years of age, hailed from the inner-city suburb of Enmore and was a cocky little larrikin who thought he was the new Al Capone around the inner west. He had fought ten professional fights, winning all including seven on knockout. A swaggering little Sharpie, his reputation was as big as his mouth and he usually came into the ring like a hurricane.

As we stood in the centre of the ring, eyeballing each other before the start of the first round, Bluey growled at me, "You'll have more than a buggered wrist when I'm finished with ya tonight, Costigan."

"In ya dreams, Bluey," I said.

When the bell for round one sounded, Bluey came out like a bull at a gate, throwing haymakers and rabbit killers left and right. It was a matter of staying clear of the maniac or getting my head knocked off.

O'Neil kept this onslaught up for the first two rounds and all I could do was cover up and avoid being knocked out. Whenever he came close I would get a jab in, but Bluey's onslaught was so ferocious that I barely had a chance to take any action.

At the end of the third round he took a swig from a port bottle and growled at me from where he was sitting. "You enjoying being softened up, Costigan? That's nothing compared to what you've got coming to ya."

Towards the end of the fifth, he clocked me with a cracking right hook on the chin which made me stagger back into the ropes before the bell saved me. I sat on my stool breathing heavily, trying to figure out how I was going to beat this mug lair.

"You're going alright, Ed," said Rory, sponging me down. "Bluey usually knocks out his opponent in the opening rounds, so you've done well to handle his onslaught."

"If I could only get a look in, I know I can knock this bastard out," I gasped.

"You just hang in there, Ed. Bluey is starting to tire and that's when you go in for the kill."

Johnny was massaging the back of my neck and he said, "Rory's right, Ed. Stay cool and you'll get your opportunity to land a knockout blow on him soon. Bluey's getting frustrated because he hasn't been able to knock you out yet. He knows he's up against a classy fighter."

When the bell for the sixth rang, I sprang to my feet and engaged Bluey in the centre of the ring. True to form, Bluey came for me, but I ducked and then hit him with a cracking straight right to the nose followed by a devastating left uppercut under his chin. Bluey staggered backwards and almost fell to the canvas before managing to regain his composure. He was in shock that I had managed to hit him with two great punches, and as he prepared to shape up to me again I said, "There's more to come, Bluey."

"You prick, Costigan. That was just pure luck that punch of yours. I'll get you for that."

For the duration of the round Bluey and I traded blows, but his punches had lost their impact as he was tiring and wary of what else I might have up my sleeve.

In between rounds, Johnny gave me instructions. "You're going well, Ed. Keep working him over and don't let up on him. He's in two minds now as he knows you've got his measure."

"Remember, Ed, you've got a knockout drop in both your hands," said Rory, as he sponged my face.

I looked up at Rory and with a voice full of steely determination said, "I'm going to finish the bastard off in the next round, Rory."

"You go and get him, Ed." Rory ruffled my hair.

When the bell for the seventh rang, I sprang out of the chair and was giving him a good workover when he hit me with a low blow. Pain rippled through my body.

"How did you like that, Costigan? I'm surprised that hurt 'cause I didn't think you had any balls," he spat.

I grimaced with pain but said nothing. While my balls were still throbbing he came for me, throwing everything he could, hoping for a knockout blow that would finish my night.

Although I didn't allow him the pleasure of knocking me out, he managed to hit me a number of times in the head, with one punch opening a small cut to the corner of my right eye. The referee looked at my cut and although concerned, he did not stop the fight.

I stayed clear of Bluey until the pain subsided, but inside I was seething that he had hit me with such a cheap shot. It didn't help that the cut was such a doozy. I sensed that the referee might stop the fight if my eye became any worse, so I made a decision to go for the knockout blow. I came for him and hit him with a ferocious straight right to his nose which opened him up. I followed that by hitting him with a left uppercut to the chin and a murderous straight right to the mouth which sent his head rocking backwards and ultimately through the ropes and into the crowd.

The auditorium roared and it took Bluey a couple of minutes before he came to his senses. He had ended up with his head jammed between two chairs and his arse in the air. It took his supporters some time before they were able to dislodge him from his rather unfortunate predicament.

Bluey was away with the pixies when they finally freed him. I looked down on the demoralised figure and with a big wink exclaimed, "They'll have to take you to the wrecking yard, Bluey!"

Bluey gave me a wild-eyed look, resembling somebody who had just seen a ghost, but said nothing. The bloke was non-compos mentis anyway.

I made my way to my corner where Johnny and Rory were standing with huge grins on their faces. Johnny slapped me on the back and exclaimed, "That was a gutsy effort, Ed! You handled that fight so well. I am proud of you, son."

Rory's grin had grown even bigger by this stage and he slapped me on the shoulder. "I told you that you would knock him out, Ed."

I grinned back and said to the pair of them, "That's just the start of things to come."

After the fight, my entourage ventured back to the O'Grady's to celebrate my win. They included Sandy, Julie, Stumpy, Noel, as well as Thumper, and my boss, Reg Steel.

Once at the O'Grady's, Nana waddled up to me from the kitchen where she had been preparing food with Aunty Eunice and said, "So, did you win?"

Before I could answer, Les O'Grady chimed in. "He was unbelievable, Nana. He knocked the thug out and sent him spiralling into the crowd."

"Hmph. Congratulations, Ed, but don't let it go to your head," Nana said grudgingly.

"We've got the makings of a champion, Nana," said Noel, slapping me on the back.

Sandy nudged in close to me and landed a big kiss on my cheek. "He's my knight in shining armour, is my lovely Ed."

"And who may this slip of a thing be?" said Nana to me without acknowledging Sandy.

"This, Nana, is my girlfriend, Sandy," I said, putting my arm around Sandy and trying not to let the old bat spoil the mood.

"So, you're the young lass who has been stealing my grandson's affections."

"I am," Sandy said confidently.

Nana stared her up and down, dismissed her out of hand and turned back to me and said, "Well, you make sure she doesn't keep you from your apprenticeship and doing your Sunday masses, Ed."

Aunty Eunice, who was never backward in coming forward, was standing nearby and exclaimed loudly, "Sandy is a lovely girl and has been a wonderful addition to the family, Nana. She has been nothing but a positive influence on Ed."

Sandy gave Nana a huge smile, but Nana said, "Well, let's keep it that way." She then about-faced and went to her bedroom.

Stumpy, who was standing nearby listening to the conversation said, "Listen, we're all here to celebrate Ed's win and that's what we're going to do. There's bigger things up the track for this lad." Stumpy slapped me on the back and led me to the dining table where a magnificent spread was waiting.

***

"That was one hell of a baptism of fire against Bluey O'Neil, Tim," I said.

"So, you're not bullshitting me," Tim said. "He actually ended up with head jammed between the seat?"

I smiled. "As true as I'm sitting here, that's exactly what happened."

Tim gave me a slight grin.

"He was a mug lair, was Bluey. He did a stint inside Long Bay in the mid-seventies for belting the crap out of some innocent bloke outside the St George Leagues Club one Saturday night. Apparently, he had just had an argument with his girlfriend and stormed out of the club in a rage and cleaned up the first person he saw," I told him.

Tim nodded but said nothing.

I shuffled in my seat. I was craving a cuppa, but I didn't want to say anything just yet. "By my 19th birthday in March of 1965, I had fought eight more bouts, managing to win them all, with five by knockout."

Tim raised his eyebrows. "Nice."

"Yep. I never lost a fight. There was some tough ones among them but I managed to win 'em all."

"That's a bloody good record," Tim said, sounding impressed.

"I was really fit and rarely went near the drink at that point. After losing out on the Olympics because of my night out, I steered well clear of the piss. Besides, I had Sandy by my side and she was a great girl and we had a lot of fun together."

"What sort of fun?" Tim said with a slight grin.

I smiled. "Sandy was the first woman I ever had sex with, if that's what you're asking. I felt guilty about it at first because I was brought up a Catholic and sex before marriage was seen as a mortal sin in the eyes of the Church and you could go to hell. It might seem trivial now, but it was big deal back then. Besides, I had nosy Nana O'Grady constantly on the prowl, checking up on me." I waggled my eyebrows. "As you can imagine, finding privacy was a bit of an issue. We did it on Maroubra Beach one Saturday night after we left the club."

"It was that good, was it?" Tim noted my smile and rolled his eyes.

"It was like I went to heaven, Tim. Sandy was sensational." I closed my eyes and recalled that most intimate moment all those years ago. "Anyway, enough of all those carnal thoughts," I said with a grin. "Now where was I? Oh yeah, boxing. Things were moving along so well in that department, that the opportunity arose for a crack at a title."

***

In early June of 1965, I had the opportunity to fight for the New South Wales middleweight title against the reigning champion from Balmain, Alby Daubert.

By this stage of my boxing career, I had built up a considerable following and there was a large contingent, including some of the Eumungerie mob, to watch the bout which was fought on a Monday night at the Sydney Stadium.

Before the fight, Johnny gave me explicit instructions. "Alby has got a devastating right hook that has sat plenty of blokes on their arses, Ed, so make sure you keep your guard up."

"I'm ready for this fight, Johnny. I really want this, it's a stepping stone to the Australian title."

"Good. Like you, he's a southpaw and a classy boxer, but if you're smart you'll have his measure," Johnny said.

I nodded in agreement.

Rory chugged me on the shoulder. "You've got enough tricks in your bag to beat this bloke, Ed."

It was late in the first round when Alby almost derailed my plans. I was concentrating on winning rather than boxing when he came at me, swinging like an orangutan. He clocked me with two cracking big punches to the side of my head that knocked me down. It was the first time that I had been knocked down in the ring and it shook me to the core. The referee gave me the standing count while I was on one knee and I only just managed to get myself back on my feet before the bell for the first round went.

Johnny gave me a spray when I got back to my corner. "What are you doing out there, Ed?"

I sucked in the big ones. "I just went in for the kill and *whammo*! He hit me."

"You were prancing around the ring like a show pony with your guard down and wha*ck!* He cleaned you up!" spat Johnny. He was furious.

"I just wanted to knock him out, Johnny."

"You're thinking about the belt and not what you have to do to win it, Ed. Listen, you'll get the title, but you have to stay switched on if you want to win this fight. Get your mind back where it should be or else Rory and I will be dragging you off the canvas."

Rory sponged me down. "Come on, Ed. You're too good a boxer to get knocked out. Start using all those combinations we've practiced."

I came out for the second round and concentrated on boxing rather than going for the knockout, and same again for the round after. Alby and I went toe to toe over the ensuing rounds and I managed to avoid his knockout right hook. It was a tough fight and he didn't leave himself open, but through a process of attrition I slowly worked him over and gained the advantage. Then in the eighth, I had him trapped in the corner while I belted him with combinations. It was one of the few times where I really had the opportunity to hit him freely and continue my onslaught without giving him a chance to counter. I was about to deliver a knockout punch before the referee stopped the fight because of a badly cut eye to Alby.

The belt was mine!

I stood in the middle of the ring surrounded by my supporters, holding the New South Wales middleweight belt high above my head. It was a very satisfying moment for me considering all the hard work that had gone into achieving this milestone.

As I grinned from ear to ear, Johnny whispered in my ear, "There's an Australian title waiting for you just up the track, Ed."

That night a whole group of us celebrated at The Silver Spade Room at the Chevron Hotel in Kings Cross. The euphoria of winning the title was heightened by having Sandy on my arm, the atmosphere of the club and the great music that was playing. Things had never seemed better. I had been focussing so much on my boxing career that I didn't hit the drink that much. As much as I liked going out with Sandy and our friends, I was always very conscious of keeping myself in good shape as boxing was an important factor in my life.

That particular night, however, was an exception. I got drunk with Noel and Sean O'Grady. Sandy, who had seen me drunk on a few occasions, didn't particularly like what she saw.

"You have a few drinks and you're witty and charming, and then you go over the top and you have a change in personality, Ed," she said, the day after I won the title fight.

"A change of personality, Sandy? I just thought I was having a good time, that's all," I responded with a shrug.

"To be honest with you, Ed, you just become plain ugly when you've had too much to drink. You're such a warm and sensitive man when you're sober. I much prefer you like that."

I was surprised by her disappointed expression. "Gee, I think you're being a bit of a sourpuss, Sandy. After all a man's allowed to cut lose occasionally."

"Well, you had better think about how you behave around me when you're on the drink, Ed." She gave me one more disapproving look and then walked off in a huff.

Our disagreement left a bitter taste in my mouth, as I thought she was being a spoilsport after the euphoria of my victory.

With Sandy's thoughts still ringing in my head, I decided to take a couple of weeks off work. I ventured back home to Eumungerie for the first week of my break to celebrate my victory with family and friends.

Stumpy always had breakfast at Mum's place ever since Grandma Costigan had passed away in 1959. It was breakfast the day after I arrived home and all the family were there except John who was away at the seminary studying for the priesthood. Mum was busily preparing breakfast, ably assisted by Margaret and Anne, and the spread of bacon and eggs, lambs fry and copious amounts of toast made me very happy as it brought back fond memories from when I was growing up. After all, I was only a lad when I was popped off to Sydney, and there was nothing like Mum's brekky.

This particular breakfast was a special occasion on two accounts for not only was it a celebration of my victory, but later that morning Margaret was leaving to work as a nurse in an Aboriginal community in Arnhem Land in the Northern Territory. She had been trying to make up her mind whether to become a nun or a nurse, and had decided to spend a year in Arnhem Land while she came to a decision. "It wasn't a hard choice, Ed," she told me when I asked what swayed her. "I could see where I was more useful to God."

Mum had been so proud of her, but worried too. "You be careful, Margaret," she warned her. "Don't go anywhere alone."

Stumpy placed a copy of the Dubbo local newspaper, *The Daily Liberal,* on the table. "What do you think of that, Ed?" he asked, grinning as he pointed to the front page.

Taking up half the page was a photo and article of me holding my New South Wales title high above my head with Stumpy also in the shot, his arm around my shoulder.

The caption read:

A SALUTE FROM ONE HERO TO ANOTHER

The opening paragraph underneath read:

WORLD WAR ONE VICTORIA CROSS RECIPIENT AND EUMUNGERIE FARMER JACK 'STUMPY' COSTIGAN CONGRATULATES HIS GRANDSON, ED COSTIGAN, ON WINNING THE NEW SOUTH WALES MIDDLEWEIGHT BOXING TITLE.

"What a great photo, Stumpy!" I said, grinning from ear to ear. I was chuffed.

"I thought you'd like that, Ed." He looked pretty proud himself.

"Can I keep this as a memento, Stumpy?"

"You do that, Ed. It will be something to look back on with your own kids in years to come."

I passed the article around the breakfast table where Noel and Anne had also joined in and were tucking into brekky.

"Who knows, Ed?" said Noel with a smile. "There might be a world champion in you yet."

"Is that true, Noel? Could Ed really be a world champion?" Anne replied.

Noel was about to open his mouth, but Mum got there first. "Anything is possible if you put your mind to it, Annie. Ever since Ed was a boy, he would go morning, noon and night if he was interested in something. There is nothing to say that Ed can't go all the way with his boxing career if he applies himself." She paused, then looked over her reading glasses and gave me a solid look before continuing. "As long as he doesn't let other things like drinking distract him from what he is trying to achieve."

Mum had seen the problems that booze had caused in her own family, and was well aware that if I was not careful that could be my fate also.

"I can handle the drink okay, Mum," I protested. "I can take it or leave it."

"Let's hope so, Ed, because I know you're partial to a drop. We all know you missed out on Olympic selection because you were out on the drink the night you damaged your right hand," she countered.

Everyone stopped and looked at me, almost like they were wondering how I would respond.

I gave Mum an icy glare and immediately felt resentment

as my missing Olympic selection was still a sensitive topic with me. "You won't be saying that if I win a world title, Mum."

That effectively shut down the conversation, so I went back to the newspaper and was perusing other articles when I noticed a small heading in the bottom right hand corner of the paper.

AUSTRALIAN TROOPS CAUGHT IN FIERCE FIGHT WITH ENEMY IN VIETNAM

After reading the article, which concerned a platoon of Australian infantry having a skirmish with a number of Viet Cong troops in Vietnam, I sat back in my chair and contemplated my own possible fate.

I had registered for National Service when I turned eighteen as it was required by law, and it had been in the back of my mind ever since that I might be called up, especially with the ever-increasing hostilities taking place in Vietnam.

As I sat there deep in thought about my possible fate, Anne, who had been watching the terse discussion quietly and was ever so intuitive, said, "You're not angry with Mum are you, Ed? After all, she only wants the best for you."

Mum looked at me with the love that only a mother can give and my resentment faded. I gave them both a reassuring smile. "Nah, I am thinking about something else, Annie."

"A penny for your thoughts, Ed," said Margaret, giving me a penetrating stare.

I pointed out the newspaper article. "That's what I am thinking about, Marg."

Mum zeroed in on the article and her mouth tightened. "Pity help us if you have to go and fight in that war, Ed. There have been enough Costigans and O'Gradys who have served this country. Stumpy's eldest brother Joe was wounded at Gallipoli and we don't need another Costigan getting wounded, or heaven forbid, killed in Vietnam."

"Well you know *my* opinion on war, Mum," said Margaret, who got up to rinse her plate.

"We are *all* aware that you're a pacifist, Margaret," I interjected. I loved her, but I did find some of her views tiresome.

"Absolutely, Ed. There is no reason for Australians to be in Vietnam," she responded.

Stumpy who had been sitting quietly at the table, gave me a serious look before I could reply. "You know, Ed, I don't talk much about the battles I was in because it was a ghastly situation. I don't like the threat of communism though, and I can see its evil hand spreading throughout the world. As much as it would pain me to see anything happen to any of my grandchildren, sometimes it's necessary to go and fight an enemy. After all, that's what my generation did. We stood up for what was right."

Stumpy's views might seem draconian now, but in the 1960s many people saw communism as a genuine threat and its eradication a necessary step to world peace. The cold war was on everyone's mind.

I looked at the worried faces around the table. I tried to reassure them, despite my own concerns. "You needn't worry about me, you lot. If I'm called up, I'm prepared to do my bit. After all, both you and Dad went to war, Stumpy. I won't shirk my responsibilities if my marble is drawn."

After I arrived back in Maroubra, I met Sandy at her parent's house one evening where we made up after our argument and she gave me a big hug. While I was at the house, her parents invited me down to their holiday house at Werri Beach for the weekend, which was situated on the south coast near Gerringong.

It was the middle of winter, so in the early evening of the Saturday night, Sandy and I walked up the beach and made a roaring big fire. Sandy wrapped her arms around mine as we snuggled up and kept warm around the fire.

As the flames lit up Sandy's beautiful face, I kissed her on the forehead. Sandy smiled and said, "How romantic is this, Ed? A cold winter's night with a roaring big fire, snuggled up with my boyfriend. Life couldn't be any better."

"You're not wrong, Sandy. Along with winning the title, having you in my life is the best thing that's ever happened to me. I sure hope we don't have too many more arguments because everything feels so right when you're around." I pulled her tighter.

Sandy grinned and then kissed me passionately on the lips. It was a kiss that seemed to last an eternity and I was in a state of ecstasy when we broke apart. This girl was something special. She snuggled back into my arms.

"I feel so sorry for Julie. She just broke up with Reg."

"Oh, I hadn't heard about that."

"She rang me in tears when you were home in Eumungerie."

"That's no good, Sandy. I thought things were fine between her and Reg. She's the nicest girl you would ever wish to meet. I hope she finds somebody else."

I was suddenly overcome with thoughts of Vietnam again. I don't know why, but I just had this feeling that I would be going there. "There's a good chance I might get called up for national service when my birthday comes around next March."

Sandy sat bolt upright. "Oh, Ed! That's terrible. I don't want you to go away!"

I sought to pull her back into my arms. "I can't do much about it, Sandy. If my marble gets drawn, then I'll go into the army."

"Then what, Ed?" She pulled away and stared at me fearfully.

I shrugged. "Then there's a possibility that I might end up going to Vietnam."

There was dread etched on her face. "Oh, Ed. I don't want to even contemplate that."

"It's okay, Sandy. I always manage to look after myself."

"Still, the thought of you being killed over there is just terrible."

I sought to reassure her. I gently stroked her face and said, "It hasn't happened yet, and there's no guarantee that it will, so let's just enjoy the moment. Besides, I've got that Australian title in my sights and I'm not going anywhere before I have a crack at that."

"I hope so, Ed. Anyway, I don't want to talk about the army. I just want snuggle up next to you around this cozy fire."

I smiled as she fell back into my arms. I kissed her on the forehead and she smiled, then buried her head into my chest and murmured, "I wish this moment would last forever."

While my boxing career was moving along in leaps and bounds, my apprenticeship was moving along steadily too. Reg Steel now had a fleet of ten trucks. I worked mostly on petrol motors and had a natural aptitude towards my trade. It helped that I had been brought up on the farm, so I had been tinkering with machinery since I was a kid. Reg was involved in interstate transport with his trucks too, running them from Melbourne to Brisbane. The highways were rough and ready in those days and the trucks would often break down. It was nothing for us to take a trip to the country to fix a truck that had broken down in the middle of nowhere. It certainly added some variety to my day which was great. It was interesting and I worked hard, and although Reg ran a tight ship he was flexible and knew my boxing was important, so he always made allowances so I could get to Johnny's gym to train after work.

By my twentieth birthday in March 1966, I was in the final year of my apprenticeship and concentrating on an upcoming bout when I arrived home from work one day to find a letter on my bed. The envelope was from the Department of Labour and National Service and it requested me to report for national service.

As I stood in my bedroom reading the letter in the dim afternoon light, I wasn't filled with any kind of dread, it was like I knew it was going to happen. "So, the moment has arrived, eh," I said to myself.

My feelings of anxiety were mainly for Sandy, as I knew how much this was going to affect her. For me, I could cop the fact I was going to do my bit, although I knew that being apart from Sandy was going to be very tough. I couldn't imagine spending any length of time away from the girl I loved, but rules are rules. And I had a short-term ace up my sleeve.

I rang Sandy to tell her news. She was silent for a moment and then said in a weak voice, "You make sure you take good care of yourself, Ed."

"Everything will be okay, Sandy, I always fall on my feet. Besides, there is some good news. I found out I can defer my national service till next year while I finish my apprenticeship."

I could almost feel her relief down the phone. "You can?" she said excited. "With any luck the war will be over by then!"

"Maybe, Sandy. In any case, I've already contacted the department and they gave me the okay. You haven't seen the last of me yet, sweetie."

"Oh, that's wonderful news, Ed!" she said, her voice thick with emotion.

"Besides," I told her confidently, "I've got a bit of boxing to take care off before I go away."

Johnny and I both knew that I was a serious contender for the Australian middleweight title which was held at that time by George Dunlevy from Newcastle. To prepare me for a tilt at the title, he organised a number of interstate fights during the year. I had won all of them by knockout.

George Dunlevy's camp were playing cat and mouse with me and trying to delay our inevitable fight, as they sensed I had his measure.

Instead of an easier final lead up bout to the Australian title, I had to fight the hard-hitting Hector Saunders, an Aboriginal boxer from Casino, with the winner given the chance to fight George for the title. The fight was in early December of 1966 at the South Sydney Leagues Club, and was hands down one of the most punishing fights that I ever fought. The bout was a brutal affair with both of us badly knocked around.

We slugged it out before I knocked him out in the tenth with a right uppercut to his jaw. When it was over I looked in the mirror. I wasn't even sure if I had won because I had severe bruising to my ribs, a broken nose and my face was badly swollen. And that wasn't the worst of it. I had fractured my right wrist once again, and as a consequence, I couldn't fight for the next couple of months while I recovered.

I was dirty with myself, as I knew time was running out before I would have to start my national service. I was even filthier because I knew damn well that the problem with my wrist was a direct result of the fight that Thumper and I had with the Sharpies.

"I should never have got on the piss with Thumper that night," I said to my brother Dan one day in a fit of anger. "It cost me a spot in the Tokyo Olympics and now possibly a shot at the Australian title."

"You can't undo the past, Ed. Besides, you're still young enough. You'll get a chance at the title when you get out of the army."

"That's if I don't cop a fuckin' bullet while I'm over there."

"Don't be stupid, Ed," Dan said. "No bloody Viet Cong's gonna waste a bullet on you, mate."

My chance to fight George Dunlevy never eventuated. My year was up. After I recovered from my wrist injury, I was called up for national service in April, 1967.

Hector went on to decimate George in May 1967 and win the Australian middleweight title. I was left with a bitter taste in my mouth because I knew that I could have beaten George, but instead I was about to start my recruit training for the army.

***

I looked at my watch and saw that I had been talking for over an hour. I looked at Tim and he seemed much calmer now. "Tell us, Tim, you couldn't manage to rustle up a cup of tea, could you?"

Tim looked at the mess behind him and said, "Yeah, I

should be able to manage something." He got up and stared rummaging around the little kitchen.

I snorted. "I don't know how you manage to find anything in here."

"Yeah, well, things have been a bit hectic lately so the place is out of order."

"You're not kidding," I said.

After a few minutes, Tim returned with a packet of ginger snaps and a pot of tea in a cozy.

I grinned. "Well I'll be buggered, that is a blast from the past! You hardly ever see a pot of tea these days."

"I hate those tea bags," he said, turning up his nose. "This is the only way to have tea—in a pot."

"Karen always made a pot of tea," I said, a distant smile on my face. "I can still remember when we first started going out. She brought me a tea pot with a cozy that her grandmother had knitted."

"My mum always had one on the table when I was growing up," said Tim.

"You and I have one thing in common, Tim, and that is we're both from the bush and people from the country like their tea in a pot." I smiled at him and he looked blank for a moment before he relaxed and nodded, a slight smile on his face. I contemplated how strange it was that such a small thing like a pot of tea could prompt a tighter connection between two people. Tim spun the pot around on the table and I was mesmerised by the ritual. I could see Karen doing the same thing as we sat outside at *Shiloh* having breakfast on the weekend.

Tim poured the tea and passed the ginger snaps over to me. I took a couple out of the pack and immediately dunked one in my cup of tea. A sip later and I was in heaven. "That's a nice brew, Tim. You and I are singing off the same hymn sheet when it comes to making tea." I sat back in my chair and savoured the brew, and then I looked back at the painting. "Can you paint like your old man?"

Tim looked at the painting then at me. "Yeah, I could always paint, ever since I was a kid, but photography is what I really like."

"So, it just came natural to you?"

"Yeah, my mum had a big influence on me. She's a brilliant artist and she taught me how to sketch as a kid."

"What did she paint?"

"Australian landscapes. In particular, native wildlife."

"What's your mum's name?" I asked. I didn't want to be doing all the talking, the lad needed to speak too.

Tim paused for a moment, looking fidgety again. "Louise."

"Do you have a close bond with your mother?"

"Yeah, she's a great lady. She's pretty smart too. She wanted to go to Sydney Uni and do an arts degree when she was younger, but she met Dad shortly after he got home from Vietnam and that put an end to all that."

"Where was she from?"

"Narrabri."

"How did she meet Finno?" I asked curiously.

"She was working as a nanny on a big property just outside of Walgett and Dad was shearing on the same place at the time."

"What did she see in your dad do you think?"

Tim made a face. "For all his madness, Dad was intelligent and witty and he loved photography. Mum could see that he had a creative streak and they clicked straight away. Dad loved her artwork and she liked his photography. I suppose they were soulmates."

"Yeah, your old man always had an eye for photography. Probably not surprising he went for a creative type. He so often he managed to capture the right expression on someone's face. Looks as though you got a bit of both of your parents' talent," I said, pointing to his photograph of the birdlife. I took another sip from my tea and looked up at my old battalion insignia and went into deep thought. Memories of Vietnam came flooding back. I felt a shiver run down my spine.

"You know, there isn't a day that goes by when I don't think of Vietnam," I said quietly.

Tim stopped what he was doing and looked over at me. His expression had changed and he gave me a look of recognition. He was in Iraq, he knew the deal. It was also a look that suggested he wanted to know more of what had happened to me in Vietnam. And although he probably wouldn't admit it, I was pretty sure he wanted to hear about his dad.

"Seeing this insignia again has brought back a lot of memories," I told him, putting down my cup. "It seems like a lifetime ago when I first travelled to Wagga to commence my recruitment training."

Chapter 4

April 1967, 1 Recruit Training Battalion (RTB) Kapooka,
Wagga Wagga, New South Wales

I T WAS DAWN when the Greyhound bus pulled up outside the Kapooka Recruit Training Centre just outside
Wagga Wagga in south-western New South Wales. I was
dressed in a thick jacket, denim jeans and was wearing a beanie
on my head, but this still didn't keep out the early morning
cold.

Some of my family and friends including Nana, Mum,
Noel, Anne, Dan, Stumpy, Sandy and Julie McCabe had held
a farewell lunch for me at the O'Grady's in Maroubra the
day before.

Julie McCabe sat next to me at lunch and we reminisced
about some of the great times we shared at Maroubra before she
gave me a warm embrace and told me to stay safe.

It was after lunch and well into the afternoon when we
were sitting in the lounge-room and Aunty started to voice her
opposition to the Vietnam War. She was part of those young
Labor intellectuals who started to shape the party in the 1960s.

She was the daughter of an IRA member, Poppy Driscoll, who had escaped to Australia in 1916 as the English had a price on his head after the Dublin Easter Rising, and some of that fire burned in her.

"The Australian Government have no right to be sending our young men to go and fight in Vietnam," said Aunty, her tone fierce.

"If we don't go and fight those commies, Aunty, who the hell will?" Stumpy interjected.

"The Australian Government is just a bunch of puppets for the Americans, Stumpy."

They argued back and forth over the next fifteen minutes with neither of them giving an inch. Me, on the other hand, I sat opposite Sandy. I was annoyed with Aunty's ranting and stared at Sandy from across the room. "I love you," I mouthed.

Sandy smiled and was about to blow me a kiss when Mum interjected. "Eunice, I don't think it's right and proper you talking this way in front of Ed. He's about to go to recruitment training and he doesn't need this sort of talk cluttering his head."

Aunty's face clouded. "You may be my sister-in-law, Monica, but I won't have you talking to me like that in my own home," she said coldly. Mum by nature was reserved, but when it came to protecting her brood she could arc right up.

Mum glowered at her. "Ed's my son and we're all proud that he is going to serve our country."

Nana decided to get involved at that point. "Have you made a confession, Ed? You need to make one before you leave for Wagga."

"I'll make one when I get down there, Nana."

"You mean you haven't been to confession, Ed?" She looked

shocked. "If you get killed in Vietnam in a state of mortal sin then you'll perish in hell, Edward John Costigan!"

"There's plenty of time to go to confession, Nana," I said, trying to appease her. "They'll have a priest at Kapooka."

"There isn't time if you are in a state of sin," she spat back.

I'd had enough of this conversation. I motioned to Sandy to come outside to backyard while Nana was still rabbiting on about going to confession.

We walked out under the clothesline and as I held Sandy by the hands, she smiled at me and I felt my heart soar.

"I'm so glad I met you, Sandy McKenzie," I told her. "I want you to know that if I go to Vietnam and something happens to me that I will always love you."

The tears started to well up in Sandy's eyes and she put her arms around my neck and said, "You're the loveliest boy that a girl could ever wish to meet, Ed Costigan."

I wiped her tears away with my finger and the question burst out of me, "When I'm finished my two-year stint in the army, Sandy, will you marry me?"

Sandy started to cry and through muffled tears exclaimed, "Yes, Ed. Yes, I'll marry you."

I kissed her on the lips passionately and as we embraced, the warmth of her body was soothing balm for the pain that was yet to come.

But the moment of ecstasy was interrupted when Nana come onto the back verandah.

"What's this going on?" she grumbled in her thick Irish brogue, making her way down the steps and into the backyard. "What do you two think you're up to?"

Sandy was startled by the sudden apparition of Nana and exclaimed, "Oh, I'm just saying goodbye to Ed, Mrs O'Grady."

Nana glared at her. "Just saying goodbye, are you? Well you can keep your lecherous little hands off my grandson you little slip of a thing."

"Easy does it, Nana," I said, holding up a hand. "Sandy won't be seeing me for a while and just wanted to say goodbye."

"Say goodbye, hey? Well, there are more appropriate ways of saying goodbye than getting involved in the devil's embrace!" She glared at us both.

"Devil's embrace?" I scoffed. "Come on, Nana, you've gone too far this time. Sandy's my girlfriend and we're in love."

"Love!" Her eyes glinted. "What would you know about love, boy? The love of Jesus, Mary and Joseph is the only love you want to be worrying about."

Nana's sanctimonious garbage coupled with Aunty's left wing rant after lunch was all I needed to tip me over the edge. My blood was boiling and for the first time in my life I gave it to Nana with both barrels.

"Listen here, you cantankerous old bog-Irish lunatic, I've had a gutful of you sticking your nose into my business. No wonder Grandpa O'Grady kicked the bucket early!" I shouted. "He wasn't afraid of going to hell because he'd already been there living with you in that broken-down railway shack in Dubbo. Drink be damned. Why don't you get the hell out of Maroubra and go back to Dubbo where you belong?"

Nana was stunned by my outburst and temporarily lost for words. Never in her life had she heard such insolence from one of her grandchildren. It didn't take too long for her to regain her composure, and when she did her steely gaze focussed on me and she growled, "You ungrateful little coot. After all I've done for you, this is how you repay me?"

"Repay you?" I scoffed, incredulous. "I'll be glad if I get sent to Vietnam just so I can get away from you!"

Nana was about to retort when Mum appeared on the verandah. "Yoo-hoo! Ed! Sandy! It's time to go. It's time to catch the bus."

I glared at Nana with steely resolve. "One other thing, Nana. I won't be going to confession when I get to Wagga."

This was too much for Nana. "Be gone with ya, lecherous little pagan scoundrel, and may the Lord Jesus himself have mercy on your soul," she barked at me.

I was still smoldering when we arrived at the CMF (Citizen's Military Force) Barracks at Marrickville late in the afternoon. Julie had joined us to say farewell and support Sandy, as she knew that my girl was doing it tough and would otherwise be going home alone.

I was still annoyed, but Sandy tried to cool me down with some reassuring words.

"I'm very proud of you for standing up to Nana like that, Ed. It's about time somebody put her in her place."

I looked at Sandy and smiled. "You're a one in a million, Sandy. Unfortunately, that old Irish bigot is so entrenched in her narrow little world that I doubt if any of it registered."

Sandy kissed me on the lips, but our lovely moment was interrupted by a strange scene being played out in front of our eyes. A group of women calling themselves SOS (Save Our Sons) were protesting rather loudly about their boys being taken away to fight a dirty war in Vietnam.

They weren't the hippy university student types that were the typical kind of protester. These women were conservatively dressed middle-age mothers holding up blue and white banners, protesting loudly about the government taking their sons away to war.

There was a real kerfuffle taking place as the women dressed in their gloves, hats and long skirts jostled with the military authorities. To my horror, Aunty had joined the group and was walking towards me. She was holding up a blue and white banner and yelling out on top note.

"This is my nephew, Ed Costigan, and I don't agree that he should have to fight a dirty war for the Australian government in Vietnam!"

"Turn it up, Aunty," I muttered in her ear. "You've had your say back home, but this is a bit too much."

She gave me a fierce glare. "This is wrong, Ed. You shouldn't be made and go and fight this war."

"I'll be the judge of that, Aunty," I told her. I shook my head and turned to Sandy and Julie, who were standing close to me, and exclaimed, "See what I have to put up with? These O'Gradys are a weird mob."

I put my hands in my pocket and was talking to Sandy and Julie when this tall, lanky bloke appeared out of nowhere. He was in RM Williams dress boots, moleskins and a checkered long-sleeve shirt, and I knew straight away he was from the bush. They say first impressions count and before he had even opened his mouth I felt an affinity towards him.

"Hey, mate, excuse me for interrupting, but did that lady holding the banner says your name is Ed Costigan?" he asked, speaking with a distinctly laconic Australian drawl.

I was intrigued by him. "Yeah, I'm Ed Costigan."

He beamed at me. "I thought I recognised you. I just want to say that I saw your photo on the front page of *The Daily*

Liberal after you won the New South Wales title and I reckon you're a real champion," he said in all sincerity.

A smile came over my face and all the venom I had felt concerning Nana seemed to dissipate as the tall, lanky fella looked at me with a grin etched on his face.

"Well, that's real nice of you, mate. Thanks for the compliment," I said.

"I've been following your career for a while now and I reckon you can go all the way," he told me.

"Thanks, mate. What's your name, anyway?"

"My name's Bob Rowe, but everyone calls me 'Rowy'. I'm off a big property out near Coolabah in western New South Wales."

"Well, Rowy, it's real nice to meet you."

"Likewise, Ed."

We gave each other a firm handshake and I knew I was onto a good thing with this bloke.

"Are you going along for this little ride down to Wagga also, Rowy?"

"Yeah, mate. My marble came up and I got a guernsey to this show also." He looked over my shoulder at the two girls, his smile getting brighter.

I grinned at him. "By the way, Rowy, this is my girlfriend, Sandy, and her best friend, Julie."

"Hi, Rowy," said Sandy. "How are you?"

"I'm good, thank you." Rowy replied politely, then focussed his attention on Julie and he said awkwardly to her, "Where are you from, Julie?"

"I'm from Maroubra. I heard you say to Ed that you're from Coolabah. Where is that?" Julie said with a smile.

"Oh, it's out between Dubbo and Bourke. Our family's got

15,000 acres out there. It's pretty flat country where we graze sheep and we also grow some wheat if the season is good," Rowy said, fidgeting and shuffling his feet.

"Wow, that must be amazing, living on such a big farm. My mum's family are off a property at Gunnedah, so we go up there for holidays sometimes."

While Rowy and Julie continued to get acquainted, Stumpy approached me with the framed photograph of him in front of the pyramids in 1915.

"You look after yourself, Ed. I want to see you come home in one piece and have a crack at that Australian title," he said, clasping my shoulder.

I shook his hand. "I will, old man, and thanks for everything you've done for me over the years." With that, Stumpy slapped me on the shoulder and stepped back.

I gave Mum a final embrace, as I did Anne and Dan, and shook Noel's hand.

I could see the pain in Mum's eyes and I guessed she was thinking of the possibilities of what might happen to me, but she gave me a stoic look before farewelling me. Anne, Dan and even Noel looked worried, but I kept up my smile. I even managed a wave in the direction of Aunty.

As I said my final goodbyes to family and friends, I noticed Rowy and Julie still talking. When I walked up beside the two of them, I heard Rowy say to her, "Perhaps we can meet up sometime down the track?"

"Yeah, that would be nice, Rowy. Maybe you can show me around your big farm one day."

"You got a deal, Julie."

I turned around and Sandy was standing on her own with

her hands held tightly in front of her, looking at me with the saddest of eyes.

I walked over and hugged her. "I'll call you when I can, sweetie."

"Please, Ed. I want to hear that you're safe and well," she said, tears welling up in her eyes.

"You don't have to worry about me, Sandy, I'll look after myself." I kissed her, gently wiping the tears from her cheek.

I picked my bag up and walked into the night to the bus. Behind me, I could hear Sandy crying, but I did not dare turn around lest she see the tears welling up in my eyes.

It was a long bus ride down to Wagga that night. Rowy kept a seat for me when I got on the bus. He could see that I was upset and tried to give me solace.

"Gee, Sandy seems to be a real nice girl, Ed," he said.

I looked at Rowy and said, "She sure is, and I am pretty cut up that I have to leave her."

"You can have a yarn with me, Ed, if that'll soften the blow," he offered.

I could see that he was genuine and said, "That's real decent of you, Rowy. I appreciate that, mate."

"That's what mates are for."

I fidgeted. "You know, I asked her to marry me today."

Rowy nudged me in congratulations. "What did she say?"

"She said 'yes'. But I told her it wouldn't be until after I got out of the army."

"You lucky bugger, Ed. I've never really had a serious girl-friend. Between growing up on the farm and boarding school, it didn't leave much time for that sort of caper," he said wistfully.

"Julie certainly had an eye for you, Rowy," I said with a grin.

"Yeah, she seems like a real beaut girl, hey, Ed?"

"You wouldn't go far wrong with her mate. I've been mates with her for a while now. She's from a real nice family. Her old man's the local GP at Maroubra."

"Yeah?"

"She loves her sport and..." I trailed off, teasing him a bit.

"And, what?"

"She broke up with her boyfriend sometime back, so she's been pretty lonely."

A grin slowly formed on Rowy's face and he exclaimed, "I might be in with a chance!"

I nodded my head and grinned at Rowy.

***

"That one simple statement of Rowy's meant so much to me, Tim," I said, sneaking another ginger snap.

"What statement?"

"'You can have a yarn with me, Ed, if that'll soften the blow.'"

Tim nodded his head.

"I believe that's where our friendship was cemented that night. I could see right from the start that Bob Rowe was a decent bloke. A real genuine country bloke. It may seem old-fashioned now in this sophisticated world we live in, but he was definitely the salt of the earth," I said, seeing that Tim was paying plenty of attention. It was all about the army and mateship now, something that he understood.

"We had a lot of time to talk on that bus trip and I soon found out that we had a lot in common. We were both brought up on the land, had the same interests like footy, boxing, shooting, and both of us had an elder brother who was running the property. Rowy wasn't real sure what he wanted to do with his life. He had been working on the farm and supplementing his income as a professional 'roo shooter, but he knew that he would have to move on as the farm couldn't support both him and his brother. In the end, it was more than a stroke of good luck that our paths were to cross because down the track, when we were in the heat of battle, Rowy and I covered each other more than once, and in battles beyond the army too."

Tim nodded again. It was fast becoming a custom for him.

I gave him a little grin. "And then there was Sergeant Holt."

"Sergeant Holt?" asked Tim, with a raised eyebrow.

"Yeah. He saw that Rowy and I were as thick as thieves and gave us hell right from the start."

***

By the time I stepped off the bus at Kapooka, I was dog-tired because I had hardly slept. Rowy and I had talked well into the night about all things. I gazed around and surveyed the motley rabble of fifty men who had disembarked the bus with me. My initial impression was that we didn't look like would-be soldiers. There were all shapes and sizes and most of the recruits were just milling around with their hands in their pockets and a look of bewilderment on their faces. In the distance, through the early morning fog, I could see the outline of a number of igloo-shaped buildings which I subsequently learned were named Nissen huts. My initial thought was that they might be mechanics workshops. You can imagine my surprise when I found out they were where we were going to live.

My own case of sleep deprivation was abruptly terminated when out of the early morning fog came an immaculately attired soldier, dressed in a neatly pressed khaki uniform, spit polished boots and a slouch hat. He had three stripes on his arm. He was well over six feet tall and had a jaw shaped like a house brick.

"Righto, you dickheads, cut the chatter, this isn't a CWA meeting we're holding here!" he roared in a gravelly voice.

The rabble suddenly became quiet as the khaki-clad man barked more instructions at us, indicating that he wanted us to line up in formation.

"Line up! Five ranks of ten in each!"

The feeble attempt to get orderly seemed to aggravate him even more. He walked slowly and deliberately in front of our lines, his boots crunching on the gravel beneath his feet. The sound made me feel uncomfortable. He roared more instructions at us.

"My name is Sergeant Holt and that's exactly what you fuckwits will do when I address you! Is that clear?"

We collectively let out a feeble 'yes' before he came back with another barrage of verbal abuse.

"What sort of a response is that, you lame pricks? This time say it like you've got balls!" he bellowed.

"Yes, sergeant!"

"At the moment you're all just lumps of shit and it's my job to turn you into soldiers!"

We all looked at him with blank faces. Personally, I wasn't too impressed with his verbal abuse as Sandy was on my mind and I was feeling melancholy.

"When I tell you to shit, you shit, when I tell you to sleep, you will sleep, and when I tell you to jump, you will say how high. Is that clear?"

"Yes, sergeant!" we collectively yelled.

Meanwhile, as the sergeant was off-loading his abusive spiel, I turned to Rowy who was standing to my left and whispered, "Now I know what the yowie sounds like after listening to this joker."

Sergeant Holt's head snapped back in my direction. He came marching over to where I was standing and with his face no less than two inches from mine, he barked, "Have you got something to say, smartarse?"

"No, sir!" I said with a look of disdain.

"What did you call me, dickhead?"

"No, sir!" I replied once again.

"Do I look like an officer, you fuckin' dimwit?" he roared.

"Ah, no, sir!"

"Stop calling me 'sir'! Can't you see I have three stripes on my shirt? I am a 'sergeant' you dumb shit!"

"Yes, sergeant!"

"Hit the deck and give me a hundred pushups, fuckwit!"

He stood in front of me and made me do the pushups slowly and although I felt out of sorts I did them with ease.

This got up right up Sergeant Holt's nose as he was expecting a lame duck. "What's your name, smartarse?"

"Costigan, sergeant!"

"Well, Costigan, you seemed to perform those pushups with ease, so you better give me another hundred pushups just to be on the safe side."

I got down and performed another hundred, never raising a sweat.

Sergeant Holt then turned to Rowy, who was trying hard to conceal a grin that was emanating from the corner of his mouth.

"You find it amusing do you, dickhead?"

"No, sergeant!"

"You'd better give me one hundred pushups to wipe that grin off your face."

I was surprised at how easy Rowy performed his punishment, but I shouldn't have been. We'd spent all night talking, and I knew his strength came from years of hard toil on the farm and playing rugby at the Shore School in Sydney.

***

"After Kapooka, the army spent the next twelve months knocking us into shape. Rowy and I chose to join the infantry and we were sent to Enoggera Barracks in Brisbane where we joined 12 Platoon, D Company, 11 RAR. I was given the job of handling the M60 machine gun. I soon developed a keen liking for the weapon and Rowy became my second on the gun. As well as covering my arse, he carried spare ammunition and a spare barrel," I told Tim. "I was as strong as an ox by this stage, as my boxing and mechanical apprenticeship had honed my physique, not to mention training at Kapooka."

"Bloody Kapooka! I know all about those NCOs. I had a couple of those arseholes rip into me while I was there," said Tim, a sour look etched on his face.

"Well, if you'd been through Kapooka like me, Tim, and then into the infantry you know what happened next," I said pointedly.

Tim looked at me knowingly and said, "They call it the Land Warfare Centre now, but I believe it was called the Jungle Training Centre back in the day. At Canungra, up in the Gold Coast Hinterland."

"You got in one, son. You'd know all about the four-week Battle Efficiency course that we went through?"

"I'll never forget it. That was an absolute ball-tearer."

"Well, I knew by the time we finished at Canungra that I was ready for battle. Everything in Canungra was to orientate you to things you would encounter in Vietnam. Some blokes even reckoned that Canungra was harder than Vietnam," I said with a shrug.

Tim nodded in agreement and said, "Yeah, well, I gotta agree with you there. By the time I was finished at Canungra, I knew I was a fair dinkum soldier."

"We became a tight unit and forged strong bonds with the blokes we were training with. You had to because you knew you were going to have to rely on them when you were in battle." I smiled at him and added, "There were two blokes in particular, who alongside Rowy, became my best mates in the battalion."

"Who were they?"

"Your old man and that other joker who was in that photo that your old man took while we were in the boozer."

"What was his name again? Schooner something?" Tim said with a quizzical look on his face.

"Pat Rooney, or Schooner Rooney, as we called him. He got that name for his fondness for the amber fluid."

"Yeah, that's him." Tim folded his arms.

I grinned. "That Schooner Rooney was a laugh. He was training to be a stock and station agent in his old man's business at Condobolin. He had a quick wit which lightened many a situation when the going got tough. We were the four boys from the bush and we were a tight bunch." I gave Tim a rueful look and tapped my fingers on the table. "But despite all this, Sandy was never far from my mind, Tim. I thought about her constantly and I wrote to her when I got a chance, as did she. Although it was hard to call each other on the phone, whenever we had a chance, we did. I told her I loved her in my letters and she rang me to tell me she had got a promotion at the bank. Those letters from Sandy, and from my family, in particular

Stumpy, Mum and Anne, made all the difference. They were a great source of strength and comfort, especially after I had been through a gruelling drill or had an NCO niggling me about something."

"My mum was the only one who ever wrote to me while I was in the army," said Tim.

"Have you still got any of those letters, Tim?"

"Yeah, some of them."

"You make sure you hang onto them," I said, giving him a serious look. "They are absolute treasures that you'll look back on in years to come."

"My mum's the best. She's always had a word of encouragement for me even when I was doing it tough," he said, his face softening as he thought of his mum.

I gave Tim a reassuring smile. "Well, mums aside, there was plenty of training we had to go through in the months ahead of deployment, including our final exercise at Shoalwater Bay, just north of Rockhampton. This exercise was to allow the umpires to assess the performance of the various platoons and companies for the benefit of the battalion commander before we were deployed to Vietnam." I gave a slight laugh. "All the training in the world could not have prepared me for the surprise I got once I arrived in Vietnam. For a kid who had been brought up on a farm and had seen little else of the world, it was an eye-opener. Other than Sydney, and a few trips up north to go camping and fishing with Stumpy, I had seen bugger all of the world. I was about to receive the biggest culture shock of my life."

Chapter 5

April 1968, Nui Dat, Phuoc Tuy Province, South Vietnam

AFTER ARRIVING AT Tan Son Nhat Airport in Saigon, we made our way over to the Caribou aircraft that would get us to the 1st Australian Task Force Base at Luscombe Field in Nui Dat, Phuoc Tuy Province. Standing on the ground, not far from the Caribou, were members of the Australian infantry battalion which we were replacing.

They were drawn out, fatigued and thin, and had a vacant stare about them. They appeared to be looking through us, as though we didn't exist. Their uniforms seemed to have been ironed and starched recently, but they were covered in sweat. I felt a shiver run up my spine. It was as though I had been given a premonition of what I would end up looking like at the end of my 12-month tour.

"Look at these poor bastards. They look like they've been through the ringer, Cozzy," said Schooner Rooney.

"You're not wrong, Schooner. They look totally rooted. I hope I fare a bit better than them when my tour's done," I replied.

"I wonder how much action they saw?" said Finno, who had lumbered up beside us.

"A fair bit I'd say, Finno," said Schooner in a laconic tone. "They didn't get that 'I just stood on a jumping jack mine' type of look from singing in the local church choir."

We all let out a muffled laugh before Rowy prophetically quipped, "I dare say there will be a bit of action waiting for us, Finno, once we're in the jungle."

Before my departure to Vietnam, I had no idea of Vietnamese culture let alone where Phuoc Tuy Province was. It consisted mainly of flat rainforest, grassland country, and to the south there were cave-ridden mountains where the enemy hid out.

The ATF was given the job of protecting the highway between the seaside port of Vung Tau to the south, and Saigon, as well as dominating and securing the province from the enemy which consisted of the Viet Cong and the North Vietnamese Army. Nui Dat, which in Vietnamese means 'small hill', was to become our home for the next twelve months. It was a former rubber plantation, and the countryside was filled with a red clay which turned into a sticky mess when it rained and stuck to the soles of our boots.

Nui Dat had 10-kilometre perimeter and housed our battalion, as well as 15 RAR. Within its confines could be found the headquarters for the SAS, armoury, Centurion tank squadron, Australian Field Battery, as well as engineering units. There was also a field ambulance, Air Force squadron of Iroquois helicopters, Salvation Army hut, military police and post office. The outside of the base was protected by wires, mines and heavy patrolling.

The tent we were given was an old World War II issue and in very poor condition with holes in the roof and sides. Around the outside of the tent, which was approximately five metres by five metres, was a sandbag blast wall which was encased in corrugated iron. The floorboards were old timber with 105 mm shell case holes which gave us some ventilation from the stifling heat and humidity. Each man had a cot, metal table, locker and a trunk.

My tent was shared with Rowy, Finno and Schooner Rooney. No sooner had we settled in when Schooner quipped, "Okay, you lot of wild bastards. Since this tent of ours is such a classy establishment, only the best will do. Cocktails will be served at 6.00 pm sharp."

"Cocktails, my arse. A cocktail would be as rare as rocking horse shit in a place like this, Schooner," said Rowy, a grin on his face.

"What would you prefer to drink, my distinguished friend from the back of the Black Stump?" said Schooner, as quick as a flash.

"How about a Reschs DA?"

"A Reschs DA? That's absolute cats piss, Rowy," said Schooner with a snort.

"You wouldn't feed that stuff to your dog," chimed in Finno.

"If you did you'd be charged with cruelty to animals," I added.

"Where I come from, it's seen as rather a posh drink. The old man used to always serve that when we had guests over," said Rowy.

Schooner, Finno and I cracked up with laughter, and after I had regained my composure, I said, "A posh drink? Who are you trying to kid, Rowy?'

A broad grin spread over Rowy's face, as we realised that he was taking the micky out of us. I threw a pair of socks at him.

"In all seriousness, Rowy, why would you drink that stuff?" said Schooner.

Rowy looked at us with a poker face and exclaimed, "Why you blokes, it's the beer that won the war!"

We cracked up laughing again. This type of banter between the four of us was a regular occurrence. We often took the piss out of each other but never with any malice.

We were given a week to settle into the base at Nui Dat before our platoon was sent on our first patrol. This was to be a short operation of just five days to allow everyone to acclimatise to the local conditions. At the last moment there was a change of plan because Schooner Rooney, who was Finno's second on the gun, had four of his wisdom teeth removed and was out of action. They reshuffled things around and moved Rowy over as Finno's second on the M60, and brought a gun crew across from 10 platoon to take my place.

They gave me the job as batman for our company's commander, Major Brian Milroy. This was a letdown for me as I was itching to get out into country. It was with mixed emotions I was given the job of making the major's bed, starching and ironing his clothes, as well as a multitude of other tasks. I was resentful because I had to hang around the other POGOs, a cheerful nickname for the boring real title of Personnel On Garrison Operations, while the boys were out there getting among the action. Also, Milroy was a pedantic bastard who liked everything done with perfection.

"When you iron my shirts and trousers, Costigan, I don't want to see a crease. Do you understand?"

"Yes, sir," I replied.

"And when you shine my shoes, I want to be able to see my reflection in them. Is that understood?"

"Yes, Major Milroy." I was barely able to hide my disdain.

Milroy was a pencil pusher who had seen no action before arriving on his first tour of Vietnam. I resented him from the start, and the fact he was a career desk jockey who had next to no practical experience only exacerbated my dislike for him. I was bitter when I returned to my tent that night.

Schooner, in deep discomfort due to his swollen mouth, was still able to manage a smartarse comment. "Well, well, if it isn't old lag-arse Costigan, prince of all the batmen in Nui Dat, having a nice cushy life, cruising around and tending to the major's every want and need."

"Be fucked, Schooner," I said with a growl. "That Milroy's a right arsehole. I'd give anything to be out in country having a crack at those nogs."

"Not so hasty, Cozzy. After all, we don't want you getting yourself all shot up so early in your tour. You may as well take it easy around here while you have the opportunity," he replied.

"It would be lot more favourable if I was over in the boozer sucking on a few cans, Schooner, rather than working for this bastard."

"Now you're talking, Cozzy. What's the chances of getting a couple cans for me on the sly next time you're out and about? Purely for medicinal purposes," he said, trying to force a grin through his swollen mouth.

I gave Schooner a huge smile. "I don't like my chances, but I'll see what I can do."

It was late afternoon on day three of my duties as a batman when I managed to scrounge four cans of beer.

"Here you go, Schooner, get ya laughing gear around a couple of these little icy cold beauties," I said, smirking at Schooner's frozen expression.

Schooner's eyes almost fell out of his head when I placed the cans in his lap.

"You little ripper, Cozzy! Your blood's worth bottling, old son. How did you manage to get these?" he whispered as he looked around cautiously.

"Trade secret. I can't reveal too much, Schooner," I said with a wink.

Schooner opened the first can and was slurping down the froth with a straw I had managed to rustle up when he said, "Oh, almost forgot, Cozzy. The mail arrived and there's a stack of letters for you."

Schooner handed me the envelopes which included letters from Mum, Anne, Stumpy, Thumper and even Noel. In among my mail was one letter that got my attention. It was a pink envelope which contained handwriting which was instantly recognisable to me.

"Sandy!" I exclaimed.

"You lucky bugger," said Schooner, lying on his bunker, merrily slurping away on his beer.

"You betcha, Schooner. I wonder what my girl has been up to?"

I almost tore the envelope to pieces. Sandy's letter was jam-packed with information on all the goings on at home, in particular the bands that had been playing at the Maroubra Surf Club. She also included a detailed account of her recent 21st birthday party which she had celebrated with family and friends two weeks previously at her parent's home in Maroubra.

I read her closing lines again and again.

I miss you so much, Ed, and I wish you could have been with me on my special night to celebrate such an important milestone in my life. I have included a colour photograph of me taken during the speeches at my party. Keep safe, my darling man.

Love,

Sandy

I placed the photograph of Sandy on my locker next to my bed, and it lifted my spirits immeasurably. As I lay back on my bed, I felt all the resentment I had towards Milroy melt away. I thought about Sandy and all the great times we had shared together. After a while, I fell asleep and when I woke later on, it felt like a load had been lifted from my shoulders.

My thoughts of Sandy were abruptly terminated when around lunchtime on the fourth day I was called out to join the rest of the platoon.

Milroy had appeared quite unexpectedly at his tent, which had taken me by surprise. I was busy dusting his locker and trunk and I'd initially thought he was going to reprimand me for the way I'd ironed his trousers that morning, but instead he said in an agitated tone, "Costigan, your platoon has been involved in a fight with the Viet Cong out in the jungle. One of the gun crew has been killed. Get your gear together quick smart and be ready to leave in 15 minutes."

"Gun crew! Which gun crew, sir?" I said in an anxious state. I feared the worst and hoped like hell it wasn't Rowy and Finno.

"What?" he said abruptly.

"Do you know which gun crew was killed, sir?"

"I don't know, Costigan. Don't pester me with details. Now hop to it and get your gear together."

Milroy turned quickly and before I knew it he was out of sight.

"You dickhead, Milroy. You know full well which gun crew's been killed," I said when he was out of earshot. My thoughts quickly turned to both Rowy and Finno. My mind raced at a million miles an hour, as I tried to fathom the huge calamity of whether or not they had been killed.

I tried to gather snippets of information from whoever I could, but all I could learn was that our platoon had engaged the enemy that morning and had incurred some casualties. No one could tell me who had been killed.

As I grabbed my gear out of my tent, I spied the photograph of Sandy stuck to the side of my locker. "I hope to God it's not Rowy and Finno who's been killed, sweetie," I said to her. "I'll be devastated if it is." I kissed Sandy on the forehead and left in a hurry.

The reinforcements and I were trucked down to Eagle Farm, which was the helicopter landing zone inside Nui Dat. As the RAAF Iroquois gunship landed, I could see the door gunner, who manned an M60, frantically throwing packs out the door that had once belonged to the killed and wounded from our platoon. I counted seven, and as he tossed them onto the ground I could see that they were shot to pieces and covered in blood. My heart thundered in my chest.

I then looked up and saw two body bags inside the helicopter. My eyes were transfixed on the both of them as two military personal grabbed the limp bodies and carried them into the back of a waiting vehicle.

"Hey, mate, do you know the names of the two blokes killed?" I said to one of the soldiers.

"Buggered if I know, mate. Apparently, it was one of the gun crews from 12 platoon that copped it off the nogs," he replied.

With that the two privates jumped into the vehicle and hurriedly sped off. As I watched the Land Rover disappear down the road, I glimpsed my own mortality and was overcome with fear. I was hit straight between the eyes with the reality of the Vietnam War and it was a sobering thought. I felt the hairs stand up on the back of my head. I swallowed hard and hoped like hell those two bodies weren't Rowy and Finno.

My state of anxiety was exacerbated when the door gunner screamed at us, "Get ya fuckin' arses in here quick smart!"

We hustled on board, and as the chopper flew off, my eyes were transfixed on the packs which were lying on the ground in tatters. I looked around to the other men in the helicopter and saw that everyone was ashen-faced.

I had seen plenty of animal blood in my life, after all, I grew up on a farm, and it had never bothered me. We slaughtered our own sheep and cattle to eat and I had always seen that as part of the natural routine of life, but this was different. My mind had been blasted from a mundane scene to a totally different one and the transition had numbed me. What I had just witnessed suddenly reminded me of those departing Australian soldiers I saw just after my arrival in Saigon. It spooked me.

We flew just above the tree tops, and the door gunner leaned across to speak to me as I was the closest to him. It was hard to hear him and he had to scream on top note as his voice was being drowned out by the chopper's engine and the rotor blades.

"This could be a hot pad where we are about to land, so I

don't want any fuckin' arsin' around when we get there. Is that clear?"

I nodded in agreement.

"Pass the message on!" he screamed at me.

"This could be a hot pad when we land, so watch your arses!" I screamed to the others in the Huey.

The chopper was violently tossed from side to side as we flew above the tree tops. We flew five kilometres south-west of the task force base where the pilot landed in a small clearing in the thick jungle. Fortunately for us, there was no enemy fire as we landed.

I scrambled off the chopper fully laden with my pack, M60, as well as spare ammunition for the gun. I had a 100-round belt of ammunition in the gun with the safety catch off, ready to fire if I encountered any trouble.

When we got to 12 platoon, they were lying deep inside the jungle, camouflaged beside a well-worn track. They had two machine guns set up in front of their position and a series of claymore mines, just in case the enemy came walking towards them.

I frantically searched the surrounding jungle for any sign of Rowy and Finno, until I spotted Chooky, who was one of our platoon's rifleman.

"Chooky, have you seen Rowy or Finno?" I asked frantically.

Chooky, who was off a poultry farm at the oddly-named town of Bob's Farm on the central coast of New South Wales, wasn't the sharpest tool in the shed and replied in a flustered manner, "Gee, Cozzy, it was pretty confusing out there. I think Rowy and Finno copped it. Sorry, mate, but I think it was them that they put into the body bags."

Chooky slung his SLR over his shoulder and walked away

into the jungle. Meanwhile, I was paralysed with fear as I contemplated the fate of my two mates.

Standing not far from me was our platoon's 2IC, Sergeant Wally Kingston, who had heard the conversation between Chooky and me. He came over and put a hand on my shoulder.

"Chooky's talking out of his fuckin' arse, Cozzy. It wasn't Rowy and Finno who copped it. It was the replacement gun crew from 10 platoon, Wilko and Slugger Jones, who got zipped. Your mates are over there in the jungle," said the tough little ex-abattoir slaughterman from Blayney.

I sighed with relief and replied to Wally, "Thank fuck for that, Wally. I thought those two had it."

"Nah, they're all right, Cozzy. It would take a bit to kill those two bastards. Especially that Finno. He's a tough prick and mad as a cut snake. You head over there and then get bunkered down."

I made my way in the direction that Wally had pointed, and after frantically searching the jungle for a few minutes, came across Rowy eating out of his American ration pack. I'd never been so relieved in my life.

"Rowy! You're in one piece, mate!" I said frantically.

"Yeah, mate, Finno and I are okay, but poor old Wilko and Slugger Jones both copped it from those nogs who we ran into," Rowy said, as he devoured what was in his ration pack.

"Shit, mate, thank fuck." I put a hand across my heart.

"We both came out of the dust-up unscathed," said Rowy, his voice quite casual. "These Yank ration packs shit all over ours, Cozzy. There's a heap more stuff to choose from."

I looked at Rowy, surprised at how calm and casual he sounded at such a dire situation. I gave him a nervous grin.

"You mad prick, Rowy. A bomb could go off under you and it still wouldn't stop you tucking into a good feed."

Rowy smiled at me and said, "You know I'm as happy as a pig in shit when I'm tucking into a feed, Cozzy."

Finno, who was sitting only a short distance away cleaning his M60, said, "You're a lucky boy that you were given the job of wiping Milroy's arse, Cozzy, 'cause it could have been good night Irene for you," he said, motioning his finger across his throat.

Dread filled me. He was right. I could have been on the gun crew that died. It was then that I started to contemplate what my platoon had gone through and it was a sobering thought. Finno was dead right when he had said how lucky I had been to be given the job as Milroy's batman.

Rowy and Finno spent the next fifteen minutes filling me in on the details of the battle before our platoon commander, Lieutenant Geraghty, gathered us reinforcements and explained what had happened. Geraghty, who was a straight shooter, was surprisingly cool considering what had happened.

"Okay you blokes, this is the score," he said in a matter of fact manner. "Part of D445 Local Force Battalion (Viet Cong), which was about 30 strong, walked into our ambush position early this morning and a ferocious fight took place. Our platoon inflicted some heavy casualties on the enemy with approximately a dozen VC killed and wounded." Geraghty paused and in a more sombre tone continued. "Unfortunately, the replacement gun crew from ten platoon consisting of Bevan Wilkinson and Nigel Jones were killed, while Dave Puckeridge and Allan Simon, two of our riflemen from our platoon, were wounded. There were other casualties, but no one else from our crew got it."

After the briefing, Lieutenant Geraghty, who I got on with pretty well, pulled me aside and gave me some advice that I will never forget, and which ultimately saved my hide on many occasions.

"I want you to remember this, Cozzy, and keep it at the front of your mind at all times," he said, looking me directly in the eye. "When we are out here in the jungle, the enemy are all around us, so it's vitally important that you keep your security up at all times. Remember that they can hit you at any time and when you least expect it."

When Geraghty was finished with his briefing, I sat down near Rowy and Finno, and meticulously inspected my machine gun to ensure it was in perfect working order.

"I don't want anything breaking down if I come across any Nogs," I said to myself, but I knew at that point that I was covered by more than just good equipment. I was even willing to concede that Nana may have been onto something.

I looked up to the sky and silently gave thanks.

Thanks chief, for covering my arse!

After lunch, we moved off into the jungle in total quietness. Our platoon was on high alert after the initial engagement that morning. Chooky had gone over to Finno as his second on the gun, while Rowy had come back over to me as my second. The other causalities were replaced by our reinforcements, enabling us to have a full strength platoon again.

About an hour later, we were in thick jungle and all was quiet as we walked in single file. We were approaching a fork in the track when Heckendorf, who was one of our forward scouts, motioned with his thumb down that something was not right. We all crouched down and I placed my right hand finger on the trigger of the M60 in readiness.

I was on high alert, camouflaged, as I lay in the long grass, when approximately 20 metres in front of us I saw six Viet Cong dressed in black pajamas. They came walking onto our track from the fork. I was momentarily stunned as this was the first time I had actually seen the enemy. As I looked at them from a distance the sobering realisation that I was so close to them made my mouth go dry. Rowy was lying beside me and we looked at each other. He knew what I was thinking, such was the bond that existed between us.

I knew that the moment had arrived. I was going to have to shoot to kill for the first time. I felt the same adrenalin pump through me like when I was in the ring and I was about to deliver a knockout punch. I gritted my teeth and rubbed my finger on the trigger, itching for the moment when I could unleash my deadly round.

As the VC walked closer to our position, I could feel my heart pumping as though it was about to explode. The Viet Cong who was leading the party then noticed one of our boys hiding in the jungle and was about to fire his weapon towards him when I let rip with my machine gun. The all too familiar *dukka, dukka, dukka* of the M60 seemed to magnify in sound as I sprayed the jungle in front of me in an arc like fashion.

All hell broke loose as the jungle came alive with both machine gun and small arms fire from both sides. In front of where I laid in the long grass was a log which served as protection from the enemy fire. The combination of intense firepower from both sides ripped the small shrubs and foliage surrounding the battle site to pieces. The skirmish lasted about five minutes and when it was over, we slowly got up from our positions and inspected the situation. We were able to count two VC killed with no casualties on our side, which brought us a huge sense of relief.

When we counted the casualties, I noticed a blood trail which one of the wounded VC had left. I followed the blood trail, my adrenalin still high after the skirmish, until I was out of sight of the rest of the platoon. The blood disappeared into the bush, and as I cautiously stepped off the track and into the jungle, searching for the wounded enemy, I was unaware that Lieutenant Geraghty had followed me. I was searching the jungle with great concentration, my finger on the trigger, when I heard Geraghty scream from a distance of no more than 20 metres away, "Costigan, get down!"

I swung around towards my platoon leader while simultaneously hitting the ground. A sharp branch scratched my stomach. When I looked up, I saw a wounded VC with his weapon drawn only metres from where I had been searching the jungle. The sound of Geraghty's M16 rifle filled the air and as I looked at the wounded enemy, I saw him receive a round of bullets to the head that dropped him to the ground instantaneously.

Geraghty walked over to the mortally wounded enemy cautiously, his rifle at the ready. After he had inspected the VC's body and realised he was dead, he turned to me and said, "I told you, you had to be careful, Costigan. That bloke was still alive and he could have knocked your lights out. Like I said to you before, you have to be so careful as the enemy are all around you. Take this as a lesson of what might have been. Don't ever go wandering off into the jungle chasing the enemy like that again. Is that clear?"

"Yes, skip!" I said in a contrite manner. My heart was going a mile a minute. I had got so caught up in the moment that all my training had gone out the window. I made a mental note that should never happen again and it didn't.

Geraghty was a seasoned soldier who had already done a tour of Vietnam and had an uncanny knack of sensing danger. He saved my life that day.

I was a bit shaken by my near miss, as I walked over to the where the two dead VC lay and inspected their bodies. I had only ever seen one dead person before in my life. That was back when I was at school when our English teacher, Brother Ignatius, had died from a massive heart attack in the school chapel during mass. He had been singing a hymn with great gusto when he must have hit one too many high notes and subsequently hit the floorboards with an almighty big thud.

This was nothing like that. One of the VC had his entire jaw blown off and it was a gruesome sight. In fact, both the enemy soldiers were very badly shot up. Although I was initially taken aback by the ghastly spectacle lying in front of me, I wasn't left with too many lingering feelings as I had seen plenty of dead animals on the farm and was hardened to the nature of death and destruction. I was used to blood.

In all honesty, it wasn't so much what was lying in front of me that had shaken me up, but more the fact that I had a narrow escape. I could have been killed. That was the last thing I wanted to happen. I wanted to get back home to see Sandy. I didn't want to die in some jungle half a world away.

After we inspected the bodies for any important documents, we moved off and did not encounter any other enemy activity for the rest of the day, although everyone was extremely cautious after our two engagements with enemy.

That night we set up our harbour position in thick jungle with three M60 machine guns covering our sentry points. As well as the machine guns we also had claymore mines set up—they were nasty buggers which blasted out hundreds of steel balls in a fan-like shape at knee level. I was given the graveyard shift through the middle of the night because I was a reinforcement. It didn't thrill me, but I understood.

My senses came alive as I became attuned to every noise I heard in the jungle. It was that quiet I could hear an insect buzzing around me in the stillness of the night. As I lay on my stomach manning the M60, I could not see my hand in front of my face because the jungle was so dark. Your mind has time to think in this situation, and I went over all that had happened during the day and the fact that I had secured my first kill—the VC who had first spied one of our blokes lying in the jungle. I felt a sense of achievement that I had killed him, after all I had saved a man's life, but I can honestly say I was not full of hate for the enemy. It was more a sense that I had been doing my job and when the test came, I was able to stand up and do it well.

After a while, my mind started to wander away from fighting and to the thought of having a drink. I had kept my drinking under tight wraps back home as my boxing career demanded it. Also, I knew Sandy didn't like it when I got drunk. As I was enveloped by the night, I dreamed of an icy cold lager. I had always thought in pictures and I could see the froth running down the sides of the glass. I was filled with desire. I could almost taste it. I started to lick my lips and longed for the first sip as the chilled ale splashed against my tongue. I stayed in this mental state for some time, but after a while it became very uncomfortable as it was impossible to get a beer way out here in the jungle. I was subjecting myself to a form of torture.

"I'll be hitting that boozer when I get back to Nui Dat," I told myself.

My state of semi-consciousness was interrupted by Greg Hackett, who had come out to the jungle with me on the helicopter. He relieved me from piquet duty.

"Times up, Cozzy," he said in a whisper.

"Thanks, Hacko, it's all yours, mate."

I made my way over to my hoochie and prepared to settle in for some shut eye after what had been an exhausting day.

Before shutting my eyes, I made myself a promise.

Come what may, I'll be wetting my whistle when I get back to the Dat.

The next morning the platoon moved off after having breakfast. Lieutenant Geraghty was concerned there was still enemy in close proximity, so he refused to allow anybody to light a fire. Instead, we ate out of our American ration packs. We patrolled for the rest of the day without incident, only stopping briefly for lunch. Late that afternoon, our platoon was picked up from the jungle by the Hueys and taken back to Nui Dat.

Although I had only been in the jungle for less than two days, I felt as though I had lived a lifetime's worth of experiences in a very short space of time. When Rowy, Finno and I made our way back to our tent, I slung my pack down on the floor and lay on my stretcher. I was exhausted.

Schooner who was lying on the stretcher adjacent to mine, looked at me and exclaimed, "You made it out in one piece I see, Cozzy!"

"I did, Schooner, but I had a close call with a nog."

"Yeah?" Schooner said, sounding surprised.

"He was lucky he didn't get zipped," said Finno as he lit up a rolly.

"What happened?" asked Schooner, sitting up.

"I followed a VC down into the jungle after I saw his blood trail, and he was about to have a crack at me when Geraghty spotted him and shot him dead," I told him. I felt like a bit of an idiot about it, but hopefully he'd learn from my mistake.

"He was a lucky boy was our Ed," said Rowy, who was opening some mail left on his stretcher.

"I was a bit too eager. The adrenalin was pumping after I shot my first nog, Schooner. I learnt a big lesson out there and I won't be doing that again."

The four of us talked for the next hour about what had happened, and before I dozed off for forty winks, I said to the others from where I lay on my stretcher, "They always put a BBQ on the first night after we've been in the jungle. I could handle a juicy steak, not to mention an icy cold beer."

"Now you're talking my sort of language, Cozzy," said Schooner.

"In fact, I can taste the little bastard going down right now," I said, before rolling over and getting some shut eye.

That night in the boozer, the feeling was sombre as we contemplated the loss of the two men from our platoon. We tucked into the BBQ while the grog flowed freely, but the mood wasn't jovial. We had a limited beer selection of Fosters, Victoria Bitter, XXXX or Carlton, and they became colloquially known as the blue, green, yellow or white cans.

As I sucked down copious amounts of VB, I became melancholy thinking about the letter Sandy had sent me. How I wished I could have been at her 21st birthday party!

I had taken the photo she sent me into the boozer and showed Finno as he was sipping on a beer.

"Wow, she's a nice sort, Cozzy. How'd you manage to crack onto her?" he said, and put down his beer to draw back on a rolly.

"I met her at Maroubra Surf Club one night. She's the nicest girl you could ever wish to meet, Finno," I told him.

"You want to hang onto her, Cozzy."

"I plan to, mate. I've asked her to marry me after this show's all over."

"And? She said yes?"

I nodded, staring at Sandy's beautiful face.

"Good for you, Ed," said Finno, taking a drag and clapping me on the shoulder. "You're a decent bloke. You deserve a good girl."

I soon found that the boozer was to become my favourite place to relax when not out on patrol. Mainly because there was little else to do at the Dat. I didn't plan on spending so much time in the boozer, but it sort of crept up on me. I happened to have a couple of seasoned drinkers in my section, namely Schooner and Finno, and as our time in Vietnam went by, the members of our platoon found that we sought great solace in each other's company, but more so in the booze.

As I became hardened to the environment and the stress of being out in the jungle for up to six weeks at a time, so too did my drinking increase. My thinking started to change as it does when you spend time with hardened, battle-weary soldiers. Not only did I become tough on the outside, but I hardened up on the inside too. Any softness about me started to disappear.

***

I sat opposite Tim, deep in thought, staring into space, and contemplating my first encounter with the enemy.

"Shit, Tim, that was a close call that first day I was out on patrol. If it wasn't for Geraghty, I could have been killed."

"So, your encounter with Maoris earlier on was just like reliving old times, eh?" said Tim, stretching his arms.

I snorted. "Yeah, you could say that. But I tell you, when I turned around to see that wounded nog pointing his rifle at me that day, it fairly put the wind up me. It was the closest call I had ever had up to that stage of my life, and in retrospect I crossed over a thin red line," I told him, my expression serious. "I started to hit the piss pretty hard whenever I got to the boozer, and it was something that went unchecked."

Tim fidgeted. "What about the old man? What was he like on the drink back then?"

"Finno," I said, as I sat upright in my seat, "was usually the ringleader. He always had some mad stunt he was trying to pull off. We were all pretty crazy back then, but your old man was the craziest out of the lot."

"Yeah? How so?"

"Like the time your old man, Rowy, Schooner Rooney and I were down in Vung Tau on R and R and we got on the piss with some Yank chopper crew. The *Septics* had some firecrackers which Finno got his hands on. He started throwing the bloody things around and almost burned the hotel down we were drinking in!" I shook my head and laughed.

"Yeah?"

"Too bloody right. We got chased out of there and staggered into a nightclub that was exclusively for black men. We almost got our lights punched out 'cause of a misunderstanding, but after some smooth talking by Schooner Rooney we got on their good side."

"What did he say?"

"Schooner told them he loved Motown music. He started rattling off the names of some of the Motown artists like The Supremes, Marvin Gaye and Stevie Wonder." I grinned. "They asked what a bunch of 'honkies' like us were doing listening to their 'jive ass music' for, and Schooner in that way he had, told ' em he loved it, and loved to dance. He performed a little dance right then and there with Rowy, and it was something stupid like you'd see at a woolshed dance. The rest of us took his lead and before you knew it, the four of us were doing some of the craziest moves you could ever see." I laughed at the memory. "Those black men thought it was hilarious and then we were all hunky dory. Finno said that he was 'as dry as a dead dingo's donger' and this big sergeant lost it. He called your old man 'the funniest motherfucker I ever heard' and because of your dad breaking the ice we got on the piss with them for the next three days. They reckon we were the first white people who had ever stepped foot in their bar. By the time we got back to Nui Dat we were legless." I pissed myself laughing. I couldn't remember the last time I thought about that crazy night, but shit it had been fun.

Tim's eyes lit up, but it also looked like he was remembering something. "Bloody Yanks, they're all mad. I saw how they operated in Iraq. Some of them are total cowboys!"

"Too bloody right, they're cowboys! I only ever came across them once while out on patrol in Vietnam and it was one too many as far as I was concerned."

"Why, what happened?"

"What happened? We were lucky the Viet Cong didn't kill the lot of us, for all the noise they were making!"

***

We were to rendezvous with an American infantry unit west of Courtenay rubber plantation, near Bein Hoa Province, as it was thought there was VC movement in the area.

This was the first time that any of us in 12 platoon had been involved with American soldiers, and our initial impression of them was that they were a ramshackle group.

It was obvious they were not a professionally trained unit simply by the way they were dressed. Some of their soldiers were not wearing shirts, or some were wearing flak jackets with no shirts. Others were without sleeves on their shirts. They were talking to each other out loud and I could hear a transistor radio blaring out from the middle of their unit. Some had cigarette packets slung around their helmets and others were chewing gum, and I could smell insect repellent on some of them. They didn't even look as though they were ready for action; some had their carbines slung upside down over their backs.

I noticed a big black bloke who had his M60 slung over his shoulder and was puffing away on a Camel cigarette. When he saw that I was carrying an M60, he approached me.

"How you doing, my main man? You been killing anything other than time, brother?" he said casually.

"Just the enemy when I come across 'em," I told him with a shrug.

"Your accent is so cool. Lay some skin, brother," he said with a laugh.

I lay my hand out flat and he slapped it with his hand.

The colour of his skin was the darkest I had ever seen, even more so than the men at the bar, and I was mesmerised. I had seen plenty of Aboriginals in my time, but never had I seen skin that was so *smooth*. Its rich, silky appearance was like nothing I had ever seen before and it left a lasting impression on me. Regardless of his casual approach, I remember thinking at the time that this heavily muscled black man was one of the finest looking human beings I had ever seen. He was a handsome devil.

"Right on, brother," he said.

As I looked over the motley bunch assembled in front of me, no one seemed to be taking any notice of their platoon commander who was trying to instruct them with various orders.

Geraghty was talking to their platoon commander when a big black fellow came wandering over to where they were talking, casually brandishing his M16 in Geraghty's face. I always remember what Geraghty said. "Wave that thing in my face again and I'll shove it right up your arse," he growled. Geraghty wasn't a big man, but when his hackles were up his icy stare was unforgettable. The soldier's eyeballs opened up as wide as dinner plates after Geraghty let loose with his spray.

"Is there any chance you could get your blokes to cut out the noise? There could be enemy around," Lieutenant Geraghty asked the American officer.

The officer turned around and addressed his men, yelling out on top note, "Hey! You guys cut the crap and keep it quiet, will ya?"

Geraghty just shook his head and told their platoon commander that we would be setting up our night harbour a bit further down the track. Meanwhile, we noticed one of the American soldiers setting up a single claymore mine, as it was getting late and the Yanks were obviously going to harbour there for the night. He wandered out without a weapon and after opening up the folding legs, he casually dropped the mine in the ground.

"Is that okay?" he yelled to his platoon commander.

On closer inspection, we could all see that the claymore was facing back towards where we were standing, and as I glanced across at Geraghty, I could see that he was seething with rage.

"You goddamn asshole!" his platoon commander screamed. "You gotta face the mine the other way, goofball!"

"Oh, okay. I fucked up big time. Sorry about that," he said.

By this stage, Lieutenant Geraghty was done. He informed his American counterpart that we were moving on.

Rowy, who was standing next to me, shook his head. "Get a load of the bloke with the claymore, Cozzy. What a fuckin' idiot. With all the noise these pricks are making, they're sure to attract the attention of any VC who might be in the area."

"You're not wrong, Rowy. I betcha Geraghty is thinking long and hard about hanging around these clowns for the night." I sneered at their campsite.

"I want to get home in one piece, Ed. I got a letter from Julie before we went out on patrol and I'm keen on getting home to see her," said Rowy.

At the mere mention of Julie's name, I went into deep thought about Sandy. "I wonder what the girls are up to, hey, Rowy?"

"I dunno, Cozzy, but I bet it's a damn sight better than being out here with these jokers carrying on the way they are. This is real spooky."

Both Rowy and I had an uneasy feeling about the situation and it only highlighted the fact that we wanted to get back to Australia in one piece to see the ones we loved. We didn't need some incompetent bunch of Americans jeopardising our chances of achieving this.

It was late afternoon as we tramped our way through the thick jungle, trying to get as far away from the American unit that we possibly could.

"On any other occasion, I'd be cursing and swearing about bush-bashing through this jungle, but I don't mind this arvo. Anything to get away those fuckin' idiots," said Schooner, as he cleared vines away from his face.

"Do you reckon Geraghty will let us light up a cigarette?" said Chooky.

"You've got buckley's chances of that happening. He doesn't want anything to draw attention to our position, so you can forget about lighting up for the time being, Chooky," I responded.

When we eventually set up our night time position, a considerable distance away from the Americans, Geraghty called the platoon signaller over and spoke to our company commander, my favourite arsehole, Major Milroy, on the radio.

"Sir, I don't feel comfortable about the situation we're in."

"Why's that lieutenant?" asked Milroy.

"Major, the American platoon is creating so much noise that if there are any enemy around they will surely be attracted to their position."

"Have you settled into a night harbour position?"

"Yes, sir, we're about one mile away in a small clearing surrounded by thick jungle."

"Okay, stay there for the night and I'll be in contact in the morning to give you coordinates for a new sector to patrol."

"Roger that, sir."

"Okay, stay safe, over and out," crackled the major's voice.

Our platoon let out a collective sigh of relief when the message was relayed that we would be moving on the next day.

It was 1800 hours when all of a sudden there was an almighty big racket as the American platoon let rip with every bit of firepower they had, then everything went quiet.

"Shit, what's that?" Schooner said, as he jumped up in a startled manner.

"That's the American platoon letting off all their firepower. They do it for one minute at 1800 hours every night," said Geraghty.

"What the bloody hell for, skip?" I exclaimed. The noise had been deafening.

"That's their way of scaring off anything that might be in firing range of where they've set up harbour for the night," said Geraghty.

"You're bloody joking!"

"I'm afraid not, Cozzy. That's the Americans for you. All gung ho," replied Geraghty, his mood tense.

I felt a shiver run up my spine before exclaiming, "Talk about an open invitation for the enemy to come and have a crack at us!"

"I've seen them do this before. That's why we're over here, Cozzy, and they're over there," said Geraghty. He looked pissed off.

That night, everyone in our platoon was uneasy about being so close to the Americans and I doubt whether anyone had much sleep at all. Lieutenant Geraghty made us put out more claymore mines than usual.

It was about midnight and I was finding it hard to sleep. I was lying under my hoochie reading a letter from Stumpy with the aid of a torch. The rain was coming down hard when all of a sudden, all hell broke loose as small arms fire pierced the rain-soaked night. Everyone in our platoon bolted upright and confusion reigned as our initial thoughts were that we were being attacked.

But it became clear in a short space of time that it wasn't us but the Americans under attack, and we froze, laying still in position, listening to a firefight that lasted approximately fifteen minutes. There was nothing we could do. It was that dark and we would have become lost in the thick jungle trying to make our way over to where they were stationed.

Lieutenant Geraghty made contact with the American unit on the platoon radio, although the Americans could not make contact with their unit headquarters. Geraghty did what he could and that was to send their coordinates back to our company headquarters so they could pass it onto the Americans.

I crawled up close to our platoon signaller who was relaying messages from Geraghty to headquarters, and they decided to direct artillery support from the Australian FSB located a short distance away.

The fire support base was manned with 150 mm howitzer guns, and within a short period of time, shells started exploding near where the enemy was attacking. The artillery salvo lasted about thirty minutes and then all went silent. The American platoon commander was able to communicate that he had at least eight dead and ten wounded, but did not know how many of the enemy had been killed, although he believed the artillery had landed right on the mark.

No one slept for the remainder of the night, and at first light we packed up in total silence and made our way through the jungle to the Americans.

The sight that greeted us was one of total carnage. The

Americans had been hit very hard, with only a dozen or so of their soldiers deemed fit enough to walk. The rest were either lying dead or wounded.

Geraghty organised for choppers to evacuate the dead and wounded. It was quite clear that the American lieutenant was in shock and not fit to command his platoon, so Geraghty took control of the situation.

Geraghty had our platoon set up an ambush position while he requested reinforcements as he believed that there could be a large force of VC nearby. Headquarters agreed to send out both 10 and 11 platoons of D Company to support us, and planned on flying them in by helicopter to a safe position nearby.

When we were in position Geraghty summoned Schooner Rooney and me to come with him to survey the situation. I grabbed a spare belt of ammunition off Rowy and the three of us walked through the carnage that our artillery had caused on the enemy.

It was a mess. Some of the enemy dead were barely recognisable as their injuries were that horrific. We walked, weapons raised, out into the killing ground and amongst the dead VC strewn in all directions. Many of them had been blown to pieces from the artillery bombardment.

Then, while I was quietly walking through the jungle a short distance from the others, I came across a young VC soldier who was in a terrible state. He was dressed in blood-stained black pajamas and was lying on his back. On further inspection, I noticed that he had almost been cut in half. His intestines were on the ground next to him, displaying undigested rice, but miraculously he was still alive. He looked as though he was no older than sixteen or seventeen years of age, and as I stood over him with my finger on the trigger of the M60, I could hear him whispering something to me in Vietnamese. His eyes were fixed on me and it became a very personal moment between the two of us. As I was standing over his mortally wounded body, I was oblivious to the fact that Lieutenant Geraghty had walked up behind me.

"Ah, have a go at him, he's rat-shit," he said with a wave of his hand.

"He's in a hell of a mess, skip."

"You're not bloody wrong there, Cozzy. Finish him off will ya."

Geraghty walked off and the wounded VC continued to talk to me in the faintest of whispers.

"I don't know what you're talking about, mate, but it's not going to do you much good," I told him gently. "You're in a hell of a mess, and I'm afraid the show's over for you."

I looked into his eyes and could see the fear in them, as he knew his fate was sealed.

"Sorry, mate," I told him, my face grave, "but it's the only option."

I took a deep breath and sent a burst of machine gun fire through his heart, and God as my witness, I've been looking at those fear-ridden eyes ever since. Can't seem to get them out of my head.

I took a deep breath after I had finished dealing with him, and putting aside my feelings, I went through his pockets as was my duty. What I found in his top pocket stopped me in my tracks.

Inside was a handmade leather pouch and in it was a set of rosary beads.

I held the rosary beads up to the early morning sunlight to examine them more closely and said to myself, "Well, I'll be buggered. I thought all these bastards were supposed to be commies, but this bloke's Catholic, just like me."

Schooner approached and interrupted my reverie. "Gee, he's in a hell of a mess, Cozzy!" He nodded at my hands. "What's that you got there?"

I turned around and showed Schooner what I was holding.

Schooner looked at me and exclaimed, "A set of rosary beads? A bit early for praying ain't it, Cozzy?"

"They're not mine, Schooner, I found them on this bloke I just finished off."

"On him? What the bloody hell is a little commie like him doing with a set of rosary beads on him?"

"Stuffed if I know, Schooner, but the bloke's obviously a Catholic."

"A Catholic!" Schooner exclaimed. "Aren't all these little nogs supposed to be communists?"

"That's what I thought," I said, uneasily.

Schooner examined the beads. "They look like the set that my mum has at home in Condobilin. She always says a couple of decades in the night before she goes to bed. Probably praying that I stay on the straight and narrow." He gave the rosary beads back to me and said, "I better keep moving, Cozzy. We gotta inspect all the dead."

After Schooner moved on, I pondered for some time the fact that here I was fighting in Vietnam, and I had just killed an enemy who was of the same creed as me. It wasn't until many years later when I was older and wiser that I found out that many of the soldiers from Vietnam were Catholics and they were only fighting us because we were in their country.

After I came home from Vietnam, I often saw the image of fear in that young Viet Cong's eyes. Of all the casualties I saw in Vietnam, none stayed with me like quite like that young man who I finished off with a mercy killing.

None.

***

"It wasn't him being cut in half and all his blood and guts spilt all over the place that worried me," I said to Tim. "After all, I'd slaughtered my fair share of sheep back on the farm and I was used to seeing dead animals, it was just part and parcel of the way I was brought up. Besides, by the time I'd come home from Vietnam I'd seen plenty of death. Nah. It was his eyes, Tim," I told him seriously. "Those bloody eyes! Maybe I was given a glimpse of my own mortality. And to throw the rosary beads on top of that! Now that really threw me. Fancy me, a Catholic from a small town like Eumungerie, killing a Catholic from Vietnam. Well, I'll be buggered, Tim. There was certainly some food for thought there. Even today, when I get tired or stressed out, I still see those eyes, but fortunately not as much as in days gone by."

Tim looked grim. "So, you were at the pointy end in Vietnam then?"

"You betcha I was on the pointy end. And because I was on the M60, you always knew that if you encountered the enemy, you'd be the first one they were trying to hit which always made me edgy."

"I know where you're coming from." Tim nodded. "I felt exactly the same way handling the machine gun in Iraq."

"Too right you do. You know, we were all pretty rattled after our initial engagement with the enemy, and our platoon was particularly vigilant. You were never sure when the enemy was and when you next might engage them. Geraghty's words about the enemy being all around became increasingly true the further we got into our tour." I shook my head. Tim listened closely. I knew I had him the second we got onto Vietnam.

"Yeah, it was bloody spooky out there in the jungle some-days," I continued. "It wasn't engaging the enemy that worried me as much as the waiting for the *moment* you might encounter them."

I gave myself a moment of contemplation and a smile came over my face as I remembered something Finno did. It was sure to lighten the mood.

Tim was intrigued. "What? What is it?" he asked, venturing his own smile.

I laughed. "Out of the blue, out of the chaos." I laughed again.

"What's so funny?"

"Totally against the run of the play. When everyone is so serious and you're all stressed out, you have an incident like the chook bomb which can lighten any situation."

"Chook bomb?" Tim said with a quizzical look.

"Yeah, chook bomb." I couldn't stop laughing now. "It wasn't all fighting out in the jungle and your old man sure knew how to make a bloke laugh."

***

By late May 1968, we had been in Vietnam for two months and the wet season was among us. You could set your watch to the rain as it came in every afternoon and continued well into the night. The rain made life difficult as the red clay of Nui Dat turned into a slimy mess which stuck to your boots and infil-trated everything you touched.

By this stage we were engaged in Operation Bexley. We were

to search a village south-west of Courtenay rubber plantation, close to the boarder of Bein Hoa Province. After our rendezvous with the American platoon a month earlier, we had no other contact with the enemy up to this date.

After searching the village extensively, we could not find anything of importance. The locals were getting a bit edgy because some of them thought that a couple of our blokes were trying to steal some of the vegetables from their gardens. It was not the case, they were only searching for weapons and ammunition that might be stored in a shed near a chook pen that was standing adjacent to the vegetable garden.

While Lieutenant Geraghty was trying to ease tensions that were simmering between both parties, Finno produced one of the more memorable incidents of our tour that diffused the whole situation.

While Finno was searching the shed for weapons and ammunition, he spotted about two dozen chickens secured in a chicken coop. While Geraghty was frantically trying to calm down the situation, Finno turned to some of us who were gathered nearby and said in a whisper, "Righto you lot, wait till I show you this little party trick of mine."

"What are you scheming, Finno?" said Rowy, who was standing nearby.

"I'm going to show you a chook bomb, Rowy."

"A what?" said Rowy, confused.

"It's called a chook bomb. Here, hold my weapon will ya while I set it up."

Rowy looked around in an uneasy manner as he could still hear Geraghty talking loudly to the villagers a short distance away, and the skip didn't like it when the blokes put down their weapons.

Finno, meanwhile, had found a spade and dug a small hole in the earth big enough to lay a chicken in. He then grabbed one of the chickens and sent it to sleep by gently stroking it between the eyes.

"There you go my little chickadee, go to sleep," he purred.

By this stage, most of our platoon had gathered as word had gone around that Finno was up to something. However, they weren't the only ones watching. We had an audience of locals too, curious to see just what Finno was doing.

Finno then gently placed the chicken inside the small hole he had dug and covered it with a light film of dirt. In next to no time, the other chickens began to walk over where Sleeping Beauty was lying under the ground, as if she wasn't even there. It was spring-loaded moment, where everyone wondered what would happen next. Then, after about 30 seconds, the napping chicken suddenly woke up and realising its predicament, aka being buried alive, it sprung into the air about six foot with feathers flying, squawking like crazy, and creating a hell of a commotion. The other chooks, who were milling around minding their own business, exploded into a ball of feathers and mayhem when their friend from the grave suddenly appeared out of nowhere. This sent the platoon into hysterics and even some of the locals found it hilarious and slapped their knees in uncontrollable laughter.

Geraghty shook his head, turned to Finno and said, barely able to contain his own laughter, "You mad bastard, Finno, you've managed to diffuse a sticky situation in a couple of minutes where I've had buckley's chance of doing so for the last fifteen."

It was just the tonic that the platoon needed to lighten the situation. We'd been out in the jungle for weeks and everyone was tired and edgy and hadn't had a good laugh for a while.

**

I sat opposite Tim with a smile on my face and said, "No doubt about it. Your old man always had some mad escapade up his sleeve. That was definitely one of his best performances. Even after all these years that story still makes me laugh."

"A chook bomb, hey? Sounds like something crazy he would have done," said Tim, half a grin on his face.

"Yeah, old Finno could certainly be crazy. He was never far away from trouble."

"That would be right. Trouble was my old man's second name," Tim said, his smile now gone.

I sought to diffuse his change of mood. "I mean trouble in the sense that if there was a prank on, Finno was never far away."

"You might mean that, but I mean trouble in the true sense of the word," said Tim.

"What, that your old man was just plain difficult in everything he did?"

"Pretty much so."

"Well, I never experienced that. I think he had a lot of good qualities. He was complex. He had the ability to be extremely sensitive on one hand and then he could be absolutely crazy on the other," I said, trying to show Tim the man I knew.

"Sensitive in what way?"

"Well for starters," I began, "he had a great love of nature. I remember being out on patrol once. It was the end of the day and we settled down into night harbour position. Finno and I were cleaning our weapons and there was a beautiful red sunset on the far horizon. 'Pity we have to be fighting a war in such a beautiful place,' he told me and I've always remembered that, Tim. It was a really touching moment. Then I remember another time when we were back at Nui Dat and I was reading him a letter that Sandy had sent me. He told me that he hoped to meet a nice girl like her and it was both genuine and touching. There was no bullshit about Finno. He had a very honest side to him. But I suppose that since I've been sober, I've learnt that I have an alcoholic nature and I suspect your old man was tarred with the same brush."

"What's an alcoholic nature?" Tim asked, his eyebrow raised.

"Hypersensitive, loner, perfectionist streak, ungrounded and unfounded fears, big ego, low self-esteem," I told him promptly.

"I've never heard that before," Tim said with a thoughtful look on his face.

"Oh, yeah. The old Alkie has a distinctive personality. That's why they relate to each other so well. When they congregate together, they are among their own tribe," I told him, fidgeting with my now empty cup.

"Mmm," Tim said thoughtfully.

"You better believe it, Tim. We're a breed of our own and we're also intelligent."

"Intelligent?" He almost scoffed.

"Yeah, intelligent," I told him firmly. "Look through history and you'll find that many of the people who changed the course of human civilisation were alcoholics. Musicians, writers, artists, actors, explorers, scientists, and the list goes on. The alcoholic is a driven character and will go morning, noon and night to achieve their goals. The pity is they cause so much destruction on the way through."

Tim sat back in his seat, pondering on what I had just told him. "Well, that might be the case with Dad. I can see my old man had some of those characteristics, but where was he when I was growing up? I mean, a kid needs his old man around, but most of the time he was missing in action in the in the pub. Did he go missing in action when you were in battle?"

"I don't like that question," I said with a stern look. "He might not have been a great dad, but you just questioned the integrity of a soldier. You should know better than that, Tim."

Tim blushed and so I softened.

"Did your old man ever talk to you about what he went through in Vietnam?"

"Never."

I gave him a firm stare. "Your old man might have done some bad things in his life, Tim, but let me assure you he never went missing in action when we were out in the jungle."

Tim folded his arms. "I don't know how many times I sat in the car with a can of coke and a bag of chips in my hand while my old man got on the piss inside the pub. He was certainly missing in action then."

"Look," I told him in a calming voice, "I know you're pissed off at him, but your dad went through a lot in Vietnam and it knocked him around."

He gave me a hard look, his belligerence returning. "You know what? I think he was a gutless bastard. Us kids never saw him like any of the ways you just said. He was always away shearing and when he was home he was always on the piss."

I nodded, wanting to acknowledge his feelings on the matter, but I knew how to convince him otherwise. "Gutless was one thing that Finno wasn't. When we were out in the jungle, he was one bloke you wanted around you when the shit hit the fan."

"Like when?" Tim asked.

"Like when we attacked the Bunkers."

"The Bunkers?"

"Yeah, the Bunkers. It was the biggest battle we were involved in and I wouldn't be here today if it wasn't for your old man."

Chapter 6

Late February, 1969, 'Battle of the Bunkers', Phuoc Tuy Province

I HAD JUST OVER one month left to serve in Vietnam and was determined to get back home in one piece. I had become hardened during my tour, like most of my platoon did, and at this late stage I was increasingly vigilant that nothing should stop me from achieving my safe return to Australia.

Unfortunately, we were coming up to what was to be to be the biggest operation we were involved in. Our platoon was flown out to a landing zone well west off the main route between Baria and the Courtenay rubber plantation by RAAF Iroquois gunships in the early morning. As the Huey flew just above the tree tops, the sun shone on my face and I was overcome with a great feeling of serenity. It was a rare glimpse of sunlight in the midst of an environment which had made me so hard. It was a window to my real self and a moment to reflect on the things that really mattered, like the love of a woman like Sandy. I had everything to live for, which presented a strange dichotomy. I was mired in the hell of Vietnam, but one flight away was Sandy and the rest of my life. It was like the sun that morning was reminding me of that.

After a while, I glanced across at Rowy who was sitting on the floor beside the door gunner. Rowy had 700 rounds of ammunition for the M60 on him, which even for his standards was a lot. Normally, we would carry 800 rounds between the two of us with Rowy carrying 500 plus the spare barrel, and myself carrying 300 with the gun. The rest of our section would carry 300 rounds between them. Bob Rowe was one of the strongest men I have ever come across in my life and his big frame could carry an enormous amount of weight on it, but even I was surprised by his load.

Years later, when we went out fishing one day, I said to him, "Hey, Rowy, I've always wondered why you had so much ammo on you that day we flew out to the Bunkers."

Rowy gave me a wry smile and said, "I suppose it was just instinct, Cozzy. It just seemed like the right thing to do when I was getting my gear together. I remember Schooner querying me at the time about it too, but I stuck to my gut feeling and took the extra belts for the M60."

His instinctive feeling probably saved our lives because three days into the operation, the shit hit the fan and we needed every bit of ammunition we could get our hands on.

We were in the vicinity of the Courtenay rubber plantation once again because intelligence had reported large numbers of enemy troops crossing the border from Long Khanh Province into Phuoc Tuy Province.

On the first two days of patrol we didn't sight the enemy. It was while we were having an early lunch on the third day that the call came through from headquarters for our platoon to rendezvous with two platoons of our company.

As we made our way through the thick jungle towards 10 and 11 Platoons, Sergeant Wally Kingston brought to Lieutenant Geraghty's attention something he had observed. "Skip, just a short distance away in the jungle I've noticed a number of freshly fallen tree stumps which the enemy has tried to disguise by packing fresh mud on top of them." He pointed in the direction where he had made the discovery.

Geraghty walked over to the spot with Wally, and after observing the tree stumps said, "The cheeky bastards. The nogs are up to something." He looked around in a wide arc, trying to see any other evidence of fallen trees before summoning the platoon to keep patrolling.

As we walked further on into the jungle, we could see that the enemy had cut down a considerable amount of trees and the stumps all had that packed mud on them. Shortly after, Geraghty gathered the platoon.

"It's become evident from the amount of fallen trees that the enemy is most probably constructing a bunker system somewhere in the near vicinity. I want you to be extra vigilant as they may be preparing themselves for a big battle."

I turned to Rowy. "It could be on for young and old, mate?"

"I got the extra ammo if we need it, Cozzy," said Rowy, reassuringly.

We tramped through the jungle for the remainder of the day, sighting more trees that had been fallen before pulling up in a clearing just before dusk. After going through the normal routine of setting up a night defense position, we had a cold feed out of our ration packs. There was a definite feeling of unease among the men as we settled in for the night. I was happy that Geraghty had chosen to carry an extra machine gun for the platoon as my own instincts told me that we may just need it.

As I settled in for the night, I turned to Rowy, who was lying under his hoochie only a short distance away and whispered, "I got a letter from Sandy yesterday and she's real worried about me. I've assured her that everything is alright but she reckons I sound different in my letters and that I've become negative. Do I sound negative to you, Rowy?"

"Nah, you sound like the same old dickhead you've always been, Costigan," said Rowy, not even trying to conceal his grin.

"You'll keep, areshole," I said, smiling back at him, but it didn't stop me from feeling melancholy over the contents of Sandy's letter. I hadn't seen any great difference in my behaviour. I knew I was getting harder, but I just felt more realistic about things. Rowy interrupted my reverie.

"If it helps you out, Ed, I got a letter from Julie yesterday and she told me that Sandy said to her that you're the best thing that ever happened to her, and she can't wait to tie the knot with you."

I felt relieved in one way, but as I lay there contemplating on what Rowy said, I blurted out, "I love that girl to bits, mate, but so much has changed in me since I've been over here that I don't know if I'm ready for marriage quite yet."

"We've all changed, Ed," whispered Rowy. "It's pretty hard not to after some of the things we've seen and done. I'm sure everything will settle down once we get back to civvy street."

I looked around our dark camp and felt unease. "I hope you're right, Rowy, but I got a tell ya I've got an uneasy feeling at the moment. I think something really big's gonna go down out here."

"If it does we'll make sure we stick together like glue. After all, you're the one bloke I want on my side if all hell breaks loose out here."

"Thanks, mate, I appreciate that. If anything happens to me out here, Rowy, I want you to know that you're the best mate a man could wish to have," I told him sincerely.

Rowy leaned across in the dark of the night shook my hand. "Thanks, Ed. Your blood's worth bottling, mate."

I lay back, content in the knowledge that whatever lay ahead of us, I was with a bloke who I could trust with my life.

I dropped off into a deep slumber.

I awoke early the next morning to be met by Rowy, who had a serious look on his face. "Let's go and face the music, Cozzy," he said in his customary laconic drawl.

I stretched. "I slept well last night, Rowy. Probably a good thing because I think this may be a big day," I said. He could only nod.

We packed our gear in total silence before heading off into the thick jungle towards Courtenay rubber plantation. It was extra slow going as we bush-bashed through the thick jungle, making very slow progress, and this only heightened the increasing anxiety within the platoon. On top of this was the fact that everyone was tired after eleven months of slogging it through the thick jungles of Vietnam. We were nearly at the end of our tour and this exhaustion produced tension among the soldiers. It was unusual for our crew, as it had generally been a harmonious relationship within the platoon with only the occasional argument.

We had only been walking for a short time when Finno arced up. "Hey, Chooky, will you stop letting those fuckin' branches you're walking through slap into my face? It's giving me the shits."

"What do you want me to do, Finno? Personally hold the branch back so it don't slap you in the face? This shit is as thick as buggery. I can't help it," replied Chooky, his mood testy.

"Well, start taking some more care will ya?" said Finno.

"Perhaps you want me to get the red carpet out for ya, Finno?"

"The only red carpet you'll being seeing out here, Chooky, is the piece I shove fair up your arse," growled Finno.

Finno and Chooky's argument was overhead by Wally Kingston who sorted both of them out quick smart. "You two dickheads shut the fuck up, will ya! The enemy could be right under our noses here. Besides, Geraghty's edgy as he knows the nogs are up to something. You know what he's like."

After that, we moved along in total silence. There were more and more logs from the surrounding jungle that had been cut down, and it soon became apparent that the enemy's bunker system was not too far from where we were.

It was just after lunch when we received a call on the radio from the commander of 11 platoon.

"Our forward scouts have observed a large force of Viet Cong north-west of Courtenay rubber plantation," his voice crackled on the radio.

"Any indication of the size of the force?" replied Geraghty.

"We estimate a force of approximately 300 Viet Cong troops."

"Can you confirm that? It was 300 troops you said, lieutenant?" said Geraghty.

"Yes, that's correct. 300 Viet Cong Troops."

Geraghty looked around at Wally Kingston ashen-faced and said, "This is serious."

"We won't be able to handle those numbers by ourselves, sir," said Wally.

"No. We'll need air and artillery support that's for sure."

I looked at Rowy and Schooner who were standing nearby. "Shit! We've never seen those type of numbers before," I said, the wind fair up me.

"300! Mate, this is gonna be one hell of a show," said Schooner, his eyes darting about nervously.

Geraghty got everyone to double check their heavy camouflage before we continued through the thick jungle. We walked for another 20 minutes and were approximately 500 metres from 11 platoon when we could hear what sounded like a loud firefight taking place.

We stopped in a small clearing, and I was in close proximity to our signaller. We could hear the commander of 11 platoon communicating to him through our VHF radio.

"There's about 100 Viet Cong troops engaging us in battle at the moment, with more in reserve. I've called headquarters for both air and artillery support and I need 12 platoon's urgent support, I repeat 12 platoon's urgent support, ASAP!" the lieutenant said in a voice full of anxiety.

"I read you loud and clear, lieutenant. We are making our way over to you as quickly as we can," Geraghty responded, right onto it.

"This situation is dire and we need your help urgently. Over and out."

The radio crackled then fell silent.

Geraghty and Wally Kingston exchanged a look, and then

Wally addressed the platoon and said, "The situation with 11 platoon is very serious, so stay alert."

We hurriedly made our way to where 11 platoon was engaging the enemy. We had only been walking for about five minutes when we were confronted by about 50 of the enemy.

The jungle came alive with the sound of the weapons. The noise was deafening.

As I lay on my stomach, protected by some heavy timber, it didn't take long before I screamed out to Rowy who was nearby, "Quick, Rowy! I'm running low on ammo!"

Rowy crawled up beside me and fed me a spare belt before exclaiming, "Watch over to your right, Ed! There's a bunch of nogs heading toward us!"

I swung the gun around and fired upon the advancing VC, managing to hit a number of them before the others disappeared back into the jungle.

"Shit, I thought the little bastards were going to land on top of us, Rowy," I said, my heart racing.

"Nice firing, Cozzy. You finished them off real good."

Over the next fifteen minutes, we engaged the VC in a bloody battle, managing to inflict a number of causalities with none of our men being hit before the black clad soldiers disappeared back into the dense jungle.

We got up and followed the blood trail from their wounded for about 50 metres before they once again engaged us in battle for the next ten minutes. We waited until they were just a short distance from us before Kingston gave the order and we let loose with everything we had. The amount of gunfire from both sides was unbelievable, as it completely denuded the jungle of vegetation.

A loud whine started and then the artillery and air strikes

started to come in against the enemy. As we walked further towards the hills situated near Courtenay rubber plantation where 11 platoon were, we heard the continuous sound of gunfire and I turned to Rowy and said, "This is just the entrée, just wait to you see the main menu!"

After our artillery and air strikes hit their mark, some of the enemy retreated and the action died down, albeit temporarily, as our opposing forces regrouped. It was mid-afternoon when we made contact with both 10 and 11 Platoons by radio, and our company commander Major Milroy gave orders for all three platoons to go to company headquarters which was situated just 500 metres from where the action had been taking place. Lieutenant Geraghty, along with the other two platoon commanders then went off to be briefed as to what was going to happen next.

Our intelligence had informed Major Milroy that we were situated 800 metres from an extensive bunker system which was the regimental headquarters of the 1st Battalion of 33rd NVA Regiment. The section commanders informed us that we were up against approximately 500 NVA troops, but they believed that many of the enemy had retreated from the bunker system after the heavy artillery and air bombardment. We were then told that we were to attack the remaining enemy in the bunker system, which included both NVA and Viet Cong soldiers.

We sat down in silence and cleaned our weapons while we waited for further instructions. Close by me were Rowy, Schooner Rooney and Finno, and I turned to them and said, "NVA. Mate, this is going to be nasty."

"Yep, we'll have to be on our toes fighting these bastards," said Schooner.

Rowy was sitting just across from me cleaning his SLR and checking the spare barrel for the M60. He happened to catch me glancing at him and he gave me a wry smile and a wink and said confidently, "Everything will be okay, Cozzy, we've got the spare ammo, old son."

His words sounded reassuring and it automatically made me feel better.

Our platoon was to be positioned on the right flank while 11 Platoon were to be behind us and 10 Platoon were in reserve. We were issued extra ammunition and grenades, and at approximately 3.30 pm, the bunker system was hit with an artillery salvo which lasted for about ten minutes.

The bunkers were approximately 500 hundred metres long by 200 hundred metres wide, and from above looked like a big flattened 'X'. It was a complex system of tunnels which were made up of logs and mud and dug well into the ground. Inside, the enemy used the bunkers for everything from storage to operating theaters. This particular bunker's primary purpose was as a regimental headquarters, as well as protecting the enemy soldiers from airstrikes.

Just before the start of the attack, Rowy crawled up beside me and wrapped another 200 rounds of ammunition around my neck, to bring my total to 500 rounds.

"You'll need this, Costigan, ya mad bastard," he grinned as he slapped me on the back.

Finally, after God knows how long of waiting, the order came to advance on the enemy and all three sections of our platoon moved out quickly in a battle assault formation which consisted of an extended line some 200 metres wide. We were approximately 400 metres from the bunker system when the order came through from Wally Kingston to advance in a crouched position.

No sooner had the order came down when from a small hill

approximately 50 metres to my right, we spotted ten VC who opened fire on us before making a hasty retreat. Fortunately, none of our men were injured and after waiting for fifteen minutes, we resumed patrolling until we were only 200 metres from the first series of bunkers. We were then ordered to crawl on our stomachs through the thick, long grass, which kept us well camouflaged.

I was once again on the extreme right flank of our platoon and our section was well inside the perimeter of the bunker system when, from out of the jungle in front of us, came scores of NVA soldiers, firing at us with demon-like fury.

"Bloody NVA, Rowy!" I yelled amid the chaos. That was the first time I'd ever laid eyes on them, having only ever seen the Viet Cong before now.

"Crikey, there's a stack of the bastards!" he replied.

The jungle came alive with small arms and machine gun fire from both sides, and it was at a level of intensity in which I had never experienced before. The noise was deafening as I fired round after round into the advancing enemy.

As the enemy approached my well-hidden position, I was able to dispose of many of them. Just forward of me and to my left was Heckendorf, who was firing with great precision. I saw him turn his head slightly to the right, as though to check the firing coming from my machine gun, when an enemy bullet smashed into his forehead, killing him instantly.

I did not have time to comprehend what I had just witnessed, as the firing from the enemy was relentless and the noise from so many firearms horrific. I didn't even have the time to process that he was gone.

By this stage, it was getting harder to see through the haze of smoke caused by gunfire, but surprisingly, my thinking was clear as I fired accurately at the enemy. I think in retrospect this was due to my alcoholic nature, which I subsequently learnt can be unravelled by the small things in life, but handles the big occasions with aplomb. Coupled with the years I had spent in the ring, my ability to put my head down and cop an onslaught was fierce. But in saying that, confusion reigned all around me as the battle raged on. It was exceedingly hot and humid and the sound of shredding vegetation and the groans of the wounded was never far from my ears, with everything overlaid and drowned out by the *dukka dukka dukka* of my gun.

The jungle around us was exploding now and I saw that our platoon was being hit with incoming enemy mortar rounds. This was splintering the branches of the trees above and reigning debris down upon us.

Our platoon was in the most advanced position with 11 Platoon slightly behind us and 10 Platoon called up from reserve to the extreme left of our flank. In among all the commotion I thought my ears were playing tricks on me, as I could have sworn I heard a bugle being played. At first I thought I was imagining it when 50 metres in front of me, an NVA soldier dressed in a green uniform stood up and blew his bugle. The sound of it sent a shiver up my spine, as I realised that it was the signal for his comrades to make another attack.

On they came in wave after wave, and yet somehow, our platoon's front line held as we inflicted massive carnage on their troops.

The pace of battle was so frenetic that I had lost all concept of time. It was as though my life had become concentrated in this one intense moment. I felt like everything that had gone before in my life had been a preparation for *this* moment. I was living my whole life in this one deadly afternoon. Nothing in my days before that afternoon mattered, as this was the very apex of my life's experiences, and all my thoughts and emotions were intensified to a level I had never experience before or since. It was a surreal experience.

But as much as we were inflicting severe causalities on the enemy, the sheer size of the attack was becoming too much for our company to handle. It was estimated that we were facing up to four companies of NVA troops up against just 120 men of our company. Lieutenant Geraghty realised that our situation was dire and requested artillery support from headquarters. Within five minutes, our 105 mm howitzer shells were landing behind the enemy bunkers where the NVA soldiers were preparing themselves for the next phase of the attack.

Our forward observation officers (FOO) walked their shells towards the advancing line of NVA. The carnage was indescribable as I could see the enemy being blown to pieces from where I was still lying in the long grass.

The extra ammunition that Rowy had supplied me was now coming to my aid, as I had been firing continuously for the best part of half an hour, in 20 or 30 round bursts.

"Hey, Rowy, this barrel on the gun is as hot as buggery! Give us the spare one, will ya?' I yelled out.

Rowy, who was only metres away, crawled towards me, dodging enemy fire and gave me the spare barrel. "There you go, Cozzy. Put this new one on and give it to these little bastards," he said, handing me the new barrel.

"Shit, this is hot," I said, as I ripped out the old barrel with a rag he had given me. I tried to work quick, but to make matters worse, Rowy's own weapon had become clogged with mud, taking him out of the fight temporarily and leaving us unprotected.

While Rowy was busy cleaning his SLR, I noticed Chooky crawling towards me on his stomach screaming, "Hey, Cozzy! Over to your right! You've got NVA advancing!"

I clicked the barrel into place and swung my M60 around and fired round after round into the advancing troops, managing to dispose of most of them. Somehow, one of them seemed to be free and clear and he kept coming towards Chooky's and my position, all the time firing his weapon. He was darting to and fro behind trees, and as much as I tried to get a clean shot on him, he managed to avoid my gunfire.

Chooky then lifted his head from the jungle floor to see where I was positioned when I screamed out, "Chooky, keep your head down!"

It was too late. The advancing enemy let rip a burst of gunfire from his weapon, hitting Chooky in the throat.

"No! Chooky!" I screamed.

My grief was drowned out by his screams, as his lungs filled with blood. I was helpless to come to his aid as my gun was now jammed with mud and I could not fire it. The predicament I was in would have spelled my own demise if I attempted any movement.

The sight of Chooky dying still haunts me to this day, and for years after I felt a great sense of guilt at my inability to kill the NVA soldier that had advanced while Rowy's weapon was jammed. Chooky might have survived if I'd got that nog.

As the NVA soldier was about to finish me off, a burst of gunfire came from my right which dropped the soldier dead at my feet.

I swung my head around to see where the shots had come from. I saw the lone figure of Finno lying on the ground, his M60 still smoking. He nodded his head, and I replied in barely a whisper, already starting to feel the effects of shock, "Thanks, mate."

I had no time to fully comprehend what had just happened to Chooky, no time to indulge my own feelings, because then I noticed a VC unit had got in on the action and were advancing from my left flank. As we hammered the enemy with small arms fire, I noticed Wally Kingston crawling towards Rowy, who had got his weapon working again, with another couple of belts of ammunition for the gun.

Once he had delivered the valuable ammo, he crawled away to our left where a VC soldier broke through from his advancing lines and shot him dead with a bullet to the head. In the melee, the nog soldier tripped over and was lying on the ground only metres from me.

"You little nog prick!" I yelled with fury.

I fired a burst from my M60. The result was horrific as the distinctive *dukka, dukka, dukka* sound of the gun sent bullets smashing into his head, inflicting mortal injuries.

The battle had been going for approximately two hours when the bunkers spewed forth a force of around 80 NVA soldiers. They inflicted a considerable amount of casualties on our platoon, killing two of our machine gun crews as well as three of our section's riflemen. We were in dire straits and it became clear that if we didn't get all the guns working we would be doomed.

Without even thinking, I handed my M60 to Rowy and while he supplied me with covering fire, I crawled forward on my stomach the 40 metres through the long grass towards the lifeless bodies of Shagger Edwards and Jumbo Campbell who were lying dead beside their M60. Rowy managed to keep the enemy at bay by bringing accurate fire to bear and this enabled me to secure the other gun which was only 20 metres from an enemy bunker.

When I retrieved the gun I was faced with another problem because this machine gun had also become clogged with mud, jamming it. Rowy could see the predicament I was in and rained down more firepower on the enemy before he was shot in the shoulder, taking him out of the fight.

"Rowy! Are you alright?" I screamed.

There was no response from Rowy and his body was obscured by the long grass, so I was unsure of how badly he had been hit. I agonised over the fate of my best mate before I caught a glimpse of Finno crawling through the jungle behind me with his M60. He was also supplying covering fire to my advance position, which saved my life as I was surrounded by the enemy. While he covered me, I stripped the M60 down and got it working again.

And just when I thought that matters couldn't get much worse, an enemy mortar round exploded above and showered me with shrapnel, the result being that my scalp and back was sliced open and I stared to bleed profusely. I wasn't sure the extent of my injuries and was in no position to inspect them, so I just kept firing my newly cleaned gun.

The enemy refused to surrender, even though we were hitting them with a combination of small arms fire, grenades and the occasional claymore mine thrown in for good measure.

I was the closest to the bunker from my platoon and had a couple of grenades on me, so I threw them in before I aimed my gun inside and disposed of the half a dozen occupants who were still firing their weapons, although they were seriously wounded. Those nogs just didn't quit.

But then, in the midst of the battle raging all around me, I had a very surreal experience. I felt as though I was going to be killed at any moment when a clear picture of Sandy came into my mind. I could see her beautiful smile and her sparkling blue eyes and as she approached me she said, "I'll be waiting for you when you return from Vietnam, Ed."

A feeling of great peace and serenity came over me, like nothing else I had ever experienced before, and I knew that I would be alright. Then, the image was gone, and I was blasted back into reality.

Funnily enough, when I returned home, Sandy told me one day it was about that time when I was involved at the Battle of the Bunkers that she had an uneasy feeling I was in mortal danger and said a silent prayer for me.

Evening drew close. The battle had been raging for three hours, but I felt as though I had been fighting for three days. I had not had a moment's rest. I was fatigued, stressed and wounded. I lay on my stomach and I continued to fire, even though I could see the green tracer bullets of the enemy firing over my head in the failing light, which in retrospect was a fascinating sight. Eventually, I managed to crawl back towards my platoon's position. Through this entire phase of the battle, Finno had covered my arse with continuous fire from his M60 before he was hit with a bullet and lost somewhere in the jungle.

When I could think properly again, I was in a state of anxiety as to the whereabouts of both Rowy and Finno, and my mind raced as to their wellbeing. I had to wonder. Were they dead?

Our situation had become worse, so Lieutenant Geraghty called in air support as he did not think we could handle the sustained attack from the much larger enemy for any longer. After calling up company headquarters, an American pilot flying above contacted Geraghty on the radio to inform him that he was going to coordinate the airstrike on the enemy. From where I was located forward of our position, I could hear that he had a thick southern American accent. He gave his call sign as Bronco Billy 81, and Lieutenant Geraghty returned with his which was Polo Gerry.

"You just mind your ass there, Polo Gerry, we gonna have ourselves some fun down there, okay?" he said to Geraghty.

"You do what you have to do, Bronco Billy 81, but do it fuckin' quick will ya because I don't think we can take much more of this," said Geraghty in a high state of anxiety.

"Okay, buddy. I'm just going to lay down a marker so we got something to put up to. You copy that, Polo Gerry?"

"Copy that loud and clear, Bronco Billy 81."

A white phosphorous rocket landed near the bunker position which Bronco Billy 81 had shot from his aircraft. It was only a matter of minutes before I could hear the deafening sound of three US F-4 Phantom bombers screaming overhead, and after they passed over, they let go of their pay load where the phosphorous rocket had landed. The jungle around our platoon shook so much that my teeth rattled around the inside of my mouth.

Over the next half hour, Bronco Billy 81 directed air strikes on the enemy, but he also gave us updated troop movements. He told Geraghty that scores of the enemy were starting to move around to our right flank where I was positioned on the gun.

It was also about this time that six of our Huey's joined the action and hammered the enemy down below with their twin M60 machine guns. That was nothing compared to what the Americans had up their sleeves as they brought in a dozen

Cobra helicopter gunships. They came in side by side and hit the jungle with a mixture of rockets and grenades.

Then came the grand finale. The mother of all shows as Bronco Billy 81 came back on the radio and explained what was going to happen next. I can still hear his southern drawl like it was yesterday.

"You just cover your ass there, Polo Gerry, because you're gonna have a real BBQ down there in a minute."

"Okay, Bronco Billy 81, we're all in position down here," Geraghty replied.

"Okay, partner, I'm going to send down some wall to wall to heat with a little bit of napalm to keep those gooks on their toes. Over," he said with a little snigger.

I looked up from where I'd moved to and suddenly noticed Rowy lying in the jungle some 30 metres away, so I decided to make my way to his position and retrieve him. At the same time, the enemy, who were approximately 100 metres away, started to advance to where Rowy was lying. I almost made it to Rowy when above all the noise I could hear Lieutenant Geraghty screaming orders at me. "Costigan, get your fucking arse out of there! The Yanks are about to napalm the area!"

I looked back at Geraghty, but decided to disobey his orders and keep crawling towards Rowy, trying my best to avoid getting shot. There was no way I was leaving my best mate out there. I eventually reached Rowy's position where he was lying just metres from the motionless body of Wally Kingston. Rowy was conscious, but injured and weary.

"Geraghty's probably going to have my balls for breakfast for disobeying his orders, Rowy, but be buggered if I was going to let you stay out here and let these fuckin' nogs finish you off," I told him, trying to grab him.

"You're a champion, Cozzy, ya blood's worth bottling, son. I'll never forget this," he whispered wearily.

"You're all right, mate, I'll get you back in one piece," I told him, trying not to worry about the glazed expression in his eyes.

"Thanks, mate, but go easy because I've been shot in the right shoulder."

"Okay, mate, I'll try to be as careful as I can, but we gotta get out of here quick smart," I told him in a soothing voice.

While I assisted Rowy back, Schooner Rooney had also disobeyed Geraghty and had followed me part way out. He gave us covering fire. We were crawling through the jungle at a snail's pace when some NVA soldiers saw us retreating and decided to have another go at us. Bullets exploded around us, but before they had a chance to inflict any damage on us three US F-4 Phantom jets came screaming overhead. I looked up then behind to the advancing enemy before I exclaimed to Rowy, "There's our bloody lifesavers, mate. Thank God for the Yanks!"

The jungle exploded with a horrendous bang, closely followed by a wall of orange flame as the napalm bombs exploded. The entire jungle lit up in a huge ball of fire and filled with thick black smoke. We buried our heads into the ground as we felt the intense wave of heat pass over us.

Eventually, I lifted my head up and the enemy was nowhere to be seen. They had disappeared off the face of the earth. Our surrounds was as black as the ace of spades, and the jungle in front of us had gone silent.

As the darkness of the night enveloped us, Lieutenant Geraghty made us stand to till 9.00 pm. Prior to this, we had made a head count of our platoon and of the 35 diggers who had gone out on the operation, there were 20 who were killed or wounded or missing in action.

Of our section of ten men, there were four confirmed dead and Rowy and I had been injured. We didn't know where Finno was. My face and my shirt were covered in dried blood and my clothing had holes in it where the hot shrapnel had landed on me. Our company medic patched me up by wrapping a bandage around my forehead.

As I sat in the darkness of the jungle next to Schooner, trying to comprehend the day that had been, he turned to me and said, "You've earned a beer after this day, Cozzy!"

"Mate, how I'd love a coldy right now," I responded, weary and sick in the gut.

"Don't worry, Cozzy, there'll be one waiting for you when we get back to Nui Dat."

I let out a deep breath. "Bloody Finno's out there somewhere in the jungle, Schooner. I sure hope he's okay. Bloody mad bugger saved my life out there today."

"Well, Rowy was taken out of here on a chopper just before dark so at least he's safe," said Schooner, trying to reassure me.

"Yeah, but he copped a nasty wound to his shoulder. I sure hope he's okay."

I eventually lay down, my thoughts totally focussed on Finno and his safety before I fell asleep. I was totally exhausted from what I had just been through and weary to the bone.

As the sun rose the next morning all was quiet and those of us who could walk went out to search the battlefield. Although I was injured, I was determined to find Finno. I was filled with dread as I was convinced that I would find him dead in the jungle somewhere.

The sight that greeted us was indescribable. There were hundreds of enemy dead strewn across the battlefield and around the bunker system. Many of their bodies were torn to shreds from artillery fire and the stench was already terrible.

As I hobbled through the now flattened jungle, I came across many of the enemy who were badly mutilated but still alive. Their condition was beyond help and there were a number of the enemy that were put out of their misery that morning with a bullet to the heart. I did the job myself a few times. I had to. Wouldn't let the bastards suffer any longer than necessary.

Then we had another issue—the sickly sweet, pungent smell of death all around us. Many of the bodies had already started to stink and decompose in the tropical heat. And it wasn't just the enemy. Our own slain comrades were still lying in their positions, holding their rifles and looking as though they were ready for the oncoming enemy. One of them was Heckendorf, who looked like he had gone to sleep and was resting peacefully on the ground, with his SLR still in his hand and a bullet hole to the head. I looked down on his lifeless body. "You were a good man, Hecky. It was good to know ya, mate."

Then I heard a familiar voice calling out my name. I turned around and there, propped up against the entrance of a bunker was Finno, with scores of the dead enemy around him. I walked closer and I could see that he was holding a live grenade in his right hand. He was shaking all over. Turned out, he had been shot in the lung. Every time he breathed, a big red bubble would appear out of the corner of his mouth.

He had also been shot in the left hand and could not put the pin back in the grenade.

Finno had sat there all night, holding a live grenade, ready to throw it if any of the enemy approached him. He had shrapnel wounds to his head and multiple gunshot wounds to both his legs and arms. He was in a hell of a mess, but it was a testimony to his toughness that he was still alive. He gave me a plaintive look.

"Could you take this grenade off me please, Cozzy?" Finno asked tiredly.

"Of course, old mate," I said gently. I took the grenade from his hand and replaced the pin, which had been lying on the ground between his legs.

"How the hell did you avoid getting napalmed, Finno?"

"I crawled into the bunker when I heard the jets coming over. Killed a few of the enemy before the Yanks hit the area around the bunker with napalm."

"You're a tough bastard, Finnegan!" I said, utterly shocked that he actually survived.

Finno managed a smile before grimacing in pain.

I got the medic's attention and he treated Finno as best he could. A number of RAAF Dustoff choppers landed in the jungle a short time later and took both the killed and wounded to Vung Tau, while the rest of Delta Company was taken back to Nui Dat in APCs. I went with Finno.

As the chopper took off, I looked down on the jungle below and the enormity of what we had just been through started to sink in. I went into delayed shock. How I had survived after being in the direct firing line of the enemy for such a prolonged period was beyond my comprehension. A shiver ran down my spine as the thought of how close I came to being killed. I glanced across at poor old Finno, laying on the floor of the Huey in a pool of his own blood, all shot to pieces. I still don't know how that mad bastard survived.

I looked up at the sun shining through the trees and said,

"What a beautiful day. Pity we have to be fighting in this bastard of a place."

We arrived at the Australian Field Hospital at Vung Tau where we were met by medics who attended to the serious cases like Finno first.

Before wheeling him away, Finno turned to me and said, "I kept that live grenade on me in case any of those little nog bastards were going to try to finish me off in that bunker, Cozzy."

"Do you reckon you would have used it, if it came to the crunch, Finno?"

"You betcha, Cozzy," he wheezed. "No way I was going to let them little bastards kill me or take me prisoner."

I felt tears standing in my eyes. "I owe you my life, Finno. I'll be forever in your debt."

"You're a good man, Ed Costigan. You were worth saving," Finno said with a weary smile.

For both Finno and I, our war in Vietnam was over. Before Finno disappeared through the doors of the field hospital, I shook his hand. "I'll never forget you, Bill Finnegan."

Finno smiled, his strength fading, his voice barely a whisper. "Likewise, Ed."

Shortly afterwards, he was loaded onto an aircraft and flown back to Australia for emergency medical treatment. It was the last time I ever saw him.

***

"Your old man saved my life on two occasions that day, Tim. Let me assure you that Finno was anything but gutless, and he certainly wasn't missing in action the day we attacked those bunkers," I said, pointing my finger at him. "If you're anything like your old man, then you would have been a top soldier, too."

Tim sat in silence. His face was closed off, but I thought I detected a slight tremor in his hand, and his eyes glistened. It had been so many years since I'd told that story, but just remembering what Finno had done for me was enough to set my hands trembling too.

"I've never heard that story before," he said eventually. "I had no idea my old man was in the thick of the action."

"You better believe it," I told him. "Your old man was a good soldier and never shirked from his responsibilities. In fact, I reckon he should have got a gong for his action at the Battle of the Bunkers."

"Why didn't he then?" demanded Tim.

"Like I told you, Finno was a good bloke, but he was as mad as a hatter. He used to backchat his superiors. Geraghty was a hard bastard but a good bloke and he could handle Finno, but Major Milroy didn't like your old man."

"What did he do to upset Milroy?"

"Insubordination, mostly. He went up in front of that dick-head for being insubordinate on a number of occasions and as a result, the pencil pushing bastard made life tough for your old man."

"So, was Dad recommended for a bravery award at all?"

"Geraghty recommended him for the Victoria Cross for his bravery that day, but Milroy wouldn't have a bar of it."

Tim shook his head, his eyes wide. "That's unbelievable. He was really recommended for the Victoria Cross?"

"Absolutely, Tim, but he got nothing. All because that desk jockey Milroy wanted to teach Finno a lesson." I shook my head. "No wonder he never talked about Vietnam to you.

Finno would have been cut up pretty bad that his actions that day weren't recognised. If I had to guess, I'd say this was a contributing factor to your old man's state of mind after he returned from Vietnam, and maybe why he went off the rails. I mean, a lot of us did, especially me after everything we had seen and done and all the killings we were involved in. But your old man, he got shot to bits and got nothing for it." It pissed me off even now.

Tim looked thoughtful and tapped his fingers on the table. "What you've just told me paints a lot clearer picture of my dad and why he was the way he was, but it's hard to shake the image I had of the old man when I was growing up. I mean, he was just a fuckin' bastard. I suppose it didn't help that when he died Mum hooked up with an absolute prick, which was like going from the frying pan into the fire. I grew up just plain angry because the two male role models in my life had been absolute losers."

I wanted to keep Tim talking. "What happened after Finno died?"

Tim looked agitated. "After his death, Mum got involved with a bloke named Tony Walsh who was the local motor mechanic in Walgett," he said with a frown. "He was a pisspot who beat up Mum and my younger brother and me. When I was sixteen, Tony gave Mum yet another hiding for some stupid reason, except this time he tore up a number of photos I had blown up for her. It was of a mob of 'roos feeding on a river-bank and it was pretty special to me. After the melee died down and Tony had gone to bed, I snuck into his room with a loaded shotgun which we kept in the house."

I narrowed my eyes. "Go on," I said warily.

"While he lay on his back, sound asleep, I pointed the shoty in between his eyes," Tim said. "Tony woke up and screamed at me, all in a rage, and I shouted that if he ever touched my mother or brother again, I'd blow his fucking brains out. Shoot him like a dead dog." Tim shrugged. "He seemed to understand that, but by morning I'd decided to take off. Went off to Cunumulla in Queensland. I had a mate working in a shearing team up there."

"What did you do?"

"I got a job as a roustabout initially, then I leant how to shear and after six months, started shearing full time."

"And the beatings? Did they continue after you left?"

"My brother used to keep in regular contact and he told me that Tony never touched my mum or him from that day until Mum left him a month later."

I nodded. I was glad that it worked out. "How long did you stay with the shearing team?"

"Until I was 21 and then I joined the army."

I leaned across the table patted him on his shoulder. He looked away, embarrassed.

"You certainly have been through a lot, Tim," I told him, my tone calm and gentle. "When it's all said and done, your dad was just like me. He couldn't handle the piss and in the end, it spelt his demise. You've been through a lot, but you don't have to follow that path."

Tim fidgeted, looking at the floor, the table, but not at me. He eventually got himself together. "So, you never saw my dad ever again?"

I shook my head. "Never again. I've always regretted the fact that we never caught up. I got in contact with his brother in Walgett about six months after I got back from Vietnam to see how he had recovered from his injuries, but he told me that he was in western Queensland somewhere doing some shearing. Pretty good for a bloke all shot up. I always meant to catch up with him, but I just got busy with life."

"Busy in what way?" asked Tim.

"I got married, started a family and a business, and life just took over. But I never forgot Finno. In fact, not a day goes by when I don't think of what happened in Vietnam and the Battle of the Bunkers. Meeting you today has really brought some memories back to me." I ran my hands down my face, and thought briefly about the envelope in my pants pocket. "I just can't believe that you're Finno's son."

Tim nodded. I thought about now he might have thought our conversation was done, and I wondered if I should say something about the letter burning a hole through my pants but he said, "So you were unsettled when you got back from Vietnam?"

"Oh, yeah. Like I said, I just couldn't get what happened in Vietnam out of my head."

"How?"

"Well, when you saw and did some of the things that your dad and I saw and did while we were in Vietnam, hell, you know how it goes, you fought too. You know what it's like coming home. It wasn't easy to settle back into a normal routine again. I couldn't settle down to anything and made a right nuisance of myself on Civvy Street."

"What do you mean?"

"Well for starters, I swore a lot."

"Swore a lot?"

"Yeah, in all the wrong places," I said, a slight smile on my face.

Chapter 7

April 1969, Maroubra, Sydney

I
T WAS THE day after I arrived home from Vietnam
when family and friends gathered at the O'Grady's place in
Maroubra for a welcome home lunch. It was a Sunday and
the guests were gathered on the back verandah enjoying pre-
lunch drinks. There were heaps of people there including Uncle
Kevin, Aunty, and their kids; Stumpy, Nana O'Grady, Mum,
Noel, Dan and Anne; and various other family and friends.

As I guzzled a beer, I was largely oblivious to what was
going on around me, reflecting on the surreal circumstances on
how I had awoken that morning.

I had sat up in bed, startled by my unfamiliar surroundings.
It was the pre-dawn and I was confused as I tried to comprehend where I was. The room was pitch black and the only thing
I could recognise was my army duffel bag, which was sitting on
the floor next to my bed. I looked around, my eyes straining,
until I become conscious of the sound of the surf breaking in
the distance. Then, like a light bulb being switched on inside

my head, I suddenly realised that I was in my old bedroom at Maroubra.

I eventually got out of bed and while I was sitting there on the edge, I rubbed my hand on the back of my head to feel the scar which had been left after the mortar round exploded above me at the Battle of the Bunkers. Although I was physically healed, I was fast learning that there were mental and emotional scars left from my experiences in Vietnam that were to take many years to cure. The experience of war had changed me forever, and that beautiful, simple life in Maroubra seemed so remote from where I'd just been.

I went out onto the front verandah to have a smoke, a habit that didn't leave me for many years, to be met by Stumpy, who was sitting in a seat having a cup of tea. Stumpy's familiar smile made me instantly feel comfortable, and he rose from his seat with outstretched hand.

"By the time I got to the O'Grady's late last night, Ed, you were already in bed so I didn't get the chance to say G'day."

"Good to see you, Stumpy," I said, shaking his hand. I was so glad to see the old fella.

Stumpy was never one to give in to idle chatter so got straight to the point.

"I got all your letters, Ed, and I know that you've been through a tough time, especially that last battle when you attacked those bunkers. I just want you to know that if you need to have a yarn about what you've been through, I am only a phone call away."

"Thanks, Stumpy, I'll keep that in mind," I said without any expression. I was already learning to keep some things to myself. The experiences of war weren't for everyone, and this was an Australia where men still kept many things to themselves. Much of my correspondence with Stumpy had included things that I had not shared with other family and friends. He had a better understanding of what I had been through in Vietnam than anyone, as he had been through the horrors of the Great War. Still, I didn't want to burden him.

The morning went by and as lunch approached I was sipping on a beer, reflecting on how Stumpy had coped when he came back from World War I, when my concentration was broken by the appearance of a beautiful looking woman who suddenly appeared in front of me.

"Hello, Ed! I'm sorry I'm late, but I was putting the finishing touches on a cake that I baked!"

I looked up, startled by her appearance, as I had been deep in concentration. It'd been so long since I'd last seen her!

"Sandy! How are you sweetie?" I said with a smile, rushing forward to pull her into an embrace.

Sandy hugged me tightly and exclaimed, "I'm sorry I missed you when you arrived home yesterday, but I was on the central coast for the day visiting my grandma, who is sick."

"That's okay, Sandy. I arrived home late anyway and hit the sack straight away," I told her. Sandy's embrace felt strange at first because it had been so long since I had seen her, but after a short period I warmed to her affection and held her tight. "Thanks for all your letters, Sandy. You'll never know how much I appreciated them, especially when I was out in the jungle for weeks at a time."

"Oh, Ed, it's just so good to have you home in one piece," she said, her eyes moist with tears. She searched my face, looking for signs of changes in me.

Little did Sandy know that although I looked physically

together, my mental and emotional state was not quite right. I was scarred by my experiences, no two ways about it, but I tried to put it aside. I smiled at Sandy and was suddenly mesmerised by her beauty, to the point that I was momentarily stuck for words.

Sandy managed to fill in the gaps. "Come on, Ed, it's time to catch up with the rest of the family as they've just arrived." She led me over to where my sister Anne was standing, watching us with a smile on her face. Time had done good things to her.

I smiled at her and said, "Boy, I hardly recognise you, Annie. You're all grown up since I've been away. How old are you now?"

"I'll be seventeen in December, Ed," she said, beaming.

"Crikey, Annie! You'll have every boy on the block chasing you," I said with a grin.

Anne blushed and let out a little giggle. She had grown into a beautiful young woman with a slim physique and brown hair that flowed down her back. She had a lovely nature and since she was a kid, she had always cared for other people. Nana O'Grady latched onto her early and tried to groom her for the convent, but Anne had never showed much interest in becoming a nun.

"What are you going to do with yourself?" I said.

"I'm going to study nursing at St Vincent's hospital in Sydney."

"That's great, Annie!" I enthused. "I think nursing would suit you to a tee, just like Margaret."

She beamed at me. "And guess what? I'm going to be living here with the O'Gradys, Ed."

"Is that right?"

"Robert has moved out of home, so there is a spare bedroom. Are you going to continue living here too, Ed?"

"I'd say so," I told her with a shrug. "Reg Steel told me there was always a job waiting for me when I got home from Vietnam."

"It would be nice having you around, Ed. It seems like a lifetime ago since you left home to do your apprenticeship."

I smiled at Anne. Her caring nature always made me feel good. "If you come and live at Maroubra, you'll have to be on guard for Aunty's radical political views."

"I'm sure I will be able to handle her prickly nature, Ed," she smiled, and she probably would too. Anne was just that capable.

"Yoo-hoo! Lunch is ready everybody!" came the cry from Aunty, over the din of conversation.

Anne and I made our way to the lunch table where she sat on one side of me and Sandy on the other. Seated at the head of the table was Stumpy, and Aunty was at the other end as a precaution in case they clashed.

As we tucked into lunch, I became subdued. I had been so used to hanging around blokes in the army, and was a bit out of sorts as it had been some time since I had been around family and friends. I missed my mates. The conversation at this table revolved around family, the farm, politics, footy and the weather. I stared into thin air, oblivious to most of the conversation as I tucked into Aunty's beautiful roast lamb lunch.

"Whitlam's calling for the end of conscription," Aunty said, getting right into it.

"He is a bloody radical that bloke, and if he becomes the Prime Minister of Australia, pity help us Aunty," Stumpy piped up from the other end of the table.

"The federal election is due this year, Stumpy, and don't be surprised if Whitlam wins it," Aunty said, her tone highly emotional and starting to get louder.

"Nah, Aunty, Gorton will get the nod," Stumpy said in a gruff tone.

My family were died in the wool Country Party supporters, and the O'Grady's being railway people, were equally strong Labor Party voters which led to some pitched battle arguments when we all got together.

This day was no exception and emotions ran high. With different family members pitching their political views with great gusto, it looked like another ding dong Donnybrook was about to erupt. That's when Aunty decided to ask me the question that created an uproar, the likes which had never been seen before in our household.

"What do you think, Ed?"

"Think about what, Aunty?" I said with a faraway look.

"About Whitlam bringing the troops home from Vietnam if he is elected Prime Minister," she said, exasperated at my lack of attention.

I suddenly looked up and stopped chewing on my baked potato. The dinner table went silent as everyone eagerly waited for the 'man of the moment' and his view. Stumpy looked wary.

"I'll believe when I see it, Aunty. Those politicians talk out of their arses, and as far as I am concerned, those pricks got us into this mess in the first place. Now, can somebody pass me another slice of fucking bread please."

Well.

Let's just say that the Australia of 1969 was a far different social landscape than the Australia of today. The niceties and common courtesies, which for the most part have disappeared in the modern age, were still prevalent then. So with that in

mind, to use the *eff* word while in polite company in conservative Australia, let alone conservative Catholic Australia for that
matter, were grounds for a court martial.

I can still hear the sound of cutlery hitting the plates, and
mouths dropped left, right and centre as my profanity hit everybody like a ton of bricks. Sandy's mouth dropped open, and
even Aunty was shocked into silence.

Nana O'Grady, who had been surprisingly silent during the
fierce political debate that had preceded my obscenity, saw this
as her cue to enter the stage. And oh boy, she didn't disappoint
with the little piece of theatre she was about to perform.

Nana's face looked as though somebody had just planted
a penny bunger under her arse and let it off. It was contorted
mixture of anxiety and rage as her eyes twirled around her head
like an eight-year-old who had just been let loose in a chocolate
shop.

She spotted an umbrella leaning up against the dining room
wall and with the type of manual dexterity you would expect
from a 20-year-old, she made a lunge for it.

"May the curse of Mary Malone and her nine blind illegiti-
mate children chase you so far over the hills of damnation that
the Lord himself can't find you with a telescope!" she shouted
in her strong Irish brogue, as thick as any that I had ever heard
come from her lips.

The full force of the umbrella she was holding like a cricket
bat came crashing down on the back of my neck in a show of
force that Don Bradman would have been proud of.

"By Jove, Edward John Costigan, I'll make sure you wash
out that mouth full of sin if it's the last thing I do!" she screamed
in a state of rage. She hit me around the head and shoulders

with a manic glee in her eyes which took me by surprise, but it only made me swear more.

"What the fuck are you doing Nana, you crazy woman!"

"You've been in bed with Lucifer himself, ya little pagan heathen. Wash your mouth out, you dirty little scoundrel!"

Then Mum got in on the action. "Edward Costigan! I've never heard such language come out of your mouth. You should be ashamed of yourself!"

Nana continued her onslaught with blows that were rained down upon me with military precision. And just when Nana was at the climax of her fury and I thought things couldn't get any worse, Noel decided to chime in with some well-timed remarks.

"Give him a couple more, Nana, for telling me that dirty joke about the donkey and the policemen behind the chook pen when I was ten years old," Noel said, with a mischievous twinkle in his eye.

That was all that Nana needed to let loose with another barrage of well-directed blows.

"You zip up, you lecherous little abomination, Noel Joseph Costigan, before I hit you from here to kingdom-come," said Nana, as she gave Noel a hot serve with her umbrella.

"That's right, Noel! You keep your mouth zipped. You're only making the situation worse," Mum said.

The onslaught lasted another few minutes before Nana collapsed in exhaustion on the lounge where she pulled out her set of rosary beads from her pocket. "Jesus, Mary and Joseph, dear Lord, what will I do about these heathen grandchildren of mine," she said, before reciting decades of the rosary.

In truth, I was totally oblivious to the obscenity that had left my mouth as this had become the normal mode of conversation for me during my time in Vietnam. During those early years after Vietnam, my mouth was to get me into trouble regularly, and it was some time before I finally wised up in that department. Some habits are hard to break.

When everything had settled down and most people had left the dinner table, Stumpy leant across with a serious expression on his face said, "We try to watch our P's and Q's around here thank you, Ed! I won't be lending you my Hans Heysen painting with that kind of language!"

***

I looked at Tim and said, "I can't believe I let that crazy old Irish lady hit me that day. If she was a bloke I would have absolutely snotted her."

Tim was oblivious to the cracking tale I had just told him. He looked distracted. "Did you just say Hans Heysen?"

I nodded. "What about him?"

"You said Stumpy was going to loan you a Hans Heysen painting?"

"Yeah, that's right."

His eyes were gleaming. "I love Hans Heysen. He's one of my favourite Australian artists."

"Yeah, I've seen a few of his paintings and I like them also," I said.

"He had a unique ability to capture the incredible beauty of the Flinders Rangers in his paintings."

I smiled at him. "Stumpy ended up loaning me an original of his named 'Droving into the Light'."

"Droving into the Light!" Tim said with eyebrows raised. "No way!"

"Yeah. She was a dinky di bona fide original."

"I've only ever seen a print of that painting, but I love it.

The light, the lone stockman droving sheep through the gum trees on an old dusty road in the early morning light captures the spirit of rural Australia like no other work of art I've ever seen," he said, his words spilling out.

"I asked Stumpy if I could get a loan of the painting for a few months after I got back from Vietnam, as I was pretty unsettled and he knew how much I loved it. He agreed on the strict condition that I look after it and it remained in my bedroom at Maroubra."

Tim was still amazed. "How did he get his hands on an original Hans Heysen?"

"Stumpy, being a VC winner, got to meet a number of prominent people and Hans was one of them. He told Hans that he loved the painting as it reminded him of being on horseback droving sheep at Coorigil. Stumpy had a quid in his pocket at the time so he bought it off him."

"That painting is priceless! It was thought that it was lost," Tim said, shaking his head.

"Lost be buggered!" I exclaimed. "It's hanging up on the lounge-room wall at Coorigil."

"What!"

"Yeah," I smirked. "It's been up at Coorigil for years."

"That's amazing! And you say it was hanging up on your bedroom wall at Maroubra?"

"Yeah. I went out to Coorigil to pick it up about a couple of months after I got home from Vietnam."

"You lucky bugger having such a prized painting in your family's possession."

I looked at Tim sheepishly. "You know, I almost lost the painting in a card game."

"What!" Tim exclaimed loudly.

"Well, like I said, I had to travel out to Coorigil to pick up the painting and was travelling with Anne on the train back to Sydney, as she was due to start her nurses training at St Vincent's hospital in Sydney. We were going to rendezvous with Rowy at Dubbo Railway Station."

"Why were you meeting Rowy?"

"After Vietnam, he had gone back to the family property at Coolabah, to recuperate from his bullet wound. After he had recovered he decided not to stick around, as there wasn't room for him as he had older brothers as well as his old man running the show. So he decided to try his hand down in the big smoke. He'd been in regular contact with Julie McCabe through letters while he was in Vietnam and they were pretty well smitten on each other. Let me tell you what happened."

***

While Anne and myself were waiting for Rowy to be dropped off by his parents at Dubbo Railway Station, I got talking to two shady characters in their thirties. They told me they were opal miners from Lightning Ridge and they were going to Sydney to tie on a big one. The bigger of the two, a brute named Bullfrog, enquired as to what I had wrapped up in the blanket. I looked him up and down with suspicion before I eventually relented and let them have a look, but only after they promised they wouldn't touch it.

Anne was getting nervous about me talking to them and urged me to move on but I resisted her hankering. The smaller of the two, who went by the name of Shorty, became increasingly interested in the painting after I told him it was a genuine Hans Heysen. He seemed to know it bit about his works and the fact that he had painted throughout the Flinders Rangers in South Australia.

I could see that the two of them were up to something and this was only compounded when Bullfrog propositioned me with a game of cards. If they won they got the painting and if we won we got 400 hundred quid. I insisted that Bullfrog produce the cash so I knew he was legitimate. After he did, I secured the deal, but only if we played Five Hundred, as Anne was brilliant at the game. Our family always played Five Hundred and Anne had been an excellent player since she was a kid. She had a spooky knack of wining card games, I believe in large part due to her incredible ability to remember what her opponent's hands were.

By this stage Anne was as nervous as a kitten and wanted to high-tail it out of there, reminding me that if Stumpy found out what I was up to he would skin me alive. I was as crazy as a cut snake at that time of my life after just returning home from Vietnam. Coupled with the fact that I was hungry for some cash, I eventually convinced her to stick around and play some cards.

I always kept a deck of cards in my bag and after I dealt the first hand it started off real bad with Annie and myself getting thrashed in the first two games. Annie by this stage was so full of fear she couldn't think straight and as a consequence had dropped her lollies.

I managed to settle her down a bit and we won the third game with a half decent hand of cards. Annie was thinking a lot more clearly by this stage, although she was still wary of the two louts. We also won the fourth after Annie received an excellent hand of hearts which put us on easy street, and I backed her up with the left bower which won us the fourth game.

I was eying off these two blokes going into the fifth game and while contemplating the consequences if we should lose, Annie announced that she was going to go it alone by calling ten no trumps. In doing this, she had to win all ten tricks and in doing so, 500 points and the card game.

Annie produced a masterful hand, producing trick after trick, which looked like it had been sent down from heaven. Anne was faultless as she led each trick with either aces, kings, queens and jacks on the rickety old table.

The colour was starting to drain from the faces of the two opal miners as they felt the card game slipping away from them. By the tenth trick they were beside themselves with anxiety as Anne led out with the granddaddy of all cards. Anne slowly and deliberately placed the joker on the card table as she gave the two hardened miners a wry smile. My kid sister had played a magnificent hand and saved her best till last, winning the game with the trump card.

Well, I could have guessed what happened next. They disputed the validity of the game as they hadn't shook hands with Annie. I could see there was going to be trouble, so I told Annie to high-tail it out of the waiting room with the painting while I dealt with the two rouges.

A melee ensured with me easily disposing of Shorty before Bullfrog came for me. I managed to give him some cracking big hits before he went off his rocker and came charging at me like a wounded bull. He was about to throw me onto the railway tracks when who should appear out of nowhere but Rowy. Rowy, even though he was still recovering from his wounded shoulder, with a head full of steam, picked Bullfrog up over his head like he was picking up one of his huge merino rams off the family farm. He then threw him into the waiting room wall. The brute landed on his back on the floor and lay motionless.

When the fight was over, I gave Anne $200, her eyes almost falling out of her head as she had never had that much money in her life. I pocketed the balance and we made a merry trip back to Sydney.

***

Tim shook his head.

"You almost lost a priceless Hans Heysen painting in a card game?" he exclaimed.

"I was a loose cannon straight after Vietnam, Tim, and likely to pull any type of crazy stunt." I shrugged.

He was totally bemused. "And what if you lost the card game? What then?"

"Hell, would have freezed over before I departed with Stumpy's prized painting," I told him with a snort.

"So you would have fought them anyway?"

I nodded my head in agreement. "But the card game paid off big time," I said with a grin.

"What do you mean?

"Well, it happened in a roundabout sort of a way. You see Mum found out about the card game after Aunty noticed the $200 in Anne's purse and then the inevitable happened and it got back to Stumpy, who went off his rocker. He made a special trip to Sydney on the train to retrieve his valuable painting, but not before tearing strips off me."

"What did he say?"

I waved him off. "Oh, he was all fired up, believe you me. It was all 'Where's my painting, Ed? I don't want you doing something else stupid and losing this priceless piece of art on me.' And more to the point, he also took my $200. I wasn't too happy about that, after all, I earnt that money." I laughed and shook my head. "I'd fought some tough blokes in the ring and been through hell in Vietnam, but Stumpy could still instill the fear of God in me when his hackles were up. I went to my bedroom where I had it hidden and sheepishly handed the money over to Stumpy." I shrugged at Tim and gave him a rueful look. "It had been years since I'd seen Stumpy that cranky, but it reinforced the fact that being a VC winner he was one hell of a hard bastard."

Tim snorted. "I'll say. So that was the last you saw of your $200 bucks, hey?"

"Nah," I said shaking my head. "Stumpy, the cunning old bugger, had other motives when he took my money from me."

"How?"

"Well, the family had no idea at the time, but Stumpy had been dabbling in the share market with a bit of success. He'd come across a fledgling little mining company and he'd decided to invest my $200 into it without telling a soul."

"What company?" Tim said with interest.

"Poseidon," I smiled.

Tim shrugged his shoulders.

Typical young bloke, he had no clue, I thought to myself.

"Let me explain. In early 1969, Poseidon had been exploring for nickel in Windarra in Western Australia, so Stumpy bought 500 shares at $0.35c a share with my $200. He reasoned at the time that if they made a quid then I'd receive the profits, but if they didn't then serves me right for being so stupid."

Tim looked at me dumbfounded.

"Like I said, Stumpy never let on to anybody that he had

bought the shares and that was the end of the painting saga. So we all thought."

"So, what happened then?" Tim said.

"Ah, that's jumping ahead of ourselves. I'll leave that for its right time," I said with my finger raised. "In the meantime, life went on and I struggled to keep up."

***

Not long after Stumpy came down to Maroubra to retrieve his painting, I started work back at Steel's Transport. It was early June of 1969, and I realised I had to get back to work after having the best part of two months off after returning home from Vietnam and recovering from my shrapnel wounds to the head. I had recovered from my wounds, but my thoughts were never far from Vietnam. The Battle of the Bunkers had rocked me to the core, as had the death of Chooky and my powerless-ness in not being able to come to his aid, especially after he had alerted me to the danger of the oncoming enemy. On a number of occasions since arriving home from Vietnam, I had awoken in the middle of the night with the image in my head of Chooky dying. Sleep was hard to come by in those days.

Although I was unsettled, the one big plus from this period was the fact that Rowy found a place to rent when Sandy secured a small flat for him a couple of blocks from Maroubra beach. He also found a job working for an Irish earthmoving company named O'Reilly Constructions as a backhoe operator.

With Rowy living only a stone's throw from me, we were able to talk to each other regularly about what we were think-ing, and in particular, our Vietnam experiences. Finno was well out bush somewhere and Schooner Rooney was at Condobolin, so I relied on Rowy heavily.

Rowy seemed to ride the affects of his Vietnam experiences a lot better than me. He certainly didn't get out of the Vietnam War unscathed, but he had his relationship with Julie McCabe developing nicely and a purpose. He had a desire to get enough money behind him so he could buy himself his own earthmoving machine. That gave him a solid direction to follow. He had business goals in mind and knew how to keep busy. Coupled with this was the fact that although Rowy and I were very similar in many ways, there was one striking difference that separated us. Rowy wasn't an alcoholic and didn't suffer from the hypersensitivity, perfectionism, and unfounded and ungrounded fears that one who has that particular aliment suffers from. Rowy, who had been through everything that I had been through, had the ability to ride the bumps a lot better than I did.

Meanwhile, at Steel's Transport, Thumper Fraser was happy to see me back. "Ed Costigan, you mad bugger, you. It's great to have you back in one piece," he said the morning I started back at work.

"I'm back in body, but I think my head may be somewhere else, Thumper," I told him.

"You'll be right, Ed. Nothing that a few beers and a few laughs down at the pub won't fix."

We were to engage in plenty of that in the ensuing months, but as time went on I felt like a robot going through the motions at work, as Vietnam was never far from my mind. I had been through something that those blokes hadn't and I suddenly found it difficult to relate to them on the same level as I had done prior to going to Vietnam. My thoughts often turned to Rowy, Finno, Schooner Rooney, and the other boys from my platoon.

It was during this period that I tried to make contact with Finno. I had his parent's address and phone number at Walgett, but when I made contact with his dad, he had no idea where he was, other than to say he was somewhere in western Queensland working with a shearing team. I could only assume that he'd recovered alright from his wounds, and left word for Finno to catch up with me when he could.

And as time went on, if I thought my job back at Steels Transport was different, that was nothing compared to my relationship with Sandy.

Sandy was as beautiful as ever and I still loved her, but the changes that had taken place within me since Vietnam had put our relationship on a whole new plain. For starters, the very thing that Sandy did not like about me—my drinking!—had exacerbated since my arrival home from Vietnam.

I found myself spending more time at the pub, making acquaintances with all sorts of like-minded drinkers who seemed to be on the same path as me. Prior to Vietnam, boxing had kept me on the straight and narrow, albeit I had cut loose a few times. The most glaring being the fight that Thumper and I had with the Sharpies back in late 1963 which cost me a place in the Olympic team.

"Gee, Ed, I wish you'd spend as much time with me as you do down at the pub," Sandy said to me one day.

"Come on, Sandy, a bloke's allowed to wet the whistle, especially after slogging away at work all day," I told her, thinking she was making too much of it.

"You used to box, Ed, and all the training and drive you had to be a champion kept you fit, healthy and focussed. You were such a positive man back then, now you just want drink all the time," she said.

Sandy's comments hit a raw nerve in me. Since arriving home I had lost all desire to get back into the ring. I felt as though my glory days were in the distant past and I wasn't interested in revisiting them.

When I look back in retrospect, Sandy and my relationship was really teenage love story that belonged to a carefree era when it seemed like I didn't have a problem in the world. She was a beautiful girl who had a fairly comfortable upbringing, and that's what she was looking for in the future. She could have never dealt with was the complexities of handling a person like me who had been through so many horrible things in Vietnam.

At first, she thought that all I needed was a little bit of time to adjust back into civilian life after my arrival home from Vietnam. It wasn't until the August of 1969, four months after I had arrived home from Vietnam that the end of our relationship appeared nigh. There were still glimpses of the spark that had made our relationship so special prior to Vietnam, but all in all it had become a testing union.

It was a cold night and we were sitting on Maroubra Beach around a fire where we had spent so much enjoyable time together prior to Vietnam. We were talking when Sandy brought up the question of marriage.

"If we're going to get married, Ed, you're going to have to settle down and curb your drinking."

Sandy had not mentioned the subject of marriage since I had arrived home from Vietnam. I believe she wanted to see if I was going to change back into the man she once knew and this was her way of giving me an ultimatum: shape up or ship out.

As much as I loved Sandy, the thought of marriage was the furthest thing from my mind and I had long dreaded the day when she used it as a means to determine if our relationship was going to last.

My mouth was dry, but I told her what I was thinking. "I'm not ready for marriage, Sandy. It's not that I don't love you, but I just can't commit myself to marriage at this stage of my life."

"But, Ed, we talked about it before you went to Vietnam! You loved the idea of settling down and having children," she said with emotion, her eyes welling with tears.

"I know I did, Sandy," I said with a sigh, "but too much has changed since I was in Vietnam. I saw some horrendous things while I was there and it's taken its toll on me."

"Then you need help, Ed. You need to talk to somebody about what you've been through," she told me, putting her hand on my arm.

"I'll be buggered if I'm going to see a shrink, if that's what your suggesting. Most of them are bloody mad anyway," I said, shrugging off her words.

She had tears streaming down her face. "What did they do to you when you were over in Vietnam, Ed? You're a completely different person."

I sat on the beach staring into the surf with the glow of the fire in my eyes. "I'm sorry, Sandy," I told her regretfully. "I just can't marry you at the moment. I need space and time to get myself together."

"If it was just space and time you needed, Ed, then I could give you as much as that as you want, but your problems run deeper than that. If you don't want to seek help for your problems, then I'm afraid there's not much of a future for you and I."

I looked up at her dumbfounded. I wasn't ready for marriage, but I didn't want to break up!

Sandy got up and brushed the sand off her skirt. She turned

to me with tears in her eyes and said, "So long, Ed. You had a special place in my heart for so long and I thought you were the one, but our time has passed. I wish you the best of luck in the future and I hope you sort out your difficulties."

She walked away into the darkness.

I was shocked. It was over, just like that.

"Sandy!" I called out to her. "I love you! Sandy, I love you sweetie!"

I was shell-shocked after Sandy dumped me. I believed that regardless of our difficulties, she would never leave me. I was left empty and was like a cork floating on the ocean without any direction.

As time went on, I found even more solace in the booze and dug myself into a mental hole as I tried to bury my feelings of hurt and pride. What made matters worse was not long after our break up, Julie informed me that Sandy had found a new man in the form of a young doctor who had come to work in her father's GP practice. The whole thing made me bitter.

"I'll be buggered, Rowy. Sandy's gone from a blue collar worker to the top shelf with this new fancy-pants doctor she's been hanging with," I said to him one afternoon, while we were having a beer together in the Pagewood Hotel.

He stared at me, a strange look on his face. "Hey, Cozzy, can I tell ya something between mates?" Rowy said quietly while we were perched at the bar.

"What's that, mate?"

"You're a great bloke, Ed, but mate, you've been hitting the turps a bit too much lately. I reckon it's time you slowed down a bit because if the truth be known, that's the reason why Sandy really left you."

Rowy shocked me with his comment. I'd never expected him to turn on me like that, we'd been through too much. I took instant offence.

"Some sort of a mate you are, Rowy! A bloke has a couple of cold ones, which he's quite entitled to after working his fucking ring off all day, and you blame that on a relationship breakdown. Turn it up, Rowy. I thought you were a bit wiser than that," I told him, utterly surprised at what he was saying.

Rowy gave me a placating look. "No one's telling you, Ed, that you can't have a couple of quiety's, but hey, mate, it's time you settled down a bit in that department. I mean you've let your boxing go by the wayside and let a great girl slip out of your hands. Look, Cozzy, we both saw some nasty stuff in Vietnam, but you've gotta put it behind you and get on with life."

"I'll be buggered, Bob, if anybody's going to preach to me about having a few beers. After all, I put my life on the line fighting for my country in Vietnam. If that's your attitude you can shove it up your arse." I swallowed my beer and stormed out of the pub with a major resentment against Rowy. We didn't speak for some time after that little bust up.

I walked around full of contempt over the next few days, as I felt justified in my entitlement to have a few beers. It was about a week after my argument with Rowy when the bus I was catching home from work broke down, and I was forced to catch another one, that I had something of a breakthrough.

The bus was crowded and the only spare seat was at the rear which I made a beeline towards. I sat down, only to be met by the smiling face of my old sparring partner at Johnny Hunter's gym, Rory Gilbert, who was seated beside me. Rory was coming home from work too.

"Ed Costigan, you mad bastard! Bloody good to see you!" he exclaimed with a big grin, showing off his pearly white teeth.

"Rory bloody Gilbert! Now this is a blast from the past. It does my heart good to see ya," I told him, grabbing his hand shaking it firmly.

"Likewise, Ed. I heard on the grapevine you were back from Vietnam. Why haven't you been down to the gym to do some training?" Rory asked, giving me a speculative look.

"I've sort of given the boxing away, Rory."

"Given it away! What for? You still got plenty of boxing in ya, Costigan."

I looked away. "I've had a bit on my plate since I got back from Vietnam and I really haven't had any time."

Rory looked me up and down. "I've been hearing from reliable sources that you've been hitting the piss a bit too much, especially after breaking up with that beautiful girl of yours."

"Who you been talking to Rory?" I snapped.

"Let's just say I got that black fellas intuition and I keep my ears close to the ground," he replied in a smug tone.

I looked at Rory and my demeanour changed as I growled at him, "Ah, give us a break about my drinking, will ya. I am sick to death about people bringing that up all the time."

"Maybe you're sick to death because it's the truth, Ed," he smirked.

Well, that about did it. What followed on the bus that afternoon was a screaming match between the two of us that lasted the next few minutes, and which brought the entire focus of the bus's passengers onto us.

As I saw a bus stop approaching, I picked up my work bag and got off. Rory appeared at the door of the bus and yelled at me, "That's it! Keep running away from life and hide behind the booze. You lost that girl of yours because of the grog! You owe it to yourself, Ed! You're a champion boxer and you've got unfinished business. Do you hear me, Ed Costigan? You've got unfinished business!"

As the bus sped off I could hear Rory's words ringing in my ears. *You've got unfinished business.*

When I actually stopped to think about it, Rory's words hit me like a sledgehammer. I knew he was right, and that also mean that Rowy was right too. Even though I didn't want to admit that the booze was a problem, I certainly knew that my boxing career was far from over and that I still had work in the ring I had to fulfill. I thought about how I had lost Sandy and it was this that really spurred me on to take decisive action and get back into the ring.

"I'll prove to Sandy that I'm not all washed up. I'll prove to her if it's the last thing I do that I am still a champion," I repeated to myself in the days that followed. In what was a tough decision, I decided a few days later to venture down to Johnny's dilapidated tin shed to see the master trainer once again and have a crack at resurrecting my boxing career.

Johnny was still producing champions, including Rory, who was the current Commonwealth light heavyweight champion.

I appeared at the door of Johnny's gym after work on a Friday in early December of 1969, to be met by his smiling face, just as he was putting the gloves on a young bloke who was about to go and spar.

"Well, I'll be! Look what the cat's dragged in. Still, I shouldn't be surprised because miracles do happen. After all, the Americans did put a man on the moon this year and if they can do that, then surely there was always a chance that my champion boxer might make a return," said Johnny with a wry smile.

"Yeah, well, Rory did give me a few words of encouragement when I saw him on the bus a few days ago," I said sheepishly.

"A few words of encouragement you reckon, Ed? The way I heard it he fairly put a rocket up you," Johnny said, barely hiding his grin.

"Listen, I don't want to split hairs as to how I got here, the fact is I'm here and ready to start training again," I snapped.

Johnny ignored my petulant snap, and looked at the young fellow who he was helping with his gloves and said to him, "You know who this bloke is young buck?"

He looked me up and down carefully before he said, "He'd have to be Ed Costigan, hey Johnny?"

"Spot on young fellow. Ed's one of the finest fighters who has ever graced the doors of this gym."

A smile came over my face.

"Oh boy, my dad took me to watch you fight Alby Daubert back in 1965 for the New South Wales middleweight title. It was the first fight I had ever seen live and I've never forgotten the guts you showed to win after he floored you early in the bout. You're the reason I took up boxing, Ed."

I felt a lump in my throat and I swelled with pride. "That's really nice of you mate. I really appreciate that. What's your name?"

"Lester Eggins."

"Please to meet you, Lester," I said as I shook his hand, not knowing then that I was shaking hands with the future WBC middleweight champion.

Johnny gave me a serious look. "Do you need any more evidence as to why you should be back in the ring? Now go and scoot, get changed and we'll get down to business again."

And that started my road back into boxing.

When I came out of the changeroom, who should be waiting for me in the ring? None other than Rory with a grin on his face. I scowled, but I knew what I had to do. I might have been a prideful sort, but I wasn't a bad sort.

"This isn't easy, swallowing my pride, but sorry, mate, and thanks for giving me a rev up. If there was anyone who could do it, it was you."

Rory broke out into a broad smile, showing his pearly white teeth and said, "Come on, Ed. Let's just forget about it and get into the ring. Show me what you do best."

We sparred for fifteen minutes before I was all washed up. I was rusty, but after I decided to put both the drink and the cigarettes down, by the end of that first week I started to get fit again and with it, my boxing improved. Although I went crazy for a while with cravings, I worked through them by thinking about what young Lester Eggins had said to me on my first day back in the gym. I had influenced a young kid through my actions, so my actions had to have weight. I had to get healthy.

In those early days back, I didn't know if I could return to where I had been prior to Vietnam, and was nervous, but trusted that under Johnny's tutelage, I could get back to my best. But the truth is, I grew great strength from the fact that I had so much influence on a young man's life, namely the great Lester Eggins.

***

"A few months after I started back with Johnny, Rory fought for his light heavyweight title defense at Festival Hall in Melbourne, in late November 1969, against a classy southpaw from Collingwood named Joey Desposita. The bout was a brutal affair with Rory managing a knockout in the final round when he was behind on points."

I folded my arms and gave Tim a wry smile as I remembered what happened next.

"What is it?" he said.

"The 10th of December 1969."

"What about it?"

"That's the day I got shot in the arse with a rainbow, Tim!"

"What do you mean?" He looked confused.

"It was just after Rory's fight when my fortunes took a decidedly positive turn."

"How?"

"Stumpy still hadn't told me about the $200 he had invested in the Poseidon shares, although we had long patched up our differences concerning the card game." I leant forward in my seat and looked Tim in the eye. "The 10th of December was the day that the Poseidon shares went through the roof. You remember I told you that Stumpy had bought 500 shares at $0.35c a share?"

"Yeah."

"Well, the shrewd old bastard decided to sell all the Poseidon shares he owned. He made a $100 dollars a share." I grinned.

"Bullshit!" Tim said, in total shock.

"No bullshit, my friend."

He looked at me eagerly. "How much did you make?"

"Fifty grand, Tim." I sat back with a wide smile on my face.

"Phew!" Tim said, shaking his head. "What you couldn't do with that!"

"There was a method to Stumpy's madness, and why he hadn't let on and told me about the shares at the time."

"Must have been a good one," said Tim.

"It was. He had every intention of telling me about the purchase of the shares, but knew that it wasn't the right time at the start."

"Why?"

"I was on the comeback trail!" I told him with an expansive gesture. "I had been drinking up a storm, my attitude was all over the shop and he didn't want anything to interfere with my boxing plans now that I was behaving better, so he kept quiet until what he thought was a more appropriate time." I moved further forward in my seat and looked at Tim intensely. "Stumpy had a sixth sense. He would tell me that he used to get gut feelings about things and his instinct told him that when the shares went sky high on December 10 that it was the right time to offload them. Lucky he did, because Poseidon crashed in early 1970. Stumpy told me on a number of occasions that it was his sixth sense that saved his life in World War I. He would point to the sky and say, 'It was the boss upstairs looking after me, Ed'.

I moved back in my seat with a wry smile. "Anyway, things moved on, Stumpy kept the windfall secret, and over the next six months I sparred continuously with Rory and other fighters who were training at Johnny's gym. I fought four bouts, winning two by knockout and two by points. My speed and agility had once again returned, and as it did, so did my confidence. I still thought about the drink but kept the cravings at bay, as I became totally focused on my boxing. In the back of my head was the thought of Sandy and how much I missed her. I always thought that if she knew I was off the drink and I won a big fight, she might come back to me. I didn't realise it at the time that the horse had already bolted and Sandy had no intention of coming back to me."

Tim nodded.

I made a face. "I was none the wiser though, so it led me to train hard and in September 1970, Johnny believed that the time was right for me to have a crack at the Australian middleweight title. He started me on a punishing training program which was to test me to the core, but ultimately prepare me for what was ahead."

***

It was a Friday night in early December of 1970 when I was set to meet Vince 'the Snake' Cosoleto for the vacant Australian middleweight title at the Horden Pavilion in Sydney.

My old nemesis, Hector Saunders, had retired after killing a man in the ring, leaving the title vacant.

Cosoleto, who hailed from Griffith in south-western New South Wales, had an Italian background and was reputed to be from a family with mob connections. My first impression of Cosoleto was that he was like a character out of a spaghetti western like *The Good, The Bad and The Ugly*. He had a dark olive complexion, greasy black hair, sported a twelve o'clock shadow and had very dark, sinister eyes.

The bout received intense interest in the media for the Monday night fight. The *Sydney Morning Herald* ran an article in the sports section on the Saturday a week before the fight with the heading:

WASHED UP VIETNAM VET NO
CHANCE IN TITLE FIGHT!

There were many within the boxing fraternity who believed

that if I was not called up for National Service in 1967 that I would have gone on to win the Australian middleweight title. Most of them now believed that my time had gone and I was no match for the young terror from Griffith who would destroy me when we met.

It was widely known that I had a problem with the drink and the punishing training program of Johnny's had taken its toll on me after I had put the bottle down. The general consensus was that Vince would merely have to go through the formalities before claiming the title.

Vince was 20 and I was 24, although I looked older considering what I had been through with my boxing career and my stint in Vietnam. Cosoleto was calling me a has-been in the weeks leading up to the fight, and this had caught on with the general public who thought I was no chance.

I was in Johnny's gym on the Saturday a week before the fight when I showed him the article in the newspaper. "Can you believe this Johnny? All these bastards have written me off. We'll see if I am a has-been or not!"

"I've got faith in you, Ed. I've known you were a champion from the very first day you walked into this gym, all those years ago. The general public may think otherwise, but those of us who know you well, know that Cosoleto is in for one hell of a fight."

"As Rory said to me on the bus that day Johnny, I've got unfinished business," I said with a wry smile. He grinned back and clapped me on the shoulder.

I had a huge entourage of family and friends who had come to see the fight including a surprise visit by Schooner Rooney, as well as Stumpy, Noel, Anne, Dan and Rowy, who I had long patched my differences up with. He was too good of a mate, and I couldn't let our argument end what had been a great friendship.

My sister Anne had become my personal nurse and would tend to any cuts I received due to my training and fights. After my breakup with Sandy, I sought solace in her company and her maturity and advice beyond her years soothed the blow. She helped me see just exactly what had gone down with Sandy. It had taken a while to admit it, but Anne was patient and got to the heart of the matter.

"I didn't treat Sandy real well, Annie, after I got back from Vietnam. I suppose I deserved what I got. I can only hope she changes her mind and gives me a second chance," I said to Anne not long before the fight.

"Sometimes it's best to live and let live, Ed," she said, with a level of wisdom beyond her years. Anne already knew that Sandy had hitched herself to the dashing young doctor in town and that they were a serious item.

The night finally arrived and it hit me that all my training had come down to this moment. I was nervous prior to the opening bell and Vince came out firing, hitting me with everything he had. All I could do was cover up and as a result, the crowd started to boo me for not taking the fight to Vince.

It was late in the first round and Vince had me pinned to the ropes when he got under my guard with an uppercut and knocked me to the canvas. It was only the second time that I had been knocked down in the ring, and I only just got up before the end of the count. As I staggered to my feet someone in the crowd yelled out, "You left your best fighting days back in Vietnam, Costigan! You're a fuckin' shot duck!"

I sat on my stool contemplating what he had yelled out and devised a plan to counter Cosoleto while Johnny spoke to me.

"Ed, the Snake's very fast and he's taken you by surprise, but I just want you to cover up and take his punches because he'll run out of steam sooner or later and then your opportunity will come. Remember, Ed, you're a classier boxer than Cosoleto, and you've got a lot more weapons up your sleeve than he has."

As Johnny gave me his little pep talk, I finalised my plan of attack as to how to unsettle Cosoleto. It was a plan which I never shared with Johnny, as he would of told me I was insane for even contemplating such a dangerous option.

Since I was a southpaw and he fought orthodox, he would have expected me to come out and hit him with a right jab, but I decided to break all the rules and come out and hit him with a left cross which was an insult to such a good boxer like Vince. I knew that this was the last thing he would have expected from me, particularly since I had received a pasting from him in the first round.

Seven times I hit him with a left cross and seven times I caught him by complete surprise in that second round, managing to open up a small cut just above his right eye. I looked across to Johnny in my corner, and he was standing there with his hands on his hips, shaking his head.

"What are you doing, Ed?" he yelled at me.

I gave Johnny a wry smile.

After my little experiment, Cosoleto went ballistic and for the next five rounds, he chased me all around the ring. He was insane with rage and I managed to avoid the worst of his onslaught by covering up and staying nimble on my feet.

During the fifth round, he was laying into me in the corner and I kept talking to him to put him off his fight. "You don't hit very hard," I told him, followed by, "Your mother hits harder than you, Vincey-boy."

This sent Vince into an even bigger state of rage.

The fight went on and it was well into the seventh round when Cosoleto once again had me tied up on the ropes. He was so close to me that I could feel his unshaven face up against mine and he whispered into my ear, "So what's it like to be a baby killer, you washed up Vietnam lowlife?"

Well.

It wasn't the Vietnam lowlife comment that got under my skin, rather the indignation of such an insult as 'baby killer.' After all I had been through in Vietnam—to be labelled with such a lie was grounds for war. As I looked into his sinister black eyes, I smoldered inside and came to the conclusion that there was no way I was going to let this creep beat me.

Before the start of the eighth round, I was sitting on my stool when Stumpy, who was sitting not far from the ring stuck his head inside the ropes and said to me, "I think it's time for the 'Coorigil Killer', Ed."

I looked at Stumpy and my mind went back to all those years before when I had sorted out Rory with a lethal combination of punches while we were sparring.

I looked at Stumpy before he withdrew his head back beyond the ring ropes, and with a wry smile commented, "Yeah, I think you're spot on, Stumpy. It's about time I brought some heavy weaponry out."

As the sweat ran down the side of my face, I looked out into the crowd and my eyes focused on Rowy and Schooner Rooney, who were sitting side by side. My thoughts turned to them and the battles we had fought in Vietnam together. In particular, I thought about Chooky dying in the heat of battle and it was then with a snap of a finger my thinking changed. I resigned myself to the fact that this fight wasn't just for me, but for all my mates I had fought beside in Vietnam. My title fight took on a whole new meaning and Rory's words of 'unfinished business' reverberated inside my mind.

I was ready.

As the bell for the eighth round sounded, I felt as though I had been given an extra burst of energy. I was well behind on points, but I had a strong feeling that everything was going to be alright. Cosoleto had punched himself to a standstill and I could see that he was wasted, so I came off the ropes and started to punch him hard with some killer blows to the head and body. As I did, I felt like the boxer I had been prior to Vietnam and my confidence soared.

It was in the middle of the eighth round and I had Cosoleto on the ropes when I took my opportunity and applied the Coorigil Killer to him. As my fists thrashed up and down with great speed like two pistons, Cosoleto was taken totally by surprise. As I continued my onslaught, my fists hit Vince's stomach and he was totally unnerved by my unexpected barrage. This was the turning point of the fight and Vince never recovered from my fierce onslaught.

For the next four rounds I hit him with plenty of combinations, managing to win each round. As I sat on my stool for the start of the final round, Johnny and I both knew that if I was to win the fight then it would have to be by knockout. I knew I had the right ammunition to do the job and I hoped the opportunity would arise where I could unleash a knockout blow.

"This is your moment, Ed. This is where you put your unfinished business to rest," said Rory as he wiped to sweat from my face.

As the bell for the twelfth round sounded, I was totally focussed and hoped and prayed that my opportunity would come. The onslaught, the high intensity bout, continued well into that final round when, with about 30 seconds to go, I sensed my chance had come.

Cosoleto was a spent force and was starting to drop his guard as fatigue set in. I stepped in and gave him two cracking right jabs to his jaw followed by a wicked left cross to the side of his face which made him stagger backwards towards the ropes. He managed to roll off the ropes and after regaining his composure, he came for me with a right hook to my jaw which didn't have much impact. There was very little time left in the fight and I noticed that Vince's hands were by his side so I lined him up and gave him a right upper cut under his jaw followed by a lightening quick left hook to the side of his head that sent him into a spiraling downwards motion.

As I stood over him, getting ready to deliver the final blow I looked into his eyes and said, "I'll give you 'baby killer', ya fuckin' maggot."

I delivered a devastating straight right to his face which sent his head rocketing backwards towards the canvas. As my fist connected with his face, I heard un almighty big snap and I immediately recoiled in pain. I felt an excruciating pain come from my right wrist. As I watched Cosoleto's head hit the floor, I held my wrist and I grimaced in agony.

As the referee counted him out, I walked back to my corner, cradling my arm, where Johnny and Rory were embracing each other and the crowd were going off in scenes of wild jubilation. The referee walked over to my corner and raised my good arm as the crowd went ballistic. Johnny made his way through the ropes and after embracing me, shouted, "You did it, Ed! You bloody well did it!"

"I know Johnny, but I think I've broken my wrist!"

"Oh, no! You alright, mate?" Johnny said with concern. He looked down at my arm.

"I'll survive Johnny, after all I've got the title!" I was chuffed.

With that Johnny and Rory lifted me above their shoulders and the euphoria of my victory numbed the pain in my wrist.

As throngs of people swarmed into the ring, I looked down from my lofty position and there standing only a short distance away were Rowy and Schooner. I pointed at them and screamed, "That's for all the boys we were in Vietnam with!"

They both grinned back. Schooner shouted, "They'd all be proud of you, Cozzy!"

I gave them a wink and as I looked down to Johnny and Rory, who were still holding me on their shoulders, I yelled out, "I've finished my business, you two!"

It was morning, the day after the fight, and there was a northeast breeze blowing as I sat overlooking Maroubra Beach. In my hand was a copy of the *Sydney Morning Herald* with the sports heading which read:

COSTIGAN'S WIN WAS THE GREATEST COMEBACK SINCE LAZARUS!

After I read the article, which both praised my title fight win and highlighted the sportswriter's own mistake by writing me off, I exclaimed, "Washed up Vietnam vet, hey? I proved you wrong, ya silly prick."

As I sat on the park bench reflecting on my victory, I was conscious of my throbbing right wrist which I knew was broken.

The previous night after my victory I had been carried into the Maroubra Surf Club on the shoulders of Johnny, Rory,

Schooner Rooney, Rowy, and my brothers, Noel and Dan, as I held my Australian middleweight title above my head.

I was greeted by scores of well-wishers and I was offered free drinks by many who had gathered to celebrate my victory, but declined all as the euphoria of winning was running through my veins and I needed no other high. There were no victory banners or streamers decorating the inside of the club, as no one had honestly thought I had a chance of bringing home the title.

As the night wore on, I hoped that Sandy would make an appearance as this was the only thing missing from my moment of glory. The title was the very pinnacle of my boxing career and I wanted her there, but alas she wasn't to appear. Although both Johnny and Rory had hinted that night that a shot at a world title may be just around the corner, I knew that this was the sweetest victory of all and I could hang my gloves up then and there and be satisfied. To come back when all the odds had been stacked against me was cause for great jubilation.

In among all the festivities of the night, Stumpy had pulled me aside. "I need to have a talk to you at some stage, Ed."

"What about Stumpy?" I said with a look of concern." Is everything alright?"

"It's fine. It's best I talk to you tomorrow when the festivities are over. I'll meet you down at Maroubra Beach at 8.00 am tomorrow morning."

"Maroubra Beach! What for?"

"I've got some good news for you, Ed, but it's confidential so it's best if we talk down there. In the meantime, you enjoy yourself tonight. I'm heading home to get some shut eye."

Stumpy about-faced and walked away without another word, leaving me hanging.

"What good news, Stumpy?" I called after him.

"I'll tell you tomorrow, Ed," he said with a wave.

I knew from past experience that once Stumpy made up his mind, you were wasting your time pursuing him, so I went back to my party.

As I sat on the park bench, wracking my brain as to what Stumpy wanted to tell me, when true to form, he arrived at 8.00 am sharp.

"Punctual as usual, Stumpy."

Stumpy smiled at me and said, "How'd you pull up?"

I held up my dodgy arm. "I think I've broken my wrist."

"Mmm, that's no good. I hope it's not a bad break. You better get that attended to quick smart," he said, taking a seat.

"I'm going up to the hospital after I've seen you to get it sorted. I think this is a bad one, Stumpy."

"Let's hope it heals okay, Ed, because the way you fought last night, I think you've got a good chance for a crack at the world title."

I leant back on the park bench and put my wrist problem to the side. I could see a smile had come over Stumpy's face and after I enquired as to what was going on, he let the cat out of the bag.

It all came out. Stumpy told me how he had bought some shares from Poseidon for a pittance with the $200 I had won from the card game. I almost fell off the park bench when he told me he had sold the shares for $100 a share, making me a tidy sum of money. Stumpy also divulged that he too had invested in the Poseidon shares, making him a some serious coin, but would not let on the amount to me.

"I've got a cheque for you, Ed," he told me.

I thanked him for his generosity to which he insisted that

we should keep it as our little secret, lest the whole world find out about it. He then took out a bank cheque from his wallet and handed it to me. I almost choked when I saw my name on it and the sum of $50,000 written on the cheque.

I had never seen that much money in my life and after Stumpy slapped me on the knee he insisted I spend it wisely before giving me a wave and walking away. I was still thanking him profusely when he disappeared up a side street and out of sight.

***

As Tim sat there in silence, I told him that I never mentioned my Poseidon windfall to anyone in those early days, except for Rowy, as I knew he was one person who could keep a secret.

"As for Stumpy, the cunning old bugger, in the years that followed, the story came to light about how both of us had made a packet on the Poseidon shares, but nobody was ever able to ascertain how much Stumpy himself had made on the sale of his shares. It was a generally accepted rumour that Stumpy had probably become a millionaire. Although Stumpy never lived an extravagant life, and there was no outward sign of his wealth, the farm never suffered, not even in the recession, and in the years that followed, Coorigil was able to sustain itself through drought and hard times."

Tim nodded his head. "Unbelievable."

"Too right," I agreed. "You know, Tim, I couldn't believe how a bloke like me had been so lucky."

Tim was speechless.

***

I sat on the park bench for some time, my mind working overtime as to how I should spend my new-found wealth. I had made a quid out of my boxing and gave serious thought to buying a house for myself. It was overwhelming to say the least, as never in my wildest dreams had I imagined having that amount of money, and back in those days having $50,000 was like having a few hundred thousand now.

As I sat there with sound of the surf breaking in front of me, I suddenly felt a throb of pain and realised that I had better get up to the hospital. "Shit, my wrist. I had better get it looked at."

I caught a bus up to the Prince of Wales Hospital at Randwick, where I waited forever before I was attended to. The battle of the previous evening was starting to catch up with me as I was battered and bruised all over from the tremendous hammering that Cosoleto and I had inflicted on each other.

I had an x–ray done on my wrist and eventually a doctor came and saw me with the results. He was a man in his midsixties with grey hair who wore black-rimmed spectacles. He got me into a cubicle where he sat down in front of me for a discussion.

"I hear that was one hell of a fight of yours last night, Ed," he said in a deep voice.

"Yeah, Doc. It was a fairdinkum mauling, but I came up trumps in the end."

"Congratulations. I didn't get a chance to see the fight but I read about it in this morning's paper."

"It's the most satisfactory victory of my career, Doc. I could hang my gloves up now and be satisfied," I said in jest.

"Is that so?" he said, peering over his spectacles.

With his dark tone, the smile left my face and I instinctively knew that he had bad news for me.

"It's interesting that you should say that, Ed, because this is serious fracture you have incurred."

"It is?"

He nodded. "You've seriously fractured both the radius and ulna which are the two lower forearm bones which meet your hand. The damage is that severe that you risk irreversible damage if you break it again."

I looked at the doctor like I was waiting for a killer blow.

He gave me a sympathetic look. "Ed, I'm sorry to tell you this, but your boxing days are over."

Knockout!

His words hit me like a sledgehammer. "Are you sure, Doctor?"

"I'm afraid so, Ed. I hate to be the bearer of bad tidings, but it's not worth the risk. It's time you hung up the gloves."

I sat there in shock for a moment, but then he coaxed me up and put a plaster cast on my lower arm. He gave me one more sympathetic look and I wandered out of the hospital in a daze. I stood on the steps of the hospital and said out loud, "My boxing career, over! I can't believe it!"

I contacted Johnny on the phone that night and told him the bad news. Johnny spent the next half hour consoling me before adding, "Ed, you have to look at the positive side. You've gone out as the Australian middleweight champion and no one can ever take that from you. You're a champion and your name will be forever etched in history. It's better you go out on top rather than some I've seen who didn't know when to hang the gloves up and ended up like punch-drunk zombies."

Johnny words, although positive, were cold comfort as I felt like the bottom had fallen out of my world. Hard to imagine with a massive cheque burning a hole in my wallet, but over the next few days I contemplated my future and spent time at Maroubra Beach, as I was unable to work because of my injury.

Things only got worse when Rowy informed me that Sandy was now engaged to the dashing young doctor. This was the final nail in the coffin and a bittersweet blow after the good news I had received from Stumpy about the shares.

In the days that followed, I seriously thought about tying on a big one and getting pissed. I found myself on a number of occasions outside the Pagewood Hotel debating with myself as to whether or not I should go in, but talked myself out of it, as I knew that was the reason why I had lost Sandy.

Then, the following weekend I couldn't help myself and finally broke out as I went on a bender that lasted all weekend. The O'Gradys were none too pleased about my performance which included me vomiting all over their front verandah. It was only after I had come off my bender that Anne was even able to talk to me.

"Christmas is next Friday, Ed. We'll catch the train back up home together. The break will do you the world of good. You'll be able to spend some time with the family."

I was morose and miserable and had already made one big decision. "I've already made up my mind, Anne. To hell with Maroubra. I've lost Sandy, I've lost my boxing career. I've already given my notice at Steel's Transport. I'm staying up at Coorigil indefinitely, until I figure out what I want to do with myself."

She gave me a reassuring hug. "I'm sure Mum will be glad to see you."

So it came to be that on Wednesday the 23rd of December,

1970, I packed my bags and left the O'Grady's home in Maroubra for the last time. As I waited at Central Railway Station for the train with Anne to take us back home, I turned to her and said, "I have a lot of happy memories of Maroubra, Anne, but this part of my life is finished. I don't have a clue what the future holds for me, but I can only hope that I fall on my feet again."

"You always have, Ed. Let's just hope there's a nice girl waiting for you down the track," Anne said, as she held me by the arm.

"There's no doubt about you, Annie. You always know when to say the right thing to cheer me up. Come on, let's enjoy ourselves at home over the Christmas break," I said and we boarded the train for Dubbo.

I spent a booze filled Christmas at Coorigil with my family, wallowing in self pity about the demise of my boxing career.

To make matters worse it was mid-afternoon on Christmas Eve when I was standing on the front steps of Coorigil and spotted Sean O'Grady's white EH Holden sedan approaching the homestead up the gravel driveway. To my horror, sitting beside him in the passenger seat was Nana O'Grady. Noel and Dan both ribbed me about the last-minute decision for Nana to spend Christmas at Coorigil. It was a great sense of mirth to both my brothers that Nana always managed to get under my skin while they took her grating nature like a grain of salt.

Nana struggled out of the car with Christmas presents in her hands, but it didn't take long for her to sink her claws into me, blaming me for the breakdown of my impending marriage to Sandy. Long forgotten was Sandy's lack of Catholicism.

Nana's arrival signalled the start of a festive season where I spent a fair bit of time at the Drovers Dog Tavern at Eumungerie, wetting my whistle. It was there I got reacquainted with Dad's elder brother Uncle Mick, who was a woolclasser and a Rat of Tobruk. The fact that he was a bachelor and part of the woodwork of the hotel didn't help matters. I was ably assisted in consuming plenty of booze by Noel, Dan and Sean, which only exasperated Nana even more.

Christmas day was a day to be forgotten, as I had spent Christmas Eve in the pub with Uncle Mick and Sean getting so pissed that I was too crook to go to mass at Gilgandra.

Members of the family including Mum, Stumpy, Nana, Noel, Dan, Anne and Uncle Mick were gathered around the table for Christmas lunch. Also there was my sister Margaret and her fiancé, Dr Geoff English, who had flown down from Arnhem Land to be with us as a celebration of their recent engagement. She'd long since decided that nursing was the way to go and was doing great things up north.

Mum was busily preparing a Christmas roast, assisted by Margaret and Annie, and had just taken a phone call from my brother John, wishing us all Christmas greetings. John was the curate at the parish of Warragamba on the outskirts of Sydney, and for obvious reasons could not make it home for Christmas.

Once Mum got off the phone, Nana saw it as her cue to admonish me in front of the whole family about my drunken state and how I had missed Christmas Day mass. She reminded me time and time again during Christmas dinner that I was in a state of mortal sin for missing mass and if I should suddenly die then I would burn in the entire fires of hell. She insisted that I should make a confession the next day, which I blatantly refused to do. The result of my stubborn refusal to obey her command saw everyone marched into the lounge-room as soon as lunch was finished where we recited decades of the rosary for the next hour.

In between reciting the rosary, Nana kept referring to Anne as the absolute example of Catholic purity, as opposed to my immoral behaviour. I took this as an opportunity to rib Annie, mouthing that she was a teacher's pet when Nana was looking the other way. Anne could barely contain her laughter at my humour and had to leave the room which brought even more wrath down upon me from Nana for corrupting such an innocent child.

By the time Nana eventually departed Coorigil on New Year's Day, 1971, I was a spent force. I had spent more time at the Drovers Dog Tavern than at home, trying to avoid running into her.

Before Nana had arrived at Coorigil for Christmas, I had seriously considered coming home to work for Noel, especially after he had purchased a semi-trailer for contract grain carting. But I had scrapped any idea of coming home to live after my Christmas experience with the mad old Irish lady.

Only a day or so after Nana had departed Coorigil, I received a phone call from Schooner Rooney that was to alter the course of my life.

***

I shook off the shudders that came from remembering that Christmas. "I can still hear Schooner's voice down the other end of the line like it was yesterday, Tim, and wasn't it a breath of fresh air."

"Why? What did he say?" asked Tim.

I grinned. "He said, 'Cozzy, ya mad bugger! I hear on the

grapevine ya at a loose end!' And I said, 'Schooner, I am as confused as a chook in a pillow factory at the moment. I don't know what to do. All I know is I want to get away from Coorigil.' Schooner, being the confident sort, said, 'Never fear, Cozzy, I may just have the answer to your woes.'"

"And what did you say to that? What did he have planned?" asked Tim.

"Well, it turned out that Schooner had a cousin named Denis Rooney who lived up at Kendall on the mid-north coast. The bloke had recently purchased a couple of tip trucks as the breakwalls were being extended on the Camden Haven River at a little place named Dunbogan, not far from where he lived."

"So you went up there did you?"

I nodded. "Sure did. I was as keen as mustard for a clean start, especially when Schooner told me that Denis was also looking for a mechanic."

"Kendall, eh? I know the spot. Passed through there a few years ago and did some fishing off the beach one arvo. Real nice spot, got some good photos," said Tim.

"Yep, sure is good for both of those things, Tim." I nodded at him. "I thought this was to be the beginning of a brand new chapter in my life but for one thing."

"What was that?"

"I took myself with me."

Chapter 8

WITHIN DAYS OF talking to Denis Rooney, I had packed my bags and made my way to the mid-north coast of New South Wales in my recently acquired EK Holden sedan.

It was late afternoon when I drove into the small village of Dunbogan, nestled alongside the Camden Haven River.

As I drove into town, I took in all the sights, including the old boat shed which was situated on the river opposite a small shop. I was immediately struck by the beauty of the village and its simple charm. It's fair to say that I loved Dunbogan right from the very start, with its river and beaches having a very calming effect on me.

However, as much as I loved Dunbogan, I got off to a rocky start thanks to a shonky real estate agent. I had responded to an advertisement in *The Sydney Morning Herald* for a granny flat to let. It was advertised as a 'Fisherman's Paradise to Let', but when I got there the dwelling resembled a dilapidated cubby house. An argument ensued with the result being that I stormed out of there and walked down to the local shop to cool down and to try work out what to do next.

I was in the shop, telling the owner about my predicament when unbeknownst to me, the local postmaster who was also in the shop overhead my conversation. He was a man in his early fifties and as he addressed me I could not help but like the cut of the man. He told me about a house down the road, opposite Googleys Lake, which he managed and was presently empty.

Within 15 minutes we were standing on the front steps of the dwelling. It wasn't until I walked up the steps of the two story house and onto the front verandah that I fully appreciated the view. The dwelling overlooked Googleys Lake with a spectacular view of North Brother Mountain in the background. Although the place was a bit tired, it was fully furnished, neat and tidy, and it had a great feel about it. "I'll take it!" I said, with a grin from ear to ear.

"It's yours," he smiled. "No need to come down to the post office to get the keys, you can just keep this set."

"That real decent of you, mate," I enthused, caught by the view. "By the way, my name's Ed Costigan. I've just travelled here from the Central West to start work with Denis Rooney out at Kendall, driving one of his tippers. Do you know Denis?"

"Oh yes, I know the Rooney family. They're certainly a bunch of characters. Burt Leech, by the way. I'm the Postmaster here at Dunbogan," he said, shaking my hand. "Come down to the post office tomorrow sometime and pick up the other set of keys. You can fix me up with the rent at the same time."

"Not a problem, mate."

Burt smiled and as he made his way down the steps, he stopped and said, "I don't think you'll be disappointed with *Lakeview*, Ed. It has a lovely feel to it."

I watched him leave, and that night as I sat on the verandah sipping on an ice cool beer, I reflected on how lucky I was to have fallen on my feet and found this place.

"You lucky bastard, Costigan," I said to the clear night sky.

The next morning, after I had fixed Burt up with the rent and picked up keys, I went out to Kendall to meet Denis Rooney.

As I approached the front door of his house, I noticed a man walking over from a machinery shed about 100 metres from the main dwelling. I could see that he was a strapping big country lad, with sandy red hair and a battered felt hat on his head.

He saw me and as he got closer, he started to shadow box. "So, the champ has finally arrived!" The man grinned at me. "I tell you, Ed, I've been looking forward to this moment. Schooner told me all about you. I saw you fight Cosoleto for the middleweight title. What a fight! What a champion! Whoo-haa, it's great to finally meet ya!"

I broke out into a big grin myself, but before I had a chance to say anything, Denis said, "Hey Cozzy—I can call you 'Cozzy' can't I, Ed?"

"Yeah, mate, go for your life," I told him with a wry shrug. "Everyone else does."

"Cozzy, I can't believe it's you actually here in the flesh." Denis continued to shadow box and pretended to hit me around the midriff with a few soft punches. "I don't want to hit the champ too hard otherwise I'll probably get flattened, hey Cozzy?" Denis said with a big grin.

I gave a cynical laugh. "I wouldn't be too concerned at the moment, Denis. I've just got out of plaster from a broken wrist thanks to the Cosoleto fight. I couldn't hit a fly off a chop at the moment."

"That's a shame, mate!" said Denis, but he didn't look too cut up. "Anyway, Cozzy, come over to my machinery shed and have a look at my equipment."

It was apparent that Denis had a fairly easygoing nature. At 27 years of age he was two years older than me, but after inspecting his equipment, I soon concluded that his easygoing ways extended to his machinery too. It was all fairly run down, and I could see I had my work cut out for me.

Denis owned two clapped out tipper trucks. One was an old Leyland and the other a Mercedes. As well as his trucks he also owned a couple of D8 Caterpillar bulldozers, as well as an old backhoe, all of which looked like they had been thrashed. His shed, in general, resembled a wrecking yard. "Your gear's looking a bit tired, Denis!"

He waved me off. "Nah, Cozzy, just run in, that's all."

"Who services your gear, Denis?"

"Little Dicky Foster who works for me."

"Doesn't look as though he's had a spanner over this gear in a long time," I said, inspecting the backhoe.

Denis gave a little shrug. "Dicky's had a few problems in life. You see, Cozzy, he spent four years in Changi at the hands of the Japs and it knocked him around a bit. I feel responsible for him. He isn't the best mechanic there is, but he turns up for work every morning."

I nodded, but I wasn't feeling too good about the prospect of working around so much clapped out equipment, especially when I was so used to working at Steel's where everything was always kept in tip-top condition.

Denis could see by the look in my face that I was none too

pleased about what I had seen, so he said to me, "Come around the back of the shed, Cozzy, I've got something to show ya."

I followed him out back where I was met by the sight of a gleaming green B Model Mack Bogie tipper.

"Crikey, Denis! Nice rig! Who drives that?" I said, staring at the beauty in front of me.

Denis grinned. "That's yours, Cozzy."

"Yeah?" I exclaimed with surprise, looking over at him.

"That's what you'll be driving as you cart rock from North Brother Mountain down to the breakwalls on the Camden Haven River."

I walked around the outside of the rig, running my hands over the bonnet of the truck before looking at Denis with a big grin on my face. He looked smug.

"It's yours to look after, Cozzy."

"That I certainly will, Denis."

I enjoyed working with Denis. The nature of the work was good, but I liked that Denis was essentially a bushy like me, who let me run my own race. It suited me right down to the ground.

Denis was well-liked and had established his business in the late 1960s when the breakwalls on the Camden Haven River were extended. He had bought himself the first of his tip trucks and started carting the huge rocks from up on North Brother Mountain to the breakwalls. It was from here that he had slowly built his business.

As well as driving his Mack tipper, I also became the business's mechanic, and in time straightened out his shed, tossing out a lot of unnecessary mechanical parts Denis had collected over the years which had been cluttering the inside and making it resemble a dog's breakfast.

What I loved best was going up and down the mountains. North, South and Middle Brother Mountains gave the region a unique geographical aspect. As well as the mountains, there were Watson Taylor, Queens and Googleys Lakes which, alongside the Camden Haven River, provided those who loved the water with plenty to do. North Brother Mountain towered 500 metres over the surrounding towns of Laurieton, Dunbogan and North Haven. The local inhabitants had come to see North Brother Mountain and its panoramic views as more than just a mountain, but the very essence of what made the area such a special place to live in. I was no exception.

I had been at *Lakeview* for about a week and was unwinding after a hard day's work with a cold beer on the verandah, when I noticed the lone figure of a man trudging up the steep driveway towards my dwelling. In his hands were two longnecks of beer.

"Thought I better introduce myself!" he called cheerfully. "There's no better way to do it than with a couple of beers for my new neighbour."

As I had been back on the drink since my boxing career ended, I welcomed his offer. "Yeah, come up onto the verandah and enjoy the view. We'll knock the top off a couple of coldies," I said, extending my hand.

"I heard on the grapevine I had a champion living next door to me, so I thought I had better make myself known. The name's Reg Kearney," he said, shaking my hand.

"Ed Costigan."

"Oh, I'm well aware of who you are," Reg said with a smile, taking a seat.

"There's no airs and graces around here, mate," I told him.

"I might be the current middleweight champion but someone's bound to take that crown shortly. My days in the ring are over."

"I heard all about your busted hand, Ed. My commiserations because I loved watching you fight. It's a real shame we won't be seeing you ply your trade any longer."

"I wasn't a real happy chappy at first, Reg, but I've got over the worst of the disappointment. After all, I ended up going out when I was still on top and I can't complain about that."

"Nicely said, Ed," Reg said, nodding his head in agreement.

He was a man in his early thirties with a slim build, dark hair and sharp features. After talking to him for a while, I could see that he had an easygoing nature and loved a yarn.

"What do you do for a crust around here, Reg?"

"I own the butcher shop in at Laurieton."

"You lived here long?" I enquired.

"Born and bred in Dunbogan, Ed. My old man, God bless his soul, was a local pro fisherman."

My ears perked up. "You fish much around here?"

"Been fishing all my life. I've got a tinnie I fish Googleys Lake with, and a bigger boat I go deep sea fishing in. You keen on a fish, Ed?"

"Yeah, I love fishing," I told him.

He raised an eyebrow. "I'm going out on the lake tomorrow arvo. I'll take you out if you want?"

"Yeah, count me in."

I was chuffed. Even though I had done a bit of fishing with Uncle Kevin back in Maroubra, it wasn't until I met Reg that my passion for the pastime really took off. I was to spend many hours with Reg either fishing the many beaches and rocky headlands of the area, or taking his boat up Googleys Lake, or out to sea, or mooring up beside an oyster lease where with a little burley we might catch a nice haul of bream.

Reg taught me so much about fishing, and showed me so many great local fishing haunts that it became an important part of my life. Fishing had a great calming effect on me and it became a great source of sanctuary if I was travelling rough and needed to collect my thoughts.

As well as showing me many of his special fishing spots, Reg also introduced me to his local watering hole, the Laurieton Hotel, and many of its inhabitants. Among the collection of seasoned drinkers were Wombat the concreter who was rarely seen out of his Jackie Howe shearer's singlet, blue King Gee shorts and straw hat. There was also Billy, the local milkman, whose perpetually flushed face suggested he was always topped up on booze, and Digger the Plumber, who if he wasn't drinking, was betting on the races.

Within a month of arriving at Dunbogan, I had secured a permanent lease on Lakeview and managed to put the worst of the trauma of breaking up with Sandy and retiring from boxing behind me. I slotted into a routine of work, fishing and drinking, and that's the way I believe it would have permanently stayed, until my life was quite unexpectedly turned upside down one sunny Sunday afternoon in September of 1971.

I had been in Dunbogan for the best part of nine months and had met all of the Rooney family except for Denis's younger sister, Kim. She had been teaching at the primary school in Ballina on the far north coast of New South Wales and had recently returned back home to take up a teaching position at the convent school at Kendall.

It was a Sunday when Denis invited me over to his farm to

celebrate his birthday with a BBQ lunch. I arrived on my own with an esky full of beer and a box of potato chips. There were about 30 guests mingling in the backyard, and I was talking to Little Dicky Foster. He was telling me a story in his jockey-sounding voice about the time he jack-knifed a timber jinker coming down a mountain road out the back of Wauchope. Dicky was right in the middle of his story when this beautiful girl with strawberry blonde hair and blue eyes approached us. She was in her early twenties, five foot six, slim, and was wearing a white blouse with khaki shorts. In her hands was a plate full of cocktail frankfurters, and I was completely blown away by her beautiful smile.

"Have some frankfurters, boys," she said quietly.

"Thank you," I said, as I gave her a smile. Our eyes met and she returned the smile.

"So, you're the one I've been hearing so much about," she said.

I suddenly realised who she was. "You must be Kim?"

"I am indeed." Kim had a very quiet, feminine voice, which I was immediately attracted to.

"Well, I've heard a lot about you too," I said, turning on the charm with a cheeky grin, "but I didn't realise you were as beautiful as you actually are from the stories."

Kim giggled and said, "Flattery will get you everywhere, Mr Costigan."

I laughed. "Good."

"So," Kim said, the frankfurters in her hand forgotten, and Dicky Foster too. "You were in Vietnam with my cousin Pat, were you?"

"Yeah, that's right," I told her, as a flood of memories arose within me. I pushed them down. "Schooner and I did our tour together."

"Schooner?" Kim said, confused.

"Yeah, that's the nickname we gave him because he was partial to a drop of the amber fluid."

"Yeah, well, we all know he likes a drink," Kim said, her expression tightening.

It was like the spell had been broken, and she hurried away to serve other guests. I could not take my eyes off her. It didn't take me long to realise that she was popular with the guests, as she was constantly engaged in conversation. I wanted to talk to her again, but I didn't want to hassle her, so I continued to chatting to other people, and hoped she'd come back around to me.

The BBQ had been going for a few hours when I felt a hand on my elbow. When I turned around, she was standing there with that same beautiful smile on her face. I felt a rush of blood through my system.

"Let's sit down on the picnic rug and have a chat," she said.

"Okay." I followed her to the rug and settled myself on the ground.

Kim tucked her legs up under her. "Denis told me that you were off a farm out west?"

"It's just a dot on the map," I shrugged. "Eumungerie."

"Never heard of it," she said, shaking her head.

"It's in between Dubbo and Gilgandra, on the Newell Highway."

"What type of farm is it?"

"My family has got 3000 acres out there. Mainly wheat, sheep and cattle country."

She smiled. "Denis said you were living in Maroubra before you moved up north?"

"Yeah, I served my trade as a mechanic before I went to Vietnam and then I went back to Maroubra after I got home." I felt like I was being grilled, but in a way it was good. We could get all the nitty-gritty out of the way now.

"I imagine Vietnam must have been pretty tough?" Kim said gently.

"Yeah," I said, looking away. "It was pretty tough, but I'm trying to put it behind me now."

She made a face. "I thinks it's disgusting that all the protesters are giving you fellows such a hard time, when it was our government that sent you there in the first place."

I smiled at her. "You're not wrong, Kim. I've had it up to my eyeballs with those leftie ratbags."

Kim smiled.

"So," I said, wanting to talk about something else, "how come you came back home to live?"

"I broke up with my boyfriend." Kim looked at me seriously, her eyes full of warning. I could sense something painful there.

"Why?"

"He was a drinker, and he was giving me a hard time," she said.

I felt a shiver run up my spine. "A hard time in what way, Kim?"

"Verbal abuse when he would get on the drink. He never hit me, it was always just verbal. I had enough." She shrugged, as though it had been a simple matter, but the look on her face was heavy.

I looked at Kim, but said nothing. I felt anxious as this was a little too close to the bone.

"What about you, Ed? Why did you move up north?"

I flexed my wrist. "I was pretty devastated after I broke

my hand. I'd just won the Australian middleweight title and to learn that I'd never box professionally again just killed me. I needed a fresh start."

"Is that the only reason?" Kim said, peering into my eyes. She seemed to sense there was something else going on.

I looked at her long and hard before answering. "Yeah."

"That's not what I've heard, Ed," she told me, her tone gentle, but probing.

"What have you heard?" I said, startled.

"I heard you broke up with a girl."

I was embarrassed, and looked away. "That's true, Kim."

"Why don't you want to talk about it?"

"Because it cut me up pretty bad." I had to wonder how things had suddenly gotten so serious. She didn't stop her probing.

"Why, Ed?"

I picked up a leaf on the ground next to me and started to play with it. Eventually, I looked up and said, "Before I went to Vietnam we made plans to get married, but when I came back I just couldn't commit myself. I couldn't go through with it."

"How come?"

"A lot happened to me while I was over there, and I just felt things had changed between Sandy and me. I saw a lot of nasty things, Kim. Things I don't really want to talk about. I still loved Sandy, but when I got back from Vietnam, I felt as though I had left the innocence of my youth back in Maroubra. I wasn't the same man. Things were just different."

"I know how you feel, Ed," Kim said. "I was totally devastated after breaking up with Brian. I really thought he was the one for me, but when he started getting abusive I knew it was time to get out of there. The future I thought we had was gone."

I looked into Kim's eyes and I could see the common denominator that linked us. Coming out of emotionally devastating relationship breakdowns allowed us to relate to each other. Although, Kim didn't know that it was the drink that had really sealed my fate with Sandy. I didn't really want her to know at that point, not after what she'd been through. I smiled at her. It was time to lighten the mood.

"Now you're a free woman, I suppose I'll have to ask you out."

Kim gently slapped me on the wrist, but she was grinning. "You're not backward in coming forward, are you?" she said, giving me a look. I could see she was interested.

"Nothing ventured, nothing gained," I gave her a huge smile.

Kim leaned forward and whispered in my ear, "If you want to chase me, then you'll find me on the golf course tomorrow." She got up off the rug.

"You play golf, do you?" I said, watching her unfold her slim form and stretch.

"Sure do," she said, and she smiled as she walked away.

"I've heard golf destroys a good walk!" I called after her.

Kim laughed and looked back at me. "Then I'll have to prove you wrong. I'll be teeing off for a social hit tomorrow morning at 8.00 am. Be there or be square."

Up until that stage, I had only ever had a half a dozen games of golf in my life, and had hated every one of them. Of course, nobody had ever shown me the basics of the game, and the last time I played, some ten years earlier, I vowed I would never grace a golf course again as long as I lived. Put me in a fishing boat any day of the week.

With that in mind, no one was more surprised than me

when yours truly lined up at the first tee at the Camden Haven Golf Club, with a set of clubs that I had borrowed from Denis.

Although I would have preferred it to be just me and Kim, playing with us that morning were Kim, her dad Cyril, a tall, slim man in his early fifties with sandy hair, and Kim's cheeky fourteen-year-old brother, Tom.

Kim not only looked great in a pink top and tartan skirt, but I knew as soon as she hit the ball that I was playing with a serious golfer. The ball came off her driver with a sweet-sounding ping and flew through the air, straight down the fairway, and landed within striking distance from the green.

"Not bad, but I had a little bit too much of a fade on it," she mused.

"I wouldn't be too harsh on yourself, Kim, it was a pretty good shot," said Cyril.

I immediately felt totally inadequate, as I could only imagine where my ball might end up when it was my turn to tee off.

I didn't learn until later that Kim played off a handicap of three. She was a great golfer. If not for her teaching profession, Kim could have become quite a successful professional golfer. But of course, it was 1971 and women's golf had not progressed significantly enough for her to be able to make it a full-time career.

In fact, it wasn't just Kim who was good at the game, all of the Rooneys were fairly handy golfers, with Cyril managing a third place in the 1955 NSW Open. Even Denis, who when you saw him for the first time gave you the impression that he couldn't hit a fly off a chop, hit a golf ball very well.

After spending a considerable amount of time lining myself up for my first shot, I took a huge back swing and attempted to knock the paint off the ball. To my shame, I topped the ball and it dribbled about ten feet in front of me.

I felt myself flush with embarrassment, and walked away ashen-faced. My pride was severely dented, especially as my humiliation had been witnessed. "The things you have to do to chase a woman," I muttered to myself.

"That was a terrible shot, Ed," said Tom, not holding back.

"Tom, mind your manners," said Cyril sternly.

"Yeah back off you little smartarse," I muttered to myself, but not loud enough to be heard. "It's bad enough being in the spotlight up here let alone you giving me a hard time."

I felt totally embarrassed for making a fool of myself. Kim, however, looked at me earnestly and said, "You've got everything upside down, Ed. Here, I'll give you some pointers." She then showed me some basics in grip, stance and how to swing the club, but this only confused the matter even more. As I went around the course that morning, my game became steadily worse, and with it, my frustration at not being able to hit the ball.

Added to this was the constant snide remarks from Tom about my total inability to play the game. "You've got it all wrong," he said time and time again. "You're the worst golfer I've ever seen, Ed."

My muted mutterings were becoming louder. "You keep that up kid and I am going to kick your arse from here to Bourke."

When it was all over, I could have buried myself in a big hole. We parted well enough, it was all smiles and laughter, but I consoled myself with a beer later.

"I doubt if Kim will want to see me again after my performance today. I made a total goose out of myself," I told

Reg Kearney. We were knocking back a quiet beer on my front verandah.

"It's not an easy game to master, Ed. You gotta remember that Kim's being playing golf since she was knee high to a grass-hopper. You need some practice if you're going to achieve any type of success."

"I can't ever imagine being good at that game. It shits me no end," I told him bitterly.

"That's because you haven't been taught how to play the game. What you need is some lessons," said Reg reassuringly.

With my disastrous performance fresh in my mind, it was with total surprise that I received a phone call from Kim mid-week.

"If you're interested, Ed, I can give you a golf lesson on Saturday morning at the club," said Kim, her pretty voice calm and relaxed.

"As long as that smart-alec brother of yours isn't around, Kim," I told her. A man could only take so much!

"You needn't worry about him, Ed. Tom's been read the riot act from dad and he won't be around to annoy you. I promise."

I was relieved, and decided to fess up to how I viewed my last performance. "I felt like a total clown, dribbling my way around the course last Sunday."

"You didn't become a champion boxer without lessons and hours of practice, did you?" she reminded me.

"True."

"Well, the same applies to this game, Ed. It's a difficult game to master and unless you're shown the basics, you'll be forever groping in the dark."

"If you can improve my game, Kim, then you're a mira-cle worker," I told her in a cynical tone, but the next Saturday morning, I had Kim show me the basics. As I lined up for my first lesson I felt like a four-year-old being told how to tie my shoe laces.

"Okay, Ed, I'll show you what I want you to do," said Kim.

With an eight iron in my hands, I tried my hardest to apply what she had just shown me, but after half an hour it just wasn't registering, and I was getting frustrated. Kim, however, was a teacher by profession, and she wasn't about to give up. She changed tactics.

"Right, I'm going to stand behind you, and we'll grip the club together and take a back swing. Okay?" she said.

"If you reckon it works, go for it," I said with a shrug of my shoulders. I was getting despondent. That soon changed.

Kim moved behind me, wrapped her arms around my hips, then placed her hands over mine indicating how I should grip the club. Then we slowly took a backswing together, her fluid style like poetry in motion.

I hadn't felt a women's body up against mine since breaking up with Sandy. It felt lovely to have her warm figure leaning into mine. I could feel her beautifully formed breasts up against my back and my mind was instantly transported to erotic places.

"Now, your feet should be shoulder-width apart, Ed," Kim said.

Kim words brought me back to the present. I shook my head to clear away the salacious vision.

"Are you concentrating, Ed? This is important. If you don't get your stance, grip and backswing right, then you can forget about the rest of your game," she said in a serious tone, completely oblivious to my distraction.

I could smell her perfume as she continued to give me instructions. I was in a state of ecstasy, barely able to concentrate.

She suddenly released her grip on me and said. "Okay, Ed, did you take all of that in?"

"Most of it, including the beautiful perfume you're wearing. What's it called?"

Kim gave me a slight smile, and placed her eight iron back in her golf bag. "It's French, Hermes. 'Caleche'."

"Well, it's very beautiful," I said. I looked at Kim, and walked over to where she was standing beside her golf bag. I wanted her, and when I caught her eyes she saw that and suddenly became defensive.

"This is only supposed to be a golf lesson, Ed."

"I know, but I can't help being struck by how beautiful you look, Kim."

She looked around, almost as if she was looking for a way out, but when she returned my heated gaze, I realised she was checking for spies and before I knew it, we were kissing passionately. When we broke apart, her eyes were wide, and she looked uncertain. I was suddenly filled with guilt.

"I'm sorry, Kim, I was out of line. I shouldn't have taken advantage of you, but it's been some time since I kissed a girl and you're just incredible. You blow me away."

"Don't be sorry, Ed," she said eventually. "It was totally unexpected, but it was beautiful, it really was."

I reached out and embraced Kim. She melted into my arms and before too long we were kissing again.

Over the next few weeks I took another couple of lessons from Kim, and although lacking in passion from our initial outing, it was something that I was starting to find enjoyable.

My inability to play golf well, and my ambition to try to prove myself in front of Kim, spurred me on and I concentrated to improve my game. Golf filled the void that boxing had left, and my wrist tolerated the strain just fine. Under Kim's tutelage, my game improved and I started to enjoy myself. We spent a lot of time on the golf course together, and it wasn't long before we were soon an official item.

With my new-found stability in love and at work, I had been thinking about buying a home with the money from the shares. I loved *Lakeview*, but the possibility of owning it was remote as the elderly farming couple from Walcha who owned it wanted it as their retirement home.

Serendipity, however, often steps in to intervene, and as fate dictated this time, the husband of the elderly couple suddenly passed away. It was Burt Leech who informed me of his death and so I asked as to whether I could buy it. I assumed that the wife would want to sell, now that the old fella was dead.

"Buy it, Ed?" Burt had said, with a look of total surprise.

"Don't worry, Burt," I said in a reassuringly tone. "I didn't rob a bank. Let's just say I inherited some money."

"Oh, sure whatever you say, Ed," Burt said cautiously.

After I convinced him that my financial gain was legitimate, he set the wheels in motion, and two months later, the title deeds were mine.

As our relationship developed, Kim still didn't know yet that getting hitched up with me was like getting involved with a ticking time bomb. If the truth be known, neither did I, as I was totally ignorant as to what I was suffering from.

She had discovered early in our relationship that I had issues with regards to the Vietnam War, but didn't know much about PTSD. I didn't either. I didn't have much knowledge of psychology, I was more of the 'get on with it' type. However, it didn't stop my subconscious working hard. The catalyst for my sleepless nights and occasional nightmares was the young Viet Cong soldier who I had mercy killed. It was something about finding those rosary beads on him that affected me. I had killed somebody of my own creed and I felt guilty about that. No matter how hard I tried, I'd wake up from nightmares. Add Chooky to the mix and I was quickly falling down the rabbit hole.

Kim now also knew that I liked a drink, and she laid it on the line that if our relationship was going to go any further then I was going to have to address that topic. After her last relationship, she had little tolerance for alcohol.

"Ed, I don't know what you have in mind for the future between us, but if you're thinking of marrying me, then you're going to have to address a particular issue," Kim said quietly, one morning.

"What may that be, sweetie?" I said, as we sat on the verandah at *Lakeview*.

"Ed, I love a good time, you know that," she began cautiously.

"Absolutely, Kim," I agreed. "I've never seen anyone move quite so well on a dance floor as you do."

Kim smiled. "And I love your wit and charm and you're always the life of the party. And I, of all people, am anything but a wowser."

I was now filled with concern. Where was she going with this?

"So, with that in mind, I am the last person in the world who would try to stop you from having a good time." She fidgeted with her hands, now hedging.

"What are you trying to say, Kim?"

"I know you work hard and you believe it's your right to

enjoy a drink, but you just seem to change when you've had *too* much to drink."

"Me, Kim?" I said in astonishment, completely forgetting that Sandy had told me the same thing once upon a time.

"I'm afraid so, Ed," Kim said cautiously.

"I'm just having a good time, that's all. I never mean to scare anybody," I told her, surprised by her admission. Her smile became tight.

"I really like you, Ed, but I've already had one bad relationship end because of the booze and I sure as hell am not going to go through another one. I don't mind you having a drink, I really don't, but if we're going to stay together then you'll have to tone it down a bit. Have a good time, by all means, just know your limits."

I was stunned into silence. I was in conflict, because although I loved her, I loved the booze too. I stared out at the view. "You know I can take it or leave it."

"You can?" she said, with a hint of trepidation.

"Sure. If I want to give it up, I will," I told her.

She looked relieved. "Well, if you can that would be great, because I don't want to go down that path again. It hurt too much."

I took her hand and squeezed it. "She'll be right Kim. I'll practice my golf instead of drinking. Don't you concern yourself, sweetie, everything's going to be okay."

Kim gave me a nervous smile. "If we're going to settle down together and have kids, then we have to provide them with a stable home life, just like you and I had." She rose from the deck chair. "I've gotta go and do some shopping in Laurieton. I'll see you later."

She kissed me on the cheek, satisfied with the conversation, and then left.

Me, though, I was stunned by what she had said, but happy that she hadn't completely banned me from drinking. I spent a number of hours agonising over my fate, but I realised I was left with no other choice. I had to tone down if I wanted to keep her. I had lost Sandy through exactly the same circumstances, and didn't want to lose this special lady the same way.

It was the beginning of a new pattern. I'd have years of staying off the drink and then busting out periodically, usually when I was stressed out. Although I kept an air of civility about me when I was sober, I was never really happy because lurking in the back of my mind was that time bomb. It was always focused on the next drink and when I could have it.

I wanted to prove to Kim that I could take or leave the booze so instead of drinking, I started spending hours both in the backyard and at the golf course. I was so obsessed with these tasks, focussing on both with intense single-minded determination. It wasn't until later that I learned that this kind of behaviour is a classic alcoholic characteristic. Improving my golf became my new obsession and I went at it like a man possessed. Of course, I hadn't even admitted to myself I was an alcoholic at this point, all I knew is that every time I wanted a drink, I would grab a club out of my recently acquired set and practice my swing in the backyard, even if it was well into the night.

On the upside, my game started to get better, and those people down at the golf club who believed I had next to no chance of improving were forced to eat their words as my handicap came down.

As time went on, if I wasn't with Kim or at work, I was playing golf.

It was difficult, but I managed to stay sober over Christmas of 1971, and in the months that followed. Although Kim was glad to see me off the booze, she was bemused by my obsession with golf.

"When you said you were going to practice your golf, I didn't think you would become a total fanatic about it. Still, if it keeps you on the straight and narrow then keep doing it," she said to me one day. "It's a good way to stay healthy."

Like most of society, and just like me at the time, she was totally ignorant about alcoholism and thought it was just a matter of putting the cork in the bottle and everything would be hunky dory. What she didn't realise was that taking the booze out of the alcoholic was not enough. I was left with the '*ism*' of the disease. The loner, the perfectionist streak, the ungrounded and unfounded fears, the big ego and low self-esteem, and the relentless drive which makes the alcoholic a unique creature. When left untreated, an alcoholic could be as productive as everyone else, but ultimately, the desire to drink is still there. It's just temporarily channelled elsewhere.

I remember an old phrase. 'You can take the booze out of the fruitcake, but you're still left with a fruitcake.' It was totally applicable to me at that stage of my life.

Anyway, that type of philosophy was way ahead of where I was in 1971. We thought that just putting the drink down would be sufficient for my continued wellbeing. Me and Kim had a powerful chemistry and love, and so I proposed to her on Easter Sunday of 1972 at her parent's house. She agreed and we were to become man and wife.

From just before Christmas 1971 to my wedding day in September 1972, I had managed to stay sober and Kim was all the happier for it.

Reg Kearney, however, my next door neighbour and one-time best drinking mate, had been a constant thorn in my side during my abstinence, always trying to get me on the drink with him.

"Come on, Cozzy, give the golf a break and come over to my place and have a drink will ya," he would often say when he spotted me around the yard.

"I've told you before, Reg. I've put the cork in the bottle and I am getting on with my life," was always my standard reply.

"Getting on with ya life?" he'd say with a snort. "You've always got that bloody golf club in ya hand. Ya must sleep with the bloody thing, do ya?"

With a stoic wave of my hand I would continue on my way.

I had managed to ward off his advances on numerous occasions, but with the added pressure of my impending marriage, Reg managed to get under my guard on my wedding day with disastrous consequences.

I had awoken on our wedding day early to make sure that all the arrangements were in place for the 3.00 pm nuptial mass at Kendall. My brother Noel, who was my best man, was staying with me in the house while Rowy and Schooner Rooney, my groomsmen, had booked a motel room in Laurieton. I had tried in vain to get in touch with Finno as I really wanted him to share in my important day, but no one seemed to know his whereabouts.

After breakfast the four of us, including my brother Dan, went down to Wash House Beach at Dunbogan for a swim before returning to my house. I told the boys that I was going into Laurieton to do some quick shopping and then we would meet back at my place for lunch.

Everything was going to plan, and after some quick shopping, I went to the petrol station to fill my car up with fuel before returning home. I was about to leave the service station, when who should drive in but Reg Kearney.

"How are you, Cozzy? Getting ready for the big day, old son?" he said in a laconic tone.

I felt a sense of anxiety on seeing Reg and answered, "I'm all ready to go, Reg. I'm just going home for a quick bite then it'll be a one-way ticket to the alter for me."

I was about to get back in the car and drive off when Reg said, "How about coming to the pub for a lemon squash?"

"I don't think so, Reg."

"Listen, mate, I didn't get a guernsey to the wedding and that's understandable because I know you've been trying to stay off the grog. I know you haven't wanted me around lest you were tempted."

I nodded, feeling a touch of guilt. The bloke had picked it in one.

"So," he continued, "I'd like to shout you a lemon squash as a gesture of goodwill." He gave me an earnest look. I could see there was hurt in his eyes that he didn't receive an invitation to the wedding. I recalled the good times we shared when we had first met, especially after he had taken me fishing on countless occasions. The better part of my nature felt sorry for him, and so I relented and accepted his invitation.

"One lemon squash, then I'm going, Reg. Do you understand?" I said, with my finger raised in resolute finality.

"Absolutely, Ed," he said with a grin. "Just one and you'll be on your way because I know you've got a big day ahead."

It all started off innocent enough with Reg and I reminiscing about the times we had spent together fishing. I felt grateful that Reg had shown me some of his secret fishing spots so I shouted him a beer while I bought myself a second lemon squash.

I was mid-way through my second lemon squash when I excused myself and went to the toilet. When I came back a few minutes later, I saw that sitting on the table where my lemon squash had been was an icy cold middy of Tooheys New. Reg was sitting on the other side of the table with a sly grin on his face. I protested but Reg would have nothing of it. He was adamant that I should drink the beer as it was my wedding day and that as a true blue Aussie it was my God-given right to knock the top of a cold one occasionally. I protested even louder to which Reg replied, "You know what the old crowd in the pub are saying about you, Ed?"

"What are they saying, Reg?" I said glaring at him.

"They reckon you've got no balls. That you've gone all soft and you're only half the man you used to be. A couple of 'em reckon you couldn't fight your way out of a wet paper bag now you've gone all 'born-againish'."

I fell into Reg's trap like a piece of bait. "I was born-againish?" I demanded, my fury rising. "I'd like them to say that in front of my face, Reg. I'd punch the fuck out of 'em," I grabbed him by the shirt front and hauled him close.

He grimaced. "Go on, Ed, it's ya bloody wedding day, so do yourself a favour and have a beer before you blow a head gasket," he said, pushing back against me.

I released my grip on Reg and sat back down in my chair. I pointed at him and said, "Next time you're talking to any of those lame fuckwits, tell 'em I'll take 'em all on blindfolded behind the pub. Even with a fucked up wrist I'll still beat the crap out of all 'em."

I picked up the middy of beer, and as natural as a duck taking to water, I took a gulp.

"Ah shit, that tastes good," I said, as I felt instant relief from my highly agitated state.

Reg grinned at me from where he was sitting and said, "There you go, Ed. You're looking more relaxed already."

It was Denis Rooney who discovered me a few hours later. I had Reg pinned up against the wall next to the bar with his feet six inches off the ground. Denis had gone to the Laurieton Hotel to get some more supplies of booze for the post-wedding celebrations and was surprised to see me.

"St George won eleven straight premierships, ya dickhead!" I was screaming at Reg.

We had been arguing about how many grand finals the St George rugby league side had won during their golden era of the 50s and 60s. Reg was adamant that it was twelve, but I was trying to convince him it was eleven, which I knew was correct.

"Hey, Denis! Get Ed off me will ya, he's gone fuckin' berserk!" cried Reg.

Denis rushed over and pulled me off him. "What are you doing, Cozzy? You're supposed to be married in a few hours and you're off your head, as pissed as a chook."

I staggered away. "This fuckin' smartarse has got it coming to him, Denis! Thinks he knows everything. Well I am going to punch his fuckin' lights out!"

"Stop him before he murders me!" Reg shouted, shaking with fear.

Denis rounded on him. "How did he get back on the piss, Reg?"

"I bought him a beer for his wedding day, Denis," said Reg, looking away.

"You what?" Denis screamed.

"I thought one wouldn't hurt him."

Denis glared at Reg. "You won't have to worry about Cozzy murdering you because I'm going to do it! He's been off the piss for months and you've got him back on it!"

Denis punched Reg out cold and then picked him up and flung him across the room, glaring at the unconscious man.

"I got to get you back to *Lakeview*, Ed," said Denis. "We gotta clean you up."

"I'll be alright, Denis," I said in my inebriated state.

Denis looked at me up and down. "No, you won't, not if I don't get you cleaned up. If Kim finds you like this there'll be hell to pay."

When we got back to *Lakeview*, Noel, Rowy and Schooner were pacing up and down the house, desperately trying to figure out where I had got to. They rushed to the edge of the verandah, dismay on their faces as they saw my terrible state.

"Ed's neighbour Reg Kearney got him back on the piss," Denis said to Noel, as he dragged me up the steps and onto the verandah. I swayed unsteadily.

"He fuckin' well what?" Noel screamed.

"Yeah at the Laurieton Hotel," Denis told him. "There's no time for get squares at the moment, Noel. We've gotta get Ed cleaned up before he walks down the aisle."

After chucking me in a cold shower for half an hour, the boys tried to sober me up by pumping me full of Vitamin B and icy cold water.

"Sober up will ya, Ed," said Rowy, as he slapped me on the face.

"I'm alright, Rowy," I slurred.

"Be buggered you are, Cozzy. Ya look ratshit," said Rowy. He was irritated.

Meanwhile, Schooner had found some smelling salts in the bathroom, left over from my boxing days, and was holding the bottle under my nose and insisting I take a decent whiff.

I came down slightly over the next few hours, and somehow, they got me into my suit and bundled into the car.

Even to this day, Noel often recalls how he was trying to settle me down as we prepared to go into the church. "Okay, Ed, suck the air into your lungs and you'll get through this."

I started to breathe deeply, all the while looking at my elder brother for calm assurance. My situation was starting to hit home. "Crikey, Noel, if Kim finds me in this state she'll kill me." I was starting to get agitated. I realised what a big mistake I'd made and was starting to panic.

"Don't worry about Kim," said Noel calmly. "You just concentrate on sucking that air in and keeping calm and everything will be alright."

"That's right, Ed, just stay calm and you'll breeze through this," said Rowy who was standing close by, his mood nice and relaxed.

"Rowy's right, Cozzy, you're not as pissed as you think you are. Kim won't know the difference," said Schooner Rooney.

"Who you trying to kid, Schooner?" I said with a look of concern. I knew that Kim would pick it in an instant.

"I know my cousin, mate, she'll take it like a grain of salt," he replied, slapping me on the shoulder.

I disagreed.

As I walked up the aisle of the church, I was so stiff with apprehension that I felt like one of Madame Tussaud's wax models. Then I spotted Stumpy, who was sitting with my family towards the front of the church, and as I looked into his eyes, I could tell by his animated expression that he knew that all was not right with me. When we reached the front of the church I let out a huge sigh of relief that I had managed to even get to that point without a drama.

My brother John, who was celebrating the nuptial mass, walked from the sacristy to where we were standing and in his typical condescending tone said, "Okay, is everyone up to speed with the format of the ceremony?"

"No worries, John, we've got everything down pat on our side of the ledger," said Noel with his typical air of authority.

Noel gave me a subtle wink which John noticed, and turning to me while gently stroking his vestment, he said, "Are you alright, Ed? You look like you've seen a ghost."

I was conscious of the alcohol on my breath, so I replied in a barely audible tone, hoping to keep the fumes inside, "I'm okay, John, just a bit nervous."

John looked at me long and hard before answering, "Yes, well, just relax your mouth and take some deep breaths and that should help you."

"That I will." I felt like my mouth had been glued together with Tarzan's Grip, the best superglue of the day.

We stood there for the next ten minutes in nervous anticipation of Kim's arrival, saying very little lest we let the cat out of the bag as to my state. Noel was steady at my elbow, and he'd prod me occasionally, just to keep me focussed and upright.

Then, like a bolt of lightning had just hit the church, the organ started up with a sound so loud that my heart skipped a beat. I looked around nervously to see if Kim had entered the church, but all I could see was an empty aisle with heads turned from the congregation towards the back of the church eagerly awaiting the bride.

I started to sweat and my anxiety levels went up when a gasp went up from the congregation. I finally looked around to see the beautiful sight of Kim entering the church on her father's arm.

She was dressed in a resplendent full-length white wedding gown, with a veil that trailed halfway down her back. Kim looked absolutely stunning as she beamed at me. To her, this was the happiest day of her life. This only made things worse for me as I was drunk and scared to hell that she'd find out. I started to suck the air into my lungs like I was in between rounds of a championship bout.

Noel looked at me startled, before giving me a reassuring wink.

John eyed me curiously. "Are you certain you're okay, Ed?"

"Yeah, I'm okay, John," I squeaked.

John glared at me, his nostrils flaring. He looked at me suspiciously. "You're drunk!"

"Not really. I've just had a couple of settlers before the main event."

John stared at me, it was almost like he was forcing down a Nana O'Grady style tongue-lashing, before he forced his attention back to Kim and her father, who were fast approaching the front of the church. He gave a forced smile to the bride, who was beaming with joy.

When Kim finally reached me, her smile receded as I resembled somebody who had been hit in the back of the head with a coconut.

"You look great, Kim. I've never seen you look so beautiful," I said to her, stumbling over my words.

She gave me a slight smile, but she knew that all was not right with me and her look of felicity changed to one of concern. She looked at me carefully, then she looked at Noel, Rowy and then to Schooner, and even at her bridesmaids, trying in vain to find an answer to how I had arrived in my present condition.

I managed to stumble my way through the wedding service and although I believe most of the congregation were none the wiser to my inebriated state, Kim had certainly twigged and her look of indignation was enough to set alarm bells ringing.

When we left the church, Kim was able to give an obligatory smile to the waiting well-wishers. I knew though that she was steaming underneath and that at some stage up the track I was in for it. I tried to nip it in the bud early, so quipped when we had a quiet moment together, "That went off without a hitch, didn't it, Kim?"

Kim glared at me and with her upper lip curled in disdain, she said, "How could you, Ed? After all we talked about? This the most special of day for the both of us, and you just had to go and have a drink."

"Relax, Kim, I've only had a couple."

Kim shook her head and said, "A couple too many by the look of you."

I started to get frustrated. "Look, we're going to have a good time tonight, so lighten up will ya."

Kim looked away in disgust, but then she turned back to me and said with a look of scorn, "You better behave at the wedding reception, Ed, or there will be hell to pay."

Well, by that stage the genie had been let out of the bottle and all that self-control that I'd managed to exert during the ceremony was gone. That first drink with Reg Kearney earlier in the day had set the wheels in motion for a wedding reception that those invited were to talk about for years to come.

After the speeches had been made, which I had managed to blunder through without too many dramas, I was busted sneaking a drink out of the punch bowl. My brother John had spied me from a distance and hissed, "If you weren't my brother, Ed, and if I didn't have so much respect for Kim, I would seriously consider putting an application into the ecclesiastical tribunal to have your marriage made null and void." John looked around, making sure that no one was listening before continuing. "The fact that you were non compos mentis during the ceremony are grounds enough for an annulment of marriage."

I had been having a good nibble at the punch trough by this stage, and all inhibitions over my performance at the wedding had gone out the window. "Listen here you fuckin' pompous bastard with ya big Latin words. I knew exactly what was going on during the mass, so take a hike, will ya?"

"Don't you swear at me, Ed, I am a Catholic priest," John said, glaring at me.

I scoffed. "You're my brother first and foremost, John, so I'll say what I fucking well want to. I couldn't give a shit about some Catholic tribunal that wants to burn me at the stake. I'm more worried about smoothing things over with Kim, and I reckon I'll have a good dig at that when this show's over." I said glancing back to where Kim was seated at the wedding table. "For now, I'll continue to enjoy myself."

John was about to take me to task once again, when who should approach but none other than Nana O'Grady. I couldn't help myself.

"Well, look what we've got here, the daily double. Father

O'Pompous and Nana O'Crazy," I said with sarcasm. I took another sip of the punch.

"Don't you start giving me lip, you lecherous lout," said Nana, her castigation face on. "Look over there," she said, pointing towards Kim. "Your spouse is sitting over there with her bridesmaids while you're over here, sipping away on the devil's syrup. Be gone with ya and go and talk to her will ya."

"Anything to get away from you, ya crazy Irish woman," I told her.

Nana waved me off and I approached the wedding table in my ever-increasing intoxicated state. "Come on, Kimmy, let's hit the dance floor, sweetie," I said in a laconic tone.

Kim was totally taken by surprise, but before she had time to react, I had her in my arms and was on the dance floor with her.

"No, Ed, I don't want to dance," she pleaded.

"Let's get up and have a bop and blow them cobwebs out of your system, Kim," I told her, trying to pull her in tight.

Kim shook her head. "I don't want to."

I ignored her. "Righto, you bunch of lame ducks," I said, yelling at the band, as the room fell silent. "Stop playing that boring shit and put a bit of life into this party. What have you got in your repertoire that I'll bring this shindig to life?"

"What about *Dizzy Miss Lizzy* by The Beatles?" said the lead guitarist.

"Sounds good, son. Let it rip then!"

With the opening sounds of The Beatles hit I proceeded to fling, twirl, spin and sway Kim around the dance floor. If there was one thing that Kim loved it was dancing, and as we rock and rolled ourselves silly, her expression changed from one of umbrage to a broad smile as the gathered crowd clapped on the fringes of the dance floor.

"Righto you lot, you're not here to be spectators! Get up and get into it," I said to the gathered ensemble. I might have been a disheveled and drunken mess, but I could always kick-start a party.

The dance floor became a swirling mass of wedding guests as we danced ourselves into exhaustion. Kim's anger eventually disappeared, and as we danced cheek to cheek she said to me, "Costigan, I don't know what I am going to do with you. You do these things to make me totally mad then you constantly redeem yourself by making me laugh."

"We're here for a good time, not a long time, sweetie," I told her. I kissed her before picking her up and twirling her around in the air, making her shriek with delight.

When I brought her back down to the floor, she looked around happily. "Look at this place, Ed, they're all having a ball."

"See, I told you everything would be alright, Kim," I told her, pulling her close, secretly relieved that things were panning out.

Kim hugged me and buried her head in my chest. "You're a rogue, Costigan, but I love you."

We were mid-dance when Denis, who was acting as master of ceremonies, tapped me on the shoulder and said, "I hate to break up the party, but it's time for the bridal waltz and the cutting of the cake."

"Yeah righto, Denis, let's do it." I said, but while I was walking back to the wedding table, I suddenly conceived a bright idea. "You keep going, Kim, I'm just going to have a talk to the band."

"What are you up to, Ed?" Kim said with a look of concern.

"Just putting in a request sweetie."

I jogged back over to the band, and asked the lead guitarist if he break into *Don't Be Cruel* by Elvis Presley, about three quarters of the way through the bridal waltz.

After Denis introduced Kim and I as Mr and Mrs Costigan, I walked onto the dance floor with my new bride. We were dancing cheek to cheek to Elvis Presley's *Can't Help Falling In Love* and it was a very tender moment between us when right on cue, the band struck up *Don't Be Cruel*.

With the opening notes of the song, I sent Kim into a spin which received unanimous applause from the guests. Over the next few minutes we both carved the dance floor up, but the my ever-increasing alcohol consumption was starting to take effect on me, and rather than quit while I was on top I decided one last move.

My confidence was up and so I decided to put Kim into a spin which she managed very well, but in the midst of it I lost my footing and went spiralling out of control. I would have landed on the dance floor and simply dented my pride, but unfortunately for me, the three-tiered wedding cake had been moved for the cutting, and was in my direct path. As I went spiralling out of control, I caught a glimpse of Stumpy, who was sitting at his table with a look of angst on his face. Before I knew it, I struck the table the wedding cake was sitting on with such force that it sent the top tier of the cake hurtling through the air, managing to land on Nana O'Grady's lap who was seated nearby. I landed with my legs spread eagle on either side of the cake, which by this stage was sitting on the floor.

"Oh, shit!" I blurted out.

As I looked around, I could see Kim standing some distance

from me in tears. Before I had the chance to say anything to her, Stumpy who was standing in front of me with his arms folded and feet set apart. He was sporting an expression on his face that suggested he meant business and as I looked up he said, "You just don't know when enough is enough, do you, Ed?"

"You just don't know when enough is enough, do you, Ed?"

I had awoken on the lounge at *Lakeview* to Stumpy's parting words at the wedding reception. They were ringing in my ears.

"What were you thinking of, Costigan? Trying to pull a stunt like that," I muttered to myself.

It was mid-morning and I was still dressed in my wedding suit. My mouth was as dry as the bottom of a cocky's cage and my head was throbbing like I had been hit with a sledgehammer.

Eventually, I lifted my head off the lounge and looked around the room where I realised I was on my own. I struggled off the lounge and after staggering a couple of steps, I walked towards the front door where I could see Kim sitting with her back to me on the front verandah.

As I approached her, she turned towards me and with her arms folded across her front she glared at me. "Just brilliant, Ed. Just an absolutely brilliant performance last night!" she said with a look of complete contempt.

"How's the cake, Kim?" I said, trying to diffuse the situation.

Kim looked at me with total disdain. "Oh, it's just wonderful, Ed. In fact, it was in such good shape that we decided to let the wedding guests eat it off the floor," she said with sarcasm.

I felt like I wanted to crawl under a table. My guilt was starting to hit me now, and Kim staring at me wasn't making it an easier.

"You're just lucky that the top tier was still unbroken and

we were able to attach it to the rest of the cake which was relatively unscathed," she said.

"Phew that's lucky. I thought it must have been destroyed."

Kim's look of contempt only increased as I tried to make light of the situation.

"I am seriously considering cancelling our honeymoon, Ed."

"Don't do that, Kim!" I said with angst.

"I am. I mean, who knows what other party tricks you've prepared for our honeymoon? Perhaps you'll feed me to the sharks once we get to Magnetic Island," she said, throwing her arms in the air.

Her words hit me deeply and as I stood in front of her feeling very remorseful, I said, "I'm sorry, Kim. I guarantee I'll make it up to you."

"Make it up to me, Ed?" she hissed. "I doubt if you'll ever be able to make such a performance up to me. Yesterday was the most special day of my life and you went and wrecked it for me. How could you do such a thing?' Kim said, the tears now welling in her eyes.

"Don't cry, Kim," I pleaded.

"Don't cry, Ed! What do you expect me to do? Dance around the room shrieking with joy?" she said before breaking down.

I tried to console her, to hold her hand, but she pushed me away. "Don't you touch me," she said, pulling her hand away from mine.

I went into the kitchen to get a glass of water when I remembered that I had bought Kim my own wedding gift, which I had planned to give to her today. I walked down into the garage where I had the wedding present hidden. It was in a white cane basket with a beautiful assortment of flowers. In the front of the basket was a bottle of her favourite Hermes Caleche eau de toilette perfume.

I walked back onto the verandah, and presented the gift to Kim, placing it on a small table next to wear she was sitting and crying.

"I hope you like this wedding gift I bought for you, Kim," I said hesitantly.

Kim looked up, her face expressionless as the tears rolling down her cheeks. She looked at the gift for some time before saying in a caustic tone, "Leave it."

I about-faced like I was back at Kapooka in recruitment training and walked down the steep driveway and across the road to the steep rough track that led through the bush down to Googleys Lake. Once by the water, I sat on a flat rock, wallowing in a deep sense of remorse.

To say I was in the doghouse was an understatement. I had never felt so guilty and remorseful in all my life. I tried to sleep, but I kept replaying that awful moment with the cake. I felt like crawling into a cave and hiding.

It was late afternoon when I decided to venture back up to *Lakeview*, and even though I owned the dwelling, such was my feeling of guilt that I felt like a stranger in my own house. As I skulked up the side path to the back of the house, I heard Kim's voice.

"Ed, are you there?"

I felt a shiver run up my spine as I was certain I was in for another hot serve.

I walked into the house through the back door, nervously preparing myself for what I thought was the inevitable tongue lashing from my bride. As I walked into the lounge-room, I noticed her calmly sitting on the lounge with my wedding gift in front of her.

"They're beautiful flowers, Ed, she said, pointing to the gift.

"I thought you'd like them," I said nervously.

"Here, sit down next to me," she said, patting the lounge beside her.

I sat down next to her, my shoulder rubbing up against hers. I needed the contact, and even though I was still nervous, her tone was reassuring.

"I'm sorry if I was a bit short with you this morning."

"Well, that's understandable considering the circumstances," I mumbled.

"You always pick the most appropriate gifts for me, Ed, and this is no exception," she said pointing to the bouquet of flowers. Her tone was conciliatory and I realised that I had my moment to make it up to her. She had given it to me.

I looked Kim in the eyes for some time before I said, "I swear on my father's grave, Kim, I'll make sure that never happens again."

Kim returned the gaze, looking deep into my very soul. "Let's just say that was a hiccup and we'll wipe the slate clean, Ed."

I leant across hesitantly and kissed her, lightly at first, but when she returned the kiss, it turned into a passionate embrace.

When we broke apart, Kim gave me a sultry look and as she nudged closer to me she said, "If you weren't such a romantic man, Ed Costigan, I'd throw you in Googleys Lake."

I smiled before Kim added with a laugh, "You should have seen Nana O'Grady's face when the wedding cake landed at her feet. Boy, Ed, she was truly horrified."

I chuckled and said, "Then it was worth knocking the cake over just see the old crow's reaction."

Kim laughed. "Come on we've got a long drive tomorrow. We had better pack our bags."

I looked at Kim with a huge grin and said, "Not before we consummate our marriage, dear."

Kim let out a gasp and said, "Ed Costigan, you behave yourself!"

I picked Kim up in my arms and carried her into our bedroom where we made love till the sun went down.

***

Tim sat in his chair, shaking his head. "You knocked the wedding cake over?" He was trying not to smile, but it was hard not to. The wedding was a shambles.

"I know, Tim, it still makes me cringe even after all these years," I told him. I shook my head.

"What did all the wedding guests say?"

"Ah, it was terrible," I said with a wave of my hand. "I had 120 sets of eyes all bearing down on me as I sat on the floor in front of the busted-up wedding cake. I tell you, I could have curled up and died at the Camden Haven Golf Club that night I kid you not. I mean, I can see the amusing side after all these years, but I can assure you it was no laughing matter at the time. I always got on with Kim's parents, Cyril and Clare, but that night they were disgusted with my performance."

"So, how did it all pan out after you knocked the cake over?"

I laughed. "Well, it was my cousin, Sean O'Grady, who broke the ice in the end. He was always good for that. He came bounding through the crowd, shouting that Nana O'Grady had saved the best part of the cake for him, picking the top tier out of Nana's lap. Naturally, everyone started laughing. I swear it just was the ice-breaker we needed as the crowd lost it."

Tim gave me a slight smile and sat back.

"Oh, that crazy Sean," I said with a grin. "He certainly saved my hide that night and somehow, after the cake was reconstructed, we were able to cut it without any further embarrassment."

"I'm surprised Kim didn't leave you. I mean, you messed up a girl's wedding. That's grounds for a divorce."

I gave him a wry smile. "I know, but right from the very beginning of our relationship, I had an uncanny knack of using my humour to get me out of trouble with Kim. Kim loved to laugh and it did not sit well with her when she was angry for any period of time. As the years progressed I was to use my sense of humour to save my hide on countless occasions."

"So how did you get on with your honeymoon?" said Tim.

I waggled my eyebrows. "If our wedding was a total disaster, then our honeymoon was the total opposite as I romanced Kim for our entire stay on Magnetic Island. We spent the days swimming and the tropical nights dining under candlelight," I told him. I still had fond memories of that trip, even now. "It was funny though. When we got home, our family and friends were surprised to find that rather than being one step closer to divorce, we were very much in love. I had stayed off the drink for the entire length of our honeymoon and it turned out to be a beautiful time between us."

***

After we returned from our honeymoon we both knuckled down and tried to create a nice future for ourselves. All I ever wanted was a happy family life, but for some reason the wheels would always fall off and my dark side would rear its ugly head. I'd promised, even sworn on my father's grave that I'd behave, but like I said, you can take the booze out of the fruitcake, but you've still got a fruitcake.

I recall one night in particular, in early 1973, when Kim experienced the effects of my Vietnam trauma first hand.

I had a big day at work and was irritable when I got home, so I decided to go to bed early. I was clear of the drink at this stage and had fallen asleep quickly. I was sound asleep, dreaming about being on piquet duty in Vietnam, when Kim came to bed and snuggled up close to me. I immediately woke up in a panic and swung around as quick as lightening, flinging Kim out of bed and landing on top of her, pinning her to the ground.

"What do you think you're doing? Sneaking up on me like that when I'm in ambush position?" I screamed.

Kim freaked out as she had never before seen me like this. She started crying before I came to my senses and apologised. My heart was racing and I had no idea what I'd done at first, and I was filled with regret that I'd scared her. From that moment on she was always cautious about approaching me when I was sound asleep.

As time went on, Kim started to understand the triggers that would send me off, and most of the time avoided trouble, but occasionally she let her guard down and felt the consequences. I was a fruitcake, not knowing that subtracting booze wasn't my only problem.

I never hit a woman deliberately or cheated on my wife, as this was against my morals. What they missed out in physical abuse I made up with my tongue. Although I could be bright, witty, generous and charm the pants off a woman, it was my caustic tongue, especially while on the drink that would belittle them and dress them down to nothing. Kim was starting to bear the brunt of that, this strange Jekyll and Hyde show.

Kim's concerns about my drinking prior to our marriage went out the window, and I broke my promises to her. I would periodically hear the call of the wild and break out and hit the drink once again. Yet right through my life I had always had a conscience, and knew deep down inside my soul when I had done the wrong thing. I had a philosophical view on life in the sense that I believed in a creator, but that I was accountable for my actions. I had always carried the philosophy with me that one should look after those who were less fortunate than oneself. I always tried to help some poor unfortunate whether it be family, friend or stranger if they were in need, by providing them with material benefits. Then, out of the blue, I would undo all my good work by getting on the drink and performing some misdemeanor that would put me in the doghouse once again. It was like my conscience took a holiday and then it would come back with a vengeance. For me, it was a totally confusing situation which I felt like I had no control over. It constantly challenged the very essence of my manhood as I fought within myself over the drink. I thought I was weak for my lack of ability to say no, but then I would succumb to the amber fluid and it wouldn't matter until the next time.

Meanwhile, life went on and before too long Kim and I were to be preoccupied with other more important issues, as the sound of a screaming child could be heard around the Costigan household.

Michelle Erin Costigan was born on June 20, 1973. She was a beautiful girl and like her mother, she had strawberry blonde hair, a fair complexion and a beautiful smile.

Michelle's birth was like a breath of fresh air and I couldn't recall ever having so much joy in my life. The tears streamed down my face the first time I held her in my arms and it ultimately brought Kim and I closer together.

Over the years she proved to be a smart kid who loved the girly things like dressing up and helping her mum in the kitchen, as well as fishing with me in the boat or collecting oysters down by the shore of Googleys Lake. We were really tight. Michelle and I had a close bond, and I know she felt the great love I had for her.

It was the little things that I have the fondest memories of these days. She liked holding my hand when we were crossing the street, us packing her schoolbag together, or our special time each evening when I would read her a bedtime story.

Then periodically, our beautiful bond was broken, as I would hit the drink and carry on like a lunatic. Michelle would hide under the bed when I was on the drink, and when I sobered up she would call me Doctor Jekyll and Mr Hyde after one of the bedtime stories I had read her. It didn't occur to me that she was witnessing the same show as Kim.

By June of 1974, I was back on one of my periodic dry spells, although the thought of giving the grog up forever would have been inconceivable at that stage of my life.

I had not had a drink for seven months and was feeling the best I had for ages. I was working on my golf and things were good on the home front as I had the house looking spick and span and Kim could guarantee where I would be each day. This new-found stability was about to change though, and our family's life was to be turned upside down as I was about to take a look for what I thought was greener pastures.

The catalyst to this change happened in a quite unexpected way one Friday morning in June. I was tipping a load of large rocks at a bloke's property out the back of Wauchope. I was on level ground and had the hoist fully extended when the right hand rear bogie wheels sunk into the soft ground. I put the truck into gear, but it lurched to one side and all of a sudden the whole rig toppled over. I managed to brace myself inside the cabin and although I avoided any physical injury, it put the wind up me and I was fairly shaken up.

I was coming home from work later that afternoon and still had the jitters thinking about how close I had come to serious injury, when I noticed little Dicky Foster getting out of his car outside the Laurieton Hotel.

I pulled my car over and wound my window down to say g'day as I hadn't seen him all day. He'd been working at Dunbogan.

"Denis told me you rolled the truck over today, Cozzy?" Dicky said leaning on my front door as he took a drag out of his cigarette.

"You're not wrong, Dicky. It scared the shit out of me to be honest with ya. I fairdinkum thought I was going to get crushed to death."

"Yeah, mate, I know the feeling. I rolled one onto its side about ten years ago and it scared the living daylights out of me," said Dicky.

"I managed to ring Denis. He was pretty pissed off about it."

Dicky scoffed. "Fuck the truck, Cozzy, as long as you're alright that's the main thing."

Dicky asked me if I wanted to come across to the pub for a lemon squash and a yarn as he could see I was a bit jittery after the truck rollover. I thanked him, but told him I had better be on my way as it was Michelle's first birthday and I promised Kim I would be home early as we had friends coming over and I was to cook the BBQ.

I was about to drive off when to my total amazement, who should come driving down the street but Schooner Rooney. After he got out of his car he informed me with his customary quick wit that he had come across to Dunbogan for the weekend for a surprise visit for Michelle's birthday party. Schooner told me he was going into the pub for a couple of quiet beers and invited me to join him for a lemon squash. I was still a bit wary about going to the pub considering what had happened on my wedding day. It was only after Schooner assured me that we would go straight to *Lakeview* after a couple of lemon squashes that I relented and agreed to come into the pub.

When we walked into the pub I noticed Reg Kearney involved in a shout with Digger the plumber and a few other blokes. Reg had fear etched all over his face, as memories of my wedding day were still fresh in his memory. From a distance he nervously inquired if I was back on the drink, fearful that I might land a punch on him. I informed him in a defensive manner that I was not and that I would be venturing home shortly as it was Michelle's birthday.

I was talking to Schooner when who should walk in but Denis himself. He noticed me and with a scowl on his face, approached where Schooner and I were sitting. Denis had been under a bit of pressure lately as he had some financial worries with the business. As a result, he hadn't been his normal jovial self. He had been a bit testy to deal with in recent weeks and rolling the truck over had only exacerbated his already bad-tempered mood.

It didn't take long for Denis to show his displeasure for

what had happened that day at work and he proceeded to tear strips off me. A huge argument erupted between the two of us due to the fact that Denis was more concerned for his truck than my wellbeing. The argument lasted for the best part of ten minutes with the end result being that I resigned on the spot.

Denis could see that I was stirred up and after I shaped up to him, he feared the worst so he high-tailed it out of the pub. I stormed off to the toilet where I was in filthy mood with a head full of resentment. I was resentful not only because of Denis's lack of concern for me, but also because I had spent a lot of time servicing his machinery without much in the way of appreciation.

There was steam coming from out of my ears when I left the toilet and with that amount of anger twirling around the inside of my head, I went to the bar without one thought of the consequences and ordered myself a beer. I downed the beer like there was no tomorrow and bought another one.

Schooner couldn't believe it when he saw me with a beer in my hand but didn't protest. He knew I was on the wagon, but if the truth be known he always liked getting on the drink with me. I made my way to the pool table and insisted that Schooner join me for a game of doubles.

What ensured for the rest of the evening was some very heavy drinking after we won free beers as a result of holding the pool table for the duration of the night.

It wasn't long before closing time and Schooner and I were as pissed as chooks when a couple of bikies we were playing against decided to start a blue with us. They accused us of cheating which we vehemently denied. After they came for us with pool cues, we managed to knock the shit out of them with little Dicky Foster even getting in on the act with some handy haymakers. Schooner and I eventually staggered out of the pub at closing time, barely able to stand, minus a bit of skin.

I was also feeling the heat as I'd well and truly missed Michelle's birthday party.

"I am going to be up shit creek in a barbed wire boat when I get home, Schooner," I moaned.

"Don't you worry about a thing, Ed. I'll be right behind you if Kim has a go at you," mumbled Schooner.

"Has a go at me, Schooner? Has a go at me?" I slurred. "She's going to skin me alive when she sees the state I'm in. Not to mention the fact I've missed Michelle's birthday party."

Schooner left his car at the pub and travelled with me for the drive to *Lakeview*. Lucky he did because I spent most of the trip barely able to see over the steering wheel, while Schooner gave me directions from the passenger seat to home. I couldn't even remember how to get there.

When we finally arrived home and staggered up the steps of *Lakeview*, Schooner and I were so drunk that we had to support ourselves. My work shirt was covered in blood and when I turned the lounge-room light on, Kim was sitting on the sofa in her dressing gown.

"Look at the state the pair of you are in! And what's all this blood over the two of you?" she screamed.

"Easy does it, Kim, I can explain everything," I said, barely able to talk.

"Easy does it, Ed!" she snapped. "I invited a dozen guests over for tonight's birthday celebrations and you were suppose to cook the BBQ. Instead, poor old Dad had to do the honours while you were busy getting on the grog with Schooner. I've never been so embarrassed in all my life!" Kim screamed.

Before I could get another word in, Schooner decided to

butt in, which rather than helping the situation made matters worse. "Kim, Ed rolled the truck over today and he was under a lot of stress and I don't blame him for getting back on the drink."

"Rolled the truck over?" Kim said in a state of shock.

"That's right, I rolled it over and the truck's stuffed and to make matters worse that brother of yours tore strips off me." I was rambling now. "What a bastard! After all I've done for him servicing his machinery and the like. Not one thank-you. I've had enough, Kim, so I quit my job."

She gave me an icy glare. "You what?"

I waved a pompous hand. "You heard me right. I pulled the pin. I don't need to cop this sort of crap from an unappreciative prick like Denis."

"Are you mad, Ed? You've got a perfectly good job with Denis and you've thrown it all away!" Kim yelled.

Schooner interjected. "Mind you, Kim, Denis was pretty heavy handed with Ed."

"You butt out, Pat," Kim barked.

"It's okay, Schooner, I've got this under control, mate," I said.

Kim glared at me. "Under control, Ed? Under control. Oh, this is a catastrophe. First thing tomorrow morning you're going to front up to Denis and ask for your job back. Do you hear me, Ed Costigan?"

"Not on your life!" I bellowed.

What followed was an argument for the next ten minutes with neither Kim or I giving an inch.

Just when the argument was at fever pitch, Michelle started to cry from inside our bedroom where she had been asleep.

"Look what you've done, you couple of ratbags," said Kim

in a rage. "Michelle was sound asleep and now you've gone and woken her."

"Perhaps Uncle Schooner can read her a bedtime story," said Schooner, as he walked towards Michelle's bedroom.

"You keep the hell out of Michelle's bedroom, Pat Rooney!" Kim screamed.

I realised that things were at a breaking point, so I motioned to Schooner that we should make tracks for the downstairs bedroom which I knew would put us out of the path of Kim.

It was mid-morning when I eventually awoke. I looked across to the single bed beside mine and noticed that Schooner had already left. "Wise move, Schooner. There's going to be hell to pay when I get upstairs and face Kim," I said out aloud.

I staggered out of bed, my head throbbing and my mouth as dry as the bottom of a cocky's cage. I got dressed and as I made my way upstairs I said to myself, "Better go and face the music, Cozzy!"

I was in the kitchen, boiling the kettle and preparing myself a cup of tea when Kim entered the room with Michelle in her arms.

"Hello, sweetie," I said to Michelle.

Michelle started to cry and Kim glared at me, shaking her head. "See what your drinking does, Ed? It upsets the entire household."

"Relax, Kim. Michelle's just hungry that's all," I said.

Kim looked at me long and hard before she said. "Well?"

"Well, what?" I said with a confused look.

"Well, are you going to go and see Denis and ask for your job back?"

"No, fuck him, Kim!"

"Don't you swear in this household, Ed Costigan. Especially in front of your daughter," Kim said pointing her finger at me.

I ignored her. "I'm not going to see Denis, Kim. Bugger him! I don't need to work for a bloke who doesn't appreciate all I've done for him."

"Ed, you know that Denis has been under a lot of pressure lately with the business. You know he really appreciates all you do for him. He just finds it hard to say it. Besides we've got bills to pay and a daughter to look after and we've been talking about having another child. What do expect us to live on? Thin air?" demanded Kim.

I looked at Kim long and hard before I said, "Na, Kim, bugger him. I've made up my mind. I'm not going back."

My pride was so strong at this time of my life that there was no way I could go to Denis, cap in hand, and ask for my job back.

Kim looked exasperated, shaking her head, and with a sigh said, "Why do you always break your promise not to drink, Ed?"

I was stunned into silence. I hadn't expected her to get straight to the point. "It's this party town, Kim. Maybe we need a fresh start away from all the people that keep dragging me back onto the drink."

"Where do you suggest we move?"

I sighed. "Kim, I was talking to Stumpy on the phone a few weeks ago, and in the midst of the conversation he mentioned a bloke from Dubbo named Rex Wilson who owns a transport business."

"And?" Kim said with a bewildered look.

"Stumpy told me that Rex's business was growing rapidly

and he was looking for blokes who owned their own semi-trailers to subcontract to him."

"What are you saying, Ed?"

"After I spoke to Stumpy, it got me thinking about buying my own rig," I said quietly, "and heading back out west."

"You want to go to Dubbo?' Kim said with a look of angst.

"Absolutely. Look, I've still got enough cash left over from the sale of my Poseidon shares. I could buy my own semi-trailer and if we sold *Lakeview*, we could buy a house on a few acres. What do you think? I could be my own boss," I said. I was really excited by the prospect.

The look on her face didn't mirror my own though.

"No way, Ed," she said, shaking her head. She looked concerned. "This is my home and all my family and friends are in this area."

"Kim, I'm sick to death of working for somebody else, and as much as Denis has been good to me, the way he spoke to me on Friday afternoon really annoyed me. I didn't trash the rig, it was an accident. They happen. He didn't have to turn on me." I sighed and gave her a serious look. "I know he's your brother and he's a good bloke, but I've run my race here and I just feel inside my bones that it's time to move on."

"And what would I do out there, Ed?" she asked. She didn't like the idea at all.

I gave her a thoughtful look. "Well, since you're not teaching and you're at home looking after Michelle, how about running the books? Doing the admin."

"Run the books," she said flatly. "I wouldn't have the faintest idea of how to run a business."

I smiled at her. "You're a smart girl and I'm sure you could work it out." Flattery had always worked wonders with Kim. "Besides, they have a great 18 hole golf course out there…"

Kim rolled her eyes. "Trying to butter me up, are you?"

"Come on, Kim," I cajoled. "It's a great opportunity to sow a little nest egg for the future. Besides, it'll keep me off the drink because I'll be too busy at work to be boozing on."

"Do you mean it, Ed?" She gave me a hesitant look.

I took her hand. "Absolutely. It'll be just what the doctor ordered. No more boozing. I'll knuckle down and establish the business."

I spoke to Kim for the next few hours, trying to convince her of all the advantages of setting up my own business.

Finally, she looked me straight in the eyes and after what seemed like an eternity, she said, "If you reckon going to Dubbo will keep you on the straight and narrow, then yes, I'll agree, because I'm at my wits end of how to stop you going on your benders."

I felt flooded with relief. "Thanks, Kim. I'll guarantee you won't regret it."

Finally, I would have the opportunity to really make something of myself, and despite all the turmoil in our lives revolving around my drinking, Kim still loved me and she desperately wanted to save our marriage. She agreed to move out west, albeit reluctantly, as all her family and friends were based around the small community we lived in.

***

"I wasn't all bad you know, Tim. At least, in general. I might have been walking a dangerous line, but others were doing really well."

"How so?"

"Well, our move out to Dubbo also coincided with Rowy and Julie McCabe getting married in July, 1974. They'd held off getting married as they were saving to buy a property, but they eventually found an old fibro house in Sutherland. Rowy asked me to be his best man and I was on my best behaviour for the duration of the reception, drinking lemon squash for the entire night. I didn't want to jeopardise our move out to Dubbo by getting on the piss and blowing it with Kim after all my hard work convincing her to go out west."

Tim snorted. "He got married? That was the only good thing?"

"Well, there was more than that," I told him. "Rowy was mortgaged up to his eyeballs, but he wanted to start his own business. When we got back from Vietnam, I'd introduced Rowy to an old Polish Jew named Josek Warski who ran a textile manufacturing business next door to Steel's Transport. I had known Josek for a number of years and the old bugger was a very wealthy man." I gave Tim a look. "No small feat considering that all of his family had been exterminated by the Nazis in Auschwitz. He arrived in Australia in the early 1950s with next to no money and a battered old suitcase. Anyway, Josek offered Rowy all of his excavation work on a set of industrial units he was building at Campbelltown, but only if he had the machinery. Like I say, Rowy was in it up to his eyeballs and was a bit short. He knew about my Poseidon windfall and so when he needed $5,000 for a decent backhoe, I gave it to him. He refused, naturally, but he was my best mate, and I wanted to see him get started in the world. From little things, big things grow, Tim," I said. "Rowy's earthmoving business out at Campbelltown became a very successful enterprise indeed."

"So you leant him the money," said Tim, almost disbelieving, "even though you were about to buy yourself a semi-trailer?" He looked bewildered.

"I did," I nodded. "I'm not telling you that story to big note myself, just to note the fact that Rowy never forgot my generosity. When the shit really hit the fan later on, Rowy stayed true to me, even got a roof over my head when I had less than nothing. What might seem like a little thing to us, can be a big deal for someone else. Besides, I had saved his life in Vietnam. Dragged him out of the jungle when he'd been shot and the Yanks were about to drop the heat, and Rowy never forgot that."

Tim nodded his head in agreement. He looked thoughtful.

I smiled at the younger man. "You see, Tim, that was the great paradox of my life. I could do an absolute bastard of an act like miss my own daughter's first birthday and ruin my wedding, and then lend a mate some money in the next instance. It used to totally perplex me, as I knew I was capable of great acts of generosity and equally great acts of bastardry." I shook my head. "It kept me in a very confused state of mind for years."

***

I contacted Rex and told him I was interested in buying a rig and contracting to him, and he offered me one of his prime movers, a 1971 F model Mack, for a really good price. On my first weekend back out west, I met with him, and both Stumpy and Noel were there also, so they could also inspect the rig with me.

Rex Wilson was a large, thickset man in his early thirties who had an easygoing nature. He had been born and bred in Dubbo and owned three prime movers which pulled both semi-trailers and roadtrains locally and to Darwin. Rex's younger brother, Donny, also worked for him, usually pulling a double roadtrain on the Dubbo to Darwin leg.

"Well, it looks tidy enough, Ed, but you're the mechanic, so I'll let you make the final decision," said Stumpy, as he walked around the primemover.

"It looks like everything is in order, Stumpy," I said as I looked at the motor with the cabin tilted. "There doesn't appear to be any water loss in the radiator and the head gasket appears to be okay."

"Any oil loss, Ed?" said Noel.

"Nah, it appears to be okay in that department also."

After inspecting the truck for another hour, I agreed on a sale and the four of us spent another hour talking to Rex about his business.

That night at Coorigil the family were having a cup of tea and a yarn in the lounge-room after dinner.

"He's a pretty straight-up bloke is Rex, Ed. As long as you do the right thing by him and be of sober habits he'll look after you," Stumpy said, giving me a pointed look.

If only Stumpy could have foreseen the future, he would have eaten his words on the spot. The very thing I promised Kim I wouldn't do when I got to Dubbo, I was to indulge myself in ten-fold.

In July 1974, we moved from Dunbogan and were living in a rented house in Dubbo while we found a buyer for *Lakeview*. It wasn't until October that we purchased a 100 acre property five kilometres out of Dubbo on the Narromine road. It consisted of a three-bedroom home with wide verandahs and a large iron shed which became the base for my business, named *Costigan's*

Transport. I was sad to sell *Lakeview* because I had enjoyed living there, but I was optimistic about the future.

I had enough left over cash to buy myself a 1969 HT Holden Monaro with a GTS 350 V8 under the bonnet. Its black and red colour made it the envy of all the petrol heads in town, and cured any lingering regrets I had from selling our dwelling at Dunbogan.

Rex soon had me very busy carting everything from cattle, sheep, hay and everything in between, to places as far flung as Bourke, Wilcannia, Coonamble, Walgett, Parkes and Condobolin, to mention just a few.

I soon learnt to enjoy the solitude of the open road and the huge distances that went with it. It was on one of these trips out to Wilcannia that I bought a Blue Healer pup which I name Snog. In the years that followed, Snog was to become my constant companion and I never went on a trip without him. I became very attached to my dog and he became my great mate as I drove through many isolated areas of the outback.

Within no time at all, I got my roadtrain licence and this saw me making regular trips from Dubbo to Darwin. It was also the start of my boozing while on the road as I was out of Kim's sight for long periods of time. I didn't even think twice about it. I wasn't around Kim, so where was the harm?

Clearly, if I thought moving out to Dubbo would cure me from my alcoholic tendencies, I was deadset wrong because it did nothing of the sort. All I did was take myself with me. As time went on I turned into an even bigger pisshead, and I also developed a nice little addiction to pills to keep me awake while on the road.

I was rarely at home, and as a result I saw most of Australia, including the aftermath of Cyclone Tracy.

Chapter 9

Early January, 1975, Darwin, Northern Territory

I T WAS EARLY morning when I first saw the complete devastation that Cyclone Tracy had wreaked upon Darwin. My double roadtrain was loaded with an assortment of freight which included beer, tobacco, guns, car tyres and bags of potatoes which I was due to drop off at a Government stores facility where my contact was some army captain.

As I drove through the suburbs, my mouth was fixed open. I had never seen anything like it. There was nothing left standing as house after house had been totally destroyed by the sheer force of the wind. Telegraph poles had sheets of mangled corrugated iron wrapped around the tops of them, while there were wires down and strewn all across the roadway. Everywhere there was twisted debris, and it looked as though hell had visited earth.

As I drove along through the near deserted streets, I noticed a woman in her early thirties sitting in the gutter, crying uncontrollably. In front of her was a white Renault sedan with its right hand front wheel bent outwards and its boot lid up.

For some reason, this battered old car is one of the strongest images I have of Cyclone Tracy. The memory has stayed with me all these years.

I stopped my rig I walked over to where she was sitting. "You right there, love?"

She looked up, surprised to see me standing in front of her, so I sat down beside her and wrapped my arm around her shoulders.

She wiped the tears from her eyes. "The police have just shot my dog."

I was horrified. "What? They just shot your dog? Why?"

"They don't want any dogs walking around scavenging food, so they're rounding them up and shooting them," she said through more tears.

"Crikey, that's severe," I said to her as I patted her back.

"I lost my husband and only child in the cyclone, and the family dog was the last reminder I had of them. I've come back to see if there was anything left on the property and there he was! Cowering in the bathroom."

Apparently, no sooner had she retrieved the dog that the police had taken it away and disposed of it. Her sobbing was uncontrollable and I felt bad for her. The poor lady had suffered too much. I pulled out my wallet, grabbed two $50 notes and handed them to her. She looked bewildered, but grateful at the same time. She wasn't above accepting charity and I could feel the relief steaming off her.

"Thank you very much," she said through muffled sobs. "You're a very kind and decent man."

"That's okay, love," I said, giving her a hug. "It's the least I can do after all you've been through."

"What's your name?" she asked, wiping the tears from her face.

"Ed Costigan."

"Who do you work for?"

I smiled at her. "I work for myself. See the writing on the door of my truck? It says, *"Costigan's Transport Dubbo."*

"Well, Ed, you're a fine man. Thank you for your generosity."

"You're welcome, love." I spent the next 30 minutes with the lady and tried to console her the best I could, considering the dire circumstances facing her, and then I said, "I had better be off now, as I have to deliver these goods."

"Thank you, Ed. I will never forget your kindness."

"You sure you'll be alright, love?" I said. The poor thing was a wreck and I was hesitant to leave her.

"Yes, thank you, I'll be alright. I feel a bit better now."

I smiled and bade her farewell. As I drove down the road I looked into my side mirror at the devastated figure I had left behind and my heart went out to her. That night I talked to Rowy on the phone and shared with him what I had witnessed. I needed to talk to a familiar voice, as what I saw in the aftermath of the cyclone had affected me greatly. It actually brought back memories of Vietnam, as I compared the carnage that I saw in the steaming jungles to the wreck that was Darwin. I knew Rowy would understand. And he did. Chatted half the night, we did.

Eventually, I drove into the Government Supply Depot, which by all accounts was a busy establishment before the cyclone, but now it resembled a dilapidated ghost town. I could see a lone figure in the distance wearing a sweat-stained Australian officer's uniform, standing in front of the remains of a large storage shed. All that was left was the building's stumps. There was debris strewn all across the yard.

As I drove closer to the lone figure, I suddenly realised that he looked familiar to me. As I pulled the rig up and stepped out of the cabin I was met with the wry smile of none other than my old platoon commander from Vietnam, Lieutenant Paul Geraghty.

"Private Costigan reporting for duty, skip," I said, snapping a lightning quick salute at him.

"Bloody hell, Ed Costigan. I hardly recognised you!" he said, looking me up and down. "You've gone and grown your hair all long! Gee, you packed some weight on, too. Looks like you're in a good paddock or you've been sucking on a schooner or three."

I looked down to the ground and shuffled my feet. "Steady on, skip."

"I kept tabs on you, Costigan. You finally won the title you kept talking about," said Geraghty.

"I did. I nailed the little bastard, but unfortunately it cost me my boxing career."

"I know, I read it in the newspaper. I was sorry to hear it, Cozzy. I honestly thought you could have gone all the way to a world title."

"So did I," I said with a melancholy look. "Still, I shouldn't be too disappointed. I ended up marrying Schooner Rooney's cousin and since then we've had a little baby girl."

Geraghty shook my hand. "Congratulations, Ed!"

"Thanks, skip," I grinned.

"How's the rest of the boys?"

"Rowy's in the earthmoving game and Schooner's still

out at Condobilin, working in his old man's stock and station business."

"What about Finno?"

"Disappeared off the face of the earth. Nobody's heard a thing about him, except he was supposed to be in Queensland somewhere working with a shearing team."

"Too bad. You know you boys showed a lot of guts that day on the Battle of the Bunkers. I always reckon Finno should have received a gong for his efforts, but Major Milroy wouldn't have anything of it."

I gave Geraghty a look of disdain. "That arsehole! I remember the time I had to stay behind and make his bed and iron his shirts while the rest of the platoon was out on patrol. What a pedantic bastard!"

Geraghty nodded his head in agreement but said nothing.

There was a lull in the conversation before I asked, "What about you skip? What have you been up to since arriving home from Vietnam? You look like you've gone ahead in the world!" I said, looking at the insignia on his uniform.

He nodded. "I'm a captain now, Cozzy. I've been at Canungra since I got back, then I was sent up here on Boxing Day to help with the relief effort after Tracy went through."

Some soldiers came along and helped us unload the two trailers of freight by hand. I had a busy schedule, as I was to load a small crane onto the rig that was due to go back to Dubbo, and then on to Sydney from there.

While I was unloading the trailers, Snog had jumped out of the cabin of the Mack and had gone for a wander, ending up somewhere outside the dilapidated perimeter fence. Just as I was finishing loading the crane, I heard him let out a yelp and as I looked across in the distance I could see that a police officer had grabbed him and was carrying him to the boot of his police car.

"Hey, what do ya think ya doing?" I yelled.

By this stage I had climbed off the back of the trailer and jogged the 200 metres or so across the yard to where the cop had Snog. "Hey!" I was breathing hard and sweat was dripping from my forehead.

"Who do you think you're talking to?" he said to me aggressively,

"I'm talking to you, arsehole," I snapped. "You've got my fucking dog."

"I don't care if he's your dog, there are no dogs allowed on the streets. I'm going to have to put him down."

What followed was a heated exchange between the cop and I which ended up with him drawing his gun on me. I threw my hands up, but didn't stop my shouting. Nor did he.

"Now back off, sport, or I'll shoot both you and the dog!" the cop was yelling.

Geraghty walked over and his calm tone and uniform seemed to ease the situation. "I think we can sort this out before somebody gets killed," he said to the both of us. He noticed a Vietnam service medal on the pocket of the police officer's shirt. "Vietnam Veteran, are you?" Geraghty said to the cop casually, pointing at the medal.

"Yeah, that's right, captain," said the cop, his gun lowering.

"What unit were you in?"

"Military Police."

"Ha, I might have bloody well known you were one of those wankers," I said with a sarcastic laugh.

"What are you talking about you long-haired smartarse?"

"Put it this way, sunshine, when I was out in the jungle getting shot at you were back at The Dat in a warm bed with three hot meals and a warm shower. No doubt you were probably in the Boozer getting pissed."

He scoffed at me. "You don't look like you were in Vietnam, you dreg."

Geraghty placed a hand on my shoulder before I exploded. "I'd be real careful what you say to this man, officer. Despite his appearances, this man was indeed in Vietnam."

"You're joking, captain," said the cop with a look of disdain.

"I was his platoon commander," he said to the cop with a wry smile. "Not only was he a good soldier who did his country proud, but he was also a champion boxer."

"Hmph! He doesn't look like a soldier's arsehole. What did you win?" the cop said to me with an icy stare.

"The Australian middleweight title," I snapped.

The colour went out of the cop's face as he realised that Geraghty and I had him snookered. I could almost see him trying to figure out if he should arrest me, but with the might of Australian military behind me there was no way!

"I'll have my dog back, thanks," I said, staring at him.

He handed Snog over, embarrassed, but knowing when to cut his losses.

My impish streak came back. "Now give the officer a big lick on the face, Snoggy," I said with a laugh, as Snog, not really caring about much but pats and the attention, went to lick him happily.

"Keep that dog away from me," said the cop, before he abruptly about-faced and made a hasty retreat.

"So long, constable!" I called after him, putting Snog back in the cabin of the Mack roadtrain.

That night, Geraghty and I relived old times. We talked

about Vietnam and spoke about the devastation of the cyclone, as we hit the booze together in the temporary army barracks where his unit was stationed. I wasn't in the best of condition to drive the next morning when I hopped into my rig for the trip back to Dubbo.

"Are you sure you're alright to drive, Ed?" said Geraghty, giving me a doubtful look.

"She's apples, skip!" I told him, ignoring my own conscience telling me that I wasn't.

I hit the road anyway with a breakfast that consisted of a Darwin stubby.

About three months after that trip to Darwin, Kim showed me a letter I received when I got home from work one day. She was smiling, so I looked inside. There was a short note and a cash cheque for two hundred dollars.

Dear Ed,

Thank you for your kind deed after Cyclone Tracy. Words will never be able to express how much your generosity meant, considering the state I was in. You will always have my gratitude.

Yours sincerely,

Beverly Dewhurst

Henley Beach, Adelaide

***

I smiled at Tim. "I never told Kim about the lady in Darwin

until we received the letter in the mail. She liked the fact that I had been so generous and it gave me a lot of brownie points."

"Like making regular deposits into your bank account, so you could make a withdrawal down the track," said Tim.

I laughed. "Yeah, spot on, mate. I was like that you know. I'd mow the lawns or do some work around house to get Kim on side before I tied a big one on."

Tim gave me a slight grin. He seemed to identify with what I was saying.

"Kim would know I was trying to get on her good side and would say, 'Are you planning to tie a big one on?' I'd be really pissed off because sometimes I was just trying to do the right thing and then I'd blow it and get on the piss." I shook my head. "It was a diabolical situation. My life swung from opposite ends of the spectrum from extreme generosity to acts of bastardry."

Tim gave me a moment and then observed, "So you left Darwin in a bad way."

"Yep. It was on the road that I did the most of my drinking."

***

I drove that Mack road train from Dubbo to Darwin nearly non-stop for the next two years as the huge task of rebuilding the city took place. The city had orders for everything. You name it, I transported it. From bricks to booze it was non-stop, with Snog by my side all the way. I spent more time on the road than I did at home, and like the tide turning, my alcohol consumption rose to dangerous levels.

On one of my trips back from Darwin in early 1976, I had just arrived back in Dubbo after being on the road for sixteen days straight when Rex got me to pick up a load of sheep just near Cobar on the Barrier Highway.

I was dog-tired when I left Dubbo carrying a stock float. After loading the sheep, I was on a dirt road heading back towards Nyngan when I fell asleep at the wheel, went off the road and almost ploughed head first into a huge gum tree. I was fortunate that I had stopped on solid ground. Memories of my truck rollover while working for Denis Rooney came flooding back to me and I was a fairly shaken up.

I was able to get back on the road with no damage to the truck and decided to stop in at the pub in Nyngan to have a few beers to settle my nerves.

While I was in the pub I got talking to another truckie and told him of my narrow escape after falling asleep at the wheel.

"I've got just the ticket for you, old son," he said, rummaging through the pocket of his shorts. He produced an assortment of pills. "There you go, mate, get these into you."

For a bloke who had knocked around a bit, I was naïve as to what drugs were around. In some ways, I was a total conservative. Drugs were the epitomy of evil. In my eyes, booze, although dangerous, was acceptable, but drugs of any sort were a no-no.

"What are these?' I asked inquisitively.

"Stimulants."

"Stimulants? Mate, I hate fuckin' drugs and I hate drug pushers," I said, waving my hands in front of him, trying to rid of him.

"Steady on, old son," he said calmly. "These aren't hard drugs. These just to give you a bit of a kick while you're out on the highway."

I paused. A little pick-me-up sounded okay. "What are they then?" I asked.

"Mephedrone and tenuates, but we call them by their

slang names—shakers or Queensland Smarties," he said with a wry smile.

I eyed him off with a look of contempt. Queensland Smarties!

"Look, mate," said the bloke, "you don't have to take the whole lot at once. Keep 'em in the cab and if you're feeling a bit drowsy then take one. I'll guarantee they'll give you the lift you need."

When I thought about going off the road, I was sold. I held out my hand out and he rolled a dozen pills into it. He gave me a knowing look.

"Mate, if you're doing that Dubbo to Darwin run on a regular basis, you'll find these things are your best friend out on the highway." He finished of his middy of beer and walked out of the pub.

I sat in my chair looking around the pub warily, before stuffing the multi-coloured pills into the pocket of my shirt.

It was about a week after that I tried my first shaker. I was out near Blackall, in central Queensland, and on my way to Darwin once again. I was feeling the pinch as I had been on the road for a considerable amount of time.

I looked at the pill for some time and then at Snog, who was watching me curiously, before swallowing the pill, ably assisted by a bottle of beer. After a few minutes, I looked at my trusty pooch and said, "Well, I haven't felt the world fall in yet, Snog, so I suppose we'll just keep driving and see what happens."

It was a bit further down the road when I felt the pill kick in. I was wide awake and making a mile as I had my pedal to the metal, Darwin bound. I remember feeling over the moon with the incredible alertness the pills provided, and then my addictive personality kicked in and I was sold.

Within a very short period of time I became a regular user of the stimulants. When I used them, I found myself able to drive long distances with less sleep. At first I only used them sparingly, but as the years went by I became a heavy user. Later, the mixture of booze and pills proved to be a disastrous duo.

Although my drinking and drug use were on the increase, I was making a quid out of the business and although we were far from rich, the family never wanted for anything. I made sure that Michelle was spoiled rotten.

Kim knew that I was back on the scoot while out on the highway, but turned a blind eye to my activities as I was sober most of the time while at home. She was happy that I was able to spend time with Michelle, and she could see a powerful bound existed between father and daughter. I was there for Michelle's first day at kindergarten, which prompted Kim to remark to me, "If I could only bottle your good side, Ed, and sell it to the world. I'd be a millionaire."

This was usually followed by the negative remark.

"As for your dark side, it would surely scare the pants of Satan himself if you two ever met."

Despite any doubts, we were able to get back to the coast and have regular holidays where I introduced Michelle to fishing. She loved it, and it was where Kim felt most comfortable. She'd been settled in Dubbo, but she was a coast girl at heart. She got to see all of her family and friends and really indulge in her great passion of playing golf.

For me, it was the only time that I played golf or fished. Work kept me busy most of the time, so I didn't get much in the way of leisure time around Dubbo. My great lure to entice Kim to move to Dubbo was golf, but it never eventuated as a regular activity as my drinking and work trumped it most of the time. I could count on one hand the amount of times I played golf while living in Dubbo. Kim would often remark sarcastically, "Oh, the amount of golf you're playing, Ed, is certainly doing wonders for your handicap. No one could ever accuse you of being a burglar in that department."

The snarky comments were all that I really had to complain about, as were both really excited by our decision to have another child, and in March 1978, Kim gave birth to a little boy. I cried, just like I did at Michelle's birth, and I knew the moment I saw him that my life was complete. We were so happy and Michelle was excited to have a little brother, but tragedy was to strike.

We were all devastated when he died of cot death at just one week old.

We had named him Raymond John Costigan after my late father. This was something that Kim never fully recovered from, and in retrospect was the catalyst that saw our relationship start to take a nose dive. Kim desperately wanted to have another child, as she saw the family as the main component that kept our marriage together.

For me, it was very painful as I desperately wanted a boy to carry on the Costigan surname. My alcohol consumption increased after my infant son's death, and Kim didn't do much to curb it. I just didn't know how to come to terms with a loss that struck at the very core of my being. Drinking was the only thing that kept me from falling to pieces. It kept me functional.

I spoke to Stumpy regularly after young Ray's death, trying to seek solace in his wisdom.

"Sometimes there are things on this earth that are beyond our comprehension. All we can do is hand these things over to the Almighty and ask for the strength to get through it," Stumpy said to me one day.

Stumpy, although a knockabout bloke, was a man of deep spiritual conviction, something which had been sown in the midst of the carnage he had witnessed during the great war. At that stage of my life, I did not share his philosophical views. I felt that I had been cheated by a god I had come to vehemently distrust. Unknowingly, Stumpy had poked the bear.

"It's easy for you to say, Stumpy, he's not your kid," I snapped, my civility at breaking point.

"Ed, I'm only trying to share with you my own way of comprehending such a tragedy. I am not trying to hurt you, rather aid you through your period of bereavement," he said calmly.

"Yeah, we'll just leave it at that," I said tersely before hanging up the phone abruptly. At the time I'd forgotten that Stumpy himself had lost a son.

It was one of the few arguments that Stumpy and I had. Despite me needing his consolation, I couldn't handle his reaction. As a result, I carried a resentment for the old man to the point where I didn't really talk to him for some time.

I know that young Ray's death affected the rest of the family, especially Mum, who always felt incredibly close to her grandchildren. Mum was also of the opinion that a son would be just the ticket I needed for a more stable home life, but she too was ignorant of my deeper malady.

It was after my argument with Stumpy that my intake of pills started to increase with serious side effects. One incident in particular scared the living daylights out of me.

It was around November of 1978 and I left Dubbo one evening bound for Darwin. I had loaded myself up with shakers before leaving and washed it down with half a bottle of port.

I had been working hard and was tired, so I gave myself some extra pills to give me a lift.

I was crossing the Darling River at Bourke, well after midnight, when I stopped the roadtrain in the middle of the bridge. I swore that I could see pink elephants crossing the road, and it was only after the bloke in the roadtrain behind mine stopped his rig and climbed up the step of my Mack that I realised all was not right.

"What's going on, mate?" I said aggressively, still freaked about the bloody elephants.

"What the fuck are you doing stopped in the middle of the bridge? You're blocking the whole bloody highway, ya dickhead," he growled at me.

"You don't expect me to drive across the bridge when there's pink elephants on it, do ya?" I yelled at him. I pointed out my window.

The truck driver looked at me in astonishment, then looked at the road in front of us with an amazed expression on his face. He turned back to me and shook his head. "Mate, you're a fuckin' shot duck. There's nothing on the bridge except oxygen. Here, get out of the driver's seat before ya kill somebody and let me move your rig off the bridge."

He pulled up my rig on the other side of the bridge at north Bourke, bundled me back in the cab and he took off. I sat talking to Snog, off my head hallucinating for the best part of four hours before continuing my journey. It wasn't until later that I realised just how bad it was, but worse was still to come.

The scariest incident that happened to me was in between Cammoweal and Mt Isa one night when I pulled the road train up in the middle of the highway and disconnected the prime mover from my three trailers. In my drug induced state, I thought I was back at home in my trucking yard after finishing a trip from Darwin. I had actually pulled the Mack into a parking bay beside the highway and gone to sleep while I left the three trailers parked in the middle of the Barkly Highway. Another roadtrain driver travelling up the highway almost slammed into the back of the trailers before coming to a screeching halt just in the nick of time. It took him a while to convince me that I was in the middle of Australia, and not back in Dubbo.

I just wasn't with it and with my ever-increasing substance intake I started to become oblivious to what was going on around me. Like the time just before Easter in 1979, when I was in between Winton and the small town of Kyuna in Central Queensland. A bloke in a roadtrain passing me, contacted me on the radio to tell me that I was missing a wheel off my back trailer. I had been driving for kilometres and hadn't noticed it was missing.

I pulled the road train up and left Snog in the Mack while I walked down the road to look for the stray wheel. It was half an hour before I eventually found it lying in a table drain just off the side of the road. I rolled the wheel onto the shoulder of the road and sat on it while I waited for a passing motorist. I had been sitting in the blazing sun for about 15 minutes when a white Mini Minor pulled up with a local called Marie Edwards behind the wheel.

Marie and her husband Jock owned the pub at Kyuna which was situated five kilometres down the road. They were good friends of mine since I was a regular customer of theirs on my trips up to Darwin. I asked Marie if it was possible for Jock to bring his ute out so as to pick up the wheel, and in the meantime, bring me a hot feed with a bottle of beer because I was starving. I was in luck. It was lunchtime and the pub was busy serving meals and within 20 minutes Jock and Marie's daughter, Denise, arrived back in the Mini Minor with her black poodle, Shadow, by her side. Denise had a rump steak and veggies and an icy cold bottle of XXXX beer for my dinner. She informed me that her dad would be out shortly in his ute, to take me and the tyre back to my rig before leaving.

In the meantime I was sitting on the tyre, tucking into my delicious steak while swigging away on a bottle of beer, oblivious to the ludicrous sight I must have appeared to any passing motorist. A HG Holden station wagon towing a caravan pulled up alongside me. Inside the car was presumably Mum, Dad and three kids, and by the look on their faces, I could see that they were apprehensive about speaking to me.

"G'day. It's bloody stinker of a day, isn't it?" I said.

They nodded in unison, watching me warily.

As I sat there dressed in my blue shearer's singlet, shorts and thongs, I said to them with a chuckle, "Geez, this is a top feed."

By this stage their eyes were as big as dinner plates. I got off the tyre to approach their car when they simultaneously locked their doors and the dad planted his foot on the accelerator and they took off like a bat out of hell.

It was part of a slow unravelling of my sense of reality and how I had become detached from it.

Despite my dependence on booze and shakers, our business continued to grow over the next few years, in no small part due to Kim's diligence in the office. If the truth be known, she was the real brains behind the day to day running of the business, always managing to secure work while I sat behind the wheel of the truck and kept the rig moving.

It was December of 1981 when Annie came to stay with

us for a few days. She was still working as a nurse at St Vincent's Hospital in Sydney. Turned out she was engaged and was excited to share the news with everyone.

"I'm 29 and finally getting married," she said, beaming at Kim and I.

"It couldn't have happened to a nicer girl, Annie," said Kim, planting a kiss on her cheek.

"I'm so happy," said Anne with a smile. "Bill is the loveliest man you could ever wish to meet."

Anne had met Bill Kennedy while he was playing number eight for the Randwick first grade rugby side, and their relationship had flourished in the social events around the club. He also worked as a surgeon at Royal Prince Alfred Hospital in Sydney (RPA). I had met him on a number of family occasions prior to the engagement and found him to be a decent bloke. He fell on his feet when he met Annie, for she was not only a beautiful woman but lovely too. She always had been.

Two days after Anne arrived she was still excited about her impending wedding, and she was especially happy to see her favourite niece, but she was concerned about my wellbeing and didn't waste any time in telling me so. She'd been the most worried about me after young Ray's death, too.

"Perhaps you should ease up on the long hours you're spending behind the wheel, Ed," she said to me one evening.

"I've got it covered, Annie," I told her. "I've just purchased a Kenworth truck."

"How's that going to help the situation, Ed?" She frowned at me.

"Dan's going to come and work for me and drive the Dubbo to Darwin leg while I look after all the other truck work in the new rig. I'll do local stuff."

My younger brother Dan had been working for a transport company in Narromine, but I had always promised him that if I ever purchased another truck he would have first digs at driving it. Dan gladly accepted my offer when I asked him to come and work for me.

This still did not impress Annie. "I'm worried for you, Ed. I think you should lay off the booze or whatever else you're on."

"Listen Annie, everything's okay, and besides, it's of no concern to you," I snapped.

Anne started to tear up and I felt guilty. I gave her a hug and said to her, "I know you've always cared for me Annie, and I appreciate it, but I'm okay. Please just trust me."

Years later, Anne told me that she felt in her bones that some impending disaster was to fall upon me in the future. If only I'd been willing to listen.

By this stage of my life I was a workaholic, and as much as I thought I loved my wife and child, it was my business that increasingly came first. I thought that by providing food and shelter for them I'd done all that was needed to secure their love and approval. Everything revolved around trucks and I spent the majority of my time either in them or around them.

One hot summer night, just before Christmas in 1981, as if fulfilling Anne's intuition, I was 35 years of age and had never been beaten in a fight in or outside of the ring. Although I was long past my prime as a champion boxer, I could still handle myself. I could still throw a handy combination, albeit my broken hand was always in the back of my mind. I had always carried an air of confidence about me because of my ability as a fighter, but this was to come crashing to the ground.

On this particular Saturday night I decided to venture

down to The Buncha in Dubbo. The Buncha wasn't for the faint-hearted as it was a place where you could be guaranteed to get a fight, a fuck or a feed, depending on what you were partial to. It derived its name from the fact that if you didn't behave yourself, then you were likely to get a 'bunch of' fives to the head.

That night, I got a pasting off a young Aboriginal brickie named Lenny Walker after I spilt his beers and wouldn't repay him. Lenny Walker punched the living daylights out of me, and I could do nothing. I even damaged my wrist again. I didn't get a bunch of fives, more like a bunch of five hundreds as Lenny made mincemeat out of me.

For me, it was a big reality check and I laid low for a long time, not daring to enter The Buncha for fear of ridicule. After 'The Big Blue', as it became known, I went on one of my periodic dry spells where I stayed off the grog for a number of months while I recovered from my injuries. I thought I'd fulfilled Annie's prophecy, but there was more to come.

It was at Anne and Bill's wedding at Gilgandra in March of 1982 where I busted once again from my dry spell. I had every intention of behaving myself, but once the grog started flowing at the wedding reception I was like a bee to a honey pot and got myself well and truly ironed out.

Kim, by this stage, had given up trying to talk to me as she knew it was pointless. My performance at my sister's wedding was the beginning of the end of my marriage. Long gone were the days when I could use humour and wit to smooth things over with Kim. I still held the belief that Kim had not left me because she was still in love with me, but the reality was the only reason she stayed with me was for Michelle's sake.

The beautiful calm and petite girl I had met all those years ago had turned neurotic as the effects of my active alcoholism started to take its toll on her. As my alcohol obsession gathered momentum, she grew sick and stressed, trying to manage her life and Michelle's around me.

Anne and Bill's wedding was the last time that Kim and I were ever seen out in public again.

***

My story about Lenny Walker had obviously struck a raw nerve with Tim. His face had a dark glow and he gave me a steely look.

"What's wrong?" I asked.

He continued to stare at me moodily before admitting, "That's how I came to join the army. I got in a blue with the boss of our shearing team in a pub in Cunumulla one night. We were all on the piss when I got in an argument with him about my pay. I thought he was ripping me off so I gave him a hiding."

"What happened?" I asked.

"I got tossed off the shearing team and then my girlfriend left me."

I nodded. I knew there was something like this hiding in the background. "So, you thought the army might sort you out?"

"I figured that I needed to straighten myself out and the army might do just the trick," he shrugged.

I knew that issue only too well. "The only problem was that you took yourself with you, didn't you?"

"I suppose you could say that," Tim said grudgingly.

"Where did they post you?"

"I joined an infantry battalion, and I did a six-month tour of East Timor in 2000."

"And then what?"

He shrugged." I needed a more of a challenge so in 2001 I transferred to a commando unit. I was in that unit for two years before being sent to Iraq in April 2003, just after the invasion."

I nodded. "What were you doing in Iraq?"

"We were sent over as part of 'Operation Iraq Freedom' and our job was to secure the Iraq airbase in Baghdad."

"Did you like the army?"

Tim nodded. "Yeah, I liked it because like shearing I was part of a team and I was doing stuff that really challenged me, but…"

"But what?" I prodded. His face was now stony as he remembered his time in Iraq. As I watched him think, I had to wonder how he was coping with his PTSD symptoms. Every soldier had them somewhere deep within. He was clearly drinking and gambling, and he didn't look like he was eating well, or even sleeping.

Eventually he said, "I had a good mate badly injured by an IED."

Tim didn't look at me, and I couldn't help but think he was still struggling with it.

"So how did that affect you," I asked him gently.

Tim looked up. "It knocked the shit out of me. It spun me out completely and I became convinced that it was my turn next to cop it."

He spoke quickly and I felt more connected to the young man than I had throughout our entire chat.

"I know the feeling, Tim. Especially after Chooky got killed. I experienced that heaps of times in Vietnam."

Tim nodded and I sought to keep him talking. I didn't need him to withdraw now, so I changed the subject. "Did you take any photos while you were in the army?"

"Yeah, there's a couple in my photo album."

"Can I have a look?"

"If you want."

Tim grabbed the photo album and flicked through the pages until he found the photo he wanted. "There you go. That's one I took of the sun setting over Baghdad airport."

I looked at it for some time before I said, "This is a brilliant photo, Tim." It really was. The guy understood really understood light and how to frame a shot.

"Thanks," he said with unease. Who knows how many times in his life he'd actually been complimented?

"If you got your act together you could become a full-time photographer," I enthused as I looked at the photo. It really was very good.

"Who, me?" he said. He seemed surprised.

"Yeah, you."

"Nah, bullshit. You gotta be shit hot to get fulltime work," he said dismissively.

"Well, I'm telling you this is excellent work. You could sell this stuff."

Tim shrugged. "I know I'm a good photographer, but I've never seriously contemplated doing it for a living."

"Anything's possible if you really believe it, Tim. But you gotta believe it deep down inside your guts or it just won't happen," I told him. I put the photo down and looked directly into his eyes. "You gotta realise that at the core of everything the drink is holding you back from what you're really good at, same as it did me. "

Tim stared at me while the reality of what I had just said sunk in. He was hearing my story, he was listening as I showed him how my life broke down. He nodded reluctantly. "But I like drinking when I take photos. It relaxes me."

"You'd be a damn better photographer if you were sober," I told him, picking up another photo.

"I can't even imagine life without alcohol," he said quietly. "It scares the shit out of me to even contemplate it."

I looked up sharply. "If you think that life without alcohol scares the shit out of you, wait till the things you hold dearest start disappearing because of it. That includes your photography."

"And what did you lose? You had everything and you were drinking. Wife, kids, a successful business. A great dog," pointed out Tim.

I glared at him with a steely resolve. "My marriage, Tim. And my daughter."

***

It was shortly after Anne and Bill's marriage that things were at an all time low between Kim and me. I was 36 years of age, we had been married for almost ten years and we were barely on speaking terms.

Kim had contacted Stumpy to get him to try to speak some sense to me, but even he couldn't get through. I once again hung up the telephone on the old man when the subject of my drinking cut too close to the bone. I wasn't prepared to listen to anything about my drinking, and was squarely convinced that people were making too much of things. I honestly thought they were a bunch of do-gooders poking their noses into things that did not concern them.

As a last ditch attempt to try to save our marriage, Kim had made contact with a visiting Southern American evangelist who had been in Dubbo conducting faith healing services. Michelle had a friend at the local convent school in Dubbo whose mother had used the evangelist to address her husband's excess drinking, apparently with some success. It was a measure of how desperate Kim was that she had even contemplated contacting the man because she was not that way inclined in the slightest, and regarded people like that as total spinners. However, my alcoholism had affected her that badly that she was clutching at straws, trying to help me in any way possible. To have contacted someone like him was a measure of how nuts she had become in trying to deal with my alcoholism.

It was a Tuesday afternoon in March when I received the visit from the preacher man. I was changing a tyre on the Kenworth when he approached the workshop through the front entrance.

"You must be Edward John Costigan, I believe," he said in a deep southern accent.

I stood up to face him from where I had been kneeling beside the truck, startled by his sudden appearance. I was frozen to the spot and a feeling of anxiety engulfed me. His voice sounded exactly the same as the American pilot who had ordered the airstrikes at the Battle of the Bunkers all those years ago in Vietnam. His appearance was baffling to me as well. He was in his early fifties, immaculately dressed in a grey suit with a pink tie, and he had a white handkerchief in his top pocket. He looked so out of place in outback Dubbo. In his hand was a red bible and as he stepped closer to me, he said in a voice of authority, "You know why I am here, don't you, sir?"

I tried to speak but the only thing that came out of my mouth was a short, sharp yelp that reminded me of when I once stood on Snog's tail.

As I stood there in front of him, frozen stiff, I had a flashback to Vietnam. Memories of the Battle of the Bunkers came flooding back to me, and I could smell the lush jungle and hear gunshots and explosions. The vision was so real that I may as well been back there. I could recall word for word what the pilot had said to Lieutenant Geraghty all those years ago, when we had been engaged in the heat of battle.

After what seemed like an eternity, I blurted out, "Bronco Billy 81!"

"What did you say, sir?" he said with force.

"You're Bronco Billy 81," I said with wild eyes.

"Bronco Billy 81? Who in damnation is he?" demanded the preacher.

"He's the pilot who ordered the airstrikes when I was in Vietnam," I said, feeling the room get claustrophobic. I could almost smell the blood and hear the cries of the wounded.

"Vietnam! I was not a pilot in Vietnam, sir!" exclaimed the preacher, snapping his fingers in front of my face. "Your wife, Kim, told me you were in Vietnam, which is why I am here. She believes that the Vietnam War has affected you so badly that you are one sick individual. I am here to cure you from that soul sickness that you are so badly afflicted with."

I stood there, white as a ghost, my heart pounding uncontrollably, completely mesmerised by this stranger who had suddenly walked into my life.

"You're not Bronco Billy 81?" I said tentatively, shaking my head to clear the vision.

"No, Edward John Costigan, you are seriously mistaken, sir. My name is Reverend Robert E. Drucker and I am the pastor of the faith healing church that meets at Rolling Fork, Mississippi, in the United States of America. I have come here to save your soul," he said, his voice rising with every word.

"Save my soul?" I said tentatively.

"You heard me correctly."

"But my soul doesn't need saving," I protested. I was returning to the present with greater clarity.

"You are seriously wrong, sir. Don't you realise that the Lord Jesus Christ is knocking on the window of your soul, boy, and you aint hearing it," he said, now bellowing at me.

"Window of my soul? I don't know what you're talking about," I said, confused.

"What I am talking about is that the Lord himself is inviting you to join him at the table of salvation and your cancer-ridden soul is stopping you from taking up that request," he said, thumping his bible against his free hand.

"But I'm alright," I told him, looking around for Kim. "I'm a truck driver and I've got a wife and daughter and we're all happy. Besides I'm a Catholic and I've been baptised."

"A Catholic! The church in Rome and all its excesses can't save you, sir, but I can," he said, his tone condescending. "Your wife tells me that you have been indulging in intoxicating beverages for a considerable time now, and it has poisoned your soul to the extent that you are dancing to Satan's tune."

"Satan's tune," I echoed, astounded.

"That is correct. I am inviting you to come and join me in prayer to drive those demons from your soul that are so wickedly dictating your actions."

I was so mesmerised by the power and charisma of the preacher that I found myself powerless to protest. It was though my whole body had been overtaken by some powerful force, the like of which I had never experienced before. I actually let the preacher approach me and let him place his hand on my forehead, and his bible against my heart.

"Be gone with you, Satan," he said forcefully, as he pounded the bible in to my heart.

It felt as though someone was smashing me with a lump hammer, but such was his power that I didn't even let out a whimper of protest.

"Release the grip you have over this man and his addiction to the dreaded beverage you have so evilly tempted him with. Be gone with you, Satan. Be gone with you and all your evil doings," he shouted, his voice sounding like a cannon booming. He pounded the bible against my heart with such force that my head rocked back and forth.

"May the Lord Jesus Christ come down upon this man's soul right this minute, and release him from the torment of alcohol that Lucifer himself has so wickedly planted at his disposal," his said, his voice now echoing throughout the entire workshop.

"Lucifer?" I said.

"Yes, the devil himself," he said pounding the bible against my heart again.

Then he started talking in tongues for the next five minutes which only put the wind up me even further. It sounded like gibberish to me, but by this stage he could have been talking in Swahili for all it mattered to me.

Unbeknownst to me, while all this was going on Michelle had crept up from the house to see what the preacher was up to. Michelle, being the inquisitive nine-year-old she was, had often ventured up to my workshop when I was on the road to try to find where I hid my alcohol.

About six months before, through sheer diligence, she had managed to find a little compartment I had in a heap of old tyres to the side of the shed where I kept some booze. With that fresh in her mind, she walked around to the tyres and pulled out an unopened flagon of Lindeman's Montillo Sweet Sherry and walked through the side door of the workshop where the preacher was still talking in tongues, and going ten to the dozen belting me with the bible.

"Look, Mr Preacher. I've got the flagon of plonk that Dad's been hiding in the old tyres," Michelle said loudly, holding the flagon out in front of her.

Michelle's sudden appearance broke the preacher from his evangelical spiel.

"Please, Mr Preacher," she said, "stop my dad from drinking. It's wrecking our lives."

The sudden appearance of Michelle and my unopened flagon broke me from my ethereal state.

"What the hell are you doing with my flagon of sherry, Shelly!" I yelled.

My burst of anger, something which Michelle had become very fearful of, prompted her to drop the flagon onto the concrete floor. As the glass shattered and sherry spilled everywhere, I lost it. I glared at the preacher. "What the fuck are you up to, ya lunatic?"

"Don't swear, Daddy. Don't swear, will you!" Michelle pleaded with me, her eyes wide.

"He's speaking the language of Lucifer, young girl," said the preacher, sensing he was losing his moment. "Be gone with you, demon. I demand you to leave this man's soul right this minute!" he yelled, as he attempted to hit me again with the bible.

By this stage I had fully awoken from trance and a struggle ensued as I tried to stop him from hitting me with his bible.

"Be gone with you, Satan!" he screamed. "Be gone this minute! Holy Lord, rid this man of all his demons!"

The mania in his eyes made me strong and I grabbed him around the throat and pinned him up against the cabin of the Kenworth. As he pushed back against me, the evangelist was still spouting rubbish, determined to save my soul, while I was determined to find out how Michelle had found my booze.

"Please don't hurt the preacher man, Daddy. He's only trying to help you," Michelle said in tears.

"Help me? The bloke's a dead set lunatic, Shelly!" I said as I flung him to the ground.

"Please, Dad. Don't hurt him!"

"Where did you find that flagon, Shelly?" I screamed, rounding on her.

Michelle stared at me, frozen with fear. "Around the corner of the shed in the stash of old tyres," she eventually whispered.

"What are you doing poking around there, Michelle?"

"I wanted to find your booze and tip it out so you wouldn't drink anymore." She was trembling.

"What?" I shouted in disbelief. I started to approach my daughter, but fearful of what I might do, she scampered like a mouse back through the side door and ran for her life to the house, all the time yelling, "The preacher man's trying to save you, Dad. He's only trying to save you!"

I looked at the preacher who was now standing dumbfounded in front of me. I don't think he could believe what he was seeing. But my ire was up and I'd just about had enough. "Get the fuck out of my workshop or I'll kick your arse all the way back to the deep south!" I picked up a tyre lever which was lying on the floor besides the Kenworth, but before I could get anywhere near him he bolted out of the workshop and back down towards the house where he had parked his car.

"May the lord protect your soul because I sure as hell can't!" he shouted. "May the Lord have mercy on your soul!"

Once he reached his car he drove off like a bat out of hell, leaving nothing but a cloud of dust behind him.

I watched him leave and then turned to the house. I threw the tyre lever into the little garden of herbs which Kim kept, and rattled the door handle, but Kim had locked it as soon as Michelle had scampered inside.

"Kim, open this door!" I demanded.

"You're not coming into the house in the state you're in, Ed. Heaven knows what you might do," Kim said tearfully.

"I want to know what the fuck was going through your mind to pull a stunt like that!"

"Ed, don't swear, please. Michelle's frightened to death. She's hiding under her bed and won't come out."

"I'll give her frightened," I snarled, banging against the door. "What the hell was she doing stealing my flagon of booze?"

"Ed, please," Kim said in tears.

"Don't let him in the house, Mum," I could hear Michelle yell from her bedroom.

I ranted and raved for the next ten minutes before finally giving up. "Right!" I screamed through the door. "I'm going down to The Buncha. We'll sort this thing out later on. You can keep my dinner in the warmer."

I took off like a bat out of hell into Dubbo, and when I walked into the pub, who should be there playing a game of darts but my cousin, Sean.

"Ed! Come and have a beer and a game of darts," he said.

"I'll skip the darts and concentrate on the beer thanks, Sean," I grumbled.

Sean could see that I was hot under the collar and after

explaining to him what had just happened he shouted me a beer. "Don't worry about Kim, Ed. She'll settle down and come to her senses after a while." He clapped me on the shoulder.

"Yeah, you're absolutely right, cuz. She doesn't know how good she's got it with me," I said. I took a deep gulp out of my middy, sure I had the right of it.

That night in The Buncha, Sean and I got a skin-full and after the both of us were swept out of the pub with the bumpers, I drove back home as drunk as a skunk. When I arrived home, I played the final card in the pack that ended our marriage.

The place was in darkness and ripping the back door off its hinges, I staggered into our bedroom where Kim was sound asleep in bed. I was desperate to relieve myself, but somehow, I had mistaken the bedroom for the inside toilet. In my drunken state, I opened up her clothes drawer and pissed in it.

Little did I know that sitting in the drawer was Kim's wedding dress. Kim woke up from her slumber and turned her bedside lamp on to be confronted by the scene being played out in front of her.

In retrospect it was much more than a coincidence that I was caught urinating on Kim's treasured dress. It was symbolic of the fact that in ten years all I had done was piss all over our marriage. How she ever put up with me during those years God only knows, but it was the final nail in the coffin of a long, drawn-out affair that had become tremendously painful for both my wife and child.

I will never forget the look on her face as she realised what I had done. It was one of complete and utter contempt and what followed was a tirade of physical and verbal abuse towards me that had built up after years and years of putting up with my behaviour. She went ballistic as she tossed anything she could get her hands at me before belting me with the metal stoking rod which was situated next to the open fireplace in our bedroom. Her face burned with rage as she screamed the words which will be forever etched into my memory before totally breaking down.

"You're nothing but an animal, Costigan, and I want you out of my life!"

She kicked me out of the house, so I spent the rest of the night in the sleeper cab of my Kenworth. The next morning when I woke up, I thought that she would have cooled down like she normally did, but as I staggered out of the prime mover there were two burly police officers waiting for me. They told me that I was not allowed to enter the house and that Kim had taken out an AVO against me, and that other than my place of work, I was not allowed anywhere near the homestead.

***

"What a terrible scene I played out that day, Tim," I said, looking up at the ceiling of the caravan. I shook my head. "At the time I had no idea what sort of terror I had inflicted on my family. It still makes me shudder just thinking about it even after all these years. All I could think about was how Michelle had found my flagon of plonk. The fact she was hiding under the bed absolutely petrified just didn't register with me at the time," I said, looking into my empty mug. "Poor kid. I was blind, oh so blind, at the time." I sighed deeply, still filled with a depth of remorse for my actions. "If the truth be known, I was absolutely petrified to give up the grog. The booze was like my best mate and to hell with anybody who tried to separate me from it."

Tim sat in front of me, quietly listening, but when he saw

me look into my mug, he got up and put the kettle on for another cuppa.

"I was convinced that Kim would come to her senses and want me back again," I told him. "That never happened though. I had played the last card in the pack and tipped Kim over the point of no return."

I shuffled in my seat and took a deep breath. Recalling the breakup of my marriage was still very painful, even though I'd long since moved on. I had a fleeting vision of Karen's beautiful smile and a pang of grief stung me.

Tim leaned against the little stove and folded his arms across his chest, waiting for the kettle to boil.

"In the divorce that followed a few months later I lost everything, including my prized Holden Monaro. As the business and house was in both our names, Kim completely cleaned me out. I was left with a couple of suitcases and Snog," I told him, remembering how the dog had seemed confused about the whole situation.

"What did you do with yourself?" Tim asked.

I looked up at him and said, "I drove one of Rex Wilson's roadtrains and wasn't that humiliating. After owning a couple of rigs, I was left with nothing. I lived in a self-contained care-taker's cottage that Rex had attached to the back of his main workshop. It was a nightmare for me after all the years of hard work I had spent building up my business. All the money I had made from the Poseidon shares was long gone and I barely had a zac to my name."

I handed Tim my mug as the kettle clicked. "I tried to see Michelle a number of times, but the AVO that Kim had out on me prevented that. Like a puff of smoke they were gone out of my life." I shook my head, remembering that day. "Kim packed up and went back to Dunbogan. She got her old teaching job back at Kendall, and it was the last time I was to lay eyes on Michelle for many years."

I shook my head as the memories came flooding back. "You would have thought that would be enough to convince me to put the cork in the bottle permanently." I looked up at him. "Not on your life. My big problem was that you could tell me, but you couldn't tell me much."

Tim bought the refreshed mugs back to the table. "You didn't quit drinking then?"

"Hardly," I said, rolling my eyes. "To top all this off, I was involved in an incident in the roadtrain that nearly cost a young couple their lives."

***

It wasn't long after I got a job driving for Rex Wilson in May of 1982 of that my drinking nearly resulted in a couple of fatalities. I was involved in an incident, that if not for its seriousness, would have been farcical.

I had taken a triple roadtrain from Dubbo to Burketown in the Gulf Country of Queensland, fully loaded with general freight. The road from Cammoweal to Burketown was very rough and about twenty kilometres out of Burketown, I came across a Kombi Van broken down on the side of the road. Inside were an English couple who were in their early twenties and on a working holiday around Australia. They both looked very fit and had golden tans from working in the hot Aussie sun during their travels.

On further inspection, I noticed they had a broken tail shaft on their vehicle. "You'll be right. I'll get you to Burketown in one piece."

"Oh, thank you, that's very kind of you," said the girl, relieved.

I hooked a chain from the back trailer of my roadtrain onto the front of their Kombi. After we drove off, I initially kept a careful watch in the mirror of my Kenworth to make sure they were okay.

As everything appeared to be alright with their vehicle, I soon forgot they were there.

I had a flagon of port under my seat and after taking a swig, I planted my foot on the accelerator so I could make a mile as it was late afternoon. The road was in poor condition and as I drove along I was continuously avoiding pot holes. I kept one hand on the wheel and the other firmly secured on my flagon.

When I eventually drove into the outskirts of Burketown, I noticed a group of Aboriginal kids standing on the side of the road, pointing at my rig, bent over in laughter. As I drove further into town I noticed other people staring and pointing at my roadtrain with a look of disbelief on their faces.

I eventually pulled my rig up and walked around to the back of the roadtrain to see what everyone was pointing at and to my horror the Kombi Van was on its side. When I pulled the young English couple from their badly damaged vehicle, they were both trembling with fear and could hardly speak. They were both in a state of total shock.

After some time they were able to compose themselves and the young bloke explained what had happened.

"You were about ten kilometres out of Burketown, driving like a madman, swerving all over the place. Our poor old Kombi was being tossed from side to side when all of a sudden a huge pot hole tossed us onto the side," he said, trembling.

"Shit!" I said.

"We were screaming, thinking we were going to be killed at any moment," said the girl with an equal look of terror, her eyes wide. By this stage, the bloke was coming back to his senses and a wild anger filled his face.

"You could have had us killed, you dickhead!"

I stood there stunned, not knowing what to say as a crowd of people gathered around the scene.

"We've got a good mind to take you to the police," the girl said.

"Don't do that. My boss will pay for any damages," I said with a look of anxiety. The last thing I needed was the cops coming down on me.

"Too right he will!" said the man.

The crowd helped put the vehicle upright, and I found a public telephone box where I eventually made contact with Rex.

"A slight problem, Rex!" I said trying to make light of the situation.

"What is it, Ed?"

"I was towing a Kombi van which had broken down, and I broke a side mirror on it."

"That's no problem, Ed," said Rex. "Just get their details and I'll fix 'em up for the costs."

"Only problem, Rex, is that the rest of Kombi is lying on top of the mirror," I said, waiting for the explosion.

"It's fuckin' well what?" Rex screamed down the phone.

The rest of conversation mostly consisted of Rex threatening to sack me and it was only due to the fact that I had known him for so long and had helped fix his trucks over the years that saved my hide.

Rex's insurance paid for all the damage done to the Kombi and when I got back to Dubbo, Rex apologised to me and said,

"I couldn't sack you, Ed. You've helped me out so much over the years."

Regardless of my present state of affairs, I was still considered a valuable employee as I put many long hours in and had a reputation for being a good mechanic. Despite everything, I never let the quality of my work suffer.

In retrospect, Rex would have done me a favour if he'd sacked me after the Kombi incident as it would have saved me from the horrendous circumstances that were waiting for me in the not too distant future.

Anne's fear, her intuition that something dire would happen in my life, was about to unfold.

***

"You know, Tim, I sometimes shake my head because it's hard to believe that it was me that lived that life all those years ago. My life today is so far removed from the insanity of those days."

Tim gave me an appraising look, pushing the ginger snaps towards me. "I must say you look like a pretty normal bloke to me and you're in good shape. I mean, I believe what you're telling me, but it's hard to picture the type of bloke you were all those years ago."

"Oh, you better believe it was me, Tim. The big difference these days, other than the fact that I don't drink anymore, is the fact that my attitude is vastly different from that of yesteryear."

Tim nodded. "So your attitude still hadn't changed at that point?"

I shook my head. "Like I said to you before, I thought I was a good bloke having a rough trot, but what happened next was to blow all that out the window. After the accident I knew I was in the wrong."

"What accident? The one with the Kombi?"

I sighed. "No. Let me tell you about the accident that changed my life."

***

It's painful to talk about, even after all these years, but I must speak about it. It was only by owning up to my horrendous act that I was able to set myself free and rise from the darkness that alcoholism had cast over my soul.

It was the 15th of June, 1982, when my life changed forever. That date will be etched into my memory until the day I die. There's never been a day before or since that even compares with it, and that includes the Battle of the Bunkers. Because of my irresponsible actions that day, I plummeted into the depths of despair—emotionally and spiritually—to such a point that I thought I would never return.

It started the day before when I had taken a semi from Dubbo to Brisbane with a full load of freight. It was Tuesday and I was heading back down the Newell Highway empty. Kim and Michelle had been on my mind constantly, and thinking of family made me decide to pull off at Eumungerie and visit Mum and the family out at Coorigil. I had not seen them for some time, and none of them could not believe the sight of me. I was unkempt and looked terrible.

I had travelled out to their property with an ulterior motive, as I wanted to get Kim's phone number off Mum. It was coming up to Michelle's birthday, but Mum flat out refused to give it to me. We were alone in the kitchen when we had an argument.

"To the think that you were once such a handsome young man, and now look at you," Mum said, looking me up and down.

"Give me a break, Mum," I said. "I'm a truck driver. What do you expect me to look like? Some pencil pushing public servant in a suit and tie?"

She gave me a sad look. "I was so proud of you at your passing out parade at Kapooka all those years ago, and when you were boxing you kept yourself in such good shape. Now your hair's long, you're overweight and every time I see you, you've got a smoke in your hand."

I bristled. "Look, I came here to say g'day and get Kim's phone number. I want to wish Michelle a happy birthday and instead I'm copping all this crap."

"Don't you swear in this household, Edward John Costigan. I won't have it," Mum snapped. She had been devastated at the breakdown of my marriage and laid the blame squarely at my feet. "First there was Sandy McKenzie and now Kim. You've let two beautiful woman go because of your drinking and irresponsible actions," Mum yelled. "You were so much better than that!"

"Look, are you going to give me Kim's phone number or not?" I shouted back at her.

"Definitely not, Ed," she said without hesitation. "You've done your dash with Kim and you've only yourself to blame."

"Ah, bugger ya then, Mum. Good riddance," I said, as I stormed out of the house.

"You've wrecked your family's life because of your drinking," I heard Mum yell as I walked back to my truck.

Those words from Mum echoed in my mind for years to come. She had no idea how prophetic they were.

I jumped into the Kenworth and took off down the driveway of Coorigil like a bat out of hell, leaving a cloud of dust behind me.

My hackles were up and I had a huge resentment towards everyone. Instead of travelling south towards Narromine and cutting back across to the Newell highway and back home to Dubbo, I made the fateful decision to drive back to Eumungerie and then onto Dubbo.

But I was thirsty after my argument with Mum and decided to head to the pub at Eumungerie and have a few beers first.

It was the single worst decision I ever made in my life.

In retrospect, it was more good luck than good judgment on my part that I had never had a really serious accident, and because of that I had grown complacent. In saying that, I knew I was doing the wrong thing as soon as I put that first beer to my lips that fateful day, but once I got the taste I was a shot duck. I ran into some blokes I knew and it quickly turned into a full-on session. I eventually staggered out of the pub and one of the blokes I was in the shout with suggested I sleep it off in the sleeper cab of the Kenworth. I waved him off and drove down to Dubbo. It was around 4.30 pm when I arrived in Dubbo, and the traffic was thick.

Even though I was drunk, Dubbo was a town that I knew like the back of my hand, so I decided to drive down a few back streets to avoid the heavy traffic.

To this day, I can't remember seeing the give way sign that loomed up in front of me, but before I knew it I had driven through the intersection and was unable to react in time to the traffic already there. I t-boned a small brown Chrysler Galant, hitting it square in the front passenger door. I was probably only doing 60 kilometres per hour, but because of the size of the Kenworth and its huge bull bar, I made a mess of the small sedan.

"Ah, shit!" I yelled as I applied the maxi brake. "What have I done?!"

By the time I climbed down from the cabin of the Kenworth, a small crowd of people had already gathered on the intersection of the small suburban street.

"You're in big trouble, mate," an old bloke yelled out from a nearby verandah.

I gave him a menacing stare and then walked around to the driver's side where I saw a woman in her thirties slumped across the steering wheel, unconscious. She had blood coming from a severe gash in her forehead, and I was filled with panic.

"Are you alright, love?" I said frantically.

She started to moan, but other than that there was no response.

After briefly inspecting her wounds, I looked across the seat to be met with a sight I'll never forget—the limp body of a badly injured young girl in the passenger seat. Even though I could see she was terribly hurt and blood covered every inch of her, my thoughts went to my own daughter.

"Are you okay, sweetie?" I said frantically.

She didn't respond.

"Little girl, are you okay?" I pleaded.

Images of my wounded mates in Vietnam came flooding back to me as I frantically leaned across and tried to find a pulse on her. I felt like I was reaching for Chooky as I searched for a pulse. Vietnam overlaid my senses and my anxiety was heightened by the thoughts of yesteryear, coupled with the scene in front of me.

Sirens began to invade my consciousness. They were coming closer and soon would be at the scene of the accident.

I continued talking to her until I felt a hand on my shoulder.

"We'll, take over from here, thanks," said a paramedic.

"Is she okay?" I said frantically.

"We'll soon find out," he said, his fellow paramedic already leaning in the car. "Are you the driver of this rig?"

"Yeah, I am."

"I'd clear out, mate, quick smart. This crowd wants your blood."

No sooner had the paramedic said this when I was confronted by a bloke in his late twenties, easily weighing about eighteen stone, who had witnessed the accident.

"You're in big trouble, dickhead!" he growled at me.

Although I was in a state of shock, I soon reverted to type and confronted him.

"You just back off, ya mongrel," I said with fists raised.

He took a step backwards and eyed me cautiously.

Meanwhile the crowd had grown bigger, and those who witnessed the confrontation reacted by surrounding me and yelling abuse. As they did, I walked around in a circle with my fists clenched, keeping an eye on anyone who might decide to try to attack me. The hostility was rising and I thought they might attack en masse when a police car arrived.

"Right you lot, back off, we're in control of this situation," the sergeant yelled to the crowd as he got out of the car.

"But he's driven through that intersection and hurt that lady and her daughter!" yelled one lady.

"I don't care what's happened!" shouted the cop. "I don't want a lynch mob taking the law into their own hands. Now, back off!"

They retreated and he turned to me and said, "You get in the back seat of the police car before this mob has your balls for breakfast." He narrowed his eyes and looked at me carefully, sniffing the air. His look became disgusted. "You bloody stupid drunk."

Knowing it was only safe place, I got into the police car where I could see the crowd from a distance still abusing me.

Over the next fifteen minutes, I watched the paramedics work in vain to try to save the life of the young girl. They had already driven her mother away in the first ambulance, but as I watched I started to shiver in shock. Eventually, the paramedics sat back, one of them shaking his head.

My heart sank when they covered the young girl in a white sheet.

She was dead.

"You've done it this time, ya maggot," a man yelled at me from the other side of the window.

I looked at the man who had just yelled the obscenity and back at the stretcher now being loaded into the second ambulance. I was filled with terror. No words can adequately explain how sick to the core I actually felt.

I sat there in stunned silence, alcohol and adrenaline fueling me, and it was only after another ten minutes when more police arrived did the sergeant and young constable walk back to their car.

"Can I go now?" I said. I was such a state of shock that I thought I was going to be able to walk away from the scene and wipe my hands clean of the wreckage.

"Go now?" said the sergeant incredulously. "You've got to be kidding. You're in big trouble, mate. The only place you're going is back to the police station."

The only consolation I have been able to draw from that dreadful day, after years and years of contemplation, was that nine-year-old Alison Jane Mitchell was killed instantly, and spared any undue suffering. Her mother, Jenny, was badly injured but survived the accident to make a full recovery. Physically, she was okay, but her mental and emotional scars were to last for many years. The suffering it was to cause both her family and mine over the ensuing years would have been too much to bear, if I fully comprehended it at the time.

As we drove to the police station, I could vaguely hear the officers engaged in conversation on their radio.

"We've got a drunk truck driver in the back. He's just killed a young girl."

Those words were to ring in my ears for years to come.

***

"You killed a little girl?" Tim said leaning forward in his seat, shock etched on his face.

I sighed heavily, despite the amazing letter in my pocket. "It doesn't get any easier to talk about it, Tim."

Tim glared at me. "You killed a little girl?"

"Yes, I did."

"A little girl," he repeated. He stared at me with hostility. "Well, I see you in a completely different light now. That's terrible!"

"It is indeed. It's never far from my mind, especially today. Talking about it now has brought it all back in terrifying detail," I said, my heart still sore with the weight of my mistake. "And even after I did that terrible thing, I still couldn't admit what I was. That came later."

Chapter 10

I WAS IN DEEP shock while I rode back to Dubbo Police Station. The reception I received from the two detectives who interviewed me was nothing short of brutal. They thought that a bit of old fashion telephone book therapy might be just the ticket I needed.

This involved one of them holding a telephone book up to the side of my head while the other slammed his fist repeatedly into the book. This was to make sure that I was left sore and sorry without leaving any bruising or marks on me which could incriminate the officers.

"What's it like to kill a young girl, ya maggot," the older detective kept saying.

While he said this, his younger partner repeatedly administered his rough form of punishment.

I was still drunk and in a state of shock. There was no way I was showing any resistance.

"You piece of shit," said the younger detective. He flung me onto the ground and proceeded to belt me around the head, waving the phone book around like he was smashing his way through the jungle with a machete.

It was more like an interrogation than an interview. It lasted for an hour and only ended when I'd had the living shit belted out of me. Following that, I was charged with culpable driving causing death. I was fingerprinted, filled out a number of forms and was led away to the cells.

That Friday night I spent in the lockup at the Dubbo Police Station was one of the worst nights of my life. It was a cold cell with nothing but a mattress on the floor and a toilet in the corner of the room. A young constable who showed a measure of compassion brought me something to eat, but I had no appetite. I was badly knocked around, so I just left the meal on the floor.

"I recognised your name when they were charging you," he said, standing at the door of the cell.

I looked up, bewildered.

"You're Ed Costigan. My dad use to talk about you all the time. He reckons you were one of the best boxers he ever saw."

My head swirled with glorious images from my past, but I looked up at the young officer and said, "Seems like that happened in another lifetime, constable."

"You're not wrong, Ed. You've certainly had a big fall from grace. Still," he shrugged, "You wouldn't be the first boxer that the booze has brought undone."

"What's to become of me?" I said after a short silence.

"You're in for a rough ride, mate, but they tell me that you get used to jail after a while."

I was overcome with a feeling of fear as he closed the cell door and walked away. I lay back on my mattress in a state of bewilderment as I tried to adjust to the huge calamity that had taken place in my life. A thousand thoughts crammed into my mind, and I was overwhelmed by feelings of guilt and terror on my impending incarceration.

I could not get the image of the young girl and her mother inside the car wreck out of my head. Again and again I replayed it like a film; my Kenworth hitting their little car and every time it did, I recoiled in horror as I rolled like a worm on my mattress.

"How the bloody hell did you let that happen, Costigan?" I repeated to myself.

It was as though every good deed I had ever done disappeared into the ether.

I killed a little a girl.

It was in the early hours of the morning that I eventually drifted off to sleep, but it wasn't an easy sleep. It was periodically interrupted by nightmares of the accident and intense feelings of remorse and shame.

I had once loved driving rigs, but now every time I was on the road I would inevitably load up with booze and pills and it had turned into a vicious merry-go-round that I could not get off. But now, because of my impending incarceration, I was to never put another pill in my mouth.

It probably saved my life. In reality, I was around the twist after years of prolonged drug use. If it hadn't been jail, I would probably would have died in some horrible accident. As I lay on my back, staring at the ceiling I said out loud, "Thank God I don't have to get into that semi-trailer ever again."

After spending the weekend in the cells, I fronted the magistrate at Dubbo Local Court on Monday morning where I was refused bail.

Later that day, I was taken, along with ten other prisoners, still dressed in the same clothes I was arrested in, to Bathurst Gaol as it was known back then, where I was put in remand in the A wing. It's called Bathurst Correctional Complex now, a 'correct' name that doesn't do it justice.

We arrived at the jail late in the afternoon and the greeting we new prisoners got is something I will never forget. The screws treated us like garbage and belted us with batons. Their German shepherd guard dogs went ballistic as we ran the gauntlet from the prison truck to the reception room. As we were running they were yelling obscenities, calling us things like 'fuckin' maggots' and 'filthy fuckin' scum'.

It was unnerving to say the least, but frankly, it was exactly what I thought of myself after the crime I had just committed.

Our first meal was one of sausages and mashed potato, served on a red plastic plate with a lukewarm cup of tea. After I had eaten, I was issued my jail number which was 1477, but was not issued any jail clothing as I was still on remand.

I was led to a small cell which had white walls with rounded corners, a red floor, a double bunk, a table and two chairs. There was a toilet located behind the double bunk and a peep hole in the front door. It was a drab and monotonous looking cell that only served to increase my already fragile emotional state.

For the next seven days, I shared the cell with a bloke in his mid-fifties who went by the nickname of 'Slick Ray' before I was transferred to B wing. Slick Ray derived his nickname from the brill cream he had slicked back in his hair. He was on remand for a car stealing offence committed in Orange. He was a career criminal who constantly chewed gum and liked to lean forward on the bottom bunk of his bed with his fingers joined in front of him. His face displayed a distant stare like he was looking into space, and he would constantly reminisce on his old escapades.

"I got pinched out at Wellington once, after I'd stolen a hotted up GTHO Falcon. I swear this thing went like a shower of shit. I would have gotten away with it too, if it wasn't for an off-duty copper who recognised me."

He wasn't what I would call dangerous, just a scammer who always managed to get caught. He had spent the best part of 30 years in and out of 'the nick' for petty crimes like car stealing and break and enters.

He was mighty good to me though. He might have been a criminal, but he had a very calming way about him. Although I was a knockabout myself and had seen my fair share of life, he knew that I was a shot duck that first night I spent in Bathurst. Mentally, I was wrecked. He took me under his wing and told me how to handle jail life. Simple things mainly, like keeping my nose clean by not being a big mouth or sticking out like a sore thumb.

Jail was huge shock to me, even though I had been through the horrors of Vietnam. However, I never cease to be amazed at how a human being can adjust themselves to almost any situation until it becomes normal. There's a routine in jail which you get used to. You get up early, have breakfast and then go to work inside the jail for the day. You're back to your cell in the late afternoon for dinner and then locked up for the night. It's a monotonous existence, but one you get used to. It's no wonder so many people become institutionalised.

When I eventually fronted Dubbo District Court two months later, the only people I had to support me were Stumpy, Anne, Rowy and Sean O'Grady. Everyone else had deserted me.

Sean, for all his madness, was just like me. His support was invaluable. Being a drinker like myself, he instinctively had a deep bond with me and an uncanny knack of knowing what to say at the right time.

My crime had been too much for most of the family to handle and as a result, they couldn't bring themselves to see me in the situation I was in. Stumpy supported me and although age wouldn't allow him to visit me regularly, he kept his correspondence with me through his letters.

Anne was my rock of Gibraltar. She knew I had a serious drinking problem but was wise enough to realise that preaching to me wasn't going to solve my problem. She'd prophesised my downfall, but still saw the good in me.

And even though I hadn't been in contact with Rowy in recent times because of my escalating drinking, he never deserted me and was there for me when I needed him most.

Stumpy, Sean, Anne and Rowy never judged me. They knew there was something fundamentally wrong with me. They knew I was a sick individual, not a bad one, who had fallen by the wayside because of a set of circumstances that I didn't know how to my control.

The day before my sentencing, Anne brought in a suit so as I could look half presentable. "I've brought you a new suit, Ed, plus a new shirt," Anne said, barely controlling her emotions.

"You're a gem, Annie, I don't know what I'd do without you," I told her.

She looked me deep in the eyes and broke down. "You'll get through this, Ed," she said through muffled sobs. "Just stay strong."

Although Anne tried to stay positive, her words sounded

hollow. All I could see in front of me was a dark passage that led to the abyss.

My future looked bleak, but my instincts had kicked in after I had met Slick Ray. I had already gone into survival mode which I believe saved me from going insane. It was similar to what I had been through in the ring and in Vietnam, and it was because of this that I survived this time in my life. I knew I was going to jail, and mentally I was already preparing for the judgement.

On the day of my sentencing, I will never forget how I felt when the judge spoke to me.

"Yours is a heinous crime, as you had no regard for other people that were using the road. A drivers licence is not a rite of passage but a privilege. You, of all people, with the responsibility of driving a heavy vehicle, should have realised this. As a result of your irresponsible actions that day, causing the death of Alison Mitchell and serious injuries to her mother, Jenny, the only option I have for you, Mr Costigan, is a custodial sentence," he said in an authoritative tone while he peered over the top of his spectacles.

The judge gave me eight years with a non-parole period of four years. There was an automatic remission system running at the time and it was because of this that my sentence was reduced to three years on the bottom with the eight years still standing on the top.

It was like I went into slow motion as everything around me seemed to freeze. I looked around for some type of consoling answer to my predicament, only to be met by an ashen-faced Rowy and my sister weeping uncontrollably.

Jenny Mitchell, who still bore the scars of her accident, yelled at me from across the court room. "I believe you have a young daughter, Costigan? How would you feel if she was taken from you?"

Her words felt as though somebody had knifed me through the heart with a dagger. I had a sudden vision of Michelle lying under that white sheet on the stretcher.

"Rot in hell, you bastard," yelled Alison's father, shaking his fist.

A man seated at the front of the courthouse screamed, "You've got it coming to you once you get inside, you peace of filth, Costigan. They'll fix you up well and good."

I looked around the packed courthouse and felt like a Christian in the Colosseum during Roman times, about to be fed to the lions.

Eventually, I was carted away to the cells, and as I was I looked up at Anne's tear-streaked face. She mouthed the words, "Stay strong, Ed."

After my sentencing I was returned to B wing where I was over-come with a depth of despair, the like of which I had never experienced before. To hear those big steel gates clang shut behind me in that cold hole of a place was a harrowing experi-ence, and I knew then that this was serious business.

Shortly after arriving back in B wing, I was issued with my prison clothing which included two beige shirts, two bottle green trousers and a jacket. To slip into my prison uniform for the first time made me feel sick to the core. I had always felt great pride when I was dressed in my army uniform, and my prison garb only reinforced how low I had sunk.

I used to lie on my bed repeating the same statement over and over in my head. How did a decent bloke like me end up in a place like this?

The fact of the matter was that I was anything but a decent bloke and my irresponsible actions had led directly to where I was presently stationed.

After about a week, I went in front of the classification board where I was classified as a C1. Because I was a fully trained mechanic, I was given the option of staying in Bathurst and being transferred to X wing or going to the Metropolitan Training Centre in Long Bay Gaol, these days known as Long Bay Correctional Centre in Sydney. There was a mechanic's workshop in the 'Big House' and they wanted to utilise my mechanical skills.

I choose Long Bay as I knew I would be close to both Rowy and Anne. It made the most sense to me, and I was well clear of the family that way.

The Maroubra O'Gradys went missing at this stage of my life. Not once did a member of the family visit me in Long Bay. This disappointed me immensely, but it only reinforced how far I had fallen from grace from those heady days of my youth spent in Maroubra.

When I arrived at Long Bay, I was sent to A wing where I shared a cell with a psychopath named Terry Peel. He was a head case who was doing a life sentence for raping and murdering a mother out at Brewarrina in far western NSW. Peel was tall, well-built and had a deep scar on the front of his chin. He had hands-down the most frightening eyes I have ever encountered.

This is just great, I thought to myself when I realised who I was sharing a cell with.

Terry wasted no time in telling me how his cell was going to be run. "I am on the bottom bunk and no snoring, do ya hear," he said pointing his finger at me directly.

That night I wondered if I was going to get out of the cell

alive, as Peel kept me awake by walking up and down our cell all night, muttering obscenities into the night air. I didn't sleep a wink as I had my back to the wall with the blankets up around my eyeballs all night.

I subsequently learnt that he was a schizophrenic. His hair stuck straight up in the air like he had just put his finger in an electrical socket. The top button of his prison shirt was always done up and his eyeballs were as wide as dinner plates. He would pace around and come straight up to your face and tell you in no uncertain terms how he wanted the cell run.

"Don't fuck with me, do ya hear me, arsehole?" he kept repeating to me.

After a week with Terry, he told me just before lights out, "I heard you snoring last night, Costigan, and if I hear you tonight I'll stick you in the jugular." He produced a sharpened toothbrush from his trouser pocket.

I bristled. "I'd be real careful about where you flash that thing around, Terry, because someone might get injured with that and it won't be me," I said, hoping to get on the front foot.

"You threatening me, Costigan?" he said, his face only inches from mine. "I've heard all about your abilities in the ring, but that don't mean nothing to me. Where I grew up out at Wilcannia we fought on the streets. I've knuckled with plenty of hard black fellas, so you don't scare me."

I said nothing, but eyed off his menacing stare.

That night as I lay on the top bunk, I knew I had to do something about him or I might cop that toothbrush in the jugular. I knew I couldn't stop myself from snoring. Who can? I didn't get a wink of sleep that night and while I lay on my bunk, I devised a plan to fix him up.

At breakfast the next morning, I got up and totally unannounced, hit Terry with a combination of devastating punches to his head and body that made him choke on his 'moosh', which is the porridge they serve up in jail.

Terry went ballistic and came for me with his sharpened toothbrush. He threw me up against the wall and was about to drive the toothbrush into my neck when I kicked him in the balls. While he was lying on the ground in agony, I sat on his chest and knocked him senseless with a lethal combination of punches to his head. When I got up, I felt pain in my right hand. I looked down at Terry lying on the cell floor with an expression on his face that suggested he had just been hit by a freight train.

I walked over to sit on my bed and inspect my hand to see if there was any damage.

One of the screws opened the peep hole on our door and said, "You're getting your right whack now, hey Terry."

He disappeared, and as I sat on my bed panting heavily, I said to Terry, "Bottom rail on top now, hey dickhead."

Terry didn't come within cooee's distance of me after that incident. He spent most of his time cowering under his blanket, such was his gutless nature.

After that incident, Terry Peel was moved out of my cell and not long after he was involved in an incident with another inmate where he slit the other bloke's stomach open with a sharpened toothbrush. He was tipped back to maximum security.

I never saw Terry again, but I heard he ended up in the segregated section out at Goulburn where they send the worst of the worst.

My altercation with Peel had earned me respect from the other inmates, especially the lifers who ran A wing. On top of that was the fact that my reputation as a boxer had followed me into jail and I was a Vietnam Veteran. That alone ensured that I was never threatened by any of the inmates. I was off limits.

In saying that, I was desperately lonely as my incarceration had left me in very bad headspace. In fact, if the present situation had gone on any longer I don't know what I would have done as the guilt surrounding Alison Mitchell's death had sent my mental state spiralling downwards. With the problem of Peel handled, all I had left was my own headspace. It was not a safe space at that point in time.

After the incident with Peel, I was transferred to another cell. I was anxious as I didn't want another cellmate like Terry Peel, so I approached the move with caution.

When I entered my new cell that afternoon in late August 1982, sitting on a chair reading a book on fishing was a man in his early forties with rough features and a medium build that indicated he'd been around the traps. He said nothing, but looked at me with a hard stare before indicating with his eyes that the bottom bunk was mine before continuing to read his book.

I sat on the bed with my arms folded for the next few minutes contemplating the lack of hospitality from my new-found cellmate before I said to him, "You like a spot of fishing, do ya?"

He glanced at me before looking back at his book and continuing to read.

I sat on my bed twiddling my thumbs before I made another attempt to break the ice. "The name's Ed."

He looked at me long and hard before responding in a gruff tone. "I know who you are."

"So, if you know who I am, do you mind me asking your name?"

He gave me a hard stare before he said, "The name's George, George Murdoch."

He then continued to read his book.

If first impressions count, I wasn't exactly overjoyed with my new cellmate. As I lay there, looking up at the top bunk for the next five minutes, I felt that well of loneliness envelop me once again.

Unexpectedly George suddenly said, "You're Ed Costigan, ex-Australian middleweight boxing champion and Vietnam Veteran!"

I looked up at him, startled, and George gave me a slight grin. "Nothing gets fuckin' past me in here. Besides, I saw you fight. You could certainly handle yourself," he said, looking me up and down. "I know why you're doing your lagging. You killed a young girl while you were drunk behind the wheel of a semi."

I glared at George.

"Don't worry, there's no saints in here," he said. "There's pricks in here that have done a lot worse so don't bash yourself up too much about it."

"Easy for you to say," I burst out, the words just spewing from me, "but I feel like the lowest prick on the face of the earth for what I've done."

"That may be the case, but you can't undo the past. You can only do something about the future," said George dryly.

I gesticulated bitterly. "Some future I've got in this shithole."

"You'll fit in. Just keep your nose clean and do your time. You'll get through it."

I nodded. "What are you in for?"

"Armed robbery," said George, turning a page in his book.

"I'm six years into a twelve year stretch. Consider yourself lucky. Yours is only a short stay compared to some of us."

"How did you get caught?"

George put the book down and told me about the day he had got nabbed. He began by telling me about his life before the robbery. He had been a career soldier who was invalided out of the army through an injury while in training at Canungra, after he had returned from Vietnam.

After he had got out of the army, his marriage fell apart, and in his own words, he was 'pretty screwed up' and fell in with the underworld up at Kings Cross where he worked as a doorman at an illegal casino.

He had racked up some big gambling debts through his boss who ran the illegal casino and the word was out that George was a marked man if he didn't square up. Desperate to get out of the red, he met a couple of blokes who were planning to rob a branch of the Commonwealth Bank in the inner west of Sydney. They needed somebody to drive the getaway car. George saw this as his way of getting out of trouble, so regardless of the consequences, jumped at the opportunity. The only problem was that the day before the robbery was ANZAC Day and George had got on the scoot with some of his Vietnam Veteran mates.

So, when they decided to rob the bank mid-morning of April 26th 1976, George was still under the weather. The robbery went off fine with $80,000 in cash comfortably stolen. They even made their way to George's getaway car okay, but in his inebriated state, George got lost and ended up down an inner city cul-de-sac. It didn't take long for the police to find them and they all got nabbed and ended up inside.

Despite our frosty introduction to each other, I found that

I liked George and even felt that maybe I had found a kindred spirit, which somewhat eased the dark mental state I was in. He played his cards close to his chest, and seemed as though he had a hard shell of indifference around himself, but I soon learnt when I scratched the surface that George was very much like me. He had a family he had not seen for a long time, a sensitivity about him, a dry sense of humour, was an ex-soldier, and the most important similarity of all, he liked a drink.

This became apparent within days of meeting him. He worked in the kitchen and was in charge of the 'boob booze'. This was a filthy concoction of old vegetable and fruit scraps which were mixed with yeast and hops stolen from the baker's shop. It was rank stuff but it had the desired effect. The grog was brewed in a secret place in a big cavity inside the butcher's block in the kitchen.

He had a system working where if any of the inmates wanted a drop, they would give him a container with a secured top and it would be delivered to their cell on the quiet by one of the sweepers.

I was riddled with guilt about the fact that it was my drunken state that had caused the accident, but I was desperate for a drink to drive the blues away.

"I was wondering how I was going to get a drink inside," I said to George, shortly after I found out about the boob booze.

"You'll be right, Ed, this stuff is guaranteed to knock ya fuckin' socks off," George said with a snigger. He brought some back to the cell one night.

"Fuckin' hell, I can't breathe," I said the first time I took a sip. I'd drank a lot of things in my life, but this was the most revolting stuff I had ever touched. It tasted like rotten vegetables and I couldn't get the stench out of my nostrils.

"You look like someone who's just had their arse up lit up with a blowtorch," said George with a chuckle.

I found talking to George about Vietnam and other experiences very cathartic. It took the edge off my negative feelings I had surrounding Vietnam and the accident in Dubbo.

It didn't take the screws too long to realise that George and I were tight. This coupled with the fact that they had their suspicions that George was involved in manufacturing of the boob booze soon brought the heat down upon us.

About a month after I moved in with George, two screws came in at 3.00 am and ramped our cell. Everything inside was turned upside down. They basically trashed the room.

"Righto, Murdoch, where have you got the ingredients hidden?" one of the screws yelled at him.

The screw giving George a hard time was new to Long Bay. He was a big pommy bloke from Lancashire, who went by the name of 'Jumbo' Marsh because of his big ears. Jumbo Marsh had earnt himself a reputation as one of the meanest screws inside the jail and this was my first encounter with him.

"I've got nothing in here, I'm as clean as a whistle," George protested.

"Bullshit, Murdoch! We've known for ages you've been brewing that shit," he said, belting George in the ribs with a massive blow.

George shrieked in pain, and the screws turned to our mattresses, which they sliced up with a knife to see if they could find any hidden contraband.

As George and I stood with our hands up against the wall, I could see through the corner of my eye that Jumbo Marsh had taken a small colour photo I had of Michelle and Snog off the wall beside my bed. I was concerned, as this was the only photo I had of my daughter and I didn't want it damaged.

"Hey, go easy, sir, that's the only photo I have of my daughter," I said anxiously.

"You shut up, dickhead," said Jumbo Marsh before he hit me in the side of my head, fracturing my cheek bone.

The pain was excruciating, but before I could retaliate, George yelled out, "Leave it, Ed. You'll be up shit creek in a barbed wire boat if you go the knuckle."

"That's right, Costigan. Take Murdoch's advice and keep your fists to yourself, not unless you want a shot at the title," said Jumbo Marsh, his face only inches from mine.

"Don't tempt me, Marsh. I could take you on blindfolded," I said through gritted teeth.

"Your glory days are well and truly behind you, Costigan. You're a has-been, and what's worse, a drunken has-been to boot. Don't you forget that!" Jumbo Marsh said before delivering a massive blow to my ribs which dropped me to the floor.

As I squirmed on the floor in agony, George turned to Jumbo Marsh and said, "You won't find anything in this cell, sir. We're all clean."

"You shut up, Murdoch, we know you've got stuff hiding in here. We'll be back," he said ominously. They left our cell, leaving behind a trail of destruction.

George winked at me where I was still lying on the floor in pain and said, "You done well, Ed. You definitely earned yourself some brownie points today."

Our altercation with the two screws only forged our friendship even further, and as the months passed, we realised that a rock-solid bond had formed between us. In time, it was this bond that was to play a part in straightening out myself for good.

It was a couple of weeks before Christmas of 1982 when I was re-classified to a C2, which allowed me to work in the mechanic's workshop. Within a week of being re-classified, Jumbo Marsh approached our cell, just before lights out one evening. George and I initially thought that he was on the hunt for contraband, but he soon eased our fears when he indicated what the visit was for. He had a lawn mower that wasn't working and wanted me to fix it.

The next day, just after breakfast, one of the screws took me down to the mechanic's workshop where Jumbo Marsh was waiting with his hands on his hips. Sitting on the workshop bench was a Victa two-stroke lawnmower. He informed me that the mower wasn't working and wanted to see whether I could breathe some life into it. After I tried to start the mower to no avail, I spent the best part of ten minutes pulling it apart. I soon noticed that the membrane inside the carbie was corroded and blocking the fuel supply. It took me a while to convince the tough screw that he needed a new carburetor kit from the local lawnmower shop, as he didn't want to go spending his hard earned cash unnecessarily.

The next morning I spent fifteen minutes installing the kit. I blew the fuel lines out and put everything back together. I pulled the zip cord and the mower spluttered and came to life.

Jumbo Marsh gave me a slight grin and said with a hint of sarcasm that I was more than just an ugly face.

A few days later, Jumbo Marsh strolled into my cell and placed the latest copy of *Rugby League Week* in my hands.

"The mower works like a treat, Costigan." He gave me a wink and left.

It wasn't my only delivery that day, I also had a Christmas card from Anne.

Dear Ed,

Regardless of what has happened, you will always be my favourite brother. Stay strong over this Christmas period, Ed. You are in my thoughts and prayers.

Love, Anne

I read the words to George and he said, "You're lucky to have somebody who still loves you, Ed. My mob have completely deserted me." He pulled a small plastic screw top bottle out of a slit in his mattress and proposed a toast. "Here is a happy Christmas to you, Ed."

I nodded and raised the container. "Here's to you George, and my family, and especially my beautiful daughter Michelle, who I haven't seen in way too long."

As I took a swig out of the container, I looked at the photo on my wall. As I touched the photo I became melancholy and I hoped that one day we might be reunited. I smiled at my dog, too. I had no idea what happened to Snog, but I missed hearing Michelle's laugh and reading her stories. She was never far from my thoughts.

Fixing Jumbo Marsh's lawnmower changed my whole outlook as I felt I was doing something worthwhile. It kept me away from the dark places in my head and was a prelude to bigger things to come. Shortly before Christmas, he approached me about working on his car. This was no ordinary car, it was an immaculate, cherry red Torana XU-1. It was a gift in itself to be working on something so fine.

I also got visits from Stumpy, Anne, Rowy and Sean just prior to Christmas which lifted my spirits. Although my situation was anything but perfect, I felt that I had been transported out of that dark hole of depression I saw myself in after arriving at Long Bay.

For the remainder of my time in Long Bay, I worked on Marsh's as well as a couple of the other screws' cars. This brought me some special privileges which usually consisted of books and magazines. I shared some of them with the other inmates which they much appreciated.

***

"Like I said, Tim, jail was anything but perfect, but it was better than what some of the other inmates had."

"Well, I suppose being in the workshop got you out of your cell."

I nodded. "It certainly did. I was actually working in my trade which did my head a lot of good. Made me feel useful. Jumbo Marsh soon learnt about the Monaro I once owned which interested him. Don't get me wrong, there was never any close bond between us because he was a hard prick, but he grudgingly respected me."

"I reckon I'd go crazy, locked up in a cell all day," Tim said with a faraway look.

I shuddered. "Being locked up in a cell is the least of your problems. When I was in the nick I witnessed the brutality of life inside and it's not pretty."

"Yeah? Like what?"

I gave him a serious look. "Like the beatings and the rapes and the intimidation from the heavy inmates to the weaker ones. Jumbo Marsh had it in for a pedophile in there and one night hung him with a bed sheet."

"Shit!" Tim said. "He killed a bloke?"

"Yeah, I saw the bloke hanging up in his cell the next morning and it wasn't pretty. Dead as a door nail he was with his eyes wide open." I glared at Tim. "I kid you not, the nick is a heavy place. It's a dog eat dog world and you better make sure you never end up there."

I told Tim a few other anecdotes of what I'd seen inside and it fairly put the wind up him. When I was finished, Tim sat back in seat his with fear in his eyes.

"And finally, my moment of truth arrived," I said to him.

"What do you mean?"

"The booze, Tim. I finally saw it for what it was."

***

The days went by and as 1983 went and 1984 came, I had adhered to George's suggestion and kept my nose clean. In saying that, I found being in jail the absolute pits and the most degrading experience I had ever been through.

Many like myself were there because they committed their crimes under the influence of alcohol or drugs, and did not know what they were doing at the time. I am not making any excuses for what I did, because in retrospect I certainly deserved to go to jail, but I didn't think that at the time of sentencing. I really didn't. I admit that.

The fact of the matter was, I was addicted to booze but I didn't know it. Hell, I wouldn't have accepted it, either. I honestly thought that I had ended up in jail because I had gone to the pub, not because of alcohol itself.

So, when Skinny Lambert approached me one Friday morning in November 1984 about going to an Alcoholics Anonymous meeting inside the jail, I treated him with complete contempt.

"Why the fuck would I want to go and listen to a bunch of lame ducks like those jokers, Skinny? I mean, what do you think I am, a complete loser?" I growled.

Skinny wasn't the sharpest tool in the shed, but he just thought I might want to go because there was a chance for a free smoke and some time away from A wing.

That certainly made me think, as anything to break the monotonous routine of jail life would be too good to let pass by.

I thought about it and agreed to join Skinny at the Sunday afternoon AA meeting for my free smokes. In saying that, it did not stop me from having a drink of some boob booze that morning before the meeting.

About 12 of us went to the meeting, and true to form we got our free smokes. There were two blokes there to talk to us, an old Aboriginal fellow named Jack and a bloke in his mid-thirties named Roger. Roger looked as though he had just come out of a private school and was obviously uncomfortable about being there.

Jack spoke about things I had never heard of before like, 'the first drink does the damage' and 'living a day at a time', as well as other AA clichés.

It was as though he was talking some other language and I was utterly confused. I leant forward in my seat and performed a character assassination on him for I thought he was talking a load of shit.

I wasn't the only inmate doing it. A couple of others gave Roger a hard time with comments under their breath such as, "Who are you trying to kid, ya fuckin' dickhead," and "I've spilt more piss than you've drunk, ya poof." But a few other inmates were genuinely interested in what he had to say and were on the program.

Jack, the old Aboriginal bloke, never missed a beat. He was very calm and I remember him telling us about how he ended up in Long Bay and then Kenmore Mental Hospital at Goulburn, all as a result of him drinking huge quantities of metho.

As far as I was concerned, it was all over my head and I wasn't interested in attending another meeting.

That night as I lay on my bottom bunk I told George what I thought about AA.

"I got my free smoke as Skinny Lambert suggested, George, but I got bugger else out of it."

George said nothing but I could hear him turn in his bunk so I continued. "Wouldn't that be the absolute pits if you had to go to AA for the rest of your life like those two mugs I heard today."

He didn't respond.

"What do you reckon, George?" I said quietly. "I might have had a few problems with my drinking, but I've never been that bad to think I'd have to go to AA."

There was a long moment of silence before George responded carefully. "Seems to me, Ed, that you might be walking around blindfolded."

"Blindfolded!" I said in shock. "What do you mean?"

"Have you forgotten why you ended up in jail?"

"That was only because I went to the pub in Eumungerie

that day. If I had driven back to Dubbo directly, then I wouldn't have been involved in the accident."

"Oh, gee, mate. You are away with the pixies," George said sarcastically.

"What are you talking about, George? You robbed a bank because you've got a problem with the punt. It's a bit rich you pointing the finger at me isn't it?" I snapped at him.

George launched himself off his bed, landed on the floor beside me and pulled up a chair in the darkened cell.

"Listen, you arrogant prick," George snarled at me with his finger raised. "I've never told anyone about this and I don't want you to repeat it to anyone, do you hear me?"

I nodded my head cautiously.

"A few years ago I went to AA after I ended up in a rehab. There was a lady psychologist there nicknamed 'Bev the Butcher' who was as tough as nails, but she helped me to get off the booze and AA was a big part of that."

By this stage I was leaning on my elbow, listening carefully.

"I got off the drink and was doing all the suggested things like going to AA meetings on a regular basis, getting a home group and a sponsor."

"A sponsor?" I said inquisitively.

"Yeah, somebody to show you through the AA program. Anyway, I was just shy of my first birthday and the group members were preparing to give me a birthday cake and a card to celebrate my achievement."

"A birthday cake! That's kid's stuff!" I scoffed.

"Listen, smartarse. Getting a year up is a big achievement in AA. It's like scoring a ton in cricket. The group members give you a cake and make a big fuss over you. You feel like you're king shit and I only had a month to go before the big day. Anyway, this good sort came into the rooms. She was in a bit of a state when she first came in and I wasn't attracted to her at first, but after a couple of weeks she detoxed off the booze. Well, I saw a different woman. She was in her early thirties, blonde, great body and a good personality. She told me she was a legal secretary and she had recently left her husband. Well I was as toey as a tick because I hadn't had a 'Wellington Boot' for a while, and she was as keen as mustard so we went for it."

"What happened?"

"What do you think? The sex was great, but then my sponsor cottoned onto what I was up to and pulled me aside after she busted and got back on the piss. His name was 'Wharfie Jack' and he was a real straight shooter. He told me in no uncertain terms that I shouldn't be screwing a new female member, or as it's commonly referred to in AA circles, 'thirteenth stepping'. Well didn't I get a huge resentment about this old bastard telling me who I should be screwing."

"What did you do?"

"I told him to go and get fucked and ended up back on the piss. You see, Ed, resentment is suicide to the alcoholic and it puts more Alkies back on the piss than anything else. I wasn't totally honest with myself when I put the drink down because I continued to gamble. It was after I got back on the piss that I racked up my huge gambling debt that ultimately landed me in here."

I looked at George with my hand on my chin contemplating what he had just told me.

"Just remember this, Ed. Those two blokes who came to see you today went home after the meeting to their wives and families while you went back to your cell. Now you tell me who's the fuckin' mug now?"

He let that sink in for a moment.

"I'm only going to say one other thing about this, and then I never want to talk about it ever again. Don't ever knock AA, Ed, because at the end of the day it may be the only place you've got left to go. Remember, your best thinking got you inside this jail."

I looked at George long and hard. "If AA is so terrific, George, then why don't you give up the piss and go back to it?"

George glared at me, but his eyes were bright. He wiped his nose and with a voice full of emotion exclaimed, "Because I fucking well can't."

He got up from his chair and launched himself up onto the top bunk.

George's words rang in my ears for sometime afterwards, as I knew deep down inside me that his truth was also mine. It was hard seeing George so upset, and I couldn't get to sleep.

After a while, George leaned down and passed me a slip of paper. "Wharfie Jack gave me this poem years ago and it helped me. Who knows, Ed, it may help you also."

I read the poem in the dull light of the cell.

They shall feel it, they shall know it

Who, when from the sky of azure, that dread thunderbolt was hurled

Made me drunkard who was sober, made me devil who was poet,

Made the girl wife and boy husband, man and woman of the world.

Henry Lawson

I lay back on my bunk, stunned by what I had just read. Even to this day, it still astounds me how powerful the impact those words from one of our nation's greatest poets had on me. At the time they hit me like a ton of bricks. It was like those words had been waiting just for me. The tragedy of my life was summed up and it was the turning point for me.

They say that the alcoholic has a moment of sanity, a moment when they see themselves exactly for what they are. That happened to me at that precise moment. It was then that I realised for the first time in my life, the very first time, that all my troubles had been because of booze.

I had done terrible things because of alcohol, lost everything. The loss of my wife and child, the loss of my home and business, the loss of all my material wealth, and the loss of a girl that I killed while under the influence of alcohol. And finally, the loss of my very dignity, my spirit and most importantly, my hope. Old King Alcohol had been having a merry old dance at my expense and I had only just woken up to the fact.

I didn't sleep a wink that night as George's story and Henry Lawson's poem reverberated around my head. I felt a great sadness envelop me and the tears welled up in my eyes. It was as though I had been given a new state of consciousness and I saw myself for who I really was.

It sure wasn't pretty.

As I lay on my bed in the dead of the night I kept repeating to myself, "Look where the booze has led you!"

Then, in the early hours of the morning, a thought came into my head that hit me like a bolt of lightning. "Maybe those people in AA *have* got the answer. Maybe they aren't the mugs I thought they were!"

The thought of AA didn't enthrall me, the principles the members had been spruiking may as well been sent from planet Pluto for all they meant to me. But it was this small realisation that the AA members might be right, which ultimately saved my life.

It led me to swallow my pride and make the important decision to go to another meeting, even though I wasn't really sure what the future held for me.

It was the eleventh of November 1984. Remembrance Day. I didn't know it at the time, but that day was the last time I ever took a drink.

***

"As fate would have it, a couple of days after the conversation with George, our cell was ramped once again by Jumbo Marsh and another screw. Some dog who had it in for George tipped a screw about him carrying packets of yeast into his cell, and as sure as the sun rises, they found the contraband in the slit in George's mattress. They also found other ingredients inside the butcher's block in the kitchen and the sly grog production came to a screeching halt," I said.

"No more booze?" said Tim. "What a blow."

"In more ways than you'll know, and beyond the booze," I agreed. "They transferred George to Goulburn and I never saw him again. I don't know what happened to him, but I owe him a debt of gratitude for planting the seed of sobriety in my mind. It was the following Sunday, with fear and trepidation, that I went to another meeting of AA. Instead of being indifferent to what the speakers were talking about, this time around I became surprisingly receptive to their message."

Tim looked thoughtful. "Why? You hated it the first time. I would too, despite that bloke telling you not to knock it."

I shrugged. "Well, it was at this meeting that I met the man who was to have a profound influence on my life."

Chapter 11

S INCE MY TALK with George, I had lost the desire to drink and although fearful as to what the future held, I walked into the AA meeting the following Sunday with a new-found attitude.

Waiting to speak to us that day was Jack, the old Aboriginal man, young Roger, as well as another addition. What got my attention with the third man was how he was dressed. He was wearing a white short-sleeve shirt, black trousers and I could not help but notice that on his collars were two distinct gold crosses. I immediately thought to myself that he was a ring-in brought to the meeting to remind us inmates how bad we had been. My new-found attitude for sobriety was abruptly terminated. Bloody priests.

"Of course there would have to be one of these bloody bible-bashing bastards here!"

Skinny Lambert, who was sitting beside me, heard my

utterance and said, "You may be surprised, Costigan. This priest has a good story!"

I turned to Skinny, full of arrogance and contempt, and snarled, "You've got to be fucking kidding, Skinny!"

The meeting started with Roger as opening bat, and just like the previous week, I was not too enthralled by what he had to say. When he was finished speaking, Skinny Lambert was asked to share his story which became a long-winded tale of woe about a broken home, abuse and bender drinking before an armed robbery landed him in the nick. Next cab off the rank was another inmate whose tale got my attention. I could relate to much of his story, especially his alcohol compulsion and his inability to say no to the first drink. Jack the Aboriginal spoke and once again told the room a story about years of metho drinking and countless amounts of rehabs before he found himself at The Mathew Talbot Hostel for homeless men in Woolloomooloo, where he had got sober.

By this stage the tension had gone out of my shoulders and I felt relaxed. Surprisingly, I identified with much of what was being said, but then the chairmen turned to the priest and said, "Father Frank, would you like to share?"

I murmured to myself, "All good things must come to an end!"

I crossed my arms and buried myself low into my seat, pulled my collar up and prepared myself for the lecture on morality which I was sure was about to come. Instead, Fr Frank surprised me with his opening remarks, which were quite humorous and which I was not expecting.

"Well, good afternoon everyone, my name's Frank and I'm an alcoholic. I've just heard Skinny share his story and if someone was running a book in here this arvo, I'm sure we would win a race with this bastard, because he's coming ahead leaps and bounds."

The room erupted into spontaneous laughter and I sat upright in my chair. The priest's quick-witted earthy spiel grabbed my attention.

Fr Frank smiled at the group. "Believe you me when I tell you that I could have quite easily ended up in here because I drove motor vehicles around paralytic for years and years. It is a miracle that I never killed anybody for there were times I couldn't see the road. After years of drinking, my alcoholism eventually took me to the gates of hell."

Frank said that in 1962 he was brought to a private hospital for alcoholics in Strathfield, Sydney. He was strapped to a stretcher in the horrors, as he had been seeing snakes crawling out of the ground, and was sweating and shaking to the point where he thought he was going to die. All this was an accumulation of years of drinking which saw him smash cars as well as suffering from anxiety, fears and the shakes.

I sat upright in my seat, as I identified with Frank immediately.

He was brought up on a wheat and sheep farm at Bingara in northern New South Wales and first picked up a drink in 1940 when training as a tailgunner in a Lancaster Bomber in the RAAF. As he went on active service in Europe his drinking increased. In 1943, returning from a bombing mission over France, his whole crew was killed when hit by an incendiary round fired by a Messerschmitt 109.

Frank parachuted into occupied France where he made contact with the French Resistance and was put under the care of a young French priest who was a member of the Resistance. Eventually the priest was betrayed by a traitor and Frank was taken to Buchenwald Concentration Camp in Germany. At war's end, Frank was liberated by the advancing Red Army.

After the war he went woolclassing and in 1948 ended up in hospital after a serious car accident. While recovering in hospital and reflecting upon his life, he thought about the young French priest who had saved his life and decided to study for the priesthood.

It was over the next fourteen years that Frank's drinking steadily increased, ultimately landing him in the private hospital in Strathfield in 1962 where he recovered from alcoholism. As the priest told his story, it suddenly occurred to me that he was identifying as an alcoholic and not a man of the cloth, and that he was at AA for exactly the same reason I was. From where I sat I found it hard to believe that a priest could end up in such a state, being a man of God and all, but his story had my total attention.

"I was devoid of all spirituality. I had to come to AA to learn about God. When I was on the booze, my only concern was how I was going to get my hands on the next drink. After my recovery from alcoholism I spent time in a number of Sydney parishes before I was made Parish Priest of St Patrick's Catholic Church in Sutherland in 1970." The priest looked at his watch and said, "I've probably spoken too long this afternoon, but I felt compelled to tell you a little more than usual about my story. Who knows, there may be one among you today who needed to hear my message."

Frank sat down and was met with generous applause. His parting words had struck at the heart of my being for I knew that he was put there for me, so as *I* could hear his message.

That night as I lay in bed I went over everything that Frank had spoken about that day. His honesty had pierced my soul like nothing had ever done before. I realised I stood at a cross-roads in my life and that I had two choices: to either keep on drinking and suffer all the consequences of alcoholism or accept the philosophy of AA.

It was there in that cell in Long Bay that I accepted my alcoholism without any reservations. I felt a great weight come off my shoulders, the likes of which I had never experienced before, and somehow, I instinctively knew I would be alright.

***

"It all began there, Tim. That's when my life finally changed, when I finally admitted that I had a problem and that problem was booze. Fr Frank's story was the catalyst for change and unbeknownst to me, he had given me the key that opened the door to a brand new way of life. Can you see where I'm coming from Tim?"

Tim nodded, his intense gaze indicating that what I had said was finally registering. I continued. "Little did I know, Tim, that as time went by, Fr Frank and I were to have more in common than I could have ever imagined."

"Like what?"

"He liked boxing and footy, but more importantly there was a natural affinity between us. Quite simply we were on the same wavelength. His message to me was that regardless of the dire predicament I was in, there was an answer to my question of how I could recover from my present circumstances. He gave me hope and that was something I had not experienced for a long while."

"Hope!" Tim said. "I'd give anything to get out of the circumstances I'm in."

Tim's sudden acknowledgement of his situation made me

sit upright and I leaned forward across the table kitchen table. "You can, Tim. This is the beginning of a brand new way of life, if you'll only admit that the booze has got you licked. Can you understand where I'm coming from? Do you see?"

Tim looked me in the eyes for some time. "Yeah, I can understand you, Ed."

I sat back. "You and I are on the same level. I know that deep down you understand what I have been trying to tell you. You know that denial underscores your actions. It's stopped you from seeing and accepting the truth about yourself."

Tim sighed. "You're right. I've been too petrified to let go of the very thing I thought was my best mate. It's my worst enemy, isn't it?"

I resisted the urge to smile. I was proud that he'd reached this space, but I didn't want to trivialise the moment. "I knew you'd eventually come around, Tim. But it doesn't stop when you've admitted the truth. The work then begins in earnest."

He nodded in agreement.

***

During the next week I was eager to get back to AA, so as I could hear the priest speak again.

Once again, I identified with him and it was after the meeting, I approached him warily for the first time and introduced myself.

"How do you do, Father, my name's Ed."

"G'day, Ed, you can call me Frank," he said casually.

"I really related to what you've said the both times I've heard you, Frank," I told him directly.

He smiled. "Well, thank you, Ed. This gift of sobriety is open to anybody who is willing to accept their alcoholism."

I nodded. "I didn't believe that I had a problem with booze until recently. Your story has had a huge impact on me. If the truth be known, I was a bit wary of you at first because my brother's a priest and we don't get along."

"What's his name?" Frank said with narrowed eyes.

"John Costigan."

Frank smiled. "Well I'll be buggered, you're John's brother. How is he anyway?" Frank said.

"I don't know, I don't talk to him. He's a pompous bastard," I said tersely.

"I know he can be a bit pedantic at times, but he means well," he said with a smile.

"You could have fooled me!"

"Don't be too harsh on him, Ed. After all, he's helped a lot of people." Frank looked at me and placed his hand on my shoulder. "I know who you are, Ed."

"You do?"

"Indeed I do. In fact, I was there the night you beat Vince Cosoleto at The Hordern Pavilion for the Australian middleweight title."

"You were?" I said, surprised.

"I certainly was. In fact, I followed your boxing career closely."

"Seems like another lifetime when that all happened," I said, feeling the old regrets stronger than ever.

"I'm sure it does, Ed. That was one of the best fights I ever saw," said Frank.

I smiled. "Thanks, Frank, I appreciate that. You like boxing, do ya?"

"Oh yeah. I fought in the ring when I was a younger man." He stared at me. "You know you're from pretty good stock, Ed

Costigan. You've got a grandfather who won the VC and you won the middleweight title."

I was surprised. "You know about my family?"

"Yes, I do. In fact, I know what happened for you to end up in here, Ed," said Frank. He didn't pull any punches either.

"Then you know I killed a young girl in truck accident when I was drunk," I said, my hands closing into fists.

Frank nodded his head. "I know all about it. I read it in the newspaper. It was a great tragedy."

"I am a shattered human being, Father," I said, my eyes glistening. "I've been hammering myself with the booze for years and look where I've ended up." I pointing to the walls of the jail.

"I can see that you've been to hell and back, but you need not worry because there is an answer," he said. His voicing sounded reassuring and a feeling of warmth and safety came over me, similar to what I had experienced from my mother when I was a small boy.

"Look where I am. Stuck inside this place. There's no answers for me here. My life's been a complete waste," I said, breaking down in tears. I was overcome with emotion.

He put a hand on my shoulder. "I'm sure it hasn't been a complete waste. Everyone has some redeeming side to their life, no matter how far they've gone down."

"It's hard to see that where I am at the moment." I wiped a hand across my face.

"You're an alcoholic, Ed. You can't take the first drink, and that's why you've ended up in jail," said Frank with his hand on my shoulder.

I gathered my composure. "I know that now, Frank. I been

fighting the booze for years and I've only just come to the realisation that I can't drink anymore. I just can't."

"Well then. You've fought a big part of the battle if you've been able to accept that simple fact. You see you have to give in to win, if you want to arrest your alcoholism. It's a paradox, but it's the truth, Ed."

"I don't know if a wretched bastard like me can be helped," I told him.

He caught my eye. "No bastard is too wretched that he can't be helped."

I wanted to believe him, but I knew what I'd done. "I killed a young girl. That's an unforgivable sin, Father."

"No sin is unforgivable," he said. When he stared at me with those reassuring eyes, I felt the truth of his words. He fully believed them. He believed that *I* was worth helping.

I took a deep breath. Somehow, things suddenly seemed so much lighter. "Thank you, Father. I appreciate your kindness."

I spoke to Frank for another fifteen minutes before the guard indicated that it was time for me to make my way back to my cell.

***

"Do you know why I leant you the money Tim?"

Tim looked at me, surprised and said, "No. Why?"

"Because a total stranger extended the hand of friendship to me and passed the message of sobriety onto me. I wanted to do the same for you."

"Friendship?" His face contorted, like he was confused.

I nodded. "Yeah, friendship, Tim! There's no other way to explain it. Frank gave me unconditional love. No strings attached. He wanted nothing in return but to help me. The fact he was a priest, and I had a contempt for the clergy at the time, made his act even more pertinent. I was in no position to be critical of this man, as my best thinking had landed me in jail. Frank spent a lot of time with me while I was in the nick. He showed me the way to a better way of life." I took a sip from my mug.

"But you were locked up in jail! How's that a better life?"

"He gave me a new philosophy to live by and in doing so I was able to free my mind," I told him.

"Bloody hell, this is getting a bit trippy for me. I mean you were in fuckin' jail, not some Indian Ashram."

I looked at Tim over my mug. "You know the first lesson I learnt on my road to recovery?"

"What?"

"That I have to give away what I've got to keep it. It's a paradox, but it works. I've put it to the test on too many occasions to know otherwise."

Tim frowned as he tried to figure it out in his head. "So, what you're saying is that by helping me, you're actually helping yourself?"

"Bingo. You've hit the jackpot."

He fidgeted for a moment and then blurted out, "Why do you believe I'm worth helping?"

I smiled. "Because I believe that you're a decent bloke. And you're the son of the man who saved my life. You're worth it."

He threw his arms wide open. "Why on earth do you believe that? You don't even know me."

"Because that priest believed in me on a day when I was incapable of believing in myself. Believe you me, Tim, I was the most unlovable creature you could have ever laid your eyes on when I finally pulled the plug on my drinking."

***

I continued to go to my one AA meeting a week while I kept myself busy reading what I could on the disease of alcoholism.

Since George had been transferred to Goulburn, I had been left in the cell by myself which was a back-handed way of Jumbo Marsh saying 'thank you' for looking after his car. When I mentioned this to Frank, he commented that things were looking up for me and it would only get better if I stayed sober.

Time passed, as it does, and 1984 lagged away as slow as watching water drip from a tap. I kept myself busy by educating myself on alcoholism, mechanics and other similar material.

Then, in April of 1985, I received a visit from Annie who came with the news that Nana O'Grady had passed away. Both Anne and my cousin Sean had kept me abreast over the last few months of Nana O'Grady's worsening condition. I was neither surprised nor cared about her health, such was my level of resentment for the woman who had been a thorn in my side for the majority of my life, but what I did not realise until Anne visited me that day, was that during those last few months of Nana's life, she had undergone an epiphany. Apparently, her attitude had changed dramatically and as a result, so had her whole demeanour. Anne told me that Nana had shared many things about herself that had remained hidden from those who knew her.

Before Anne departed she gave me an envelope from Nana addressed to me. I placed it on my bunk and looked at for some time before eventually opening it and reading it later that evening.

Dear Ed,

I know this letter will come as a total surprise to you and I would not consider ill of you if you did not avail yourself to read it, considering our relationship has been anything but the best for as long as I have known you.

The fact is that I am not long on this earth as I am terminally ill and the end is nigh. In these last months of my life I have had plenty to reflect upon, and I realised I owed much restitution to those I have been in conflict with. My remorse has been unbearable.

Soon after I was informed by my doctor that my cancer was terminal, I had a profound experience where I realised how my hard shell of indifference has caused much angst to those who have been closest to me. It is you, Ed, that I owe the greatest apology to as my abrasive nature has caused you much animosity and indignation towards me as far back as my memory goes. I hope after I have shared some of my life with you that you can please forgive me for my injustices towards you.

As a girl in my late teens growing up in the town of Kilmallock, in county Limerick in Ireland, I was full of the joy of life as any young lady would hope to be. It was my dearest wish that a knight in shining armour would come into my life and sweep me off my feet. As fate would have it my beau did appear in 1912 in the form of Thomas Joseph O'Grady when I was 19 years of age and he was 22.

It was in the shadows of World War I that Tom finished his degree in civil engineering and I could not have been more delighted at my station in life for my heart was full of love. But alas the great calamity which was about to sweep the world took precedence over our affairs of the heart and Tom enlisted in the army. He was commissioned as a lieutenant in the 1st Battalion Royal Munster Fusiliers, where he landed at Cape Helles at Gallipoli on the 25th of April, 1915.

After Gallipoli, Tom's battalion was then sent to the Western Front where he served in both France and Belgium. Although Tom fought to the end of the war, he was a wreck from shelling and gas attacks, not to mention the constant grind of battle.

We settled down in Limerick City where Tom found a job as a civil engineer and we had our two eldest children; your Uncle Kevin and your mother, Monica. The dash and witty sense of humour which had attracted me to Tom had gone and I was left with only the shell of the man I once knew. More children followed.

Tom took to the bottle and could not work in his profession, so with the children in tow we decided to immigrate to Australia and settled in Dubbo, where Tom had a number of cousins living.

Within four years of arriving in Dubbo, I had given birth to two other children and by the time of the Great Depression hitting in 1929, we had a total of eight which only exacerbated Tom's alcoholism.

We battled on over the next few years and it was in 1932 that the great tragedy took place. Contrary to what was the official cause of Tom's death, it was not an industrial accident that caused him to be run over by a steam train but suicide. During this era suicide was a taboo subject, even more than today, and as Catholics it is seen as a mortal sin where one goes to hell, so I dare not mention the true nature of his death to anybody.

Regardless of Tom's worsening alcoholism, I was devastated as he had left me with eight young children and as a result I plunged in to a state of depression. I never forgave Tom for taking his own life and as the years went on I developed into a neurotic woman.

Ed, I know you are in dire straits and the tragedy of your crime has rocked our family to the core, not to mention the poor girl's clan who you have devastated. I have been told by Anne that you have recently sought help for your drinking whilst in jail and I commend you for your stern actions in addressing your problem.

I ask for your forgiveness for my past indiscretions towards you.

I have not been able to visit you in jail as I am too frail, and by the time you have finished your sentence I will have left this earth.

God bless you, Ed, and may the good Lord keep you safe.

Your Nana,

Bernadette O'Grady

I recoiled in shock at seeing Nana signing off her letter with her Christian name, as the years of animosity had severed any affection I had towards her and I had completely blotted it out.

I sat on the chair in my cell for ten minutes, my head spinning with a multitude of thoughts, all the time trying to comprehend what I had just read.

"Did I just read what I thought I read?" I said aloud to myself. "Was that Nana who wrote that?"

"Are you alright in there, Costigan?" said one of the screws as he walked past my cell.

"Yes, sir. Everything's fine in here."

"Keep the noise down then will you!"

"Yes, sir."

I continued to ponder in silence on the enormity of what I had just read, in particular the revelation that my grandfather had committed suicide and not died of an industrial accident as the family had been led to believe.

I delved back into the envelope where I found two black and white photographs which I had never seen before, and which left me confused as to who they could be.

The first one was of a beautiful young woman with shoulder length brown hair in a formal dark dress, seated with a floral bouquet. I looked long and hard to try to identify who it may be, but to no avail. It was only after I tuned the photo over that I learned the name as I read the neat handwriting.

Bernadette O'Shaughnessy. Taken in 1912 aged 19 at Kilmallock, Limerick.

I covered my mouth lest I let out a gasp of shock and disturb the guard once again.

I continued to study the beautiful woman in the photograph, trying to correlate the fact that this was actually my crazy nana, who I only ever pictured as a hagged old crow.

After a considerable amount of time viewing the photograph, I turned to the other one which left me in a state of even more perplexity.

It was Nana and Thomas on their wedding day. Nana was as beautiful as I have ever seen a woman look on her wedding day, dressed in a beautiful white wedding gown. Next to her was my grandfather looking resplendent in his officer's uniform.

On the back of the photograph was written

> *Thomas Joseph O'Grady and Bernadette Francis O'Shaughnessy on their wedding day, December 1915, Limerick.*

I lay on my bed and held the letter and photographs in my hand. I breathed heavily as I contemplated what I had just read and seen. I was overcome with a feeling of great melancholy for what Nana had been through, and spent a restless night tossing and turning as I thought about what I had read in the letter. By the morning I was worn out by my sleepless night.

I was overcome with a great feeling of compassion for my nana, and for all that she had been through in her life. Nana's words to me about seeking help for my alcoholism touched me deeply and the fact she had shown me a great level of commendation for my actions had allowed me to see her in a new light. Nana's letter was timely, as it further highlighted how a change in attitude can change one's life for the better.

I shared the letter with Frank and he noted that even while

in jail, things were looking up for me. I felt a huge amount of regret that I had not been able to see Nana before she died and express to her how appreciative I was to receive her letter. Because I was. I really was.

Her letter had caused me to reflect about my own predicament and I had determined that I would do my utmost to never grace this hellhole ever again. Jail had been the very antithesis of everything I was or thought I was. I was a man who had been brought up with a moral code, was a hard worker, loved my freedom, loved the company of a woman, and especially liked wide open spaces. Jail was the opposite to all these things and I loathed it.

By the time of my parole board hearing in June 1985, I had been inside for three years and when I was granted early release, I will never forget the feeling of euphoria that came over me.

My early release was on the proviso that I adhere to strict conditions for the next 12 months which included reporting to my parole officer, abstaining from alcohol and attending at least one AA meeting per week.

A month before my release, Frank had asked me if I would like to come and live in the presbytery with him while I found my feet in civvy street once again. I agreed, for although I was excited about my release, I was still nervous about how I would handle the outside world as a sober man.

As I picked up my belongings, leaving the Big House for what I hoped was the last time, Jumbo Marsh turned to me and said, "Keep off the piss, Costigan, and keep those AA meetings up. I don't want to see you back here."

I looked at him long and hard before responding. "I don't intend to come back."

"That's the shot, Costigan. You're not a bad bloke and you're a bloody good mechanic. That's more than some of these jokers have got going for them."

"I'll be right, sir. I always manage to land on my feet," I told him.

I was amazed to hear those kind of words coming from one of the hardest screws at Long Bay. It was the closest I had ever heard him come to praising somebody.

With Jumbo Marsh's words still ringing in my ears, I entered the free world for the first time in three years, a bitterly cold sou-wester blowing in my face.

Waiting in the carpark for me was Annie.

As I walked towards her, I could see the tears welling in her eyes. I was only metres from her when she could not contain herself any longer and lunged at me, throwing her arms around my neck and hugging me while she sobbed.

"Oh, Ed, you're free at last!" she said, planting a kiss on my cheek. I held her tighter than I ever have before.

"I am indeed, Annie, and it's the sweetest of feelings."

A magpie, perched up in a tree not far from where we were standing, let out a fluty song that pierced the mid-morning sky. I stood there with my eyes closed, absorbing the magnificent sound of a bird I had not heard for three years. A huge smile came across my face at such a simple pleasure.

"There is much to catch up on, Ed," said Anne, taking me by the arm.

"There sure is, Annie. Let's get away from this place," I said, glancing back once last time at the big house.

"You can put that place behind you, Ed, and make a fresh start," said Annie patting me on the shoulder.

"That's exactly what I intend to do."

***

"Nana O'Grady's letter had a profound impact on me, Tim."

"How?"

"I suddenly realised that if Nana could forgive me after all the bile she had spewed out during her life then perhaps I could forgive those I resented, too."

Tim considered it thoughtfully. "Sounds like a pretty big ask!"

"You're not wrong, but at least I tried to soften my approach towards those who had done me wrong. I'm not saying I succeeded all the time, but I tried."

"You're a better man than me." He shrugged, and I couldn't help but think of how I was, and how I'd build up resentment at the drop of a hat.

"I'm no bloody saint, but I've come to learn that resentment is a cancer to the soul. It destroys you inside," I told him.

Tim nodded. I wondered if he was seeing the upward swing on all this.

"Anyway, with that in mind I had a big task in front of me as I tried to adjust to life outside without a drink."

Chapter 12

I SPENT MY FIRST weekend of freedom at Anne and Bill's house. They lived in a beautiful four-bedroom home overlooking the Pt Hacking River at Gymea Bay in Sutherland Shire in Sydney. My first night spent there was very strange as I was sleeping in a queen size bed in such magnificent surroundings compared to where I had been cooped up for the last three years.

Anne and Bill's kids, Peter and Samantha, were wary of me at first as they barely knew me, but by the Sunday they had warmed to me and were disappointed to see me leave.

Now I was a free man and of sober habits.

I thought there might be a possibility of seeing Michelle, but after discussing it with Anne, I soon realised that Kim and Michelle wanted nothing to do with me. My actions and drinking had affected them too greatly.

I discussed the issue with Frank on number of occasions while I was in jail and his advice to me had always been to live and let live.

"There has obviously been a lot of damage done to your family, Ed, and you have to accept that it may take years before it sorts itself out. Give it time, and if it's meant to work itself out, it will," Frank said to me.

On Monday morning, Annie dropped me off at St Patrick's at Sutherland before making her way to work. Frank was there to meet me and after showing me to my bedroom, I soon settled in to life at the presbytery.

After a few days, I took the initiative and became the handyman around the parish. It started off simply enough when I noticed a leaky garden tap in the school grounds one day and replaced the washer. I'd never felt like I'd achieved so much. Such a simple act, but in retrospect it still amazes me how something as simple as fixing a garden tap meant so much to me. It struck at the very core of my being and it made me feel human again. I was a mechanic and had always felt the most satisfied when I was repairing things.

I started going to AA meetings on a regular basis all over Sydney. As I had no car I took the train or the bus, and as a result, got to know Sydney like the back of my hand.

I was just grateful to be a free man after those years in jail, and didn't want for much. Such is the way of recovery though, that little gifts of sobriety landed in my lap.

Like when I caught up with Rowy a couple of days after landing at Frank's. He invited me out in his tinnie to do a spot of fishing up the Port Hacking River. We spent about four hours up the river fishing and I was as happy as I had ever been, indulging in such a simple pleasure with a great mate. We talked about the old days and everything that had happened since I met Frank. That little fishing episode with Rowy meant so much to me and I still think about it after all these years.

"I don't know what you're doing, Cozzy, but bloody well keep doing it because it's working. Anything's better than what you were like on the piss," he said to me in the boat. Little comments like that were a reminder of what I was, and made me even more grateful for those who had stuck by me.

On top of this, Anne and Bill would pick me up on a Sunday where I would spend the afternoon at their place, followed by a baked dinner in the evening. It was amazing to see those who loved me most rally to my cause and do everything to ensure my wellbeing. All I had to do was repay that faith.

My simple lifestyle of meetings, work, and friends provided a good foundation for the future. As Frank said to me one day, "The type of sobriety you want in five years time, Ed, depends on the foundation you build right now."

Life went on. It was a huge adjustment to become a sober man after so many years of drinking. If the truth be known, I was relieved to be off the drink, but also scared at what the future held for me.

It was July of 1985 and I was a month out of jail when Frank approached me about an AA meeting he wanted me to go to.

"There's a meeting on Sunday down at Woolloomooloo, at the Mathew Talbot. It's a hostel for homeless men, but they also run AA meeting's there. I think it would do you the world of good to go down there, Ed. It would be a great reminder of where you have come from."

"As if I need to be reminded of where I've come from, Frank. I mean to say, it's burnt into my memory," I said dryly.

"That maybe the case, Ed, but it is my experience that the alcoholic can very easily forget their last drink and a good old-fashioned reminder never did them any harm," Frank said with a wry smile.

I looked at him and a smile came over my face. "You know how to get under my guard, don't ya?"

"That's my business, Ed. To reinforce the message to you."

The Mathew Talbot was run by the St Vincent de Paul Society and was established for disadvantaged men from the streets. It was quite a disturbing sight to see all the stiffs sitting on either side of Talbot Place in all manner of states, and as Frank suggested, it was only when I looked at the human carnage did it truly reinforce where I had come from. Many were yelling abuse at each other and some were fighting and it brought home how crazy I had been.

"Fuck the state government. Those pricks couldn't organise a fuck in a brothel," said one bloke lying in the gutter, sucking on a bottle of Sting.

Then there were others who were away with the pixies and just talking to themselves. It was a stark and sobering reminder of where I could end up if I decided to drink again.

No sooner had I sat down in my seat when a large man who I learned went by the name of Stanmore Mick approached me. "Would you like a cup of tea, sir?" he said in a rapid fire tone.

I noticed a twinkle in his eye which made me smile. "Yeah. Thanks, mate," I replied.

He poured me a tea and shoved a couple of cigarettes into my top pocket. It was the sweetest brew of tea that I had ever tasted, but that didn't matter because my attention was focussed on the circus that was being played out on in front of me.

"Don't you ever tell me I've got a fuckin' problem with alcohol ever again," said one skid row dero.

He was holding a bottle of plonk while screaming at another

similarly well-dressed man. He stormed out of the meeting into the street and even though I went back to the Matthew Talbot regularly, I never laid eyes on him ever again.

After ten minutes the meeting started, and it had been going for a short time when an old Aboriginal woman interjected, "I want to fucking well speak, chairman!"

"You can talk to me after the meeting," said the chairman patiently.

"I want to fuckin' well talk now," she bellowed.

"Sit down, ya fuckin' black bitch," said an old dero from the back of the hall.

"Don't you call me a black bitch, ya fuckin' white prick," she screamed.

"Go on piss off," he spat back.

Losing all patience, she got up and threw her cup of tea all over him before walking out.

The old dero laughed his head off before screaming, "It was a shit cup of tea any way!"

I was to later learn that he was an old metho drinker who lived at the Mathew Talbot. There were people from all walks of life in there, from white collar workers to tradesman to the skid row alcoholics off the street. It was a bunch of liquorices allsorts.

The chairman spoke at length, then after a while he turned his attention to me. "Hey, mate. Yeah, you in the flannelette shirt and jeans," he said as I turned around. "Would you like to share?"

I froze in my seat. I had never shared at a meeting before.

"It's okay, son, we won't bite you," he said.

Frank gave me a dig in the ribs and whispered, "It's about time you shared your story, Ed."

I got up from my seat, my heart pounding and my hands

full of sweat. I nervously made my way to the front of the meeting. I stood there in front of the 60 or so people, frozen like a 'roo stunned by the headlights of a roadtrain.

I was about to open my mouth when the old dero who had abused the Aboriginal lady yelled out some encouraging advice to me. "Sit down, ya dickhead. Ya full of shit!"

The room erupted into raucous laughter and it was a number of minutes before things settled down and I was able to start. It was like that bloke had kicked me back to life and I was ready. I directed my first comments to the dero. "Remember mate, your best thinking has got you here."

The place erupted into more laughter before the Aboriginal lady reappeared out of nowhere. "You give it to the fuckin' smartarse, mate. He's full of shit."

"Who you calling a fuckin' smartarse, ya bitch," said the old dero.

"I'm calling you a fuckin' smartarse," said the Aboriginal lady.

And then it was on. The old dero launched himself at the Aboriginal lady. She managed to sidestep him before hitting him with a combination of punches that I would have been proud of if I'd thrown them.

The end result was a foregone conclusion. The old dero was left lying on the floor motionless, and the Aboriginal lady stood over him and growled, "Got what was coming to ya, hey prick."

When the commotion eventually died down, I looked at the crowd gathered in front of me, who were now focussed on me, and totally quiet.

I said those immortal words.

"My name's Ed, and I am an alcoholic."

I felt a huge sense of relief come over me, as though a heavy weight had been lifted off my shoulders. I'd never said those words before in front of a meeting and just hearing them come out of my mouth gave me instant relief.

The words came much easier now. I started to tell my drinking story and once I started talking, I couldn't really stop. I went for about ten minutes and when I finished my share, everyone erupted in huge applause.

The Aboriginal lady, who by this stage had resumed her seat, yelled out, "Great speech, son, you should be running the United Nations."

The whole room erupted into howls of laughter.

No sooner had I sat down than a giant lump of a man came in, dressed in filthy clothes. He was crying uncontrollably and as he made his way to the front I could smell that unforgettable sweet aroma of stale alcohol coming from the pours of his skin. He pulled a chair out of the front row and turned it about face and knelt in front of it. He cried uncontrollably for the remainder of the meeting and when it was over, he stood up, picked up the chair up and hurled it down the length of the hall. It went flying through the air and narrowly missed a man sitting towards the back of the room. He then stormed out, punching and shoving people in an aggressive manner. I was surprised.

Frank turned to me and said, "It's not all peace and serenity in AA, Ed. There are a lot of sick people in here."

I nodded my head in agreement.

When the meeting was finished and we were gathered down the back of the hall talking to other members, Frank made a suggestion. "I occasionally come down here on a Sunday morning to say mass before the meeting starts. When the meeting's finished, I stick around and help serve lunch to the homeless. Would you like to give me a hand, Ed?"

I looked around at the swirling mass of people and a grin came over my face. "This place is an absolute nut farm, Frank, but I feel right at home here. Yeah," I agreed. "Count me in."

So was to start another phase of my recovery, and a very beneficial one. As Frank was to constantly say to me, "You got to give this thing away if you want to keep it, Ed."

The Mathew Talbot soon became a regular part of my life. I got to know many of the characters who graced the walls of the establishment and came to see them all as equals. I knew only too well that this could become my reality if I didn't keep my guard up and make my recovery the very centre of my life.

"Let's just say you're putting a little insurance policy in place against picking up the first drink, by coming down here and giving a bit back," Frank would say.

Frank was big on service which was understandable, what with him being a priest. He believed in a universal spiritual law called the 'law of abundance' which said that whatever you give away you get back. Good or bad. It was through this one principal that he believed a good life could be had if you helped those around you. I soon came to realise that this was the natural order and because the alcoholic has a naturally compassionate streak in them, I adopted it as part of my life.

As much as I enjoyed the Talbot, the job was not without its tragedy. There was one day when we had a man go into an alcoholic seizure and die right in front of my eyes. Another man committed suicide in a laneway just back from the Talbot by hanging himself. This was sobering stuff. I came to see these human discards as sick, not bad people. Under their chronic alcoholism laid much humour and intelligence, but for some the strain was too much.

This was never more evident than in the case of one older

fellow named Bruce who used to go on metho benders and end up in the Talbot to dry out. He was quite violent when he was on one of these benders, but when he sobered up you could not have met a more likable fellow. Bruce was very articulate and he was obviously an educated man, although I never found out exactly what he had done with his life as he was very shy talking about these things. It wasn't uncommon to find highly intelligent people, some with university degrees, within the walls of the Mathew Talbot. The disease of alcoholism does not discriminate among intelligence, class or creed. Some of these exceptionally talented people fall through the cracks and find their way into chronic alcoholism. Bruce was one such case.

There was an old stand up piano that sat alongside the wall of the dining area and Bruce would sit in front it and play the most beautiful classical pieces without referring to any sheet music. Frank would inform me that he was playing something from Mozart, Beethoven or Chopin. I would be working away and this beautiful music would come wafting through the building. It was a very memorable and emotional experience.

Then one day he was gone, like the wind, never to be seen again.

In time I came to like the Talbot. Underneath all the madness and human suffering there was something very special about the place. Whether it was the rawness of alcoholism hitting you in the face or the special breed of person who worked there... I do not know exactly, but it had a particular and unique spirit running through its corridors.

Bruce was only one among many who left a lasting impression on me, and through the examples that the Talbot provided, good or bad, it paved the way for my new-found way of life.

***

"It wasn't all smooth sailing in AA, Tim."

Tim looked uneasy. "That Mathew Talbot sounds like a pretty heavy place."

"It was, and it certainly wasn't for the faint-hearted," I agreed. "It's confronting. It might not be every one's cup of tea, but I related to the place because of what I'd been through myself. I had a natural affinity with the people there, because their reality had also been mine."

"How long did you keep going there for?"

I shrugged. "I still go there. I still find it beneficial."

"Even after all these years?" Tim looked surprised.

"Yep. Even after all these years. It's still acts as a good reminder of my past, even though it's been a long time since my last drink."

"Phew! I'll give you points for persistence, because be buggered if I'd be backing up to a shit hole like that."

I smiled at Tim. "Well, it wasn't all AA you know, Tim."

Tim lifted his eyebrows.

I threw my arms wide open. "It would be a pretty bland existence if recovery was all AA! I needed to get out and start living again, but I didn't know where to start because the booze had been part of my life for so long that I didn't know how to live without it."

"So, what did you?" he asked.

I sat back in my chair and mused for a moment. "Well, by August of 1985 the honeymoon had worn thin after eight months of sobriety. My initial euphoria of being sober had disappeared and I was faced with the stark reality of what I had been left with. I was 39 years of age. I didn't have a job,

I was broke, I had no woman in my life, and no house to call my own."

"Didn't you tell me that you were happy just to be free when you first got off the piss?" Tim said, shuffling in his seat.

"That's true," I agreed, "but my initial feeling of joy at getting sober had passed. I was now faced with trying to rebuild a life out of nothing. I went into a deep depression for a couple of weeks, thinking of the carnage I had left behind, so much so that I contemplated picking up a drink again."

"Even after everything you had been through?" Tim said. He looked astounded.

I nodded. "Yep. Such is the cunning, baffling and powerful nature of alcoholism. It got so bad that I found myself standing outside a bottleshop in Sutherland one Friday night, seriously contemplating going in and buying some grog to put me out of my misery."

Tim sat forward. "Well? Did you?"

"No. Fortunately, I didn't. Instead, I got on the train and dragged my arse along to an AA in meeting in Heathcote that night which at least kept me sober, albeit not very happy."

He almost looked disappointed, so I grinned at him.

"What?" Tim said with a look of intrigue.

"That's when a little miracle happened that changed the way I looked at life."

"Miracle?"

"Yep, and it came about in a most unlikely way."

***

It was the next morning and my lip was dragging on the ground, such was my depressed state, when I heard Frank whistling in the garage. I decided to investigate and when I entered the garage Frank was placing his golf clubs in the back of his car.

He told me he was about to leave to play golf which brought back memories of when Kim and I had played at Camden Haven Golf Club in the early days of our relationship. Frank queried me about my golf and I told him that Kim had taught me a lot about the game and I had been an average golfer before my drinking had put an end to my participation.

Rowy played golf regularly and had mentioned to me on a number of occasions when I had been inside that we should have a game when I was released and I had kept this thought in the back of my mind.

Frank could see that I was interested and asked me would I like a game, but I shuffled my feet and hesitated. He prodded me as to what the problem was and I told him that I would look like an absolute hacker trying to play golf.

He told me that he played in a social group that played every Saturday morning at Woolooware Golf Course and there was some real plodders in among the group and that I would not look out of place. Still, I hesitated and Frank could see that all was not right, so he prodded me some more as to my problem was.

I spent the next ten minutes telling Frank how worthless I felt about myself and that I had nothing to show for my 39 years on this planet.

Frank listened in silence and when I had finished, he crossed his arms and told me that my sobriety was the most important thing in my life and without it I was worthless to everybody, least of all myself. He told me that I had done a lot of damage to myself and it was going to take time to heal.

I felt better after talking to Frank and decided to take him up on his offer of a game. He was pleased and before he drove off he suggested that the two of us have nine holes at Woolooware the following Monday morning.

On that Monday morning, I hacked, sliced and pulled my way around the golf course, but in among all the confusion I had a ball. It was the first time I had really enjoyed myself for a long time and I was overcome with a boyish enthusiasm. I believe it was golf that served as the catalyst for me being reintroduced back into the human race. From that moment onwards, I started to feel like I was living again, and not just surviving.

It was around this time that I also had a profound change in my thinking. It dawned on me that sobriety wasn't so much about staying off the drink, but about living life. As a result I've never thought about having a drink from that moment, and my depression soon lifted.

After my game of golf with Frank, my attitude changed for the better. I had a spring in my step and I felt as though the weight of the world had been lifted off my shoulders. Within a couple of weeks I had taken up golf lessons with the club pro, and slowly, many of the basics of the game that Kim had taught me all those years ago started to come back to me.

Although things were looking up, my past was never far from my mind and it did cause me grief sometimes. An example of this was a couple of weeks later when Frank and I were having a social hit one Monday morning. "I can't believe I gave up golf all those years ago, Frank. It was the drink that ruled the roost though and eventually my marriage went out the door and I lost the love of my daughter," I said.

"It hurts you a lot doesn't it, Ed?" said Frank.

I nodded. "It sure does. I did the wrong thing by her. I

love that kid to bits and it pains me that it's been so long since I've seen her. I've missed all the important parts of her life. Her birthdays, her achievements at school and at sport. My sister showed me a photograph of her the other day. What a beautiful young lady she's growing up to be!" I said wistfully. "She's 12 years old with gorgeous strawberry blonde hair, just like her mother. I find it very sad that I can't see her."

"You haven't had any luck in trying to see her, Ed?"

I nudged at the turf. "Nah. Not a chance in hell. I don't blame her either. What I put her and Kim through was just atrocious. Still, it doesn't make the situation any easier."

Frank looked at me for some time before he said, "Time is a great healer, Ed."

"Yeah, I've heard that all before, Frank. Like I said though, it doesn't make the situation any easier."

"Go easy on yourself, Ed. You're doing your best. In fact, you are doing more than your best. I think you're a remarkable man to have come this far. If the good Lord sees fit that you should be reacquainted with your wife and child, then it will be in His time, not yours. In the meantime, you just get on with living because I am proud of you, Ed Costigan."

I smiled at Frank and shook his hand. "I appreciate that, Frank, you're a great friend."

A couple of days after this conversation I received a phone call from Anne.

"Bill and I have rented a holiday house down the coast at Vincentia for a few days and we'd like you to come along, Ed."

"I'd love to, Annie!" I enthused.

What followed was a great few days spent with my sister's family. Bill also liked his golf so we managed to get a couple of rounds in while we were down there. We were playing one day when Bill turned to me and said, "Annie and I are so proud of you, Ed. We think it's incredible how well you've come along. I think you're a really decent bloke now you're sober, and the kids just adore you now they've got to know you."

I felt warmed. "You don't know how much that means to me, Bill. I feel like I am part of the human race again."

My little holiday was just another part of the huge jigsaw puzzle of my life coming together and it softened the blow of everything that had passed in my years of drinking, especially the loss of my wife and child and the accident also.

I spent Christmas of 1985 at Anne and Bill's place, and as we entered the new year of 1986, I felt myself getting stronger.

As much as I was appreciative of all that Frank had done for me, lurking always in the back of my mind was the fact that he was a priest. I constantly wondered when he might put the heavy hand on me and try the religious angle. It never really eventuated, for he was too prudent a man and only wanted to see me sober.

"Grog's your bloody problem, Ed. Make sure you don't ever forget that!" he would remind me in his unique way.

But eventually, he did address the question of God in a very subtle way. "How's your relationship with the man upstairs, Ed?"

I made a face. "If the truth be known, I've had more hang ups than a Lebanese Deli when it comes to the subject of God and religion."

Frank gave a little laugh. "You wouldn't be the first person to enter AA with problems in that department!"

I needed to make my feelings clear on the matter. "I really hope you don't shove religion down my throat, Frank, because

I've had just about enough of it throughout the course of my life."

Frank laughed and said, "Look, Ed, I am a Catholic priest and religion is at the centre of my life, but what you believe in is totally your business. You can rest assured that I am not here to convert you at all, because your God has to be one of your own understanding. The only thing I am stressing to you, is to get a higher power that you can believe in. The whole idea of a higher power is to hand your alcoholism over to something bigger than yourself. That's ego deflation at depth, and humility is the touchstone of all spiritual progress."

Frank left that with me and never mentioned it again. In fact, it was because he never said anything about the subject again that I became open to the concept of a God in my life. I always believed in one, even when I railed against the concept of religion, and I felt that He had saved my life, but to use God on a daily basis was a new concept for me.

A few days after my conversation with Frank, I took a ferry ride from Cronulla to Bundenna. After walking for some time, I found a nice spot high up on a cliff overlooking the ocean down towards Marley and contemplated what Frank had discussed with me.

Frank's proposition of a God of my own understanding appealed to me because it wiped the slate clean from all the Catholic dogma I had been brought up with. As I looked over the turquoise sea below I began a dialogue with this God.

"I'll do a deal with you, chief. You keep me sober and look after me, and I'll do anything you want me to do. I don't want any of the bible-bashing stuff. I just want to be able to have a yarn with you, a little chat now and then about whatever is going on in my life. I think that's a pretty good arrangement. What do you think?"

Well, I can assure you the ocean didn't suddenly part and I didn't see a lightning bolt overhead and I most certainly didn't receive the ability to talk in tongues. What I did receive was a great feeling of peace and serenity wash over me. As I sat there looking at the swirling ocean down below, my new-found pact with God set my life on an entirely different course. I've heard all the piss-weak arguments over the years that religion has caused more wars than anything else, and what about all the maimed, crippled and poverty stricken people throughout the world, etc.

They can push that bullshit for all its worth. All I know was the day that I handed my life over to a higher power, this God of mine has covered this ex-pisshead's arse from Coorigil, Eumungerie, from that day to this, and I've been a better man for it.

Because Frank never pressured me on this subject, I have been able to approach him on countless occasions over the years and seek his counsel on things of a spiritual nature. I never became a religious nut, something I feared after the fearsome Nana O'Grady. No, I just came to terms with one simple fact. That there is a God, and I am not it!

This led to something else remarkable. With my new-found spirituality at the centre of my life, I soon found that I was able to *start* to come to terms with the two great calamities in my life; namely, Vietnam and the accident. I was able to hand over my innermost fears and guilt to this higher power, and the burden which I had carried around for so long was taken from me.

As Frank pointed out to me one day, "You could cry for

a thousand years and pray for a thousand years and you won't undo one single act from yesterday. I suggest you get on with living, Ed."

I learnt much from Frank's simple pearls of wisdom, and felt that I started to grow into a better man.

It was during this period that I also began to observe Frank more intently. I saw the way that he interacted with people and what I saw a man who was well-liked and respected by all levels in society. He seemed to have a very practical and natural way of dealing with people, as well as a great sense of humour. People were naturally drawn to him because he didn't so much talk about his spirituality, but lived it in his day to day life.

This I observed firsthand when I was sweeping the church one morning. It was after breakfast when I was in the church by myself, sweeping the aisles. I was in a world of my own when I heard footsteps approaching me from behind. I looked up to see Frank, dressed in his black cassock for a service. He shaped up to me in an orthodox boxing stance and urged me to have a go at him.

"Come on, Costigan, give us your best shot," he said with a grin on his face.

I looked at Frank and soon realised he was having a joke with me. I dropped the broom. "Okay, I'm up for it, Frank."

I then shaped up to him and we proceeded to shadow box up and down the aisle for five minutes, all the while throwing combinations at each other but never making contact. This little sparring session almost killed me as I was so unfit, but I found it very enjoyable.

However, it was abruptly brought to a halt when an older lady of the parish who had arrived to arrange the flowers entered the church. She nearly had a heart attack at the sight of us shaping up to each other. When she left the church in a hurry, we looked at each other and burst out laughing. Frank walked away, sniggering to himself and slapping his side. I believed this little episode had just about made his day.

It was towards the end of September, 1986, when I realised I had not heard from Stumpy for some time. This was unusual because he used to ring me a couple of times a week and now I hadn't heard from him for ages.

I was concerned for his wellbeing and my fears were verified when I received an urgent call one night from Anne to say that Stumpy was ill and that I should come home to Coorigil to visit him. They believed he did not have much time to live.

Stumpy was 89 and although he had lived a long life, age was finally catching up to him and his body was shutting down.

I was mortified at the thought of losing my great mentor and I hurriedly drove out to Coorigil with Anne, Bill and the kids.

I had not been back to Coorigil since that fateful day in June 1982 when I had driven the semi-trailer from Eumungerie back to Dubbo. I was nervous about the reception I would receive from my family, but once again Anne had come in to bat for me.

"I told Mum that you were coming home to visit Stumpy, Ed, and that there should be no animosity towards you," said Anne, while we were driving home to Coorigil.

I was relieved. "Thanks, Annie, because if the truth be known, I am bloody apprehensive about going back to meet the family."

"Just relax, Ed, Annie's sorted it all out," said Bill from the driver's seat.

We were in between Dubbo and Eumungerie on the Newell highway, and I was reflecting on my upbringing at Eumungerie when my thoughts inneviatebly led to Michelle.

"Has Michelle been up to visit Stumpy?" I said, swelling at the thought that I might see her.

Anne dashed that hope though. "She has, Ed. Michelle said her goodbyes to Grandpa a few days ago and she's gone back home to Dunbogan."

"Do you know if she mentioned me, Annie?"

"Mum told me on the phone that Kim didn't want you at Coorigil while she and Michelle were there."

My heart sunk and I fell silent. I was devastated, and Annie being Annie could sense it. She turned around in her seat.

"Give it time, Ed. She's still young and hurts about what happened." She placed her hand reassuringly on mine.

There was a long silence and I found myself deep in thought. "I suppose I can't blame her one bit. I was always on the drink or driving trucks when she needed me most. I loved that kid and she loved me, but I always managed to do something to wreck everything."

"Time is a great healer, Ed," Anne said, echoing Frank's constant refrain.

I sighed. "It will take a lifetime before she forgives me."

"When she gets older and understands the full extent of what has happened to you then hopefully she will want to make contact. Please, Ed, let things take its natural course."

We drove down the Narromine Road and turned off towards the family homestead. I sat deep in thought as the memories of my past came flooding back to me. As we approached Coorigil there was a John Deere tractor pulling a set of disc ploughs in the paddock nearest to the road. Bill slowed the car down until it came to a stop. I knew exactly who was in that tractor, so I stepped out of the vehicle and climbed through the wire fence and walked towards the tractor. In among all the dust I could see the figure of my brother Noel in the cabin. Eventually the tractor stopped and I walked to the door and opened it.

Noel looked at me and I could see his lip start to quiver as the emotion of the moment caught up with him. I was embarrassed as I was unaccustomed to seeing my brother in such a state. He had always been the gregarious knockabout elder brother, seemingly fearless while I was growing up, now he was totally undone.

"I'm sorry, Ed, sorry that I didn't come and visit you in jail," said Noel, on the verge of tears.

I grabbed Noel's hand tight. I could barely speak myself.

"I just couldn't bring myself to see you in such a place," he said with a voice full of emotion. "I feel so ashamed. It doesn't matter how bad the crime was, I, of all people, should have been there to support my younger brother."

"It's okay, mate. I understand how you felt," I said, swallowing hard.

"Please forgive me, Ed?" said Noel.

"It's all over now, Noel," I said reassuringly. "Don't beat yourself up about it."

"Thanks, mate, I appreciate it." Noel said, barely managing to get the words out.

I stood there for five of minutes, just holding my older brother's hand. I'd never felt such a connection with Noel, nor would I ever have imagined that we would end up this way, but it felt right. Eventually, his tears died down, and I patted him on the hand with a promise to catch up later. I really wanted to see Stumpy.

I went back to Bill and Anne in the car, and as we continued up the driveway, I noticed that nothing much had changed in the four years I'd been away. The main driveway was still lined with the massive poplar trees which Stumpy had planted after his return from World War I. In the fresh green paddocks alongside the driveway some merino lambs were grazing.

As we approached the homestead, I could see two people standing on the front lawn. As I got closer I realised it was my brothers, John and Dan.

"John would have to bloody well here wouldn't he," I muttered.

"Take it easy, Ed," said Anne, a warning note in her tone.

I approached John and he gave me a distant look before grudgingly shaking my hand. His look of disdain towards me only heightened my feelings of apprehension in coming home to Coorigil. Standing only a short distance from him was Dan, who still looked the same with his lamb chop side levers and brown hair sitting just below the ears. He gave me a warm handshake and his typical casual manner said, "G'day, mate, how ya been," like I'd just gotten back from some exotic overseas holiday.

I was bemused by Dan's introduction and then saw the paradox of the situation between him and John. I broke out into a smile. "You haven't changed a bit, have you?" I said, slapping him on the shoulder.

"Why should I?" he smiled. "Day will turn into night and we'll do it all again tomorrow, Ed."

I was still smiling over Dan's reaction when I saw my mother appear at the front door. She was wearing an apron and had obviously been cooking. She looked at me timidly, her mind probably working overtime as to how to react to the man standing in front of her. I wondered if she thought I was a criminal or a son, but her motherly instincts took over and her face softened.

As she walked over to me, I could see she had aged as her hair was greyer and there were pronounced wrinkles on her face. She tried to contain her emotions, but the moment got to her and she burst into tears as we embraced. I held her close, inhaling her familiar scent as I stroked her back with my right hand. From nowhere, I was filled with a swelling relief.

"Oh, Ed, I'm so glad to see you home, safe and well," she cried.

"Thank you, Mum," I said, not able to say much more as I was too much choked up with emotion.

I held Mum for some time before she said, "I made a batch of scones and a fresh pot of tea, so come inside. We'll have them while Margaret is in with Stumpy."

"Margaret's here?"

Mum nodded, wiping her eyes with the edge of her apron.

By this stage, Noel had arrived back at the homestead and pulled himself together. He reverted to his old laconic self. I said very little as I was apprehensive about John, but Noel, Dan Anne, Bill, the kids and Mum were kept busy in conversation.

John kept his distance from me and although I could sense he still had a great deal of contempt for me for what I had done, he said nothing.

I talked with the family for another ten minutes and eventually excused myself as I wanted to see Stumpy.

When I reached Stumpy's room, I knocked on the door quietly.

"Yes?" came the calm voice of Margaret.

"It's Ed, Marg. Is it alright to come in?"

"Yes, come in, Ed. Grandpa's just resting."

I walked into the darkened room to be met by my elder sister. I had not seen her for some time, as she was still nursing in an isolated indigenous community in Arnhem Land in the Northern Territory.

Margaret was equally as nice as Annie, but a more reserved version of her younger sibling. Margaret and Geoff had one daughter, who was also a doctor, and they had seen their life in the Northern Territory as a vocation. They didn't wander about too much, so it brought home how sick Stumpy was if Marg was back.

As Margaret attended to Stumpy, I mused over the fact that she had always referred to Stumpy as Grandpa. Although distance had kept Margaret and me apart over the years, I still found her a warm person who never sat in judgment of the crime I had done. Maybe that was the part of her that had considered becoming a nun.

"He's been restless for most of the day, Ed," Margaret said quietly.

I stared at the old man, small and withered in the bed. I'd seen that type of frailty before in some of the really sick ones out at the Talbot. He looked like he was near the end. "How long has he got, Marg?"

Margaret placed a hand on my shoulder and with the most gentle of smiles said, "The end is close, Ed. He's in the final stage of his life."

My head dropped and I was overcome with emotion. I groped for the chair by the bed.

Margaret rubbed my back. "He's hung on a bit longer so you could be here with him at the end. After all, you were always his favourite, Ed."

"Yeah. The best grandfather any boy could ever wish to have is Jack 'Stumpy' Costigan," I said with a voice full of emotion.

"I'll leave you alone with him now."

Margaret left quietly, in that strange cat-like way that nurses have got, and I was alone with the old man.

I listened to his heavy breathing and reflected on our life together; all the happy moments we had spent together from my earliest recollection to when I was a man.

I had been sitting there for the best part of five minutes, deep in thought, when Stumpy stirred from his slumber and spoke to me in a laboured tone. "I think the great ringer in the sky is calling me home, Ed. When my time is come, I'll be ready to pack up my swag and move on."

I looked at the old man as he smiled at me, but I couldn't say anything. At any moment I was ready to breakdown.

"I've had a very blessed life, Ed," said Stumpy, his voice weak. "When I was on the Western Front, I honestly thought I'd never see Australia again. Too many of my mates had been killed and I thought it was only a matter of time before my number was up. To think I survived both Gallipoli and France is nothing short of a miracle. I now know why God allowed me to survive the Great War, Ed."

"Why's that Stumpy?" I said in a strained voice.

"So I could be your guide and mentor throughout your life."

I couldn't say anything. The lump in my throat was enormous. I thought about all the times he'd been there with advice, and all the times I pushed him away. Somehow, he'd always been there. He stuck fat.

Stumpy pressed on. "I could see something in you, even when you were a young boy, that was very special. Even though I love all my grandchildren equally, I somehow knew that you were to walk a different path to the rest of them. I've seen you reach both the highest heights as a boxer and the lows of rock bottom. My instinct told me that one day you would rise out of the mire because the almighty has work for you to do. Your experiences, and all you have been through, will benefit many people in the years that lie ahead."

I took the old man's hand.

Stumpy breathed hard and I looked at him in alarm, but he gathered his thoughts and squeezed my hand tight. "I had a dream a couple of nights ago, Ed."

"What was it, Stumpy?"

"I dreamt that sometime in the future, a beautiful woman will come into your life. She was the most exquisite looking creature I have ever seen. "

I was bewildered. Stumpy was offering psychic predictions in his final days! Nothing in my present state of circumstances would allow me to believe that a beautiful woman would be entering my life sometime in the future. I put it one side as the ravings of a dying old man, and instead looked into his eyes. He was so weak and it really hit me, he was leaving soon.

He gave me a weak smile. "Before I leave this planet, Ed, I must stress to you this one thing."

"What's that Stumpy?"

"You have found sobriety, Ed. Don't lose it; it is a precious gift."

"I don't want to lose it, Stumpy, it means so much to me." I squeezed Stumpy's hand and my tears began to flow. "I love you, old man," I blurted out. "You've been my guiding light throughout my life."

A look of weary peace came over him. "I love you too, Ed. Let me rest for a bit, lad. I'm weary."

I shook Stumpy's hand and kissed him on the forehead. I watched him drift off to sleep before leaving the room quietly.

It was the last time I ever saw him alive.

As I lay in my old bed at Coorigil that night, I recounted my conversation with Stumpy that day. I thought about what he had said about a beautiful woman coming into my life sometime in the future and felt a strange sense of calmness when I pondered his words.

"Perhaps he could be right. Maybe there is somebody waiting for me," I whispered to myself, barely daring to hope.

I slept a deep sleep until I was woken in the wee hours of the morning. Then, like a bolt out of nowhere, I became conscious of a story that Stumpy told me when I was a boy, concerning his father's eldest brother.

His name was Declan Costigan and he was considerably older than my great-grandfather Paddy. Declan had left Ireland at eighteen, bound for America, and settled in Hampshire County, Western Massachusetts, where he worked on a farm. The American Civil War was on and he fought for the Union in the Irish Brigade. He was wounded at the battle of Gettysburg in 1863.

Stumpy told me that after the Civil War, his father received a letter from Declan where he described the carnage that took place at Gettysburg. Declan also made mention of a process that many of the soldiers, after being wounded on the battlefield, would take to prepare themselves for death. It was named 'fixin' to die', where a soldier crossed his arms over his chest while he lay on his back. Stumpy had concluded his story by telling me that's how he wanted to go out.

The next morning at 7.00 am when Mum entered his room to check on him, that's exactly how she found him. The doctor arrived not long after and pronounced him dead, and when he turned to those of us gathered in the room, he said that he'd passed away in the early hours of the morning.

I was overcome with grief. "You were spot on, old man. You left this planet just how you predicted. A soldier right to the end."

Later, when I went for a walk around the farm, I found myself staring at the setting sun. A smile came over my tear-stained face and I remembered every wonderful thing my grandfather ever did for me.

"Thank you, Stumpy, for your beautiful life."

Stumpy's funeral at the Catholic church in Dubbo was a huge affair. Among the congregation were relatives and friends, members of different religious denominations, politicians and those representing sporting, charitable and community groups. Stumpy had such a big impact on the community that everyone came out to celebrate his life.

That night as many of us sat around an open fire in the house paddock at Coorigil, reminiscing about Stumpy, Rowy, who had come out to pay his last respects too, said to me while we were seated on an old log, "I've got a proposition that might interest you."

"What is it, Rowy?" I said.

"Julie and I have been doing some thinking lately," he said tentatively.

I was curious. "Yes?"

"We want to refurbish *Shiloh*. We're getting a builder in to fix it up and he needs a hand with the refurbishment and so we suggested you."

"Yeah, I'd be interested in that," I said. I was immediately taken with the idea. I loved Rowy's property and *Shiloh* was the cream of the crop, a great little place right on the water.

Rowy looked relieved. "He's happy to employ you as his labourer, and when the work's complete, Julie and I would like to know if you want to live in *Shiloh* and rent it off us."

My eyes widened. Life certainly was moving things along, but I had no money to pay for it! "I'd love to Rowy, but I haven't got a hope in hell of paying rent as I haven't got a job."

"Well, that's the other thing I was going to see you about. When you're finished working on *Shiloh*, I was wondering if you'd like to come and work for me as my mechanic? You told me a while ago that you can get your drivers licence back mid next year. When you get it back you can start with me."

From little things, big things grow, I thought.

"Too bloody right I'd like to come and work for you," I said, eagerly shaking his hand.

"Okay then, Cozzy, it's settled," said Rowy with a grin. "The builder is starting at the beginning of November. We've got a spare room for you on the bottom floor of our house which you can live in while *Shiloh* gets refurbished."

Gratitude rolled over me in waves, and with his generous proposition, the door had been opened to a magnificent stage in my life. The years that were followed were to be some of the happiest of my life. I had transcended the darkness I was in only a short while back, to see the light of positivity. A new life was born.

***

"It must have really stung, losing the old fella," observed Tim, as I went silent for a moment.

"Yeah, mate. With my own dad long gone, Stumpy was

all I had. He was my mentor, my guide and my support," I said, thinking back on my grandfather. "We sat around the fire that night, and my head was full of Rowy's proposition, but mainly I contemplated on how Stumpy's guidance had left a huge imprint on my life. I was so happy to have known the old bugger, but I was also sad, thinking I might never have the opportunity to share something like that with Michelle when she had kids. She wanted nothing to do with me, so I thought a door had shut there."

Tim nodded and I brightened up, as it was all starting to get a bit maudlin.

"Stumpy passing on was devastating, and I felt the sting of that grief for a long time, but happiness was just around the corner."

Chapter 13

Early November, 1986, Caringbah Railway Station, Sydney

IT WAS A beautiful spring morning in early November when I arrived at Caringbah Railway Station. As I walked up the steps of the station towards the Kingsway, I was filled with a great sense of gratitude for all that Frank had done for me. The simple accommodation he provided for me had kickstarted my life, but now it was up to me.

I walked down to the carpark where Julie Rowe was due to pick me up at 9.00 am. After about five minutes I could see Julie's white Holden Commodore sedan come into view, and with a wave she pulled up alongside me. I gave her a kiss on the cheek before putting my bag in the boot.

Julie was dressed in her nurse's uniform. "I've been on the night shift, so after I introduce you to our builder I'm going to hit the sack, Ed."

"You do that because you look totally shagged, girl, and I mean that in the nicest possible way, Jules."

Julie bent over the steering wheel with laughter. "You'll

keep, Costigan, besides I've been too busy at work to be participating in any of those sort of activities lately."

As we drove along, I reflected on all the years we had known each other and the good times we had shared in our youth. Good old Maroubra. I was hit by a flood of memories.

"Have you seen Sandy lately, Julie?" I was curious about my first love.

She smiled. "As a matter of fact, I have, Ed. Bob and I went out to dinner with Sandy and her husband a couple of weeks ago. She's still as beautiful as ever, with the same beautiful nature."

"So, she's still married to the doctor?" I said with a tinge of regret. Sandy was the first person who made it clear that I was menace on the grog. If only I'd listened.

"Oh yeah, her and Andrew are still married and they have three beautiful kids."

I was beset with a feeling of great loss as I reflected on my relationship with Sandy all those years ago. "I owe her a huge apology, Julie, for the way I treated her," I said eventually.

"I wouldn't give yourself a hard time, Ed," said Julie. "Sandy's long moved on from all that."

"She might have moved on, but I've never forgotten the way I treated her when I got back from Vietnam," I told Julie.

"They were tough times, Ed. Sandy told me a number of times over the years that she knew you weren't right after you got back. She's got no hard feelings towards you." Julie gave me a reassuring look. "In fact, she told me more than once that she was devastated when she broke up with you. She just knew that she couldn't go on any longer."

I sighed. "If I ever get the chance, I would like to apologise to her, Jules."

"I'm sure she'd appreciate that, Ed," Julie said, patting me on the knee.

We eventually arrived at the Rowe house, situated down the end of Willarong Road, Caringbah. The front verandah had panoramic views of Yowie Bay, the Port Hacking River and the Royal National Park in the distance. The view never failed to blow me away. Still does to this day.

After we had a cup of tea and a slice of cake, Julie took me for a walk down the steep sandstone steps which led to *Shiloh*. I could see that the pathway was in serious need of repair and on further inspection I could see that it was overgrown with weeds and small shrubs as it zig-zagged its way down the sloping terrain towards the waterfront where *Shiloh* was situated.

About ten metres to the left of the track was a narrow gauge rail with a little carriage about two metres long which was called *The Rocket*. *The Rocket* was dark green and made of fibreglass. On the front were two round headlights and it was covered with a khaki coloured canvas canopy that was torn.

"The electric motor on *The Rocket* is broken, Ed," Julie said.

"Maybe it's something I can have a look at down the track."

She smiled. "I'm sure a man of your mechanical knowledge could breathe some life into her."

"How did *Shiloh* get its name, Jules?"

"You remember Josek Warski, the Polish Jew who Bob worked for years ago?"

I hadn't heard that name in a long time. "Sure do. I introduced Rowy to him."

"When he bought the property and built the little cottage on the water, he named it *Shiloh* which is a Hebrew word that means 'place of peace'. Considering everything he went through in his life, with his family gassed in Auschwitz and all, it was his little refuge."

As Julie told me this, I spied *Shiloh* through the surrounding bush.

As I looked at the old ramshackle cottage, I was filled with a great sense of serenity. I'd seen her before, but the idea that she would now be my home was incredible. I looked at Julie. "I've always liked *Shiloh,* Jules, but never in my wildest dreams did I think I would ever live here."

She placed a hand on my arm. "Bob and I know you liked it, Ed, that's why we're giving you first digs. And you're our friend."

I sighed and breathed the fresh air, inhaling deep into my lungs. "As it was Josek's refuge, then so too it will be for me. This is another world down here."

She took my hand. "It certainly is."

On further inspection I could see that *Shiloh* was in need of heavy repair. The roof was missing some of its red tiles and many were cracked. As we walked through the dwelling I could see that it was also trashed and looked as though vandals had been in there.

Running down the centre of the house was a hallway and on the right was a kitchen, then in front of that the living room with a round table and four broken chairs around it. On the left at the front was the main bedroom with a busted up double bed and an old wardrobe. Behind it on the left was the second bedroom. It had of a laundry on one side of the house and a bathroom on the other. The concrete pavement around the dwelling was in a bad way. At the front was a floating pontoon which looked new, and moored to it was Rowy's tinnie with its 25 horsepower motor on the back of it.

"*Shiloh* certainly needs some work done on it, Ed," said Julie, interrupting my reverie.

I stood back at a distance taking in the scene in front of me. I agreed. "It does, Jules, but this place is just what the doctor ordered. It's got a great feel about it."

I looked across to the other side of Yowie Bay where there were other waterfront dwellings, many with pontoons and boats. The water was a beautiful blue and looked crystal clear. There was no industry on the Port Hacking River, and this only added to the allure of this peaceful setting.

Julie and I spent the next fifteen minutes looking through *Shiloh,* and I made a mental list of what needed doing before we saw a barge with a large outboard motor cruising towards us. As the barge got closer we could see that it was being driven by a blonde man wearing work clothes in his mid thirties, who stood about six feet tall and who was in tremendous shape. When he tied the barge up on the pontoon he bounded off the vessel in one leap. Julie introduced us.

"Ed, this is our builder, Ian Duckett. Ian this is Ed Costigan. Bob and Ed were in Vietnam together."

After we shook hands Ian said to me, "Most people call me 'Ducko', Ed. Rowy's told me a lot about you. Sounds like you're just the man I need to give me a hand while we knock *Shiloh* back in shape," he said in a laconic tone.

"I'm up for the challenge, Ducko," I told him with a grin. "I'm looking forward to a peaceful little sanctuary when it's all done."

"It sure will be, Ed. It's a little paradise nestled down here, separate from all the hustle and bustle of the world."

I liked Ducko from the start. He had an easygoing nature and a great sense of humour, and the conversation between us flowed very easily. Our friendship was only enhanced when he subsequently told me he was from a small country town named Galong, which was situated near Harden in southern New South Wales. He was a country boy like myself.

After Julie left us and made her way back up to the house, I gave Ducko a hand offloading various tools and building supplies before he made his way back up Yowie Bay.

At 7.00 am the next morning, Ducko and I started the task of refurbishing *Shiloh*. For the first week we concentrated on stripping the place out until we brought it back to just the framework and roof trusses, and then we took numerous skip bins of construction waste away.

Over the next two months, Ducko and I worked hard and Shiloh took shape. By Christmas I had managed to put some money away. I planned to buy a vehicle once I was eligible to get my drivers licence back. By early February of 1987 the renovation was complete and I was ready to move in. Bob and Julie had supplied *Shiloh* with new furniture which they had purchased just for me.

That first night as I lay on my back in bed, I felt a quiet satisfaction at being an integral part of *Shiloh's* restoration. It was achievement, one that brought me great joy and satisfaction, much like fixing the tap washer did back at the church. Frank suddenly entered my mind and I vowed to get him over for a meal.

After I settled into *Shiloh*, I set about landscaping the track and surrounds that led to the dwelling, and fixing *The Rocket*. The months I spent landscaping were an important part in my recovery for I not only became fit, but I also spent a lot of time by myself, surrounded by nature. My life had become a chaotic mess in my active alcoholism and I was forced to stop, listen and observe the flora and fauna around me which brought me back to the here and now.

It was around this time that it first occurred to me that I should try to make amends to the family of Alison Mitchell for my crime. I discussed it with Frank and being the prudent man he was he suggested I tread carefully as it might not be wise to make contact. He suggested that the animosity towards me from the family could still be very high. I took his advice and although I made no contact with the Mitchells, I was willing to make amends if the opportunity ever arose. For me this was an important part of my recovery, but I trusted Frank's advice so I left it at that.

By the end of May 1987, the bulk of the landscaping project had been completed, although the work would be ongoing into the future as constant maintenance would be required to keep the place in shape.

It was time to take a big step forward. I went to the Department of Motor Transport and sat for my drivers licence and passed. I was so nervous and I felt a sense of guilt about getting my licence back after the events surrounding the accident. I passed though and soon after, I started work with Rowy as his mechanic.

Rowe Civil Contracting was based in Waratah Street, Kirrawee, where they had a large yard and a big workshop. I was nervous at first and felt like a duck out of water as it had been a while since I had worked in my trade. Everything in life was brand new, being a non-drinker.

Rowy sensed this and for the first month all I did was drive the fuel truck which suited me fine until I got my head around my job. In time I got the jist of what was happening, and eventually, I slotted back into my trade where I become more than just a passenger but an integral part of Rowy's operation. There was never an idle moment, as there was everything from scrapers, graders, excavators, backhoes and trucks to be maintained.

After a few months, Rowy set me up in a small service truck with everything I needed. I was happy with this arrangement because I was out on my own, going from site to site, and back to the workshop to do repairs when necessary.

Those early days working back with Rowy were an important part of my life as it helped my self-esteem immensely. Work was at the very centre of how I viewed my manhood.

**

I sat back and shook my head. "You don't know how much it meant to me to get back into my trade, Tim!"

Tim nodded. "I suppose work is a good way to keep busy."

"A lot of people out there go about their day-to-day work without really appreciating their job. For me working back in my trade was the very essence of my manhood," I said.

"Yeah, I can appreciate that."

"I felt as though I was doing what I was meant to do and what's more I was putting a quid in my pocket each week. Crikey, Tim, whoever knew that something so small could mean so much."

Tim sat in deep thought. I watched him and knew that I was getting through to him. The defensiveness had mostly left his posture and he seemed to be listening to everything I was saying. I looked at his face, his oily complexion and knew where to take the conversation next.

"It wasn't just work that added to my self-esteem!"

"What?" Tim said, lifting his head.

"Rowy left an old punching bag on the back verandah of Shiloh one arvo."

He scoffed. "A punching bag?"

"Yeah. He found it in a skip bin on a job site in the inner city. Thought it would be good if I got back into some fitness. Well, I wasn't too keen on Rowy suggesting I get fit again. Truth be known I didn't want to give up the cigarettes, and I knew I would have to do that if I was to start working out again."

"So, what did you do?" asked Tim.

I gave a short laugh. "I went through a right royal mental conflict over the next week. The better part of my nature kept telling me to get off my arse and get fit, while the alcoholic told me to keep smoking and do nothing. That's what it all boiled down to. Either I hang onto my last remaining crutch, the cigarettes, or get fit."

"You chose to get fit, right? You look fit now," Tim observed.

"Well, it didn't happen until I had a revelation one night. I was awoken by a thought that came into my head. I remembered what I had thought when I had taken up golf again, that sobriety isn't so much about staying off the drink, but living life to the fullest."

"Yeah?" Tim said with a strange look.

"Well, being the crazy Alkie I am, I got up then and there at 4.00 am in the morning and hooked the bag to the beam under the awning to the side of the house."

Tim gave me a bemused look. "At 4.00 am?"

"Yeah. I started pounding away on the bag without any bandages on my hands. I don't know how I didn't wake the Rowes up, I was making so much noise as I hit the shit out of this bag, and my hands were wrecked for a week."

Tim shook his head in disbelief.

"When I was finished, I threw all my cigarettes into Yowie Bay."

Tim sat back with a bemused look and said. "You're fuckin' nuts. 4.00 am? Tossing ciggies in the bay?"

I laughed. "Yeah, you're probably right, but it started me back on the road to fitness, Tim, and what's more I felt like a new man."

**

It took about a week before my hands recovered from my initial workout on the bag. I decided that I should start a routine of running, so I went and purchased a new pair of joggers. I was subsequently brought down to earth after I went on my first run, which was just a short jog up the street. This became most embarrassing when a little old lady in her sixties jogged past me as though I was standing still.

I persisted even though I was reduced to a slow walk on that first day. As the weeks went on, I was able to jog a little more, even though after ten minutes I was pretty knocked up. On top of my running I started to perform some exercises which included pushups and sit ups. When my hands were recovered I started working out on the punching bag and in time I started to develop speed as the old combinations that had made me lightening quick in my youth started to return. Surprisingly, my buggered right hand seemed to handle the strain of hitting the bag.

Slowly, I started to strip the weight off and my fitness improved to such a point that I could run for 30 minutes without breaking down.

In that first month or so, I was coughing up black flem as

the years and years of cigarette smoking were finally loosening their grip on me. I didn't mind. I found that by keeping physically fit, my mental, emotional and spiritual fitness started to improve. In time, I came to believe that what Frank had told me in one of our big chats about the physical, mental and spiritual inter-connection. They are all connected, and if one of those areas suffers, the others suffer too. I started to feel like a new man and became dedicated to the pursuit of my new-found health.

I found that my new-found physical wellbeing served as a catalyst for other opportunities. A change of attitude can often lead to doors opening which otherwise would have remained firmly shut. It was not long after this that serendipity visited me quite unexpectedly.

It happened in early September of 1987, when Annie came to visit me at *Shiloh* one evening. I was taken by surprise as she usually called before coming over, but her positive demeanour, which included her customary warm smile, suggested that her visit was one of glad tidings.

After inviting her in and making a cup of tea for the both of us, she let on to the nature of her visit after we both made ourselves comfortable.

"I suppose you're wondering why I've made a totally unannounced visit," she said.

"Yeah, it's a bit out of character, Annie."

"Well, it's to do with Stumpy and something he left you. But before I divulge what it is, I need to tell you something, Ed."

Over the next half an hour, Annie told me a story that took me totally by surprise and raised the hairs on the back of my neck.

When Stumpy died, unbeknownst to the family, he had left a considerable amount of wealth behind. My family had always known that Stumpy was never short of a quid as he played the stockmarket, but the full extent of his wealth was something we were unsure of, as he was very secretive of his business affairs.

Anne told me that because of the complicated nature of Stumpy's wealth it had taken 12 months for probate to be settled, and that he had made her the sole executer of his will. Anne went onto say that as well as leaving a considerable amount of money to the Catholic Church and numerous charitable groups, Stumpy had also left his family a generous amount of money. With that, Annie handed me a sealed unmarked envelope.

I looked at the envelope for some time, my hands shaking with anticipation.

"Open it," she said with a smile.

I opened the envelope and pulled out a crisp cheque which I held up in front of me. I looked at it for some time, my hands trembling.

"$50,000! Annie!"

"Yes, Ed, fifty grand, and it's yours to spend wisely."

"Well, I'll be buggered. That's the exactly the same amount I earnt from my Poseidon shares all those years ago," I told her in astonishment.

"I know, Ed, Stumpy told me not long before he died."

I was stunned into silence and all I could do was look at the amount on the cheque in wonder. "The cunning old bugger. He was looking after me right up to the end, hey Annie?"

She got up and hugged me. "He certainly was, Ed. He loved you."

I kept $10,000 of that money for myself and deposited the balance in a long term investment account. I was determined that the money should be well spent as I had experienced the pain of losing all my material wealth in my divorce with Kim, and never wanted to go through that experience again.

I contacted Noel and he informed me that he too had received a cheque off Annie, as well as other members of my family.

In the midst of our conversation, Noel informed me that my prized 1969 Holden Monaro GTS was to be auctioned. It worked out that old Cecil Grainger, who owned the property two kilometres down the road from Coorigil, had recently passed away and there was to be a clearing sale on his farm the next weekend.

After my divorce with Kim, Cecil had expressed his desire to purchase my prized vehicle and as a get even to me, she had sold it to him. This had been a real kick in the teeth as the Graingers had been the nemesis of the Costigans for many years, due to the old Catholic/Protestant friction.

The auction was a tense a fair with a number of bidders vying for my prized car, but with Noel at my side, I was able to get it back. Many of Cecil's family were at the auction, but were unaware of my presence as I was making my bids from the rear of the crowd. It was priceless to see the look on their faces when I emerged from the crowd as the successful bidder. They were ashen-faced and shattered to see a Costigan, let alone this particular one, in possession of Cecil's car.

After the auction I drove the car to Sydney like I was king of the world. It was more than just a car to me—it was symbolic of my independence.

With the Monaro in my possession, I revisited my youth and as a result, my thoughts turned back to having a woman in my life. I pondered on Stumpy's prophetic dream, about a beautiful woman coming into my life. At the time I thought they were the ramblings of a man in the final days of his life, but now I wanted it to be real.

As October drew to a close, I wondered how a bloke like me would ever find a woman like the one he described. I had been with some beautiful women in my time, but from my present station in life, it seemed like a near impossibility for me to find a woman of the calibre that Stumpy had prophesised.

***

I sighed. "I thought a lot about what Stumpy had said to me on his death bed about that beautiful woman. To tell you the truth, Tim, I wanted to believe that more than anything else in the world."

"You were lonely were you?" Tim asked directly.

I nodded my head and with a look of melancholy said, "You better believe it, but I had no answers. I just hoped that a nice lady would come into my life. Besides, I was preoccupied with other things."

"Like what?"

I smiled at him. "That upcoming weekend was going to be busy, as there was a parade for Vietnam Veterans. Little did I know, before the weekend was over my life was to take a remarkable change in direction. It was to be the beginning of one of the most beautiful chapters in my life."

Chapter 14

S ATURDAY THE 3RD of October, 1987, was a remarkable day not only for me, but for many of us Vietnam Veterans who had not been formally recognised for our service.

An estimated 25,000 Vietnam Veterans participated in the march through the streets of Sydney on that early spring morning, watched by a crowd of approximately 100,000 people.

The march was led by the next of kin of those who had not returned, with each carrying an Australian flag that represented the dead.

For me it was one of the most powerful experiences of my life. It was the first time I had seen many of my mates from Vietnam since the conflict had ended. Schooner Rooney was there, and Rowy and I had gone in together. I enquired about Finno's whereabouts. It'd been years since I'd seen him and I was eager to catch up, but no one seemed to know where he was.

Schooner shrugged. "I dunno, Cozzy. Seems to have disappeared off the planet. No one knows where he is, but crikey! The mad bugger would have enjoyed a day like this."

I agreed. "Too bloody right, Schooner. I'd love to catch up with him some day. That crazy bastard saved my life."

I was dressed in a new suit which proudly displayed my campaign medals. As I marched past Prime Minister Bob Hawke and his wife Hazel, as well as many other dignitaries, I felt a great sense of gratitude for being recognised for the part I had played in the conflict

As Schooner Rooney held up our battalion banner, a great cheer went out from the crowd and our boys were filled with a great sense of pride.

After the march, members of our battalion gathered at the Gresham Hotel in Sydney where we both celebrated and reminisced about past events. Although most of the boys in my battalion indulged in the amber fluid that day, I stuck to my lime and soda. I was just happy in the thought that I was sharing such a special day with blokes I had experienced so much with.

It was late afternoon when I decided to make tracks back home, and after leaving Rowy with rest of our battalion, I arrived back at *Shiloh* dog-tired after such an emotion charged event.

I decided to have a sleep and it was 8.00 pm when I eventually awoke.

My earlier feelings of celebration had disappeared to be overshadowed by a well of loneliness. As much as it had been a momentous day, it had brought back those events in Vietnam from so long ago to me. While asleep I had a flashback and once again it was of those devastated eyes and Chooky dying. It was the fact that I was so helpless and unable to do anything for him that affected me the most.

I had been going through these feelings over the last few months and they usually came on me when I was by myself, in the darkness of my home. This time it had a special bite to it for it seemed to drag up other feelings of inadequacy. When I woke, I sat on the side of my bed trying to shake the image of Chooky from my mind. It usually took a while, but I often felt a bit better if I did something useful. My stomach was rumbling and I knew I needed some supplies from the shop so I could cook dinner.

I knew the convenience store up on Willarong Road closed at 8.30 pm, so I quickly washed my face, grabbed my wallet and car keys and headed out to *The Rocket*. I motored up towards Rowy and Julie's place, and when I reached the top, I noticed the outside light at the back of the Rowe's house was on. I suddenly remembered that Rowy mentioned that Julie was inviting a few of the girls around that night for a game of cards.

I made my way to the Monaro and after starting the car, I noticed that the battery light on the dash kept flicking on and off. This had been happening over the past week and after further investigation, I found that the alternator needed replacing. I had picked up a reconditioned one on the Thursday afternoon and had planned to install it on the Sunday. I ignored it, hoping it would at least last for the trip to the shops.

I made my way to the shops and after I purchased what I needed I went to start the car but there was no response.

"The bloody alternator!" I said out aloud.

I rested my head on top of the steering wheel and let out a deep sigh.

"I don't need this, I really don't bloody well need this at the moment," I said to myself.

I got out of the car and contemplated what to do next. I

had the spare alternator back down in the laundry at *Shiloh* and figured that I was going to have to hitch a ride back home and grab it, then get a lift back up to the shops with Julie Rowe and install it.

Within ten minutes I had managed to hitch a ride and after being dropped off, I walked up the pathway towards Rowe's door. The back light which had been on earlier in the evening was now switched off. As I made my way slowly through the dark, I could hear the sound of laughter coming from inside the house and was about to knock on the door when through the window, I noticed a striking dark-haired lady in her early thirties walk across the living room.

It fair stopped me in my tracks.

I was taken aback by her beauty, and from the darkness outside, could only watch as she carried a plate across the room to where the ladies were at work. Sitting around a square table playing cards were Julie Rowe, Annie, an attractive blonde, and the woman with dark hair. I was mesmerised by her eyes. They seemed to have an hypnotic effect on me—I just could not stop looking at her. Suddenly, I thought about Stumpy's dream.

"I'll be buggered, old man. Is this the one you dreamt about?" I whispered.

I continued to look at her before whispering to myself, "I won't disturb them as they look like they're having a good time. I'll get a lift back up to the shops tomorrow morning."

With that I stepped backwards, intending to make a quiet escape, but unbeknownst to me, one of the Rowe kids had left a skateboard sitting on the pathway in the dark. I managed to trip on the skateboard and it took off towards the BBQ area which was situated on the next level down. I went flying down a flight of concrete steps, managing to collect a metal garbage bin on the way down. The almighty crash of metal onto concrete set the next door neighbour's dog off barking and before I knew it, I could hear the sound of chairs and tables being moved from inside the house. They were getting up to check out the ruckus.

"What was that?" I could hear Julie yell from inside the house.

As I lay there on the timber decking, I felt my right hand throb with pain and I silently cursed. The back light came on and I was met by the sight of Julie, standing at the back door with an umbrella in her hand, a fierce expression on her face, and the three other woman cowering behind her. The expression on Julie's face and the way she was holding the umbrella suggested that she was ready for action at any moment. I knew she was too, Julie had been doing martial arts for years.

Julie looked down at where I lay, trying to focus on who it was, when her eyes widened. "Ed Costigan, what the hell are you up to?"

"I tripped over on one of your bloody kid's skateboards, Julie!" I yelled.

"Oh no! If I've told them once I've told those kids a thousand times not to leave their skateboards lying around the place," Julie said. "I tell you, Ed, there's going to be hell to pay tomorrow when I catch up with them." She flung open the door and came outside. Being a nurse, she came right over, all bustle and fuss. "Are you alright?"

I winced. "I think I've buggered my right wrist again, Jules!"

Anne, who was standing with the other girls behind Julie, said, "Oh no, Ed, not your bad wrist! How many times have you damaged it over the years?" She made her way down the steps to the landing where I was lying.

"Too many times, Annie!" I tried to flex it, but the bloody thing was killing me.

"Oh, you poor man. Let me have a look at it," Anne said.

Everyone was on the landing now, ready to offer help.

I grimaced in pain as Anne gently took my wrist and inspected it to see if it was broken. I could still move it, so Anne concluded there was a good chance I had only sprained it rather than broken it. Julie nodded in agreement, then made her way back to the house to get an ice pack out of the freezer.

As I sat up, I told the girls about my car breaking down and how I had come up to the house to get a ride back up to the shops.

"And look what you got for your trouble!" exclaimed Anne.

I smiled at her, then I looked up to be met by the beautiful brown eyes of the dark-haired woman who was behind Anne. She smiled at me. It was a beautiful warm smile and I immediately felt a connection with her. I couldn't look away.

Anne, when she glanced up from my wrist, noticed and apologised.

"Oh, where are my manners. Sorry, Ed. In all the drama I didn't introduce you to my friends. This is Kylie Winters," she said, pointing to the blonde lady, "and this is Karen Monaghan," she said, indicating to the dark-haired woman.

"How do you do?" I said politely to both.

Kylie smiled at me. "You're in luck, Ed, surrounded by four nurses."

The other girls giggled and I said, "Well, I can only suppose I've died and gone to heaven." They all laughed again and were still laughing when Julie returned with an ice pack in a towel and wrapped it around my wrist.

"There you go, Ed, that will reduce the swelling," she said.

"Thank, Jules," I said, grimacing in pain.

"Come on, Ed. Let's get you back up to the house where it's a bit more comfortable," said Anne.

As the four of them helped me to my feet. My eyes once again met with Karen's, and as she smiled at me and supported me to stand, she said, "There you go, I've got you."

"Thank you. I appreciate that," I said to her.

"You're welcome."

I could see that Karen not only had a lovely smile and beautiful eyes, but also a lovely nature. Truth be told, if first impressions count then I was smitten.

Once up at the house, Julie made me comfortable and Anne turned to me and said, "One of us would drive you up to Sutherland Hospital for an x-ray, but we've all had a few drinks. We're all staying here for the night, Ed."

"That's alright, Annie. I'll just stay here for a while before I make may way down to Shiloh."

"I can drive you up to the hospital tomorrow morning for an x-ray if you like," said Karen.

"That's very kind of you. Thank you," I said. Karen smiled at me and my heart swelled.

I stayed up at the Rowe's house for the next hour and the girls were interested in what had happened at the march that day. We chatted for a while, with the pain in my wrist subdued somewhat. I put it down to Karen's presence. She had a very calming effect on me. Although she was quiet, I found her very easy to talk to and I soon realised there was some chemistry between us.

I eventually made my way down to Shiloh, reluctant to part from the girls, but I had lost my appetite and so I went straight to bed. Sleep didn't come. I lay awake thinking of Karen, with Stumpy's words reverberating inside my head.

I eventually drifted off to sleep with the vision of Karen's beautiful eyes lingering inside my mind.

I was awoken the next morning by the sound of the telephone ringing.

"How's the hand, Ed?" said Julie on the other end.

"It's still sore, Jules, but I don't think it's broken, just sprained," I told her, flexing my wrist.

"Well, you better come up to the house and we'll take a look at it. Besides we're cooking up some bacon and eggs and we've prepared some for you."

"How kind, Jules. I'll be up in a jiffy."

I made my way up to the Rowe's house with the alternator to be met by Anne at *The Rocket* who insisted she have a look at my hand. After inspecting it for a number of minutes she said, "I think you're right, Ed. There seems to be movement there, so I don't think it's broken, just sprained. I'd still get an x-ray up at the hospital though."

"You hoo! Breakfast is served!" shouted Julie from the kitchen. We wandered in and she placed a plate loaded with bacon and eggs, tomatoes and toast in front of me.

The smell was mouth-watering. "Thanks, Jules! You're a real darl," I said, eyes widening at the feast in front of me. I was self-sufficient and could make my own meals, but I loved Julie's food more.

Julie grinned. "Rowy's still in bed after getting home late from the march and the kids haven't surfaced yet. They probably heard me yelling last night after you tripped on the skateboard and know I'll read them the riot act when they eventually appear."

Karen was sitting at the table opposite me, dressed in a blue polo shirt with '1980 NSW Squash Open' written on the top.

I looked at her and said, "Good morning."

"Good morning. How's the hand?" she responded.

"A bit sore, but I hope it's just a sprain and nothing more serious." I jammed some eggs in my mouth.

She nodded. "I'll take you up to the hospital after breakfast and get it checked out."

We talked between ourselves during breakfast and every now and then I noticed Karen look across in my direction and sneak a glance at me, which she would follow up with a smile.

After breakfast, I said my goodbyes and we made our way to Karen's car. Karen was driving a very sporty looking red Toyota Celica and as we drove up Willarong Road the atmosphere between us was friendly, although Karen seemed more reserved now that we were alone.

"So, you play a bit of squash do you?" I said, commenting on the shirt she was wearing.

"Oh, yes. I won the 1980 NSW Women's Squash Open."

I was impressed. "Wow. You must be a pretty handy squash player."

She nodded. "I was gearing up for the World Squash Championships in Toronto the following year, but I had a serious ankle injury shortly after that tournament which forced me out of the game for six months," she said, glancing towards me.

"That's no good. What a bad stroke of luck!"

"Yes, I was at the peak of my career, but the injury dashed any chance I had of competing in Canada."

"Are you playing squash now?"

"I play A grade at Dick Carter's Squash Centre at Miranda." She made a face. "I was never the same after my injury, so I'm stuck with local competition."

"Well, you mustn't be any slouch playing A grade," I said.

"I still play alright, but nothing like I was before my ankle injury," she said, smiling at me.

"I know all about sporting injuries," I told her. "I just keep on damaging my right wrist. It ended up ruining my boxing career."

"Oh, I know all about your boxing career, Ed. Annie's told me all about you and my Dad was a fan."

I was surprised. "Is that right?"

"Absolutely. I know you were a champion boxer in your day." She glanced at me and we smiled at each other again.

I was smitten. Every time she smiled at me, all the empty places inside just seemed to fill up.

Karen drove me to the hospital and waited for me to have my x-ray. Fortunately for me, I was cleared of a break in my wrist as it was only a sprain. She then drove me back to the shops so I could fit my alternator. I was touched that she chose to run the full race.

"Are you going to fit that alternator by yourself?" she asked.

"Oh, yes. I'll mange somehow, buggered hand and all."

Karen shook her head. "I don't know the first thing cars. I think it's a amazing that somebody can fix them."

"Well, I'm a mechanic and I've been doing it for a long time. I suppose it's just second nature to me," I said with a shrug.

"I still think it's a miracle," she said with a grin.

I was fully expecting her to take off at that point, so I thanked her for her help and said that it would be nice to catch up again some time.

Karen smiled but said nothing, so I got down to work. She stayed to watch for a few minutes and then said, "So the car will work? You'll be able to return back to Julie's house?"

"Oh, yes. Definitely," I said.

"Okay, then."

She gave me another smile and as she went to leave, I mentioned again that it would be nice to catch up some time. She gave me a little nod and wave, but didn't reply.

I watched her leave, full of mixed emotions, and then managed to fit the new alternator with great difficulty. When I got home, I ran into Annie on the driveway as she was preparing to leave.

I couldn't hold it in. "Boy, what a beautiful girl Karen is, Annie!"

Anne smiled at me. "That she is, Ed."

"I'd love to take her out, but I got the sense she might be a bit reluctant in seeing me. I mentioned I wouldn't mind catching up but she didn't really say anything."

Anne confirmed my hunch. "You're absolutely right, Ed. Karen's been through a very difficult time lately, and she's very reluctant to start seeing people."

I suddenly filled with anxiety. "Why? What happened?"

"Karen was engaged to a surgeon. They had been seeing each other for over five years and just two months before the wedding he took off overseas with a girl he met at a party. Just left her there without a second thought," said Anne. "It hit her hard."

"Crikey, that is a tough call," I said, scratching my head. "He sounds like an absolute creep."

"That's putting it lightly. Karen was so devastated that she hasn't been with a man since."

I frowned. "So, she's a bit damaged then?"

Anne gave me a look. "Yes, Ed. Karen finds it very hard to trust a man, any man."

"How long have you know her for?"

"About twelve months. She felt that working with the dying was her calling and we soon became good friends, but even that took a while." She got serious. "Ed, Karen has a huge wall up to protect her vulnerability, but I can assure you she is a beautiful person when you get to know her. You just need to give her some time."

I smiled, thinking of those eyes. "Oh, yes, I can see that. Did you see the way she was smiling at me?"

"Yes, I could see. She liked you."

I took a punt. "Do you reckon you could get her phone number for me please, Annie?"

Anne looked at me and grinned before saying. "I'll see what I can do, but don't be surprised if you get the knock back, Ed."

I contemplated what Anne had told me after I kissed her on the cheek and bade her farewell. As I made my way down to *Shiloh,* I was determined to get to know Karen better, but how, I wasn't absolutely sure.

In the days and weeks that followed I thought about Karen constantly. I asked Annie on a number of occasions if she had any luck getting Karen's phone number, but she came back with nothing. Anne probably had her number, after all, they were friends, but Anne was a good person and she would never force anyone to do anything against their will. I respected that, but it looked as though I was going to have no chance of asking Karen out. Then, in late November, things changed. Anne invited me over to her place to celebrate her 35th birthday.

Anne had made it a hat themed party, so on the Saturday afternoon of the party I walked up to the Rowe's house and asked Julie if she had a spare hat to wear.

"Come downstairs with me, Ed. There's a box with an array of hats in there. You can take your pick," she said.

As we rummaged through the box, I disregarded hat after hat until I spotted a lone hat sitting on top of an old sports bag.

"What about that one, Jules?' I said pointing at it.

"That's a Scottish 'tam o'shanter' of the Buchanan clan. One of Bob's excavator operators gave it to him after he came back from a trip to Scotland."

I grinned. "That'll do, Jules."

"Are you sure, Ed? There's a stack of other hats you can try on if you want?"

"Nah, that'll do just fine. Besides, I happened to like this one."

She shook her head, in disgust at my taste.

It was early evening when I parked my car. I was walking down the street to Anne and Bill's place, when I saw Karen standing outside her vehicle, jiggling the handle.

She looked agitated, but as I walked closer I was distracted by her hat which was a fake pot plant and made her look very cute.

"Nice hat!" I said with a laugh.

She spun around. "Oh. Hi, Ed!" She looked surprised and then turned back to her car. "I seemed to have locked my keys in my car. What a silly goose I am," she said anxiously.

"Oh, that's no good. I can get into the car if you want me to," I told her, trying to reassure her.

"Oh, no, Ed. It's okay. I wouldn't want to inconvenience you. I'll just call the NRMA and they'll be able to open it."

"Seriously, it's no problem for me to open it. I keep a special tool in my vehicle that will get into your car."

"Oh. Well, only if it's not too much problem," said Karen reluctantly.

I smiled at her. "Not at all. Leave it to me. I'll go and fetch my 'Slim Jim'."

"Your what?" she said.

"My Slim Jim. It's a special tool for breaking into cars. I told you, I'm a mechanic so I always keep one with me."

She looked relieved. "That would be great, Ed. I appreciate this so much."

"It's no problem. I'll be back in a jiffy."

I jogged back to my car and when I returned, I held the tool up in front of her so she could see it. It was a piece of thin metal about 60 centimetres long and two centimetres wide with a hook on the top of it.

"There you go," I said, sliding it in between the door frame and the window. I hooked the lock inside and heard the click. "This will do the trick."

Within a minute the door was open.

I stood back like I'd done a magic trick. "Hey, presto! There you go, she's all open now."

Karen stood back, her face flushed with embarrassment. "I don't know how I could have been so silly to lock my keys in the car!"

"Ah, don't worry, it can happen to the best of us," I said, waving it off.

"Well, thank you very much," Karen said.

"Not a problem. I'll just run this back to the car and I'll be back in two shakes of a lambs tail."

"Okay, I'll wait for you," Karen said with a giggle.

When I returned, Karen and I walked down the street to Bill and Anne's home.

We had been walking for a short while when Karen glanced at me with a smile and said, "I like your hat, Ed. Isn't that a Scottish tam o'shanter?"

I nodded. "Yes, it is. Apparently, it's the Buchanan clan."

"Well, I reckon you look really nice in it," she said.

Our eyes met and we smiled at each other and I suddenly felt a flare of hope.

When we arrived at Bill and Anne's home, I was met with a pleasant surprise. A number of my family had made a surprise visit to the shindig that night. They were all there including Mum, John, Margaret and her husband, and Noel and Dan and their wives. There was also all of the Maroubra mob who I had reconciled with in recent times, and other assorted relatives and friends I had not seen for some time.

Karen and I were soon met by my cousin Sean O'Grady. I introduced Karen to Sean, who had a beer in his hand and he responded with, "Ah, so I see you've brought the new flame along, Ed?"

There was an awkward moment where Karen and I engaged in a bit of navel gazing and we were lost for words over Sean's tactless comment. Our embarrassing situation was only thwarted when Annie suddenly appeared out of nowhere and saved the day.

"Welcome to my birthday party, you two! I'm so glad to see you could make it," Anne said, planting a kiss on my cheek.

"Wouldn't have missed it for quids, Annie," I said.

Over the next half hour we engaged in some pre-dinner drinks and appetisers before we were all seated at the huge dining room table.

The flow of conversation and the animated mood of the evening had made me totally relaxed and as a consequence I had forgotten that Karen was seated opposite me at the far end of the table out of my sight. Dinner and desert were finished and we were enjoying coffee and chocolates when I was in the middle of telling the guests a story. It involved an incident when Noel and I were kids and we had found a pile of old newspapers and set them alight in the garage one Saturday morning, only to be discovered by Stumpy when he opened the garage door and caught us red-handed.

"And didn't Stumpy tan our backsides that morning!" I said through muffled laughter.

"Too bloody right he did, Ed. I remember he marched us into the house and gave us both a hiding," said Noel, laughing along.

I had my head in my hands I was laughing so hard, when through the corner of my eye I noticed Karen smiling from where she was sitting at the far corner of the table. Her broad smile showed her beautiful white teeth and her eyes totally bewitched me.

Karen's gaze never left me and I was totally spellbound by her look. It's like I couldn't look away, and we stared at each other for what seemed like an eternity. Out of the corner of my eye I could see Anne looking at me with a smile on her face. By this stage, the laughter from the other guests had stopped and I realised they were watching the interaction between Karen and I.

I was suddenly filled with embarrassment. "You'll have to excuse me."

I made a hasty exist into the backyard where I was surrounded by trees which overlooked Gymea Bay. An automatic sensor light came on which lit up the backyard and I paced uneasily.

What was wrong with me? I was like some nervous school-boy. The sensor light flicked off as I stood by the big gum tree, but then flicked on a moment later. I looked up and saw that Karen had followed me out.

My heart started to pound.

She folded her arms in front of herself. "Thanks for helping me with my car tonight. I was in a real pickle until you came along," she said quietly.

"That's okay. It's the least I could do," I said with a smile.

There was an awkward moment between us when we were both lost for words before Karen spoke. "I know you've asked Anne for my phone number, Ed. I just want to say that I'm very flattered that you want to take me out."

I didn't know what to stay, so I stood there, breathing heavily with both desire and anxiety, as I looked into her eyes. She looked serious.

"As you've probably already been told by Anne, I went through a very nasty relationship breakdown that cut me up pretty bad."

I nodded. "Yes, Anne filled me in on all the details as to what happened. I'm sorry you had to go through such a hor-rible time."

Karen smiled and continued. "I'm very scared of being hurt again, Ed. That's why I haven't responded. I just can't go through that again."

Even though I understood, I was stung. "Karen, I would never hurt you."

She smiled at me. "I know you wouldn't, Ed. I can see you're a decent man."

"I'd really love to take you out, but I understand if you're not ready for dating."

Karen smiled at me nervously, so I sought to give her something less intense to think about.

"Would you like to come fishing with me one day?" I said.

"Fishing?" she exclaimed in amazement.

"If you don't want to go, that's okay," I said, holding up my hands, taking a step back. "I just thought it would be a good way to get more acquainted with a nice day out on the water. We could chat all day."

She looked at me with wondering eyes. "That's the strangest thing that a man has ever asked me to do on a first date."

I stood there nervously, wracking my brain as to what I should say next, when Karen broke into a huge grin and said, "Okay. You've sold me, Ed. I'll come fishing with you."

I felt my soul soar, and the ice was broken between us permanently.

"We could get a loan of Rowy's tinnie and take it up the river and try for some bream."

"That would be nice, Ed. I could bring a picnic hamper," Karen said. "You know, I haven't been fishing since my dad used to take my brother and I up the Port Hacking River when I was a little girl."

"Did you enjoy yourself?"

"Yes, I used to love it," she mused, her eyes going dreamy for a moment, "but then I started playing squash and that took up all of my time."

I grinned. "Okay, leave it with me. I'll organise it for next weekend. Now you and I better get back to this shindig or they'll be sending out a search party for us."

"Okay," Karen said smiling at me.

We walked back into the party, all eyes firmly focussed on us and resumed our seats before I said, "Now where was I?

Oh yeah, Stumpy had just tanned our arses. How could I ever forget that!"

"Language, please, Ed!" said my mother.

"Sorry, Mum. Backside!"

The gathered guests broke into spontaneous laughter. Karen and I smiled at each other before I caught a glimpse of Anne, who gave me a reassuring wink before blowing me a kiss.

Stumpy, you old genius!

As I sat back in my seat, I looked at Karen who was smiling at me. My fate was sealed with this dark-haired beauty.

For an outsider it would have appeared that our relationship was an unusual one. For starters, at 31 she was ten years young than me, and those who knew her well understood that the few men she had been with during her life had all been professionals with university degrees. Some of her family members viewed me with suspicion at first because of the age difference, coupled with the fact that I was a tradesman. In their eyes, she was taking a huge social step backwards by hooking up with me.

Her father, Joe, was an exception to the rule though. He was originally off a farm from a small place named Yerong Creek in between Wagga and Albury in the Riverina of New South Wales, and was a self-made man. Joe had come to Sydney in his mid-twenties with not a cent to his name. From nothing, he had started a furniture and carpet business in Taren Point which had grown into a very successful enterprise.

What Joe could see from the beginning that the others couldn't was the fact that Karen and I had a very strong emotional connection. He soon realised that I was stabilising and grounded influence on his favourite daughter, who he knew had been devastated by her relationship breakdown.

Shortly after I started seeing her, I soon realised that Karen was a very principled person with strong morals and beliefs, and that she didn't suffer fools gladly.

One of Karen's characteristics which I soon noticed was that when she found something amusing, she would throw her head back and laugh out loud which I found very appealing.

It was the Saturday of the following week when I organised the fishing trip. I had waited till there was a late afternoon high tide and took her over to Costens Point at the entrance to South West Arm in Rowy's tinnie. I pumped some live nippers on the low tide at the sandflats at Mainbar, as I knew this was always a sure thing to catch bream.

Karen had met me at *Shiloh* carrying a picnic hamper that had enough food in it to feed an army. She was wearing a khaki shirt with matching shorts and white Dunlop Volleys, and even dressed simply, she looked beautiful.

I was to soon learn that Karen possessed a great sense of style and whether she was going fishing or to a black tie event she always looked sensational. In fact, I once commented to Rowy that Karen would have looked hot even if she was wearing a set of overalls digging out a trench with a pick and shovel.

Rowy had responded with, "She can dig out my plumbing trenches any day, Cozzy!"

"Okay, I've got sandwiches and freshly made chocolate cake and a hot thermos of tea for starters, Ed," she said while I helped her into Rowy's tinnie.

Once we were both in the boat I took the opportunity to make a thorough inspection of the contents of the hamper. I was astounded to see an array of food stuffs that would have been more suited to a Christmas party rather than a fishing trip.

In among the hamper there were homemade pickled olives, cabanossi, coconut slices and all sorts of tasty morsels that left my mouth watering.

"Crikey! There's enough food in here to sink a battleship, Karen!"

"Be prepared, I always say. Now, let's go and catch some fish," she said.

I soon learnt that whatever Karen did, she did with class and style and good food was an essential part of her repertoire. Karen set the bar high, but it was worth it because the rewards were always plentiful.

We motored over to Costens Point and after I baited Karens hook with a live nipper we settled down to some fishing.

"Gee Karen, you've gone to a lot of fuss with the food. I take my hat off to you for preparing such a nice spread."

She grinned. "Thank you, Ed. I got that off my grandmother. She's Italian and she never went anywhere without a nice picnic hamper."

I returned her smile. "Good. Well, now we have to be quiet because bream are very finicky fish and it doesn't take much to spook them."

Karen looked at me, and with her index finger over her mouth she lampooned me and said in a whisper, "Mum's the word, Ed. I won't say a thing."

I shook my head and with a smile said, "Smarty pants."

Karen threw her head back and laughed.

We continued to fish in total silence for the next half hour and it was right on dusk with neither of us getting a bite. Karen was starting to fidget in her seat at the lack of action and I felt awkward as I thought our first date would be doomed if no bream appeared.

"They usually come on the bite at the top of the tide," I said, trying to reassure her.

"Another fisherman's tale, I suppose," Karen said with a look of mirth etched on her face.

"No, I mean it, they like the slack water at the top of the tide."

Karen smiled and with tongue in cheek said, "Pan fried snapper would be lovely, thank you, Ed."

I snorted. "If they are going to bite then it should be happening soon."

"I'll believe it when I see it," Karen said with a grin.

Then, right when I thought I was going to look like a fool, Karen's reel gave a squeal as her rod bent over towards the water.

"There's a fish on! There's a fish on!" Karen screamed.

I laughed at her excitement. "I can see that, but don't tell the whole bloody world about it will you!"

"Sorry, sorry, it's the Italian in me. I start to scream when I get excited." She wrestled with her rod.

After a nice little fight, Karen eventually pulled in a nice-sized keeper bream to which I said, "Well, Miss Karen of Italian ancestry, it's as I said before. Rule number one when you're bream fishing in a river is that you must be as quiet as a church mouse."

"Yes, yes, I'm sorry. I won't forget that in the future."

Over the next half hour we caught another seven bream between the two of us, and every time a fish was caught Karen screamed with delight.

I shook my head to which Karen said, "I know, I know, I shouldn't scream, but this is so much fun, Ed."

It was while Karen was bringing in the eighth bream that disaster struck. I was laughing at her screaming antics, and while clambering over her picnic hamper to net the fish, I stumbled and fell head first over the side of the boat and into the water.

"Oh my God! Are you alright, Ed? Karen screamed.

"Yes, I'm okay," I said, as I bobbed up besides the boat, "but if I stay in here for too much longer there's a chance a shark might start nibbling on my toes. Give me a hand getting back into the boat, will you?"

"Okay, what do you want me to do?" Karen said, leaning over the side.

"Put all your weight on the stern while I jump over the bow and back onto the boat."

Karen did as I said and with great effort, I managed to clamber back on board, soaked to the core. I wrung my hands and when I eventually looked up, Karen was in hysterics, her hand over her mouth trying to subdue her muffled laughter.

I glared at her and this made her laugh even more.

"I'm sorry, Ed. I don't mean to laugh, but that's the funniest thing I've ever seen in my life," she snorted through howls of laughter and she threw her head back and let loose.

The more I glared at her, the more she broke up into fits of laughter.

"Oh, Ed, this is priceless. This is the funniest first date I've ever been on," she said.

I looked at her laughing from where I was sitting on the bow, and I began to laugh when I realised how funny my appearance must have appeared to her. I resembled a drowned rat as I was soaked to the core. I didn't realise it at the time, but my act of misfortune had served as a great ice-breaker and any pretense that might have still been lingering between us to that point came tumbling down.

Her laughter died away, and the nurse inside her kicked

into gear. "Oh, you poor man, you're absolutely soaked to the bone. Here, let me keep you warm," she said, wrapping the picnic rug around me.

As Karen wrapped the rug around my shoulders, her face was only inches from mine. I took in the aroma of her Red Dior perfume; she looked absolutely gorgeous as she fussed over me. Then our eyes met and as I looked deeply into them, our lips somehow touched for the very first time and we kissed passionately. I thought with her fears she might resist, or step back, but she pushed into me. I was overcome with a feeling of ecstasy and my heart tingled with joy. It was quite simply one of the most beautiful moments of my life, and no intimacy I had ever experienced before came close to the feeling I felt right then and there.

Eventually, after what seemed like an eternity, our lips parted and I dropped my head and said to her, "I'm so sorry, Karen. I shouldn't have done that. It was too hasty. Please forgive me?"

Karen placed her hand under my chin and gently lifted my head until we were gazing into each other's eyes. "Ed. That was absolutely beautiful."

"It's been a long time since I've kissed a woman like that, Karen," I told her.

To which Karen responded with a shrug. "I didn't think I would ever allow a man to kiss me like that ever again. I'm glad I did."

All my thoughts came to the surface. "You're the most beautiful woman I've ever laid my eyes on."

Karen once again kissed me passionately on the lips. "I feel so safe with you, Ed."

I smiled and felt a sense of relief. Up until that very moment

I wasn't sure if she would ever feel what I felt for her. "Well, let's get to *Shiloh* before I die of pneumonia."

I shifted around and kicked the tinnie into life, and Karen buried her head in my chest and snuggled up against me, despite the fact that I was drenched.

"Thank you for inviting me out this afternoon, Ed. It's been lovely."

In early January of 1988, Rowy invited me out to Randwick Races. I asked Karen if she would like to accompany me and she gladly accepted. We'd been taking it slow, but I was sure that what we had was rock solid and she'd say yes.

I arrived at her two-bedroom unit in Kiora Road, Miranda, at 10.00 am on race day dressed in a blue suit which I had recently purchased. I was met at the door by Karen's younger sister Sophie, who I had not met before. She was 27, and like her sister was very attractive with dark brown hair, green eyes and was very well-spoken.

While Karen was still preparing herself, I engaged in conversation with Sophie. She told me that she studied classical music at the Music Conservatorium in Sydney. It was while she was telling me that she played keyboards and organ in a blues rock band that Karen entered the lounge-room from down the hallway with a sensual sway of her hips.

If I thought she was attractive before this day, then I was astonished by how she appeared in the lounge-room. She wore a tight fitting blue and white striped dress that ended above the knee and showed off her tremendous figure. She wore a neat little short-sleeve black coat that came down to her waist with the buttons open. To top things off, she wore silk stockings and had on a pair of black stilettos. On her head was a blue and white fascinator.

Karen looked absolutely sensational and I was taken by surprise at how beautiful she looked. After she approached me with her customary beautiful smile, she kissed me on the cheek before saying, "Well, well, Mr Costigan. Who scrubs up like an absolute gentlemen?"

Karen stood back and viewed me from a distance with her finger tapping her chin and said, "Who could have ever imagined that an old salt of the sea like you could look so handsome. Especially after resembling a drowned rat when you fell in the water that night."

I laughed and we spent another five minutes talking to Sophie before we made our way to my car and to the races.

What followed was a very enjoyable day followed by dinner at a Thai restaurant in Cronulla with the Rowes.

After dinner, I drove Karen back to her unit, arriving at about midnight. I pulled the car up and left the motor running. There was an awkward moment between the two of us where nothing was said and I sensed that Karen wanted to ask me something.

"Ed, there is one thing that I have been meaning to ask you."

I turned the car off and a feeling of apprehension came over me.

"What's that Karen?"

"I spoke to Anne some weeks ago as I felt there was something from your past that you weren't telling me about. Anne told me you had a drinking problem, but that you hadn't touched a drink for a number of years. I spoke to Julie not long after this and she also confirmed this. I think you're a nice man, Ed, but I find you a bit of a mystery. Anne told me that you got into a lot of trouble with your drinking but she didn't go into any detail."

I looked straight ahead and could hear my heart pounding but said nothing. I was filled with a fear that this was leading somewhere terrible. Would she ditch me if she found out the truth?

She put me on the spot. "Ed, I had a great time today, and I've enjoyed our time together so far, but there is no way we could ever have a relationship if we kept secrets from each other. Is there anything you need to tell me?"

I stared at her nervously. "Karen, if you knew about my past then you would run for the hills and probably never want to lay eyes on me ever again."

"I'll be the judge of that, thank you!" Karen said directly.

I sighed. "Karen, I'm a recovering alcoholic. I left a path of destruction behind me that I'm still trying to come to terms with."

"Perhaps you can tell me about it," she ventured gently.

I sat in silence staring straight ahead looking at the stars. I sighed and tried to dissuade her one last time. "I've never been so happy as I've been the last couple of months, Karen, and I know you won't like what I tell you."

Karen gave me a stern look. "Ed, if you don't tell me, then there is no chance that things will go any further between you and me. I can't be with someone who lies to me, or doesn't think I'm worthy enough to know his past."

I took another huge sigh, as I felt like I was going to the executioners block. I was reluctant, but instinct told me that if I wanted to keep going with her, and I did, then I had to tell her. I pulled the keys out of the ignition.

I spent the next hour explaining everything. I told her that I was three years without a drink. I told her about the truck accident and that I killed a young girl and had gone to jail. I told Karen about my ex-wife and that I had not seen my daughter in five and a half years.

I left no stone unturned.

I wanted to be with this woman, and if the truth was required, then I would tell it. All the advice that Stumpy, Frank and Anne had given me over the years had pushed for honesty in all my dealings.

Karen sat in total silence and didn't say a word, but she listened carefully. I hoped that she'd see my regret, my guilt, and my grief.

When I was finished I felt totally washed up and sat in silence, staring straight ahead, waiting for Karen's reply. After what seemed like an eternity of silence, she finally spoke, her words carefully chosen.

"Thank you, Ed, I needed to hear that," she said. "I sensed that you had a lot hidden away that you weren't telling me about and I appreciate your honesty. I have a lot to think about with what you have just told me, and I feel that the situation between us has changed. Thank you very much for today. I appreciate you asking me to the races. Good night."

She got out of my car and I watched her walk away in anguish. She didn't look back.

I rested my forehead on the steering wheel.

"Bugger, bugger, bugger, bugger! I've just blown it! "

***

"You can imagine how I felt, Tim. Here I was with the most beautiful woman I had ever been with and she leaves me hanging in limbo."

"Crikey, that must have knocked you for a six? Especially if she was that dream girl that Stumpy told you about."

"You can say that again."

"I suppose you can't blame her though. I mean after dumping that load on her! Well, that must have been too much for her to handle?"

"That's what I thought, but contrary to what you may think, Karen didn't dump me. After a few weeks she made contact. I thought I'd lost her, but there she was," I told him, spreading my arms expansively.

Tim looked surprised. "She came back? You told her that you killed a kid and all that other stuff you've told me, and she just came back?"

"That's right. When Karen weighed it all up, when she really thought about what she knew of me, and my family, after all, she was good friends with my sister, she knew that she was onto a good thing. She knew that I had that ability to listen and give back to her, that I wouldn't jeopardise our relationship for anything. That's why she came back to me. She realised that we both had a deep attachment to each other and that she needed me just as much as I need her."

Tim sat back in his chair, folded his arms and with a look of interest said, "Well, go on then. What did she say when she came back?"

"It happened at an Australia Day BBQ at her parents' home."

***

In the weeks that followed my conversation with Karen, I berated myself for divulging too much of my past.

"You should have kept your mouth shut, Costigan! It was just too much for her to take. You'd still be with her if you'd just said nothing," I said to myself one day, but part of me knew that wasn't quite true. It probably would have lead to a worse bust up later on if she'd discovered I was holding back more.

Then, unexpectedly, Karen rang me. I had resigned myself to the fact that it was over between the two of us, and although I'd been tempted to ring her a number of times, I held back. From what I knew of Karen, she had to come to me.

"Hi, Ed. Sorry it's been so long since I've made contact, but I've been pretty busy lately. My parents are holding a BBQ on Australia Day at their place and I just want to know if you want to come over and meet my family."

I was shocked.

"Yeah, that would be nice, Karen," I said nervously. I couldn't believe she went from not talking to me to introducing me to her family!

Her parents, Joe and Fran Monaghan, lived in a waterfront home in Matson Crescent at Caringbah, which had a clear view looking right down Yowie Bay. I was as toey as a tick as I knocked on the front door of the Monaghan's residence for the lunchtime BBQ. I was met at the door by Karen's youngest sister who was as equally as beautiful as her elder two sisters.

"Oh, hi. You must be, Ed?" she said with a smile.

"That's right. Felicity?" I said, holding out my hand.

"I am indeed, please come in," she said, shaking my hand.

"Nice place you've got here," I said, surveying the inside of the home. I knew the family had been in furnishings, so it was no surprise.

"Thank you. Everybody's out on the back deck," said Felicity pointing outside.

I walked outside to be met by the spectacular sight of the full expanse of Yowie Bay. It was a stunning view, and as I was taking in the panorama, Karen sidled up to me and took my hand.

"Hi, Ed, glad to see you could make it. Come and meet the family."

She looked so beautiful, and strangely, it was like no time had passed. I smiled at her. "Thanks, Karen. It's nice to see you again."

Karen smiled and said, "Likewise, Ed."

What followed was an introduction to family and friends that seemed to go in one ear and out the other. What I did remember was being introduced to her two eldest brothers, Vince and Paul, and Karen's younger brother Peter. The Monaghans' attitude to me was initially one of cautious reservation as they were still wary of this older man in Karen's life. Karen's father, Joe, was the exception. He seemed to warm to me straight away.

"Karen tells me you're originally off a property, Ed?"

"I am, Joe. Little place called Eumungerie in the central west of NSW."

"I'm off a property at Yerong Creek down in the Riverinia."

I brightened up immediately. Joe and I had an instant rapport. We found much in common with our upbringings. Being the patriarch, he was loved and respected by all of his clan, which I believe served as a catalyst for the rest of the family eventually warming to me.

Lunch was great and it was dusk when Karen walked up beside me and said, "Come for a walk with me to the back landing, Ed, so I can show you the view."

"Yeah sure, Karen." I followed her, thinking that perhaps now we'd talk.

Karen led me down a series of steps down to a lower section

that was landscaped with rock walls and small shrubs where we stood on a neatly manicured grassed area. From here the view of Yowie Bay was expansive and if you strained your eyes you just see where *Shiloh* was situated at the other end of the bay. It was hard to believe I could basically see their house from my own.

Karen stared down at the bay before she began. "I wanted to bring you down here, Ed, so we could be in private. I have some important things to say to you."

My heart started to pound. "I figured that might have been case."

She stared at me. "I've thought long and hard about what you told me that night in the car. To be perfectly honest with you, it shocked me. I knew you had been in trouble with drink but I never, not in my wildest dreams, thought you had hit rock bottom to the extent that you did. It made me wonder if you were the right man for me."

"That was why I was so reluctant in telling you the full extent of what had happened to me Karen, but I know that I had to be honest. Telling you of my every weakness was one of the hardest things I've ever done," I said quietly.

Karen nodded her head. "I didn't think I could sustain a relationship with you after what you told me. Especially after killing that poor girl in the truck accident. I thought about that for days afterwards and I could not get the image of that poor girl out of my head."

I felt the bottom fall out of stomach. I took a huge gulp and said with trepidation, "You and me both. I can't undo my past, Karen. All I can do is try the best with what I've got left."

Karen shook her head and said, "I realise that, Ed."

"My past has made me what I am today. If I had not lived

the life I have, I would not appreciate the things I've got today," I told her.

She must have sensed I was trying to explain myself because she gave me a rueful smile. "Ed, I'm around dying people every day. I've heard some of the most putrid deathbed confessions imaginable from people who are seeking redemption in the last moments of their life. I've seen the relief on the faces of people who have finally divulged secrets about themselves that have been hidden for a lifetime," she said. "I thought long and hard about what you told me that night. I was weighing your value in the palm of my hand when it finally dawned on me that I am not in a position to judge you for your past. As much as what you've told me about yourself has shocked me, I know that you're a good man who is trying to live a decent life and rectify what he can."

The flutter turned into a sea of butterflies. I was so relieved. "I honestly thought it was over between you and me. I wasn't sure you wanted a bar of me after what I told you."

"No, Ed," she said, as she took me by the arm. "I invited you here today because I want you to be part of my life," she said with a smile.

I smiled back. "And I want nothing more than to be part of your life too."

She leant against me, and I was happy, but there was something else to be said. "Karen, there's one thing you have to understand if you and I are to have a lasting relationship. It's important."

She pulled back to look at me quizzically. "What's that, Ed?"

I gave her a serious look. "It's this. My recovery is the most important thing in my life. If I don't maintain that then I've got nothing, and that includes you."

Karen nodded. "Of course. I accept and fully support you, Ed, and I would never jeopardise your recovery. Whatever you need, you'll get."

I pulled her close. "I'd never do anything to harm you. You make me so happy, Karen, and these last few weeks, thinking it was over, really stung."

Karen ran a hand down my cheek and then she kissed me. "One of the things that I like about you, Ed Costigan, is that you are so honest."

I was astonished. "You do?"

"Absolutely! I could see that the very first night that I met you," she said with a laugh. "There was something really decent about you. I could see it from the start."

"I was mesmerised by your beauty, Karen!"

"Thank you, Ed." She nestled up against me again.

"You're a pretty special lady, Kaz, and I know you've been through a lot with your own relationship breakdown. I just wanted to make sure that you felt safe. That you wanted to be with me without any pressure."

Karen's smiled faded. "You know, Ed, I was totally shattered after I broke up with Geoff. In retrospect, I could see that he wasn't the right one for me and that it would have only ended in disaster if we tied the knot. It was only after the breakup when I went to work at St Vincent's that I was able to put my life back into perspective. It was working in the palliative care ward that helped me. You and I meeting is the best thing that's happened to me, and I missed you more than I can say while we were apart. You are the one for me."

I wrapped my arms around her and held her head against my chest while I kissed her on the forehead.

"I'd love to wrap my body around yours tonight, Karen," I whispered in her ear.

"There's plenty of time for that later, Ed," she said with a smile. She leaned up and kissed me again.

As I stood there, looking out over the bay, with every single one of my dreams coming true, I mused on Stumpy's prophecy and Frank's words of wisdom to 'just wait', I was struck. I knew what I wanted and it was this woman. Everything about her was perfect. No one else would do, there was just her. I didn't want to waste another second. If she was willing to accept me knowing what she did now, then perhaps she was in for the long haul.

"What are you thinking Ed?"

I tore my eyes away from the water and stared deep into her eyes. "Karen, would you marry me?"

"What?" Karen said, shocked.

"Would you marry me?"

Karen stood there her mouth wide open saying nothing before she finally said, "Oh, I don't know what to say."

I rushed ahead. "I've already made up my mind. There is nobody I'd rather be with than you. I can't give you much materially, but what I can give you is my love. I'll make sure I look after you for the rest of my life, Karen."

"Ed, I'm not interested in how much money you have." She was flustered, but she also looked thrilled, like maybe she was wanting this too. "I like you for who you are."

I got down on one knee and as I looked up at her I said, "Will you do me the honor, Karen, and be my wife?"

Karen looked at me for an eternity and as I looked back at her I could see the tears in her eyes and as they started to roll down her cheeks she said, "Yes, Ed. Yes, yes, yes, I'll marry you."

I got up and hugged her tight, and when we separated, I

kissed her; a deep kiss filled with every bit of love I had. Karen always used her instincts and her intuition, and despite everything we'd been through, she already knew that I was the one for her. She just need to make her sure her head had been on right, to be settled in her heart.

"Good. Then that's all settled," I said with a smile when we broke apart.

Karen threw her head back and laughed. "I insist we have a spring wedding, Ed."

"A spring wedding it will be then, my dear."

Karen set the wedding date for Saturday the 1st of October 1988, as that was the anniversary of when we first met. While she busied herself with preparations for the big day, I involved myself in another project which was to be my wedding present to Karen.

I had long wanted a little putt-putt boat to restore and I happened to come across one for sale in the local newspaper just after Easter in 1988. The bloke selling it lived at Fisherman's Bay at Maianbar on the other side of the Port Hacking River, so I went for a drive one Saturday afternoon to inspect it.

This boat was just what I had been looking for, as I had long wanted to strip one back and return it to its former glory, almost as a symbolic gesture of my own rebuilt life.

It was sixteen foot long and the hull was made of New Zealand Kauri, and despite appearances was not in very good condition. The one cylinder motor was not working and after further inspection I realised it needed a major overhaul. The decks and hull which were made of light brown beech timber were in need of replacing and after much haggling, I was able to beat him down from $1,000 to $770.

Rowy towed the boat behind his Shark Cat, and we placed it in his boatshed where I could covertly restore it with Rowy's son Luke as my assistant. I was going to present it to my darling on her wedding night.

Meanwhile, I took Karen up to Eumungerie just after I had purchased the putt putt to show her where I was brought up. Most of the family had already met Karen at Anne's birthday party and they were delighted at the news of our impending wedding.

I was the happiest I had been since my pre-Vietnam days. With my impending wedding, my boat restoration project, a good job with Rowy that was ticking along quite nicely, regular games of golf with Frank, and fishing the Port Hacking, life was good.

I spent months painstakingly rebuilding the boat after work and when it was finished in early September of 1988 it looked immaculate. I had painted the hull light blue and the deck was painted with a teak stain which only accentuated the beautiful light beech timber. The last thing which went on the boat was its name. I had thought long and hard about it and wanted the name to reflect not only Karen's beauty, but draw upon her Italian heritage.

I had one of those 'eureka!' moments one night while fishing on the pontoon at *Shiloh* when the name came to me.

After getting a signwriter to paint the name on the front of the hull in black writing, I kept it hidden from prying eyes by covering it with newspaper and securing it with masking tape.

I was all set for our weeding day and as it drew closer Karen was none the wiser of what I had been up to for months in Rowy's boatshed. Little did I know at the time how important this little boat was to be in Karen's and my future life.

***

I looked at Tim with a grin on my face.

"In all seriousness, Tim, my honesty did pay off in the long run and I got the girl. It was scary divulging my past, because I thought I had lost Karen for good, but only a relationship based on honesty will survive the test of time."

Tim nodded his head in agreement and said, "I know you're right, Ed. I've had a number of relationships end in a nasty way, and up until now I've been just plain wary of getting involved with a woman."

I made a face. "Can you blame them after the way you've been living? Let's face it, Tim, an active alcoholic isn't a real good recipe for a successful relationship. Like I said, honesty is paramount and that's something you haven't had a lot of in your life lately."

He sighed. "To be honest with you, Ed, I just don't know if I'll ever meet a woman like your Karen."

I gave him a reassuring smile. "You will, Tim. I was the most sorry sod there was, but look what ended up coming my way. You have to get fairdinkum."

"I can see that. But all the work you did, it just looks so hard."

Tim looked downcast and I felt for the lad. I knew where he was coming from. "It was hard," I said quietly. "You've seen how I tried and failed. But when I got fairdinkum, it stuck. Besides," I said with a smile, "it all ended up just brilliant. The work paid off. I got Karen and she got the wedding she had always wanted."

Chapter 15

Saturday the 1st of October, 1988, Sutherland, Sydney

I T WAS A beautiful sunny Saturday afternoon in early October when I stood in the aisle of St Patrick's Catholic Church at Sutherland.

Standing beside me was my best man, Rowy, with Noel as my groomsman.

"A lot different to the first time you tied the knot, hey, Cozzy," said Rowy as he gave me a wink.

I shook my head as I remembered that crazy day. "It still makes me shudder when I think about it, Rowy."

"The family have always said he should have won an Oscar for that performance, Rowy." Noel whispered with a snigger.

It was because of my drunken state at my wedding to Kim that I was granted a church annulment from my first marriage on the grounds that I was so drunk that I couldn't remember what I was doing. It was one of the rare occasions where my brother John showed his solidarity by coming to my aid and helping me with the process of gaining an annulment. Although, I reckon he probably did it just as much for Kim as me. Or for the church and his idea of what the vows meant. I never knew where John's motivation lay.

Celebrating the nuptial mass were both Fr Frank Casey and, yes, John. I was all in favour of just having Frank up there, but after John came into bat for me on the annulment I conceded, and Karen and I invited him to celebrate the mass with Frank.

John really had mellowed after our last meeting during Stumpy's final days. At some point he'd finally realised that I was endeavouring to right the wrongs of my past, but I suspect that Frank had kept him abreast of my progress. He respected Frank and because Frank respected me, it did wonders.

The church was packed with around 150 guests from both sides of the Monaghan and Costigan families. Also among the congregation were Schooner Rooney and his wife which made my day. I still couldn't find Finno, and I resigned myself to the fact that I might not ever find out what happened to him.

Karen was due to arrive at the church at 4.00 pm, but the hour came and went and she was late. I'd like to say it increased the excitement, but for me it only heightened my anxiety. Then, at 4.15 pm, the wedding party arrived in two white Rolls Royces. They had been held up by some minor adjustments necessary for Karen's hair.

The congregation let out a collective sigh, no one bigger than me, as both the flower girl and page boy entered the church and proceeded to walk down the aisle.

Sophie had organised a string quartet and piano for the wedding ceremony. They were all friends of hers from her years at the Sydney Music Conservatorium. As the wedding procession began, the church was filled with the beautiful sounds of Pachelbel's 'Canon in D major'.

Then Sophie entered the church, closely followed by Anne,

who was Karen's maid of honour. They looked absolutely beautiful as they were both dressed in matching turquoise strapless satin dresses with a short train.

The congregation let out a collective gasp as they took their first glimpse of Karen. As she stood in the doorway, the sunlight accentuated and highlighted her glorious figure. It looked like some heavenly angel had descended to earth. Joe escorted her down the aisle and as I viewed my wife to be for the first time, my mouth opened in awe. I was mesmerised at the sight of the gorgeous lady walking towards me. Karen looked absolutely stunning as she made her way up the aisle, occasionally glancing at well-wishers standing in the pews, giving out excited little waves to a few people.

She was dressed in a classic 1960s style figure-hugging fish tail gown in champagne satin with a net overlay of the same colour. The slight v-neck bodice was fitted with spaghetti straps with small lace details which accentuated the décolletage of the bride. Rose corsages had been added to both the shoulder and thigh to give it a romantic and feminine touch of glamour. In her hand was a bridal bouquet consisting of an arrangement of white roses and tulips, and in her hair she wore a small fascinator which was the same colour as her wedding gown. Karen's beautiful skin gleamed pure and her brown hair, which was tied back, only accentuated her beautiful wedding dress.

As she strolled towards me, she resembled some Roman goddess. I had never seen her look as beautiful as this. It was like she'd stripped away the veneer of everyday life and revealed the goddess within.

It wasn't until she was almost beside me that our eyes first met. She gave me radiant smile as Joe handed her over to me.

He whispered in my ear, "Look after her, mate, she's my pride and joy."

"I will indeed, Joe," I told him, bursting with pride.

It was during Frank's homily that I became fully aware of the reality of the situation that I now found myself in. I happened to glance down at the wedding booklet that was on my lap and noticed the lovely floral surrounds on the cover page.

Welcome to the marriage

Of

Karen Francesca Monaghan

And

Edward John Costigan

Saturday 1st of October 1988

St Patrick's Catholic Church, Sutherland

After the wedding reception, held at the Monaghan's residence at Yowie Bay, and which, I think it's worthwhile adding, I behaved myself accordingly, I drove Karen down to *Shiloh* with streamers strewn all across my beloved Monaro.

Karen was still dressed in her magnificent wedding gown and I picked her up and carried her in my arms towards *The Rocket* so as not to damage her dress. She was as light as a feather to carry and the satin material of her wedding dress felt smooth and silky in my hands. Karen giggled as she put her hands behind my neck while I carried her down the sandstone steps which led to *The Rocket*. I gently placed her in the seat and made sure that her dress was secure inside the carriage.

When we got to the bottom, I once again carried her in my arms into the house where I gently set her down on the lounge.

I fixed both of us a drink and after handing Karen her glass of champagne I walked over to my music collection and pulled out a Duke Ellington album which I knew Karen loved.

I played the track *Day Dream* as this was one of Karen's favourites. She was standing in the doorway of the living area that led out to the front screened veranda area. I walked towards her and after she put down her glass of champagne, I took her by the hands. I held her beautiful body close to mine and we danced slowly. She kissed me gently on the lips and then hugged me. I gently caressed the back of her neck. Never had I felt so happy. I could smell her Red Dior perfume and her skin felt smooth as I ran my hands down her shoulders and onto her arms. We gazed into each other's eyes and kissed each other passionately as we continued to dance.

After thirty minutes I said to Karen, "I've got something to show you."

"What is it, Ed?"

"It's over here at the pontoon."

I took Karen by the hand and hit the light switch, which lit up the pontoon. There, moored in the water, was my little boat.

"There! What do you think of that?" I said, pointing at the boat.

After focussing on the boat for some time, Karen suddenly gasped. "Oh, Ed, what a beautiful little boat!"

I smiled. "That's my wedding present to you, Karen."

She looked at me in astonishment. "For me?"

Karen walked over to the boat so she could inspect it more

carefully. Glistening in the light was the name of the boat—
Bella Donna—which was written in black italic writing on the
side towards the bow.

She bent down to inspect my pride and joy, gently gliding
her hands over the decking for a number of minutes; eventually
running her fingers over the name of the boat.

"*Bella donna*… that's Italian for 'beautiful woman'. Did you
know that, Ed?" Karen looked at me and our eyes met.

"There is only one beautiful woman in my life, Karen," I
told her.

"I love it." Her eyes were full of tears.

"I hope to spend many hours with you in the *Bella Donna*,
Kaz."

"Oh, that would be beautiful."

We held each other tight and then I looked into her eyes
and said, "I love you and I can't think of anybody else who I
would rather spend the rest of my life with."

Karen hugged me and rested her head on my chest. We
were almost dancing again, but without the music.

"Come on, there's something else I'd like to play for you," I
said. I put on the Van Morrison album *Moon Dance,* and then
we sat on the step that led to the pontoon.

The night was warm and as the light breeze blew across the
water, Karen wrapped her arms around me and rested her head
on my shoulder. We talked softly as we enjoyed the sounds of
Crazy Love. It was a very romantic setting and Karen looked
beautiful, as the lights of *Shiloh* shone on her face.

"You're very much a romantic, Ed," she whispered in my ear.

"I do my best," I said with a grin.

The night was drawing on now, and I could feel my anticipation rising. Karen had made a conscious decision once we got

engaged to save herself for our wedding night. As much as I had wanted to make love to Karen on so many occasions before, I had agreed with her wishes and now I suddenly realised it was well worth it.

She took my hand and said, "I think it's about time we got more comfortable."

I couldn't have agreed more.

Karen then led me into the house and into the bedroom where we went to bed. Her body was as smooth as silk as I wrapped my naked self around her and kissed her on the lips, and then on her breasts; first the left, then the right. She wrapped her arms and legs around me, and brought me back up to kiss me passionately on the lips.

"Yes," she whispered, and I knew everything was perfect.

That night in *Shiloh* we made love for the first time and it was absolute bliss.

After our honeymoon at Port Douglas, Karen turned my world upside down as she started the process of transforming *Shiloh* both inside and out. I am a creature of habit and get annoyed if anybody moves my Tupperware container of teabags on the kitchen bench, let alone starts to rearrange my house.

Karen was a woman of style and I believe part of that was due to her Italian heritage which gave her that special ability to add class, warmth and beauty when it came to the refurbishment of *Shiloh*.

"We're not living in this place the way it is, Ed," Karen said in no uncertain terms after arriving home.

"What's wrong with it?" I said with outstretched hands.

"What's wrong with it?" Her expression was pure disbelief. "Well, for starters it's as cold as charity."

"Cold as charity?"

She threw her arms out wide. "It lacks warmth and colour and that homely feeling."

"I think it's a fisherman's paradise, Kaz," I said, breaking into laughter.

Karen rolled her eyes and walked away shaking her head. Eventually, she started laughing. "You'll never learn, Ed," she said. She looked around thoughtfully, biting her lip.

In retrospect I should have known better as Karen had her unit at Miranda beautifully done out inside. I remember the first day I visited when I took her to the races. The warmth and colour struck me immediately and I felt very comfortable the moment I entered.

Although we were only renting *Shiloh,* Karen had no problems convincing Bob and Julie that *Shiloh* needed a makeover.

It was the Saturday morning after we arrived home from our honeymoon that Karen got into action. She was leaning against the lounge-room wall with her arms folded, when with a burst of enthusiasm she blurted out, "The colours of Tuscany!"

"The what?" I said in total confusion.

"The colours of Tuscany, Ed. That's what the theme for *Shiloh* will be."

"Where's Tuscany?"

"Where's Tuscany?" she said in exasperation. She looked at me like I was crazy.

"I know it's in Italy somewhere, but where exactly?"

"It's an area in central Italy and is known as the birthplace of the Renaissance. It's rich in history, landscapes and has a powerful artistic legacy. I've decided that in keeping with my Italian heritage it will be the theme for the total transformation of *Shiloh* from a static abode to a place of beauty and warmth."

S.E.NETHERY

"And when is this all due to start?" I said with a look of apprehension.

"Right now," she said smiling.

Over the next month the both of us spent our weekends repainting the inside of the dwelling.

The main bedroom was painted in a beautiful rich olive green tone while the spare bedroom was a dark cheery red named 'Heartthrob'.

"The kids will love that colour when they stay over, Ed. It's got a playful tone about it."

"The kids?" I said with narrowed eyes.

"Yes, all our nephews and nieces, not to mention the Rowe kids. They'll love having a night down here and I'm sure Julie will be happy to send them on down whenever she can."

I walked away shaking my head. I was used to having *Shiloh* to myself and the thought of kids zooming around the place was a bit too much for me to handle. How wrong I was on that score!

The kitchen was the last room on the agenda and Karen chose an orange-grey colour scheme which looked fantastic. When we had completed the painting, *Shiloh* had transformed so much that I felt I was living in a different home.

"This looks absolutely brilliant, Kaz. You've worked wonders here, sweetie," I said as I stood back, taking in the magnificent transformation in colour.

Karen wrapped her arms around my waist and kissed me on the lips. "I'm glad you like it," she said with a smile.

As the months went by *Shiloh* started to slowly change in character.

She added little subtle touches here and there that only added to the ambience of *Shiloh*. I would come home from work and there would be a new rug on the floor or something she had picked up from a store that kept in with the spirit of *Shiloh*'s Tuscan design.

Karen loved flowers and she always had a fresh bunch in a vase at home. She loved the bold colours and settings of Australian artist Margaret Olley and all of her nature imagery, so over time Karen picked up quite a few prints of Margaret's paintings and the colorful works of flowers adorned our walls, adding a spirit to our home that hadn't been there before.

Shiloh boasted an old brick fireplace, but I had never had it working. At Karen's insistence, I cleaned it up by re-laying the broken bricks at the front and then getting a professional chimney sweeper to clean the stack. In the years that followed, our fireplace became a central part of *Shiloh*'s identity, and many a cold winter's night was spent in front of its warming glow, either snuggled up next to Karen or sharing it with family and friends.

In essence, Karen had worked wonders in changing *Shiloh*. It was once a very simple dwelling, but now it was something that spoke to the visitor and made them feel very happy when they left.

As Karen and I settled into married life we found that there were always a couple of kids staying over on the weekends. They were usually Anne's kids, or the Rowe's, in particular Fiona, and as *Shiloh* had a couple of beds in the second bedroom, it became a holiday retreat for them.

When the weather was favourable, I often took them out on *Bella Donna* to go fishing up the Port Hacking River or explore in the Royal National Park. *Bella Donna* soon became the focus of much of our outdoor activity and it was nothing for Karen to prepare a hamper and take ourselves with a couple of kids in tow over to the Royal National Park for a picnic.

Although I had lived by myself for a considerable amount of time before meeting Karen, I soon found I enjoyed all the extra company and the constant stream of banter from having the kids around.

It filled me with a happiness that I had not experienced for many years, and although it bought back memories of Michelle. I was stung by those pangs of regret every day. Despite that ongoing agony, the constant stream of kids soothed that wound.

And if I liked the kids, then Karen absolutely adored them. She became their surrogate mother of sorts and I saw how she looked at them. I saw what was deep in her heart. Strangely, it was a topic we didn't broach for some time.

The kids and the Rowe family just loved Karen. Bob and Julie often remarked to me how meeting Karen was one of the best things that had happened in my life. While Julie wished that we'd met earlier, Bob would often say to me, "That girl's a rare diamond and you're a lucky man to have her, Ed!"

Karen's influence on my life was totally revolutionary and as much as she initially turned my life upside down, in time I was all the better for it. It was the little things like shopping for clothes or taking me to get a haircut. It was strange how I never resisted her directions because by nature I could be rebellious if anybody tried to run my life. With Karen though, I never felt as though she was dominating me. Her persuasive ability had a mystery and a power which I had never experienced before.

Even when it came to events I had no power over her. I had not properly celebrated my birthday in years, so when my 43rd birthday came around on the 17th of March, 1989, Karen made sure it was a special evening with a dozen of my closest family and friends. It highlighted to me how family were so important to Karen and how I had lost that part of my life in the years I spent in my alcoholic haze. I remember looking at everyone that night and being so full of love for them all, but there was something missing. Michelle, obviously, but those wistful looks of Karen's were starting to affect me too.

As much as we were very happy together, we both knew that our union would only be fully realised if we had a child. This issue soon became the most important thing in our lives.

When we lay in bed at night, Karen would often run her fingers across my rough hands, as she found this very sensual. She would look at my hands and comment, "If I could read your hands, Ed, I imagine they would read like an epic novel." She would inevitably smile and with a sigh bury her head into my chest as she wrapped her arms around me.

Our conversations would include our hopes and dreams and aspirations for the future and it would inevitably lead to Karen talking about her love of children. We decided to try to conceive, but to no avail. She was coming up to 33 years of age by this stage and knew that she wanted to fall pregnant sooner rather than later. She was desperate to have a child, and I still wanted a son to carry on my family name. My beloved little boy Ray was a weight that I would always carry, and I had plenty of nieces and nephews, but to have a son would have meant the world to me.

After the continuous effort of trying, we decided to see the doctor. A series of tests discovered that Karen had picked up an infection somewhere in the past that had caused an inflammation to her fallopian tubes. The doctor informed Karen that the condition was caused by either bacteria or a virus, and was probably transmitted through sexual intercourse. He then delivered the knockout blow. Her chances of conceiving were minimal.

When we returned home from the doctor and sat on the lounge and discussed our predicament. She was so angry and had only person to blame.

"That Geoff," Karen said with a look of disgust.

"The villain, hey Kaz?" I rubbed her back.

Karen nodded her head in agreement. "Had to be. I can't believe how easily I was seduced by him, Ed."

"It can happen, Kaz," I said with reassuring kiss on the forehead. "You've got nothing to blame yourself for."

Karen stared into space and tears started to well in her eyes. "I desperately want to have children, Ed, and he's taken that away from me." She broke down and sobbed, holding her head in her hands.

I wrapped my arms around her for the best part of ten minutes and just held her while she cried herself out. I grieved for myself as well. There would be no son, no little girl, to lighten up our lives. What made matters worse for me was the fact I couldn't see Michelle and little Ray hadn't lived beyond his precious seven days. It hurt all too much, but unlike me, this hurt was fresh for Karen. I had learned to live with my pain.

I sought to console her. "I know it's easy for me to say, Kaz, but we've just got to play the cards we've been dealt."

Karen lifted her head, and wiped away the tears. "I know you're right, Ed, but it's a big blow to be hit with this type of news when all your life you've been preparing to have children."

Karen sat in silent contemplation for some time and then sighed. "At least I found you, Mr Costigan, and that makes me very happy."

I wrapped my arms around her and kissed her on the top of her head. "How about I make a pot of tea to cheer us up."

"That would be nice, Ed," she said before kissing me on the lips.

Mum had hand-knitted a tea cozy and given it to us as one of our wedding presents. It was the colours of the rainbow and Karen loved nothing more than to brew a pot of tea and put the tea cozy on. We sat on the lounge, had a cup of tea, and ate some of Karen's homemade ginger cake with the lemon icing on top.

"It never ceases to amaze me the healing qualities in a cup of tea," Karen said thoughtfully.

"Yes, there is certainly something special about it," I said, relieved that Karen seemed to be picking up. I gazed into her beautiful dark brown eyes. "I love you, Kaz."

Karen smiled at me. "And the feeling is mutual, Ed Costigan."

"At the end of the day we have each other and that's all that counts," I said.

Karen snuggled up and kissed me on the lips. "And that thought makes me very happy."

"Besides," I added, "we're lucky because we do have kids in our life. With Rowy and Annie, we'll always be surrogate parents. We are part of a beautiful family."

Karen smiled and said, "Indeed we are. Indeed we are, Ed."

All of the Rowe children were close to Karen and I, so much so that they called us Aunty and Uncle. That gave us no amount of joy.

After Matt, Gerard, Martin and Luke, Bob and Julie had desperately wanted a daughter and when Fiona was born in April of 1984, they were overjoyed. Julie referred to Fiona as her bundle of joy and as soon as she could talk they knew she was very special. Fiona had an engaging personality and it was obvious from an early age that she was very intelligent. With strawberry blonde hair like her mother and a beautiful smile she bonded with Karen soon after they met.

Although the three eldest boys spent plenty of time at *Shiloh,* it was Luke and Fiona who were particularly close to us. By the time Karen and I married, Luke was six and Fiona was four and they spent much of their time down at *Shiloh.* Bob and Julie were happy for them to trundle on down to us after school and on the weekends, and we were glad to have them.

If there was a moment when Karen and Fiona's relationship became very special, it was about a week after Karen had received the news from her doctor that she couldn't conceive. Karen had told both Julie and Anne what had happened and the two girls had been like a rock to her during this very difficult time.

It was a beautiful Sunday morning. Karen had come home from mass and we were having brunch out the front of *Shiloh.* We were eating our bacon and eggs and were enjoying a cup of tea when we heard a little girl's voice calling out from a distance.

"Yoo-hoo! Uncle Ed and Aunty Karen! Are you there?"

Karen looked at me and said, "Did you hear that, Ed?"

"Hear what?" I said, savouring the bacon. I was oblivious to anything but food.

"It sounded like Fiona."

"Hello! Uncle Ed and Aunty Karen!" The voice was becoming distinctly louder.

Karen cocked her head to one side. "It's Fiona."

As we both looked up from the table in search of Fiona, she suddenly appeared from around the side of *Shiloh.*

"I thought I might find you two down here having a snack."
Her pithy comment brining a smile to our faces.

"Well you guessed correctly, Missy Moo!" said Karen with
a grin.

"That's good, Aunty Karen, because I've got something for
you," said Fiona as she tried to hide a bouquet of flowers behind
her back.

Karen could easily see the flowers but played along so as not
to disappoint Fiona's surprise.

"Now, what may that be?" said Karen trying to conceal
her smile.

Fiona presented Karen with the lovely bouquet of flowers
with an enthusiastic child-like flourish. They consisted of an
assortment of daisies, dandelions, gardenias and roses.

"For me, Missy Moo?"

"Yes, Aunty Karen. The florist told me that these flowers
would cheer you up. Mum said you needed cheering up. I don't
know what you need cheering up from because you seem fine
to me."

Fiona's words struck a chord with Karen, and in an instant
her demeanour changed and her lip started to quiver. "That's
very kind of you, Fiona. It's very kind of you indeed."

Karen then hugged her tight and as she did Fiona said,
"Why are you upset, Aunty Karen?"

"Oh, it's nothing, Missy Moo, just some grown up stuff,"
said Karen, wiping a tear from her cheek.

She gave a petulant little frown. "That's what Mum said.
She wouldn't tell me because she said I wouldn't understand."

Karen gave her a weak smile. "Maybe when you're a bit
older I'll tell you."

"I hope these flowers cheer you up, Aunty Karen?" asked Fiona, her innocent eyes so earnest and true.

"Oh, they have definitely cheered me up," Karen said, hugging Fiona. "With a visit from you, I'm always cheered up."

From where I sat on the other side of the table, I knew I had just witnessed something magical and that bond was only to deepen as the years went by.

Just as Fiona was to have a special bond with Karen, so too was I to have with Luke. He had shown a keen interest in things of a mechanical nature as long as I had known him. Rowy was happy for me to show him anything I like. In fact, it was when I started to rebuild *Bella Donna* that I first noticed Luke loved to be around me, observing what I was doing. Even though he was only a little tacker, he showed a keen interest in my project and whenever I was in Rowy's boatshed, covertly working on the boat, young Luke would usually appear like magic.

At first he would just stand beside me and observe what I was doing, until one day I dropped some nails on the floor of the boatshed and he picked them up for me.

"You got a keen interest in this little project of mine, hey Luke?' I said while he put the nails into an old ice cream container.

"Uncle Ed, when I grow up I want to be a mechanic just like you!" he said with a conviction that was refreshing..

"Is that right, young fella?"

"For sure, Uncle Ed."

"Well, if that's the case then you better start getting your hands dirty, Lukey!"

He stood up straight to attention. "Okay, Uncle Ed. I am ready for action."

I didn't realise it at the time, but that's when Luke's informal apprenticeship started. From that moment onwards he became my loyal assistant as I rebuilt *Bella Donna*.

Initially, he helped in small ways like cleaning the paint brushes or passing me nails while I refitted the hull with new timber. He got the smell of grease and oil in his nostrils just like I had at his age helping Stumpy on the farm and it grew on him.

Luke often came to work with his dad on a Saturday morning, and it was then he saw firsthand the ins and outs of the mechanical side of his dad's business. I was still working with Rowy at this point, and as I worked on machinery in the workshop, Luke would often be present, observing and learning.

In fact, it was the last thing on my mind to start my own mechanical business, but it just sort of evolved out of a very small incident. It all happened on a Saturday morning just before Easter of 1990. I was repairing a hydraulic hose on an excavator just before smoko when a bloke came strolling into the workshop. I grabbed a rag to wipe my hands and went over to greet him.

"What's the problem, mate? How can I help you?" I said to him.

"My Kenworth's just shit itself big time."

"Why, what's happened?"

"I think I've just blown the turbo on it."

"I thought I could smell smoke," I said, wryly

"You're not wrong. The streets covered in the stuff," he said.

I nodded. "Okay, I'll be with you in a tick, mate, just as soon as I fit this hydraulic hose."

When I eventually went out onto Waratah Street to inspect what had happened, I soon noticed the turbo was indeed blown.

"What do you want to do?" I said.

He looked worried. "I'm from Brisbane and I don't know anyone down here to repair it. I got to get back up to Brisbane by Tuesday night to pick up a load to go to Bundaberg. Can you recommend anybody who does truck repairs?"

"We're an earthmoving business here, mate, we don't do general repairs, but if you want I can have a look at it for you after I finish here at lunchtime," I told him.

He looked relieved. "That would be great, mate. I'd really appreciate that."

After inspecting his rig, I ordered a new turbo for him on Monday and after fitting it had him up and running by lunchtime the same day. He was thrilled by the whole deal, and I felt happy that I could get the bloke on his way.

The seed was sown for my business venture when I was speaking to Frank on the phone that night. I quite innocently mentioned the story to him when we were chatting about our day.

"You ever thought about going out on your own, Ed?"

"What, starting a mechanical business?"

"Yeah. A man of your experience would go alright, I should think," said Frank.

I was taken aback. "Gee, Frank, that's a pretty big move. I mean there's a lot to starting a business you know!"

"You've been there before. The difference this time around is that you're a sober man," he said.

I was silent for a while, to the point where he said, "Hello? Ed? You still there."

"Sorry, Frank. Yeah, you know what? I'd love to have a crack at my own business again. I always liked being at the helm and steering the ship." I was suddenly full of vim.

"I think you'd do alright, Ed!"

Frank knew more about me than I did of myself, for he could see that I had both the ability and drive to get a business started. And the thought stayed with me for the rest of the week and grew until I convinced myself that I could definitely make a fist of starting my own business. I had not mentioned it to Karen as I wasn't sure what her reaction would be, but on the Saturday night we were having dinner at a Thai restaurant at Cronulla when I brought the subject up.

"You sure, darl? I mean you've got a secure job with Bob," she said with a look of concern.

I squeezed her hand. "I know, Kaz, but after talking to Frank I am convinced it's the right thing to do."

Karen and I continued to talk over dinner about the pros and cons of going out on my own. "It's your choice, Ed. I can't tell you what to do, but I just don't want to see you getting stressed out running a business after all you've been through. I don't want you to jeopardise your health for this."

I took her comments onboard, but what Karen didn't realise was that I had always been a risk-taker and would never be fully satisfied if I didn't follow my gut instincts and act on them.

I was reluctant to tell Rowy about my plans, but surprisingly I found him to very supportive.

"Bloody oath, Cozzy. I reckon its great idea. I'll be sad to lose ya, but you and I both know that you'll never get ahead working for somebody else. You can even have that old shed up the back to work out of if you want!" He clapped me on the shoulder.

"Yeah?"

"Bloody oath, Cozzy," he said. "There's a heap of shit in it at the moment, but once we clear all the old tyres and crap out of there, she'll be like brand new."

"You're a champion, Rowy!"

He gave me a rueful smile. "Hey, Cozzy, I still remember when we got home from Vietnam and you leant me that money so I could buy that old backhoe. Crikey, you introduced me to Josek. Mate, my business started with that old clapped out machine and that old Polish Jew and I got you to thank for that. Besides you dragged me out of the jungle in Vietnam, when I was left for dead and it's the least I can do for you."

From little things, big things grow.

I looked at Rowy long and hard and felt a great feeling of comradeship for my lifelong mate. I shook his hand and felt overwhelmed by everything he had done for me. That tall lanky bloke from Kapooka, my mate on the M60, was still there covering my back.

Over the next week we cleaned up the old shed and by the following Monday I commenced my fledgling business. Rowy was flexible enough to allow me to keep working until I got myself up and running, and I had been able to buy myself the necessary equipment to run the business with what Stumpy had left me and with what I had saved.

I had not a clue where my business was going to come from, but like Frank had so often said to me, "Just stay positive, Ed, and everything will work out."

Work was slow to start with, but I was lucky to have made quite a few contacts within the construction industry since I had started working for Rowy, and little by little, they started to come to me once they found out I was up and running.

Somehow, I kept my head above water during 1990 and as my reputation grew so did the business. By Christmas time I had just about severed all working ties with Rowy as I had enough work to keep me going full-time.

Karen was supportive and we were able to relax over the Christmas period which we spent with the family at Coorigil and by the new year of 1991 I was ready to build the business up.

To this day, I still don't know where 1991 went. It just flew. I was so busy in establishing the business, coupled with managing my recovery so I didn't overdo it that it just disappeared.

I had been sober for seven years and much had changed in my life. I was living in a beautiful home, married to my soul mate, started a business and re-established old friendships.

Karen and I had a very active life but I was conscious of taking things easy because I knew that stress had a bad effect on me. Frank would often tell me not to get to hungry, angry, lonely or tired, or the 'HALTs' as he used to call them, because he knew they were a trigger for alcoholic behaviour. On top of this, he constantly reminded me to keep my AA meetings up.

By the end of 1991 the business was moving along steadily, although I had to keep my hand firmly on the tiller for it was still earlier days. Then, quite unexpectedly, my business took a different direction when I ended up with a heavy duty tow truck which I did not want.

***

"Geez, you've been through the wringer," said Tim. "After everything you and Karen went through, you couldn't have kids."

I shrugged. "Easily one of the biggest disappointments in my life, Karen's too. But what could we do? Life had to go on. We still had each other, and we had the kids dropping by *Shiloh* like it was a halfway house. We made do with the family we had."

He digested what I said, and I leant back in my seat and

gave him a wry smile. Tim's mood was dipping again. "You'll have to mind my changing the subject, but I'll say it again, Tim. You could become a professional photographer!"

"Ya joking?"

I shook my head. "No, I'm serious. There's only one thing that is stopping you."

"What's that?"

"Fear."

He looked slighted. "Never!"

"Oh, don't worry, we all have it." I waved off his indignation. "Fear's everywhere. Fear of failure, fear of the future, fear of going broke, to name just a few. But that's not the real fear."

"It isn't?"

"Nope." I shuffled in my seat and made sure I had his attention. "The biggest fear is that we may actually succeed."

Tim frowned. "What?"

"I'm fairdinkum, Tim. Fear that you may succeed is the real fear."

"How do you figure that?"

"You've been dwelling in negativity for so long that you don't believe you're worthy of success."

Tim leant back in his seat with a look of astonishment. His expression turned thoughtful.

"It's true, Tim. You haven't believed in yourself for a very long time and if you're going to succeed in life, then belief has to be paramount in your mind at the beginning of your venture."

Tim looked at me dumbfounded. "You reckon? You really think that if I believe I'm worthy of doing well, then it'll happen?"

"Absolutely, Tim! You have to stay positive and trust your gut instincts. It's always worked for me."

Tim's eyes were suddenly lit with a fire that hadn't been there all day. He almost looked shy. "You know, I think I'd love to be a full time photographer, but I'm shit scared that the whole thing would just go belly up."

I winked at him. "See? Fear of success. If photography's what you want to do then go for it. After you repay your debt to me, of course," I added with a cheeky smile. "If you stay positive everything will work out. Sure, there will be tricky situations, that's life, but remember that positivity leads to positivity and negativity leads to negativity."

Tim gave me a wry smile.

"It's either that or go and join the rat race for the rest of your life living a mundane existence, because fear has got you by the balls. Have a look around you." I said, waving my hand. "There's people everywhere caught up in a rut, too shit scared to do what their heart's been telling them to do all their life. That's why they're living unfulfilled lives. I followed my heart, trusted my gut feelings and started a business. Yes, it was scary in the beginning, and it can still be scary some days, but in the long run it has brought me success. The most important thing is that I'm doing what I really want to do and isn't that what life's about?"

Tim nodded and his eyes were bright with promise. I gave him a warm smile. I could sense there was a real bond forming between us now. He trusted me, believed I could help him. All I would do is help him to help himself.

"Let me tell you what happened when I bought the tow truck."

Chapter 16

Mid-February, 1992, Kirrawee, Sydney

IT ALL HAPPENED one Thursday afternoon in mid-February. I was getting ready to close up for the day when a skinny man in his mid-sixties with grey hair strolled into the workshop. My first impression of Neville Taylor was that he was an old bushy who was the salt of the earth. Neville spoke with a laconic drawl and I was automatically drawn to him. He reminded me of so many of the characters I had grown up with back in Eumungerie and on first meeting him I was overcome with a great feeling of comradeship.

"Are you Ed Costigan?" he said, drawing back on his cigarette.

"I am."

"I hear on the grapevine that you're the Mack truck expert?"

"I know a thing or two about them," I said in an unassuming way.

"Good, because I've got a rig on the back of this low loader outside that needs some work done to it."

I was wiping my hands with a rag when I followed him out

onto Waratah Street where he had a Mack Valueliner parked. He was towing a drop deck low loader and on that he was carrying a heavy duty tow truck.

"See, this here's a 1984 Mack Superliner tow truck. It's been in a bit of a dingle and needs some work done on it. Do ya think you can get it running again?"

My jaw dropped.

"It's been in a bit more of a fuckin' dingle, Neville! The whole front end is caved in!" I said.

He shrugged. "It's got a scratch or two on it that's for sure, but nothing a man of your ability can't fix," he said.

I shook my head. "A 'scratch'. That's a bloody understatement. What size motor is it, Neville?"

"It's got a 400 hp V8 under the bonnet with a Mack 12 speed gearbox and a tri-axle at the rear."

I stood there for some time with my hand on my chin, contemplating the huge task of what was required to get the rig up and running again.

I turned to him to deliver the news. "It's going to take some serious coin, not to mention a lot of effort to get this rig on the road, mate!"

He grinned. "Don't you worry about the money, Ed. I'll fix you up for that fair and square. I just want to know if you can fix the truck?"

I stood there for some time looking at the rig before I turned to Neville and said, "It'll take some work, but yeah, I'm prepared to have a crack at it."

Over the next few weeks I worked on the rig and Neville was true to his word, paying me in cash installments. It was only after I had been working on the truck for a month and asked for another installment that the money dried up and I never saw another dollar.

What started was a protracted argument with Neville as I tried to get the money out of him to complete the project. Neville told me he didn't have any money left as he had been left with some bad debts in his trucking business. As a result, I took possession of the truck, even though it was the last thing I wanted.

I was left scratching my head and after discussing the problem with Rowy, he convinced me to get the truck up and running and incorporate the tow truck into my mechanical business.

I decided to give it a go, but there was one stumbling block and that was Karen.

Karen had wanted a new kitchen at *Shiloh* and I had promised her one as I still had money left over from Stumpy's inheritance. The problem now was that I was going to have to pour the funds I was going to spend on the kitchen into fixing the tow truck up. I knew Karen wasn't going to be happy about that.

"This is going to bloody tricky," I said to Rowy after discussing with him my plans for the tow truck.

"Good luck, Cozzy," he sniggered. "I'd like to be a fly on the wall when you have that conversation with Kaz."

I hadn't even told Karen about the tow truck, and when I eventually spilled the beans her reception was frosty to say the least.

"And how much is it going to cost to fix, Ed?" Karen said, staring at me with her arms folded.

I shifted my feet and after staring at the ground exclaimed, "Well, it's going to take quite a few thousand dollars, Kaz."

She narrowed her eyes. "And what about my new kitchen?" Her tone was dangerous.

I paused, then swallowed before saying, "The kitchen's on hold for the time being, Kaz."

She exploded in a flurry of arms and sound. "What? But you promised me I could have a new kitchen!"

"I know I did, sweetie," I said, trying to placate her, "and you'll get your new kitchen, but this truck is a great opportunity to expand my business once it's repaired."

You could have cut the atmosphere with a knife it was thick.

It took me a couple of months to complete the rebuild on the truck, but with a fresh paint job, it ended up being one of the smartest looking rigs on the road.

***

"I would have loved to have seen the conversation between you two at the dinner table that night!" Tim said.

"It was a bit frosty, I must admit," I said, with a shake of the head.

"And you'd promised her a new kitchen. Bloody hell, women get really touchy about things like that," he sniggered.

"I had every intention of getting Karen a new kitchen, but not just then. I had to get the tow truck up and going. It meant greater returns in the long run and to my mind, more money for an even better kitchen than we'd planned."

"Still, I bet you were in the dog house for a month?"

I gave Tim a serious look. "Not only was Karen unhappy about not getting a new kitchen, but that night she brought something else to the fore that I had never fully understood. It had never even crossed my mind."

"What was that?' Tim said. His expression was curious.

I sat back. "She thought that getting behind the wheel of a big rig again was like jumping from the frypan into the fire, because of what had happened with the truck accident."

"Oh, I see," said Tim. "But she knew you hadn't had a drink for a long time."

"Too right. I kept telling her that over dinner, but she just couldn't seem to shake the idea out of her head."

"Well, what did Karen think of the truck when it was finished?"

"She was still dirty about all the money I had pumped into the truck, but she was suitably impressed. It looked like a ripper." If I had a photo of the truck, I would have ripped it out. Showing Tim an actual marker of success was one of the best ways to inspire people, and he was just so engaged in the story right now.

"So, she was happy?" Tim asked.

"Yeah, but not so much because of the tow truck." I gave a laugh and shook my head.

"What then?" asked Tim, his eyebrow raised.

"I had enough money left over for a new kitchen!"

Tim grinned. "You were in the good books again."

I nodded. "Yeah, but both the rig and the kitchen left me pretty tight for cash. I had to find work for the tow truck which wasn't easy because it's a bloody hard industry to crack. Fortunately for me, I stayed positive and a door opened at the right time."

***

I spent the first two months after I repaired the tow truck scrounging around for work for it, but to no avail. My mechanical business was the only thing that kept the money rolling in because the tow truck wasn't returning anything. I would walk into the workshop and be filled with a feeling of angst at seeing the Superliner sitting idle.

It was the big operators who had the market sown up, especially with the major insurance companies.

I had been knocking on their doors since repairing the tow truck, but couldn't get a look in. I was convinced that if only I could get my foot in the door, things would take a positive turn. That thing needed to be earning its keep.

It was a cold wet, wintry night in August of 1992 when I received an urgent phone call well after midnight from a bloke who worked for an insurance company. It was the opportunity I so desperately needed. His name was Sam Roberts and he needed a heavy duty tow truck urgently to salvage a Kenworth that had been written off up near Mount Tomah on the Bells Line Road. He briefly explained that all his regular contractors were busy as it was a wet night and there were a number of accidents around the metropolitan area.

When I got off the phone and went back to bed, Karen stirred in her sleep and wrapped her arms around my body.

"Who's ringing you at this ungodly hour?" she murmured.

"A bloke from an insurance company. There's been a truck accident and he needs a tow truck," I told her.

Karen rested her head on my chest while her arms were around my waist and it felt good. So good that I didn't want to get out of bed.

"I wish you didn't have to go out into that terrible weather, Ed. It's so lovely being snuggled up next to you."

I kissed Karen on her head. She was right. I snuggled up close to her and it felt good. So good in fact that the last thing

I wanted to do was venture out into the bitterly cold winter's night.

I lay there for another five minutes in a comfortable state and was about to go back to sleep when it felt as though somebody invisible had kicked me. I lifted my head off the pillow at a frightful pace and with an air of urgency in my voice said, "Love to snuggle up a bit longer, Kaz, but there is work to be done."

Karen was startled by sudden change in temperament. "So, you are going to retrieve that truck?"

"You're absolutely right, Kaz. This is the opportunity I've been waiting for," I said, as I started to don my work clothes.

"Well if that's the case, I better make you a cup of tea and some toast before you go."

"You're alright, sweetie, stay where you are. I'm going to hit the road."

I'm convinced that if I stayed in bed that night and not taken my opportunity when it arose then my tow truck business would have folded very soon after.

That one phone call was to be the beginning of a fruitful relationship with Sam. In particular, it was the catalyst for me in gaining regular work recovering heavy vehicles in both the metropolitan area and in the country.

I instinctively knew that things would get better after taking that job and they did. It set in motion a whole new direction for my business that was to have very positive outcome in the future.

Time rolled on and rather than being the bland future I had initially envisaged my sobriety to be, it became an interesting life.

There were opportunities the like I could never of imagined in my drinking days, which added an air of excitement to my life.

In saying all that, life was far from peaches and cream, because life is life no matter who you are, and because of my sobriety I had more responsibilities on my plate. They were responsibilities I could handle because I had been given a positive way to live my life.

Karen and I had a good relationship, and as much as we had our disagreements, we rarely argued. The one thing she never really warmed to was me operating the tow truck.

Karen wasn't keen on me driving trucks because of my past. No matter how many times I tried to convince her that those days were behind me, she still thought that some impending disaster was looming while I was behind the wheel of a truck.

On top of that, talking to Karen about things of a mechanical nature was like talking to her in Swahili. Karen's eyes would glaze over even if I started talking about maintenance on her Toyota Celica. She thought it was something akin to a miracle that a car's wheels turned around. What made the car run was a total mystery to her.

It took a totally unexpected set of circumstances for all that to change.

She had decided to take a few days off to visit relatives in Griffith. From there she was travelling on to Wilcannia where her good friend Mary Anne Gibson lived on a big property with her husband and three kids.

The two of them had been best of friends since their school days in Sydney. Mary Anne suggested that Karen visit the property on numerous occasions over the years and she had finally taken her upon that offer.

I wasn't keen on her travelling all the way out there by herself, as I knew she had next to no experience in remote driving. Being the independent person she is though, she was determined to go on the trip because it had been so long since she had seen Mary Anne.

After spending the weekend at Griffith with her relatives, she left mid-morning on the Monday bound for Wilcannia. Karen had travelled north to Hillston and was travelling west on an unsealed section of road towards the Cobb Highway when she took a wrong turn, got lost and disaster struck.

Karen broke the cardinal rule of travelling in the country. She drove through a flooded causeway. Lucky for her the Celica managed to splutter its way out of the water and stopped on the steep section of gravel road on the other side of the causeway.

Karen had no mobile phone back in those days and it was close on dusk before an elderly farmer coming home from a cattle sale spotted her stranded on the side of the road. Karen was distraught and after making sure she was alright, he attached a chain to her car and towed her back to his property which was situated about five kilometres down the road, arriving in the dark.

It was approximately 6.30 pm when I received a phone a call from Karen. She tearfully explained what had happened. Karen was guilt-ridden about what she had done to the car and how I might react. I assured her that I could fix the car and it was her that I was concerned about. I promised that I would hit the road at first light and come and get her.

It had just so happened that the day before on the Sunday, Anne had presented me with a six-week-old chocolate brown kelpie pup. She had recently been home to Coorigil and Noel had given her a pup to give to me from one of his bitches who had just had a litter. I had intended for him to be a surprise for Karen. I knew she would love him.

It was before sunrise on the Tuesday morning when I hit the road in the tow truck, taking the pup with me as I knew it would cheer Karen up.

As I travelled along, I was contemplating what to call him when suddenly I remembered a lieutenant I had met on R and R in Vung Tau during my stint in Vietnam. He had a little chocolate brown kelpie pup with him, although how he had come to have a dog, I do not know, but the kelpie was a real little cutie and I had grown fond of him in our short stay together.

This bloke was as mad as a cut snake loved a drink and was a Forward Observation Officer, or FOO, as they were called, and I ended up getting on the piss with him for the whole day and night.

Suddenly, as I was driving along, I exclaimed loudly, "Foo! That's what I'll call you!"

The pup lifted his head and wagged his tail.

I eventually arrived on the farm late that Tuesday afternoon and spotted Karen's car with the bonnet up, just outside a big machinery shed.

Karen greeted me like she had not seen me in years. After inspecting the car I could see that it had water in the motor and I would need to get it back to the workshop to fix it.

The elderly couple who owned the property had been very kind to Karen and it was dark when we said our goodbyes and hit the road, but not before handing Karen my little surprise package. She melted in adoration. "Oh, Ed. He's beautiful."

"I've named him Foo."

"Foo! Where did you get that name from?"

I explained the origin of the name to Karen and where Foo

had come from. She held him tight and nursed him on her lap as I made the long haul back to Sydney.

As we drove along, Karen apologised for getting into so much strife and with it she saw my business in a totally new light. She had never been in the cabin of a big rig before and was enthralled with the ride. As a result, she came to realise how much work I had put in to getting the tow truck part of the business up and running. From that day on she became totally supportive of my tow truck operation and never again did she doubt my enterprise.

***

"That incident with Karen's car had a ripple effect," I said.

"What do ya mean?" asked Tim.

"Well, being broken down in remote Australia was a bit of a wake-up call for Karen. From somebody who didn't give a stuff about maintenance on her car she actually became interested in looking after the Celica. She started to checking the oil, water and tyres, and funnily enough, she got a bit interested in cars after that. She was open to talking about mechanics and it really opened up our relationship." I tapped my fingers on the table. "It was just a little thing, but it worked wonders."

"What about her car?"

"It took a bit of work to get it up and running again, but the Celica lived to see another day," I grinned.

"And you got plenty of work for the tow truck?"

"Sure did. In fact, things went from strength to strength with both sides of my business. I got so busy that I put my old mate Jimmy 'Thumper' Fraser on as a mechanic. Remember? One of Reg Steel's men?"

Tim nodded. "Yeah. He got you into boxing. Still, I can't

believe all that it took was for Karen to breakdown to understand your business."

I smiled. "It's the tough times that make a relationship grow, Tim. Frank Casey often says to me that a relationship is about compromise. It's not all lovey-dovey all the time, he says. You begin to appreciate your partner a lot more when you can accept their defects of character."

"So you and Karen were all hunky dory after that," assumed Tim.

"Well, not quite!" I rolled my eyes. "Nothing is ever perfect."

"Why, what happened?"

"Well, there was the question of Foo."

"The dog?" Tim was baffled. "What's the dog got to do with it? I thought she like him."

I held up a finger to clarify. "She loved him. No, it was about where he slept."

***

When we arrived home from our rescue mission, Karen was overjoyed and well in love with our new arrival. She rang Fiona soon after we arrived home and asked her to come over as she had a little surprise for her.

True to form, Fiona was over in a flash and Karen and I were sitting around the outdoor setting having an afternoon cup of tea when we could hear her voice from a distance.

"Uncle Ed and Aunty Karen! Where's my surprise?"

Fiona walked around the corner of the house, her eyes darting left, right and centre, looking for her surprise.

"So? Where's my surprise, Aunty Karen?" she said, almost jumping out of her skin.

"You sit right down here close your eyes and I'll bring it

out to you," said Karen. She jumped up and grabbed Foo. She walked over to Fiona and luckily, Foo remained quiet.

"Now, put your hands out."

The little girl obediently put her arms out.

Karen placed Foo gently into Fiona's arms. "Now open your eyes."

Fiona opened her eyes and looked down at Foo and squealed. "Oh my goodness, a puppy dog! He's so gorgeous!" Fiona shrieked.

I grinned at her.

"He's a little kelpie," said Karen.

"What's his name?" Fiona said, almost jumping out of her skin.

"His name is Foo," said Karen with a generous smile.

"Oh, Foo, I love you to death." Fiona hugged Foo and in return he licked her on the face which sent her into waves of giggles. I smiled at her.

"Foo came off our family farm, Fiona," I said. "He's a country dog and loves being outside."

"Does he round up sheep?" Fiona said.

"I dare say he would be good at sheep work, knowing what his mother and father are like."

"Where is he going to live, Uncle Ed?"

"We're still deciding on that Fiona," said Karen with a coy smile.

I gave her a stern glare. "Yes, and we don't want the dog sleeping in the bedroom with us, do we Karen?"

"Old spoil sport over here reckons that dogs belong outside and he's being a stick in the mud over it," Karen whispered to Fiona.

"Oh, Uncle Ed, don't you want to snuggle up to Foo in bed each night?" said Fiona.

"No, I don't. I was brought up on a farm and we never dreamed of having our working dogs in the house," I told her adamantly.

She frowned. "Where did they live, Uncle Ed?" Fiona said with an inquisitive look.

"In the paddock next to the homestead, usually in a hollow log or a kennel."

"How cruel!" said Fiona. She looked shocked.

I waved her off. "Cruel be buggered, they are working dogs, not pets."

"Well this dog is a pet, Ed," said Karen. She looked at Fiona and gave her a wink. "You won't change Mr Stubborn on this one, Fiona."

As per usual, Karen's persuasive manner got the better of me, and although I refused to have Foo sleeping on the end of the bed, he was allowed to stay in the house. Initially he still stayed out at night, but I lost that battle too. He was allowed in, but only after we finished dinner each night.

Over the next two years the business grew steadily, so much so that by April of 1996 I secured a loan and bought myself another Mack Superliner, this one with a low loader trailer. This truck was a 1991 model with a 500 hp motor and a 12-speed Mack gearbox in it.

I had also put another mechanic on. Mark was in his late twenties and the added advantage of having him around was that he also had a semi-trailer licence with quite a few interstate hours up. With the tow truck and low loader getting constant work along with the mechanical workshop, Thumper, Mark and I were kept busy.

But as much as I enjoyed every moment of working my business, I realised I was pretty tired and needed a good holiday. Karen and I regularly got away for short trips but she knew I was in need of an overseas trip.

We had the money and I came home from work one night in May to find that Karen had a stack of brochures in her hands on Italy and Ireland.

The trip would be a life changing experience for me. By going to Europe I was entering a world which was so different to the one I knew.

After flying to Rome we made our way to Karen's ancestral home in San Ferdinando in Calabria, southern Italy, where her mother's ancestors had come from. Karen could trace her roots in this region back some 300 years, and she had many relatives still living in the area.

We stayed with one of Karen's cousins, Adalina, and her husband Ciro and their two children, 16-year-old Renata and 14-year-old Carlo. Adalina and Ciro had refurbished an old two-bedroom townhouse into a stylish modern residence about ten minutes from the beach.

At first I was somewhat taken back because of the language barrier, but I soon warmed to the environment as I had always loved history. Besides, Karen could speak fluent Italian and that certainly eased the language barrier for me.

Karen and I spent two weeks with Adalina and Ciro before we moved on and explored other parts of Italy including Naples, Venice, Tuscany and Rome. After a month in Italy, we travelled to Ireland to Callan in County Kilkenny to the birthplace of my great grandfather Paddy Costigan. Karen and I met some

Costigan relatives who treated us like royalty. They still farmed the same land that Paddy was brought up on.

We then travelled to Elphin in County Roscommon where Karen's paternal great-grandfather had come from, and we were also able to also make contact with her Irish Monaghan relatives.

After our trip to Ireland, we went to France and the western battlefields where Stumpy had fought, including Poziers, where he won his Victoria Cross. After that we travelled to Turkey where we stayed in Istanbul. I was not prepared for the incredible experience this city was to give me. I was to learn it is the crossroads of two major religions, namely Christianity and Islam, and the bridge between Europe and Asia. It was the museum of the Hagia Sophia which most captured my imagination. I learnt it was formerly a mosque and before that, the Eastern Orthodox Basilica named St Sophia during the Byzantine Empire.

After spending three days in Istanbul we then travelled to Gallipoli. Once again, nothing could have prepared me for what I saw there. I had seen plenty of photos and read much about Gallipoli, but to see the landscape firsthand and retrace the places where Stumpy had been before he was in France was unbelievable.

We finished our trip back in Istanbul where we spent two more days before flying home to Sydney.

Our two month trip was a life-changing experience for the both of us. I believe the trip matured me and made me take stock of what was important to me. In retrospect, I think the trip prepared me for what was ahead because I came back a much calmer person, and less prone to resentment.

***

My mind filled with visions of Istanbul. I snapped out of it. "I saw life in a different light after that trip, Tim."

"How so?"

"Well, for starters, I never fully appreciated Karen's Italian heritage until I walked the streets where her ancestors had come from. Karen explained to me her culture and I came to view her differently. It was a deeper appreciation of her as a person." I smiled, remembering the days we spent with Adalina and Ciro.

"It must be an eye-opener to see Europe. I mean it's such an older culture," said Tim, thoughtfully. "I wouldn't mind travelling again."

"Istanbul was an incredible place to visit," I told him. "Not only was the Hagia Sophia special, but so was the Blue Mosque and Topkapi Palace where the sultans lived during the Ottoman Empire."

"What did Karen think of it?"

"She was in another world," I enthused. "I mean, Karen was right in her element. You know, Tim, I used to think that walking into a bottle shop was on the same par as visiting the Hagia Sophia. I used to love all the packaging to such an extent that it was like having a spiritual experience."

Tim gave me a slight grin. He understood that.

"But in all seriousness, I could never have imagined that Europe would have such a profound experience for a bloke like me. Karen saw the change in me and she noticed that I was a lot calmer when we came back."

Tim nodded, but his eyes had gone glassy. It was a faraway look I knew. "What are you thinking of?"

"I'd love to go to Europe. Imagine the photos."

"You probably could have got there on that $7,000 you blew on the pokies," I admonished, but then I softened. "Anything's possible if you stay off the juice. If you play a straight bat you can do all that one day."

He looked wistful. "You reckon?"

I smiled at him. "Absolutely. I hope you can see how my life went from strength to strength after I got off the juice. I continued to kick goals and as an added bonus, Karen and I started to travel a lot more. The next year we bought a four wheel drive and travelled up into the Northern Territory. Karen fell in love with Kakadu and the billabongs on the Mary River. You see, I realised that life wasn't all about work and you need balance. I still worked hard, I've never given short shrift in my life, but we got away on plenty of trips which we both loved. I love nature, and I know you do too. Can you imagine just taking off whenever you need to?"

"The Northern Territory. I was up there when I was in the army. I took some great photos of landscapes up around the East Alligator River in Kakadu," said Tim. "Some of them are in the book," Tim said, pointing at the album just next to me.

I opened the album and flipped through the leaves, but I continued to talk.

"Over the next four years, Karen and I saw some more of the country as we travelled the top end from Cape York to the Kimberly. In fact, it was on one of these trips that Rowy surprised me by asking me if I wanted to buy *Shiloh*."

***

It was July of 1999 and Rowy, Julie, Karen and I took a trip up to Cooktown in Far North Queensland. Rowy was towing a tinnie behind his Nissan Patrol which we planned to fish out of on the Endeavour River at Cooktown.

It was the morning after we arrived and Rowy and I we were

up the river near a sunken wreck fishing while the girls went shopping in town. We had collected our bait back at the wharf and had anchored the boat near the wreck when *whack*! My rod bent over like it was about to break and my spool started to wiz.

As I brought the fish to surface, I could see that it was a big barramundi.

"Get a load of this little beauty, Rowy! What a ripper!"

"Steady on, old son, while I get the net under it," said Rowy with a grin from ear to ear.

We spent the best part of half an hour fishing at this spot and caught a half a dozen fish consisting of barramundi, mangrove jack and fingermark. We then moved up the river and anchored. The morning was bright as there was not a cloud in the sky and it was very relaxing as the two of us fished side by side.

Rowy cleared his throat. "Julie and I are thinking of selling *Shiloh*."

My heart missed a beat. I wasn't even sure I heard him right as the thought of leaving my much-loved abode by the water was devastating to me.

"You got someone interested, Rowy?" I said with trepidation.

Rowy took sometime before he answered and with a grin on his face he said, "Julie and I thought that you and Kaz might want to have first digs at it."

I lit up. "Are you for real, Rowy?"

"Absolutely, Ed!"

Figures and calculations rebounded inside my brain as I tried to work out how we would pay for the dwelling.

"But why are you selling *Shiloh*, Rowy?"

"Jules and I want to cash up as we want to buy a cattle property on the road to Wombeyan Caves," said Rowy.

"What like a weekender?"

"Yeah, just a place to escape the big smoke, not too far from Sydney."

"Sounds good."

"Well, Cozzy, you and I are both off the land and I've always wanted a few acres of my own where I can graze a few cattle. You know how it is. Sydney's all hustle and bustle but I miss the space of the bush," he said.

"How many acres you looking at?" I asked.

"500."

Rowy and I kept fishing for a few minutes when I asked the big question, the one that was giving me anxiety. "So how much do you want for *Shiloh*?"

"Thought you'd never ask, Cozzy."

"I'm fearing the worst, mate, because I can only imagine it's out of our league." My heart was thundering, hoping it would be affordable.

"It's a bit hard to put a value on *Shiloh* because there is nothing similar to the dwelling in the area. We had our home valued at $1,400,000 recently, so we figured we would ask $500,000 for *Shiloh*."

"Phew, that's some serious coin, Mr Rowe!"

"It is, but as they say 'location, location' and the view alone adds a lot to the value."

I thought about it carefully. "Karen just loves *Shiloh*. She has put so much work into the home I just know she would love to own the place "

Rowy smiled. "Julie and I know that you both love *Shiloh*, Ed, and we have had it in the back of our minds for some time. We wanted to let the two of you have a crack at it."

Rowy and I spent the next couple of hours fishing the river, as we chewed over the practicalities of how Karen and I could pay for *Shiloh*.

When we arrived back at the caravan park, I took Karen for a drive out to the Annan River just five minutes south of Cooktown. We were only a couple of minutes into the trip when Karen leant over from the passenger seat and said, "Guess what, Ed? Bob and Julie want to sell *Shiloh*!"

I looked at her and broke into laughter. "That Rowy, the cunning bugger, he's dropped the bombshell on me while we were fishing and Jules has done the same to you while you were out shopping!"

Karen was ecstatic of the prospect of owning *Shiloh* and set a plan in motion to purchase the dwelling. "I can sell my two bedroom unit in Miranda."

"What do you reckon it's worth?"

"I had it valued for $240,000 earlier this year."

I nodded. "We can do it. We'll borrow the rest. *Shiloh* will be ours."

***

"It was early December 1999 when we settled the property," I said to Tim. "Although Karen and I had been living in *Shiloh* for ten years, that first night after settlement was pure magic. It's one thing to rent a place, but to own it is something else."

"You mean the bank owned it," Tim said, with a hint of sarcasm.

I waved him off. "Yeah, yeah, the bank owned it, but it was our names on the title deeds," I said, ignoring his cynical tone. "Karen and I lay in bed that night like two excited children. I had to keep pinching myself to make sure I wasn't dreaming.

Karen was buzzing with ideas as to how she could make even more improvements to *Shiloh*."

He shook his head. "The way you've been talking this *Shiloh* up you'd swear it was the best thing since sliced bread!"

I looked at Tim and sensed a touch of jealousy in his tone. I smiled. "*Shiloh* is a little touch of paradise. From where I had come from it served as the perfect antidote for all that I had been through. It wasn't just a house, it was a home. A proper home."

But as much as it was paradise, its inhabitants were only human. We were coming up to that part of the story where it got hard. I felt my heart get heavy, and Tim noticed.

"What's wrong?" he asked.

"What?" I said, startled by his comment.

"You look like you're a million miles away."

I gave him a rueful smile. "Things were that good and I had made up so much ground I had lost through my alcoholism that I couldn't believe what had happened to me. Next to getting off the drink, meeting Karen Monaghan was the best thing that had ever happened to me. Life was good. I wanted for nothing, mate, *nothing*."

Tim didn't say anything, but he looked wistful. Like he wanted that too.

"Then something strange happened the year after we had settled on *Shiloh*. I can see now that it was an omen of what was to come."

I looked at Tim long and hard and once again, I felt like pulling the envelope out of my back pocket and reading it to him, but I resisted the urge. He was receptive, but we weren't quite there yet.

"Karen met a lady in at St Vincent's where she worked."

"What lady?" Tim said with a look of interest. "You mean like a patient?"

I nodded. "Karen nursed this lady for a long time, and they built up a very strong bond."

***

By early 2000, Karen had grown very fond of an elderly lady by the name of Nancy who she was nursing at St Vincent's Hospital. Nancy was in her mid-eighties and was recovering from breast cancer. Her earthy charm attracted Karen almost immediately.

Karen was a thorough professional at her job and was careful not to get emotionally involved with her patients. Nancy was different though and they had struck up a very close bond. Karen mentioned Nancy to me on a number of occasions and I found out that she was originally off a big station out at Wilcannia, but was now living in Parkes, in central New South Wales. Karen told me that she would often sit and talk to Nancy. Her simple wisdom on how to handle her condition was a source of great enlightenment for Karen.

Karen showed me a photo of the two of them sitting on Nancy's bed with Karen's arm around her shoulder. If a picture paints a thousand words then this photograph accurately summed up their relationship. Their smiles indicated there was much love and warmth between the two of them.

Nothing in Karen's conversation ever alerted me to the fact that there was a connection between Nancy and I, yet there was. Karen never told me, she was prudent in that respect, and it was something I was yet to discover. But regardless of that yet hidden connection, Nancy meant a lot to Karen, and so in April 2000, when I was sound asleep in bed, Karen came home late one night from work. After a while I awoke from slumber

HEAVY LOAD | 511

and after rolling across, I noticed that she was lying on her back staring at the ceiling. I was worried.

"Are you alright, sweetie?"

She turned towards me and I noticed there were tears in her eyes. "We lost Nancy this afternoon, Ed."

"Ah, Kaz, I'm sorry to hear that. Are you alright?"

"Oh, Ed, I'm so sad. She was such a beautiful lady and I loved her company," said Karen in tears.

That night she snuggled up a little bit closer to me and I held her tight. I could see that Nancy's death had affected her greatly, and even though I'd never met the lady, I'd heard much about her.

"I just want you know, Ed, that if anything ever happens to me I love you very much," she whispered.

"Karen, nothing is going to happen to you," I said with concern. I'd never heard her talk like that before. Her words had sent a shiver up my spine, even though they were relatively innocuous.

She was my rock and it was inconceivable that anything would happen to her. Her steady influence was so important in all areas of my life. She had the ability to talk me through the tough times, and was especially good at helping me deal with the fact that it had now been 18 years since I had last seen Michelle. I thought of my daughter constantly, and I often wondered what she looked like, who her friends were and what she was doing for a living.

My sister Anne kept me abreast on what was happening with Michelle. They kept in close contact after the divorce, which made me envious in some ways. Karen was a great source of strength and helped me to accept the situation and I hoped that in time, things would change. I stayed true to Frank's advice to wait, and she waited with me.

Karen slowed me down and made me rest when I needed a break. Once, she made me stay in bed for two days and rest as she knew I was burnt out. I had always been a driven man but she helped put balance into my life. Karen had coloured my life in like no other human being could have.

***

Tim suddenly looked wary.

"What is it?" I asked him.

"You're talking like something terrible is going to happen."

I gave him a sad look, thinking about my encounter with Foo this morning. "It's just life, Tim. Just life."

Chapter 17

December 2000, Shiloh, Yowie Bay

IN WAS EARLY December after Karen and I had thrown a party at *Shiloh* that everything changed. We had made the theme a 'back to the sixties' party and it was a fun night shared with many of our friends and relatives. It was 3.00 am when the final revellers departed *Shiloh*. Karen had been her normal jovial self at the party and although she had gone to bed at midnight because she was tired from work and some hard games of squash, I didn't think it unusual.

The next morning, true to form, I was up at sunrise, even though I had only had a few hours sleep. I took *The Rocket* up to the top so I could gather the Sunday paper. While I was up there I noticed that Rowy was up and about, so I decided to have a coffee with him on their front verandah. After a while, Julie and the kids surfaced, albeit a bit seedy, and they cooked up some hot breakfast which we all ate together outside.

After a couple of hours of good talk, I made my way back down to *Shiloh* and noticed that Karen was still asleep. After giving her a kiss on the forehead, I decided to take *Bella Donna* up towards Northwest Arm and try to catch some flathead while drifting with white bait.

It wasn't long before I had hooked up to a nice size flathead and over the next couple of hours I caught six. I knew Karen would be happy as she loved flathead. I would cook them on the BBQ for dinner that night. After a couple of hours fishing, I decided to moor the boat in the Royal National Park and went to sleep under the shade of a melaleuca tree.

It was after lunch when I finally arrived home and after securing the boat to the pontoon I made my way inside.

I walked down the hallway towards the laundry so I could wash my hands and noticed that our bedroom door was partially open. Karen was sitting on the bed.

"Hi, sweetie, how are you?" I called out as I walked past the bedroom.

Karen didn't respond and I thought nothing of it, as she had a habit of saying nothing when she was painting her nails.

As I walked back up the hallway, I stopped at the bedroom and sheepishly stuck my head through the door. Karen was sitting on the bed with her back to me still wearing her floral dressing gown even though it was now the afternoon. From where I was positioned, I could see that she had her hand on one of her breasts.

"Everything okay, Kaz?" I said anxiously.

Eventually she turned around, and I could see her exposed right breast. I looked at it intently, noticing that it was inflamed and red. I looked up at her in shock. Karen said nothing but gave me an intense stare.

After what seemed like an eternity, I eventually blurted out, "What is it?"

Karen looked at me and said, "I don't know, Ed, but it doesn't look good."

"When did you notice it?"

"Only this morning when I got out of the shower."

"It looks like it may be infected with all that swelling," I said, trying to play it down.

"Let's hope that's all it is, Ed."

I could hear the concern in her voice so I walked over to the bed and sat down beside her and placed my hand on top of hers.

"It's going to be okay, Kaz, we'll get this sorted out."

"Oh, Ed, I'm so scared," she said, and threw her arms around me. She began to cry.

I held her tight and reassured her that everything would be alright, even I was filling up with anxiety. Karen had mentioned that she had been feeling a bit tired lately, but we thought it been because of a couple of hard games of squash. Neither of us mentioned what we thought the problem was. Neither of mentioned that we both feared the worst.

The next day Karen made an appointment to see her GP in Caringbah. Fortunately for Karen, she was able to get an appointment for the following morning, and I took the morning off work and attended the surgery with her. Dr Helen Ascot was a woman in her late forties and although very formal, was a pleasant woman to speak to.

After some preliminary questions, Dr Ascot examined both breasts and noticed it was only the right one that was enlarged. She put Karen on a course of antibiotics as she thought it was only an infection. We were both relieved and left the GP with lighter hearts.

Karen started on the course of drugs, but after a week, the swelling had not reduced. She returned to see Dr Ascot the following week and after her second examination of Karen's breasts, she recommended an immediate biopsy, as she thought that Karen might have a tumor. She booked her in to see a Danish oncologist named Dr Joen Lorenzen whose practice was at Miranda.

Dr Lorenzen was in his early forties. He had blonde hair with a very athletic build and was extremely likable character. He insisted that we call him Joen and made us feel very comfortable in his presence. Dr Lorenzen took a biopsy of Karen's breast tissue as well as a sample of the skin on her breast and sent it away to pathology for an examination.

A few days later, Karen received an urgent phone call to come and see Dr Lorenzen and once again, both of us booked an appointment to see him at his surgery. The second time we visited him he was very formal and came straight to the point.

"Karen, the biopsy shows that you have a form of breast cancer called Inflammatory Breast Cancer. It is a rare form of breast cancer that only affects a small percentage of the population. It's not surprising your GP did not pick it up straight away, as it's such an unusual form of breast cancer."

My heart stopped in my chest.

He went onto explain the nature of Inflammatory Breast Cancer, or IBC as it's called, and the fact that it blocks the lymph vessels in the skin of the breast and that can cause the whole breast to become inflamed.

Both of us were in shock as we sat there in stony silence. Dr Lorenzen recommended that Karen start chemotherapy straight away, but gave us no satisfying prognosis.

What followed was a very difficult period as Karen felt as

though she had been hit by a sledgehammer. In the weeks that followed, we both walked around like zombies as the thought of Karen not surviving was too much for both of us to cope with.

Karen had to stop work while she was going through chemotherapy as she started to lose her hair and suffer from the side effects such as nausea and tiredness. It was the biggest test that our relationship had ever been through, as it had both knocked us for six.

Some nights we would just sit at the dinner table and not say anything to each other as the situation had us totally perplexed. We felt it was slowly strangling us, and despite Karen's job as a nurse, we did not know how to talk about it openly to each other.

We spent Christmas of 2000 at *Shiloh* and although it was spent with family and friends, Karen's illness had set a dark scene upon us. The celebrations lacked the festive spirit of years gone by.

In early February of 2001, after Karen had been on chemotherapy for a couple of months, I suggested we both take *Bella Donna* down to Southwest Arm for a fish. We had not done anything normal like that since she had been diagnosed with breast cancer and I felt that it would do us both the world of good.

It was a beautiful weekday and I had taken some time off work to look after Karen. The sun was shining as we motored up the river, eventually anchoring the boat in the cove about halfway up Southwest Arm. The early morning sun was shining and the faintest of north east winds was blowing across the water. There was nobody else on the river, and it was a very tranquil setting—just us and nature. I was fishing towards the back of the boat with my back to Karen and she was up the front. We weren't talking as we were both deep in thought.

Suddenly, Karen broke the silence with her familiar, calm voice. "Ed, I've done a lot of thinking lately."

"What is it, Kaz?" I said, turning towards her.

She gave me a serious look. "I've come to terms with the fact that I'll die from this illness."

I froze in my seat, not able to speak. Her words had numbed me.

Karen went on to tell me that she had had a premonition that she would die at a young age. It had happened when she was nursing Nancy. She told me that Nancy's courage and the wisdom she displayed during her own predicament had been a great source of strength for her and she had learnt much from the experience.

There was total silence as the realisation hit me that there would absolutely come a day when she would no longer be with me. With everything I had been through in my life, the thought of losing her was too much for me. The tears started to well up in my eyes and I buried my head in my hands and wept openly.

I felt Karen's hand on my shoulder and when I turned around she embraced me, holding me as tight as she could in her weakened state.

"I don't want to lose you, Karen," I said through muffled tears.

"Nor do I want to lose you, Ed, but death is part of life," she said calmly, as she stroked the back of my head. I wondered how many times she had given that speech to patients and their families.

"I love you so much, Karen, you're the best thing that has ever happened to me."

"And I love you too, Ed. But I need you to be strong for me," she whispered. "I need you."

Karen kissed me and as we embraced, we both let out the flood of emotions that had been trapped while we'd walked around in fear and confusion. After a while, we looked at each other and smiled, and it was as though a weight had been lifted off our shoulders. Both of us felt a new sense of freedom had come over us.

This episode was the catalyst that our relationship needed to be rejuvenated, for in accepting the fact that Karen would eventually die, it set us both free. There was no need to skirt around the issue anymore and we were both able to talk about it openly from that moment on. In doing this, our feelings and emotions were totally open to each other.

I had long known that acceptance was the answer to my problems. It was by being totally open to the reality of Karen's condition that both of us were able to get on with our lives.

"The attitude is the father to the action," Karen said to me one day.

I stared at her amazed. "It is indeed, Kaz. What has prompted you to say this?"

"You often quote the saying that Fr Casey once gave you, Ed. I have thought about this a lot lately, Ed. It means a lot to me," said Karen.

Karen had always had her faith and gone to mass every Sunday. She believed in the philosophy of doing to others what you would have them do to you. Not only did she believe it, she lived it. She had always understood her own mortality and believed that one day she would be meet her maker, but with the circumstances she now faced it became a lot more pertinent.

"As a nurse I've been around death all of my working life, Ed. I accept that my time will come just as yours will come," she said philosophically.

Karen's pragmatic attitude to her own mortality was a great source of strength to me for it taught me a lot about myself.

I sought great solace through the fellowship of AA during this period—it gave me strength. Karen gained strength from her Catholic faith, but I didn't want to burden her with all of my fears. AA was where I did that. Karen released her burden in church. She often said to me, "You've got to have a healthy relationship with the man upstairs otherwise life is a pretty shallow existence." And that wasn't all, she would also say to me, "Nothing else you say counts if you can't speak with love, Ed."

Karen didn't so much talk about spirituality, but lived it by her example. But at no time did you ever get the impression that Karen was holier than thou, for although she had a strong faith, she was a fun girl who knew how to party and lived life to the full, regardless of her present circumstances.

I learnt a lot from Karen over the years with regards to my own spirituality, but none more so as when she became sick.

"Let's say we both suck the marrow out of life and live each day as though it was a our last, for whatever time we have left together, Ed," she said.

"You always manage to put a positive spin on things, Karen," I said with a smile.

Karen smiled. "I'd rather go out doing what I want to do than moping and groping through each day."

"I think that's the perfect way to live our lives, Kaz," I said.

Karen's upbeat attitude coincided with the both of us spending more time with Frank Casey. We had always had him around for dinner, but his presence took on a new meaning for the both of us. It was never a depressive gathering when he was over at *Shiloh* for we were open about Karen's condition. Frank was a great source of strength to the both of us, with his wisdom and advice guiding us through this difficult situation. There was always much laughter when he was over, and plenty of tears too. We talked about death openly with Frank. Karen and I came to see with his help that death was a part of life, and the only difference between the living and the dead was that they were in different dimensions.

As a consequence of our knew found philosophy, our relationship grew to another level. We both discovered little hidden treasures about each other. Karen, although sick, could still look beautiful even with a bandana wrapped around her head. She really rose to the occasion during her illness. She was a shining example to all those who knew her on how to carry oneself with courage and dignity.

I talked to Rowy a lot during this period about what Karen was going through and he offered me sound advice. Rowy, like a lot of people from the bush, had a very philosophical view on life. Other than his secondary schooling, he had never attained any tertiary qualifications but his intelligence and wisdom was something I paid attention to.

"You just got to play the cards your dealt, Ed, and make every moment count with that beautiful wife of yours. You never know when your time is up, so live every day like it's your last," he said to me one day when we were fishing.

Karen had her down days, especially when she was sick, but she never felt sorry for herself. She was going to fight for as long as possible. After she got through her first treatment of chemotherapy, she went back to work on a part-time basis. It was amazing to see so many of the staff at St Vincent's rally around her. It was as though it was her reward for the years and years she had spent caring for those around her. There was always somebody on hand from the hospital when we needed them.

Karen and I started spending more and more time together and would sneak away for a day's drive down to Kangaroo Valley or up to the Blue Mountains. We also spent time with those who were closest to us at *Shiloh*, their friendship taking on a greater depth. Fiona was still Karen's particular favourite, and Karen's sisters also spent considerable amounts of time with us.

I loved every moment of it.

Meanwhile, my business had gone from strength to strength and as a consequence, our financial situation looked healthy. Somedays I would scratch myself on the back of the head and marvel about where I had ended up, especially considering how deep into the mire I had once sunk.

Meanwhile, Rowy had bought a five acre block in the new industrial area of Taren Point and moved his business over there. He built a new premises on the block which included a big workshop with office space upstairs. As a consequence, I moved my business from the little workshop into Rowy's old site in Waratah Street, as I had outgrown my existing premises.

In mid 2002, Karen and I bought a 200 acre property named *Goodgidgee*, which was 30 kilometres from Mittagong on the Wombeyan Caves road. The property was only just down the road from the Rowe's, and was mainly undulating cattle country. It was nestled on the Wollondilly River and it became a marvelous retreat for both of us, as well as for family and friends.

The house was rundown and I spent time refurbishing the interior. Rowy and Luke helped me with the renovations and when it was finished, it came up an absolute treat.

The homestead had wide verandahs and four bedrooms with a large open fireplace in the lounge area. The house had been the main homestead for the original property, which was much larger than the present acreage.

Karen used her time there to rest. She became easily tired the longer her illness went on, but she somehow found the energy to turn the once-dilapidated gardens at the front of the house into a beautiful showcase of native plants and landscaped areas. I did all the heavy manual work which included extensive landscaping while she organised the design, ably assisted by Fiona, who by this stage had blossomed into a beautiful young woman and started nursing at Sutherland hospital.

I did some improvements on the fencing and bought 50 Hereford calves to fatten up. They did well, as there was plenty of feed on the ground.

By late 2002, Karen had perked up and her once beautiful brown hair was growing back, even though she looked a little spiky on top.

We spent Christmas at home and then headed to *Goodgidgee* where we spent a couple of weeks. It had appeared that Karen's extensive chemotherapy may have beaten the cancer for she had seemingly recovered and gained a new lease on life.

Then, in early 2003, she had a bad turn and after a visit to her oncologist he booked her in to have a mastectomy of her right breast, as well as lymph node surgery at St Vincent's. After surgery, Karen went through extensive radiation treatment which made her extremely tired for a few months afterwards.

Karen recovered from this last treatment and came home to recuperate. She had stopped working by this stage and accepted that her squash days were behind her. I became her carer from this moment on, and I was ably assisted by Julie, Fiona, Anne and the Monaghan girls.

Once again, Karen surprised everybody by coming good and everybody was astounded by her fighting spirit. When she was well enough she was up and about, organising more landscape designs for the gardens at Goodgidgee.

We got to work and together created a magnificent landscaped garden area for the remainder of the yard. Karen designed sandstone pathways that led to a beautiful outside BBQ area which was surrounded by an assortment of native shrubs and climbing plants like jasmine.

"When my time is up, Ed, I want this garden to be my legacy," she said to me one day while we were both working in the yard. I was perpetually stunned by her ability to just keep on fighting. She was such an inspiration during this period.

When we got back to the city, she started to spend a lot more time with Frank Casey. His counsel gave her great strength. Karen's example only made me a stronger man, as I felt my own spirit uplifted by her great courage and poise. She went through her daily trials and tribulations without ever complaining.

In the middle of 2003, Karen was asked by the principal of St Vincent's at Potts Point to give a talk on her illness to raise awareness of breast cancer in younger women. Being an ex-student and always willing to give back, she didn't hesitate in offering her time.

Karen spoke about the disease and how she was dealing with it by looking after herself physically, mentally and spiritually. She later told me that she only meant to speak for fifteen minutes, but ended up speaking for an hour. Karen told me she was met with generous applause by both the staff and students.

After the talk, she was having a cup of tea when she was introduced to a number of the staff members.

That night when we were having dinner, she told me about one of the history teachers she was introduced to. Apparently, she was a striking looking woman with strawberry blonde hair in her late twenties, and was called Michelle.

As soon as she said that, my ears perked up.

Karen told me that while speaking to this woman that she felt a great affinity with her as though she knew her. She said she had the most beautiful blue eyes and lovely smile, and was very much interested in what Karen had to say and asked her many questions. At the time she thought to herself that it might have been my Michelle, but didn't want to pry.

When Karen was leaving, Michelle lent across and kissed Karen on the cheek. "You're a very beautiful woman and a true inspiration to all of us, Karen."

Karen knew then that the woman was Michelle Costigan, and just had to ask.

Michelle looked at Karen for some time before answering. "I am and I know who you are too, Karen."

Karen had smiled and said, "I just want you to know that Ed loves you very much and he feels a great deal of remorse as to how he treated both you and your mother."

"Thank you, Karen," she had said. "I appreciate that, but I need you to know that Dad's drinking destroyed Mum and me. It still pains me to think about those days."

Karen had replied, "I understand, Michelle, but if you want to ever reconcile with your father, he would love to see you again. He is a lovely man, and very different to the man you once knew."

Michelle smiled at Karen and while she held her by the

hand she said, "I appreciate that, but it's been so long since I've seen Dad that he'd feel like a total stranger to me. Mum and I got on with our lives after he left and meeting him after all these years would feel very awkward for me."

"I understand. I'll leave it in your hands. After all time is a great healer," Karen said.

Michelle nodded and said on a lighter note, "Aunty Anne has kept me abreast of all the going's on over the years. I've seen your wedding photos. You looked absolutely beautiful."

"Oh, thank you! It was the most special day of my life and your Dad absolutely gleamed that day," she said with a smile.

"She told me all about *Shiloh* too," Michelle added. "It looks like a wonderful place surrounded by the bush and the water."

Karen nodded. "We are very lucky to be able to live there."

The two of them continued to talk over the next half hour, and it was only the fact that Michelle had a class that ended their conversation. Karen said they had such a great rapport.

When Karen told me the story at the dinner table, I was filled with a desire to get in contact Michelle immediately. "You know, Kaz, I should get in contact."

Karen gently put her hand on my hand and said, "Just let things be for the time being, Ed. It would be best to live and let live as there has been a lot of hurt there. Let Michelle make the decision if she wanted to reconcile with you. Remember what Frank has always said."

I was downhearted. "I suppose you're right, Kaz. It would be difficult for Michelle if I just contacted her out of the blue after all these years. After all, she was always a sensitive kid and there must be a lot she is still dirty about."

"I think that's a wise decision, Ed," Karen said, rubbing my hand.

Over the next six months, Karen was to give a number of talks at St Vincent's about how she was progressing with her illness and each time she was met with applause.

She spoke again with Michelle and they exchanged phone numbers and caught up for coffee on a number of occasions, although I was never invited. Karen felt as though she was acting as an intermediary between Michelle and me. Although she never indicated she was interested in meeting up, Karen, with the lifelong help of Anne, was smoothing the way for a much hoped-for reconciliation one day. Karen was well aware that a lot of damage had been done, and the hurt caused by my drinking, was irretrievable. In saying that, the strong bond that was growing between Michelle and her were positive signs that one day she may want to meet me.

***

"It wasn't till Karen explained to me the look in Michelle's eyes that day that my memory was taken back to all those years ago. It brought back memories of one of my drunken rampages," I said to Tim. "She used to look at me with such fear and loathing."

Tim fidgeted in his seat, he looked uneasy. Perhaps someone had once looked at him like that too.

"I was lucky to be blessed with two great wives in my life, Tim. Kim and Karen. Kim was a top girl and I stuffed that up big time, but be buggered if I was going to destroy my marriage to Karen. I worked hard to make ours a good marriage because I knew the carnage I had left behind the first time around. I wasn't perfect but I did my best. I guess that's when I finally realised that I had no right to expect Michelle to come waltzing back into my life after what I had put Kim and her through."

"Kids don't forget that stuff," Tim said quietly, and I knew now he was thinking of his own home. He was still young enough to have it fresh in his mind.

"Too right, son," I told him. "What gave me solace was that Michelle was at least talking to Karen and Anne, too. She knew I wanted to see her, so all I had to do was wait, but at least she had the support of the family. At least she was still connected."

Tim nodded. "I guess. Did Karen's condition pick up?"

I gave him a rueful look.

***

In November of 2004, Karen went back into St Vincent's where she was diagnosed with brain metastasis. Karen went through more radiation treatment, and after a long period of time in the hospital she asked to come home again.

Karen had built up a very close bond with Foo and one of the reasons she wanted to be home was so she could be close to her favourite pooch. I am no dog psychologist, but I firmly believe canines have a highly tuned sensory function about them. They can sense friendliness and fear in humans and they can detect illness too.

Foo knew that things weren't right with Karen. When she was sitting on the lounge he liked nothing more than to lay beside her with his head on Karen's lap. Karen took great solace in this and it gave her a great source of contentment to have Foo constantly by her side.

Fiona was a great source of strength also. At 20, she had grown into a beautiful young woman who was mid-way through studying nursing. She spent heaps of time with Karen and theirs was a very special friendship that paralleled a mother-daughter relationship. The two of them would spend hours chatting away, mainly on Fiona's hopes for the future, all while Foo sat nearby. Julie was often down from the main dwelling too, doing what she could to make things easier for us both, and both Bob and Luke were great support.

It was difficult to watch at times, Karen and Fiona, for I was seeing something that Karen should have had with a daughter of her own. On top of that was the fact that it brought up memories of Michelle and what should have been but for my drinking. As much as I had come to terms with much of my past, I could still not shake the guilt I felt for the way I had treated both Kim and Michelle. I could only hope that some time in the future the door would be opened and I could see my daughter again.

Anne also spent a lot of time with Karen. Their friendship was a great source of strength to Karen, who regarded Anne as a confidante of her innermost thoughts and feelings.

We had slowed right down by the time she came home that last time, and were only making the occasional visit to our property down at Wombeyan Caves as Karen was becoming increasingly tired. She had given up work completely and although she knew this was the reality of where her illness had taken her, it still pained her as she loved her career so much.

Christmas of 2004 was a special occasion at *Shiloh* with many friends and relatives popping in during the festive season. It was a true indication of how special Karen was to so many people and how much she was loved. As much as Karen was exhausted, she was very moved by everyone's best wishes and made the effort to get involved. Secretly, it affected her deeply.

When we were by ourselves, Karen indicated on a number

of occasions that when her time came I should spend more time at *Goodgidgee*. "You've worked hard all your life, Ed, and it's time you spent a bit more of your time relaxing," she said to me one day.

"You know me, Kaz. I am not the type to be sitting around twiddling my thumbs all day. I've got to be doing something."

"You can still do the things you love and relax at the same time. There's a lot of work to be done at *Goodgidgee* and you love it when you're down on the farm."

I gave her a sad look. "I can't imagine being at *Goodgidgee* without you, Karen. So much of the gardens remind of you."

"Then everytime you look at one of the native trees we've planted, you'll be reminded of me, Ed!"

"I just hope your here a bit longer to share *Goodgidgee* with me."

She gripped my hand as tight as she was able. "There's nothing more I would love, Ed, but my fate is out of my hands."

Karen and I looked at each other and smiled. No words could accurately portray the love we felt for each other.

"You're a good man, Ed Costigan, and when my time comes, you'll be well and truly looked after."

I kissed Karen on the forehead. "You always know how to say the right thing, Kaz."

By early February of 2005, Karen had become severely ill, but was determined that *Shiloh* was where she wanted to be when she died. In those last weeks I spent some of the most precious moments that I had ever spent with her. We reminisced about the past and all the experiences we had shared together. We spoke about my future and Karen contemplated the afterlife and what it could be.

"I don't know exactly what it is, Ed, but if it's something akin to the love I've shared with you then I'll be happy," she said to me one day.

She was calm and knew that the end was near, but kept a grace about her at all times. Many of her family and friends visited her to give her comfort, but it was they who felt the most comfort after seeing her.

Frank Casey gave her the sacrament for the dying on the morning of the 14th of February 2005. It was a Monday morning and she was surrounded by her immediate family including her parents and brothers and sisters. Bob and Julie Rowe, Fiona, and Anne and Bill were with her until midday.

At nightfall, everyone was outside in the lounge-room and I was with Karen in the bedroom. Beside our bed was a bunch of roses in a vase I had given her that morning for Valentine's Day. Foo was lying on her bed with his head resting on her stomach. Karen was very weak, but she could talk and as Foo lay there she gently stroked him behind his ears.

"You're such a lovely dog, Foo," she said.

Foo wagged his tail and looked up at Karen with melancholy eyes.

"Dogs are such lovely animals, Ed," she murmured. "They bring so much joy into one's life."

"They are very special, Kaz," I said stroking Foo on the head.

Karen continued to pat Foo on the head and she smiled. After a few minutes she looked at me with her serene brown eyes and said. "I'd love to hang on a bit longer, Ed, but I'm afraid I'm just too weak to do so."

"You do what is best for you, Karen," I said in a calm voice while I held her hand.

Her voice was very strained and she was breathing heavily. It was an effort for her to talk.

"You don't know how happy you've made me, Ed Costigan," Karen said in a laboured tone.

The tears started to roll down my cheeks.

"You're such a fine, strong man with so many good qualities, Ed."

I shook my head, but could not speak for I was too full of emotion.

"You've been through so much in your life and showed great courage to overcome your adversities. You taught me so much about my life. It's been a beautiful journey with you." She had such love in her eyes.

"You coloured my life in, Karen," I said through tears. "My years spent with you have been the happiest of my life."

Karen raised her hand and stroked me on my cheek. "You're a very funny man, Ed. You've made me laugh so much over the years," she said with the faintest of smiles.

I laughed softly and Karen gave a strained chuckle before coughing.

She did not speak for some time, and then she finally said in a calm and clear voice with her head slightly raised off her pillow. "Remember, when I pass over I am only a conversation away. My memory will be on every breath of wind that you feel," she said before closing her eyes.

They were the last words that Karen ever spoke to me.

I lay down beside her in the bed with my upper body supported by two pillows and continued to hold her hand. The night went on, and eventually I went to sleep.

It was just past 11.00 pm when Foo's whimpering woke me from my slumber.

"What's wrong Foo-boy?" I said.

Foo had jumped on the bed, and he nudged Karen on her chest with his nose, as he continued to whimper.

"You okay, Foo?"

I then looked at Karen and she had a look of tranquility on her face as she lay on her back. There was total silence and I could not hear her breathing. I sat upright.

"Karen?"

There was no response. I felt for a pulse. Nothing.

Julie and Bob Rowe were asleep on the lounge next door, having stayed for the night.

"Jules! Quick! Come in here, please."

Julie was in the room in seconds and could see that I had a look of concern in my face.

"It's Karen, she's stopped breathing," I said urgently.

Julie checked Karen's pulse and her face fell. "There's nothing there, Ed."

"Nothing there?" I echoed, my words barely audible.

Julie didn't really need to say anything, her face said it all. "I'm sorry, Ed, but Karen's passed over."

I was shocked into silence, my head spinning around at a rate of knots as Julie embraced me.

"She's passed over?" I repeated, like I hadn't understood.

"Yes, Ed, I'm afraid she's gone," Julie said. Tears fell down her face and she pulled me in tight.

Rowy then entered the room and wrapped his arm around my shoulder. He said nothing, but he didn't have to. His gesture was enough to convey his feelings.

The three of us sat in the bedroom while we waited for the doctor to arrive. Nothing was said between us—we were too deep in thought and full of grief.

Foo lay on the bed with his head on Karen's chest continuing to look up for any sign of life. His whimpering never ceased.

The doctor arrived just before midnight and pronounced Karen dead. I felt totally numb and could not express my feelings at all. I was used to death and had seen plenty of it on the battlefield, but this was like nothing I had experienced before.

Rowy, Julie and I sat together for the remainder of the night in my lounge-room and drank tea. Eventually, I went to sleep as the sun was rising, and Rowy and Julie caught *The Rocket* up to their house to bed. My sleep was intimately broken as the enormity of my loss was brought home to me.

The days that followed just after Karen's death were like a daze for me. I would never want to relive that period again. It was though I went through an out of body experience. It did not seem as though I was functioning as a normal human as I ghosted about the house.

Then, I was granted a lifeline from my grief-stricken state. Fiona, who was deep in bereavement herself, had deliberately not come down to *Shiloh* in the days that followed Karen's death as she felt I needed time alone to grieve.

It was late on the Wednesday afternoon, a couple of days after Karen had passed away that Fiona knocked on the door of *Shiloh*. In her hands was a container of freshly made chicken and vegetable soup which she had made herself. Fiona wore a look of stoicism as I approached the door and on greeting her she drew a deep breath and said, "Aunty Karen always said that a warm bowl of freshly made chicken and vegetable soap works wonders when you're down."

Fiona had every intention of coming down to *Shiloh* to give me support through my bereavement. As soon as she had uttered Karen's name though the reality of her own bereavement hit her like a ton of bricks and the flood gates opened for her.

"Oh, Uncle Ed, I miss her so much." Fiona cried, almost dropping the container of soup at my feet.

"Come here, sweetie," I said, as I retrieved the soup and held her tight while consoling her.

"I'll never forget her, Uncle Ed. She was such a beautiful woman," Fiona said, weeping quietly.

"I know, sweetie. Yours was a very special bond," I said as I hugged her.

Fiona was to cry many tears of grief in the weeks and months that followed Karen's passing, but she always maintained that it was the sorrow that she expressed at *Shiloh* that Wednesday afternoon that was the most cathartic experience of her bereavement over Karen.

In a strange twist, it was Fiona's deep bereavement in the days leading up to Karen's funeral and my subsequent consoling her that helped me through much of my sorrow. It was through comforting Fiona that I was able to forget about my own sadness. Her youth and beautiful nature allowed me to see how much she was hurting and this gave me the ability to focus on her own sorrow rather than mine.

It dawned on me that Karen's relationship with Fiona was on a parallel to mine with Stumpy. It helped me understand the close bond the two of them as Karen had been a mentor and confidant to Fiona just as Stumpy had been to me.

Fiona proved to be a blessing in the days leading up to Karen's funeral and she helped me prepare a beautiful send off for her. As well as Fiona, I was lucky for the constant stream of friends and relatives who came to see me. They gave me great comfort and keep me occupied, and as a result it stopped me from going into a deep depression.

On the day of the funeral at Our Lady of Fatima Church at Caringbah, Fiona accompanied me into the church with her arm wrapped around my waist. All of our close friends and relatives who knew the close bond that existed between Fiona and Karen saw it as only fitting that she should be with me on the day of the funeral.

Frank, who was now retired and living in a unit at Cronulla, celebrated the requiem mass and a beautiful eulogy was given by Karen's father, Joe, which touched everyone present.

I had managed to hold myself together until Karen's sister Sophie closed the service with one of Karen's favourite songs. She sung the *Quiet Land of Erin* while playing acoustic guitar. This is a traditional Celtic song, sung by Sandy Denny, and it was one of Karen's favourites.

The tears streamed down my face, and many of those gathered in the church, it was brought home that the song highlighted all that was beautiful about Karen.

At the wake afterwards, which surprisingly was a very upbeat gathering as it was a celebration of Karen's life, it was Sophie's rendition of this song more than any other part of the mass which captured the imagination of those who were gathered that day.

As much as my consoling of Fiona helped me through my initial stages of sorrow, I was not immune to grief and when it hit me, it hit me hard.

Karen had been the love of my life and although we had our disagreements like any marriage does, we loved and respected one another and this transcended our annoyances towards each other. I wasn't always easy to live with as my alcoholic nature could be a challenge, but Karen's compassionate and caring nature was able to see through my foibles to the better side of my nature.

Karen once said to me in a coy manner, "Did you ever think of taking out a lady in AA before I met you, Ed?"

To which I responded plainly, "One nutcase in the household is bad enough let alone two, Kaz!"

Karen threw her head back and laughed before saying, "Oh, how cruel, Mr Costigan."

As much as that statement may seem rough, I knew that living with an alcoholic must not have been easy for Karen and it was for this reason that I loved her so much because she allowed for my defects of character. I had always thought I was a lucky man to have landed such a classy woman but it was my sensitivity and caring nature that attracted me to Karen.

The period that followed Karen's funeral was very lonely for me. My bed and my heart were empty. There were nights when I would roll over in bed and expect to feel Karen lying beside me, only to come to the awful realisation that she was no longer there. I would sit up in bed and shake my head to see if I was dreaming. But for my faith and my friends, I don't know how I would have got through.

The two people in my life who stuck to me like glue were Frank and Rowy. Whenever I needed either of them, they were there for me and Rowy especially would sit and talk with me into the wee hours of the morning. That's what I classify as a true friend. Not necessarily somebody who has all the answers, but rather somebody who will sit and just listen.

I'd like to say that the situation improved, but the fact of the matter was that it only got worse. Some people handle it better than others, but my grief was a deep well. I had lost my soul mate. I had lost my zest for life which included my favourite pastime of fishing. I didn't even bother to take *Bella Donna* out on the river.

I managed to go back to work, but all my passion for that had disappeared also. I couldn't have cared less if my whole business disintegrated into dust. I had no desire to work. I was just going through the motions of turning up and clocking off at the end of the day. Fortunately for me, Luke Rowe steered the ship ably, assisted by my loyal mechanic Jimmy Fraser, and my ever dutiful secretary, Barbara.

I stayed in this state for months and nothing that anyone said or did could break me out of my situation. That was, until I received a letter from Frank one day.

At the beginning of July of 2005, four months after Karen's death, I arrived home from work late one afternoon and opened a letter which had been posted to me from Frank.

Dear Ed,

I have taken the liberty of writing you this short note as I regard you as one of my closest friends and I realise your grief at the loss of Karen is overwhelming.

In the years that I have known you, I have come to realise that you are in, colloquial terms, 'made of the right stuff' and it is this among many of your other fine qualities that have drawn so many people towards you. It was these unique qualities that Karen could see in you long before you could see it in yourself.

None of us can fully understand death and the

passing of our loved ones, while the pain can ultimately only be tamed by our faith. It is with this belief that you must accept that Karen is in a better place and that her passing is only temporary and that one day, God willing, you will be reunited.

I know that Karen had accepted her situation and that ultimately, she would have not wanted for you to be in your present state.

Ed, I urge you to gather your resolve and to pick yourself up, as Karen would have wanted you to live again with the exuberance that you were meant to live with. You have too much to offer to those who can benefit from your life's experiences to be wasting your days in sorrow.

In closing, Ed, do not mourn too long lest you mourn for yourself.

Your close friend,

Frank C

The contents of the letter were the catalyst for a new beginning for me and I pondered on the contents of Frank's letter till the small hours of the morning.

The next morning I was still deep in thought and in no mood for work. I decided to take *Bella Donna* out for the first time since Karen's death. It was a very cold winter's morning and a thick fog covered Yowie Bay and the Port Hacking River all the way over to the Royal National Park.

As I travelled over to South West Arm I reflected on my

life with Karen, and I smiled as I thought about the many great times we shared together in *Bella Donna*.

Eventually, I motored into the little cove which was situated about half way down the Arm and which was a favourite spot for Karen and me to relax and talk. It was totally calm and there was not a ripple on the water or a breath of wind. On the shore I could see a deer feeding on the green pickings close by the water. I anchored the boat and sat in silence for some time before I pulled out the letter that Frank had sent me. As I read the words out aloud, Frank's message became more apparent. When I was finished reading, I was overcome with a grief that made me ache with a pain that came from the very depths of my being. It burst out of me in a flood of tears that felt as though they had been dammed for eternity.

I sat back in the boat and watched the fog start to lift. A beautiful, warm winter's sun broke through and it was shining on my face. I was overcome with a realisation, or a truth, for want of a better word, that I had never experienced before. It was as though I had been given a new state of consciousness in which I had never possessed before and everything in my life came into order.

The first realisation I had was that it was a miracle that I had ever met Karen in the first place. I contemplated on where my alcoholism had taken me, and but for the intervention of Frank I would have been doomed.

Here I was complaining about the fact that Karen had been taken from me, when I realised that I was a lucky man to have even spent one day with her, let alone eighteen of the best years of my life.

I was then filled with gratitude that this beautiful woman had come into my life, and more importantly, I was hit with my second realisation: *she* had chosen me. I'd transformed from a sorry sod into a man worth loving. I mattered to Karen. She chose me.

I suddenly became aware of Karen's presence and felt as though she was very close to me. I could hear her laugh and see her smile and the frosty look she would give me when I annoyed her.

By this stage the fog had completely lifted and it exposed a cloudless blue sky where the early morning sun shone down upon me. I lay back in the boat and let the sun shine down on my face. After a while I went to sleep and when I awoke half an hour later, I felt totally refreshed.

I was overcome with a new feeling of enthusiasm and so I lifted the anchor on *Bella Donna* and made my way back home.

When I arrived back at *Shiloh*, I looked at my house and saw it was a pigsty with dirty dishes throughout the kitchen and dust everywhere.

"Do you think Karen would be pleased if she saw the state the house is in?" I said to myself.

I spent the best part of the day cleaning my house and when I was finished it sparkled. I then drove down to South Cronulla to see Frank.

When I arrived, Frank was sitting in the sun on the verandah of his unit reading a book. After he made a cup of tea for the both of us, we talked for a number of hours about the contents of his letter. I thanked him for his words and how they had broken me out of my deep state of bereavement.

The next day I went back to work with Frank's words fresh in my mind and a new outlook on life. I became determined to pick myself up as I believed that's what Karen would have expected of me. As a result of my new-found attitude, a number of amazing events took place shortly after.

Not long after my epiphany at South West Arm, I received a pink envelope in the mail one day. Inside was a bereavement card and although the words written on it were brief, they were powerful, a beautiful tonic to help me through my grieving.

Dear Dad,

I'm sorry to hear about Karen passing away. I had the opportunity to meet her on quite a few occasions and found her to be a very beautiful person. Her lovely nature and kindness were attributes which attracted me to her.

I hope that the passage of time will heal your loss.

Please accept my sincere condolences,

Yours sincerely,

Michelle Costigan

Although Michelle had not come to Karen's funeral, she had been kept abreast of all that had happened through Anne.

I later learned that it was Anne who had advised Michelle to send the condolence card after she had asked my sister for advice as whether or not to send one. Michelle felt that because she had ignored me for so many years that I would not appreciate her contacting me. It was only after Anne insisted that Michelle send the card that she realised how appreciative I would be of her gesture.

"It may just heal a lot of wounds," Anne told me she had said to Michelle.

"There has been a lot of hurt, Aunty Anne, there's no denying it, but it may be what's needed to build a bridge to try to reconcile with Dad," Michelle had replied.

After I received the card, I penned a short note which included my phone number, thanking Michelle her for the card and a wish that she would call me whenever she liked.

It was about a week after I sent the letter to Michelle that I received a phone call.

"Dad, it's Michelle," she said, hesitantly.

My heart nearly burst out of my chest.

"Hi, there, Shelley! How you doing, love?" I said to her casually, like I had been talking to only five minutes before. I tried to reign in my enthusiasm. I didn't want to press too heavily and scare her off, but my girl was smart.

Michelle laughed. "You always were very casual, Dad."

"Well, there's no flies on me, girl!" I said with a chuckle.

"That's what you use to say to me when I was a little girl. Boy, it used to crack me up," Michelle said with a little laugh, but she then got serious. "I just wanted to repeat my condolences, Dad. Karen was a lovely lady."

"That she was, love, and I'm glad you got the chance to know her," I told her.

We talked for about ten minutes, mainly about Karen's funeral, before I tentatively invited her to *Shiloh*. "What about you come down to *Shiloh* for some lunch this Sunday? I can show you around while we chew the fat some more."

She laughed. "I haven't heard that saying for years. Yes, that would be nice," Michelle said.

I wanted her to feel comfortable, so I added, "I'll give Annie a tingle to see if she can make it also."

"That would be nice if Aunty Anne could join us," agreed Michelle.

"Just the three of us. It will be nice and cozy."

"Okay, that'll be great."

***

I sat there looking at Tim with glistening eyes.

"It sounds as though it was a momentous moment in your life," Tim said. He was looking a little teary himself.

"I tell you, Tim. I can't begin to tell you how happy I was to speak to my little girl after all those years," I said with a grin as wide as an ocean.

Tim smiled.

"I'd dreamed of that moment for years. Just to hear her voice was pure magic and to think I was going to meet her made me both exited and apprehensive."

Tim shuffled in his seat. "So, how did the lunch go?"

I rapped my fingers across the table. "It was great, just great! Nothing could have prepared me for the joy I felt at seeing my daughter after so many years."

***

The following Sunday I prepared a nice butt of pork on the BBQ with some roast potatoes to accompany it. Anne had said she was going to make a salad while Michelle had promised to bring a surprise desert.

As much as our initial conversation on the phone had been a casual affair, easing the tension between us, nothing could have prepared me for the emotion of our first meeting.

It was bang on midday and I was turning the pork on the

BBQ when I heard Foo let out a bark. I walked around to the side of *Shiloh* to see *The Rocket* making its way down the steep incline to the bottom.

Over the years I had seen *The Rocket* descend that incline on countless occasions. It was just a normal, everyday routine, but this day my eyes were glued to the small carriage and I felt as though I was waiting for a visit from the royal family.

My palms were sweaty and my heart pounded as I waited for my long overdue reconciliation with my one and only daughter.

Foo ran up to *The Rocket,* barking, and seeing Anne, he immediately wagged his tail.

"Hello, Fooey darling. How are you?" Anne said, patting him on the head.

Then Michelle came into sight and after patting Foo, she then focussed her attention on me.

Although it had now been 23 years since I had last seen her, I instantly recognised her. Anne had showed me photos of Michelle over the years, but nothing could have prepared me for the sight of my daughter all grown-up. Michelle had grown into a beautiful young woman in her early thirties, who had a striking resemblance to her mother with her strawberry blonde hair and slim build.

We both stood there staring at each other. I was struck dumb, shocked into silence that the moment had finally arrived after all these years. All that could be heard was the wind blowing through the trees. Annie, good old intuitive Annie, kept well back, giving us the space.

The silence between us became eerie, and just when I couldn't handle it any longer, Michelle said, "Hi, Dad."

My mouth was so dry I couldn't speak. Eventually the

words came out. "Hi, Michelle. It's so good to see you, sweetie. You look absolutely beautiful."

Michelle smiled and as she did I stepped forward and kissed her on the cheek, and she responded by wrapping her arms around me and hugging me tightly. I dropped all pretense of nonchalance and held her for all I was worth. My daughter! After so long, my little girl was back.

We held each other tightly for some time, and I couldn't hold back any more. "I'm sorry for everything, Michelle."

Michelle dug her head into my chest and said, "That's okay, Dad. It's just so good to see you again after so many years."

When we finished embracing, Michelle stood back from me and inspected me up and down. "You look so healthy and relaxed, Dad. Especially compared to what you use to be."

I smiled. "Thanks, Shelley. A lot of water has passed under the bridge since the last time we saw each other."

"Indeed it has," she said.

Anne decided it was time to lighten the situation and said, "Okay, how about I fix us some drinks!"

"Great idea, Annie," I smiled.

We talked for about half an hour before the three of us sat down for lunch. I felt there would be a more appropriate time for Michelle and I to talk in depth about the past, so I kept the conversation light. We spoke about *Shiloh* and I was interested in all that Michelle had to tell me about what she had been up to over the years, while Anne chimed in with all the latest news about the goings on with our family.

When we finished lunch, Michelle presented us a beautiful pavlova which she had made. On top were generous amounts of cream, strawberries and passionfruit.

"Shelley, my favourite!" I exclaimed.

"Mum used to always make you a pavlova with plenty of strawberries and passionfruit. I've never forgotten it was your favourite."

"You've got a good memory, Shelley." I laughed.

On hearing me call her by her abbreviated name, Michelle broke into a huge smile which warmed my heart.

After devouring a number of slices of the delicious pavlova with ice cream, I showed Michelle around *Shiloh* and told her about all the improvements that Karen and I had done to the dwelling over the years. Michelle showed great interest and asked me many questions about the little home and its Tuscan colours. The afternoon flew by and it was approaching dark when we were down on the on the pontoon and I was showing Michelle *Bella Donna*.

"Perhaps when we have a nice day, I can take you out on the boat?"

"Yes, that would be lovely, Dad."

We hugged and said our goodbyes, and as much as it had been a beautiful afternoon and gone off without a hitch, I knew that Michelle and I had much more to talk about. I felt that a day out on *Bella Donna* would be a good way for Michelle and I to talk in depth, as Karen and I had always found a trip on the boat a great way to discuss any issues we needed to air between us.

In the days that followed my meeting with Michelle, I felt a great peace come over me. Our reconciliation helped fill a great void that had been left with Karen's passing.

The opportunity to make restitution to Michelle came towards the end of July 2005, a few weeks after my initial meeting with her. The day was sunny as we set out from *Shiloh* and up the Port Hacking River. Although there was a light south-west breeze blowing, which put a nip in the air, we were able to find a protected area on the shore up North West Arm where Michelle set down a picnic rug. She'd made a beautiful picnic lunch which automatically put me at ease for it reminded of Karen's culinary delights which were synonymous with our trips in *Bella Donna*.

As we tucked into a roast chicken with a salad that Michelle had prepared, we opened up to each other about what had happened in the years we had been estranged. We spoke at depth about my time in Vietnam, which Michelle knew very little about. So little in fact, that she didn't even realise I had been wounded in battle.

Michelle spoke directly to me about the pain my drinking had brought to her and Kim and that they had felt the effects of it years after they left me. She told me about her stepdad Paul, who had died in 2003 of prostate cancer, and then showed me a recent photo of Kim, who still looked great. I told Michelle that I would like to make amends to Kim and she said that after Paul's death she had mellowed and would be more approachable now. It gave me hope that some time in the near future I might be able to reconcile with her.

Michelle and I spent the best part of the afternoon together and when we were about to come back in *Bella Donna,* she hugged me and it was a hug that was full of warmth. A warmth that I had been yearning after for years.

Reconciling with my daughter rejuvenated my life, for although I had lost the love of my life in Karen, I had found another one and that was priceless.

None of this would have been possible without Anne, who through her incredibly close bond with Michelle throughout the years had been the catalyst for our reunion. It had been Anne's cool mind, like she had always shown at the card table, which treaded the tricky waters with Michelle and through her negotiating skills, managed to help reestablish our relationship.

Michelle invited me over to her unit at Clovelly one night for dinner where she introduced me to her partner, Greg Foley, who was a science teacher at St Vincent's. Greg was a good bloke whose amiable nature Michelle was attracted to.

I was able to re-introduce Michelle to the Rowes who she had not seen since she was a girl. In particular, she was happy to meet Fiona Rowe and they quickly struck up a friendship after she realised how important she'd been to both Karen and me. I invited Michelle and Greg to a number of BBQs at *Shiloh* where they was able to get more acquainted with the Rowes. They liked Michelle and immediately took her under their wing, treating her like family.

It was September of 2005 when Michelle invited me out to dinner one Saturday night a Thai restaurant in Cronulla. It was a small affair with only Michelle, Greg, Anne, Bill, Fiona and myself there.

After we finished our meals, I went to the bar to order some drinks and Greg followed me over. "Ed, I was wondering if I could have a quiet word with you?"

"Yeah, mate, what is it?"

"I've planned to propose to Michelle this evening, and with you being her father, I feel it only right and proper that I ask for your permission."

I stood there stunned, trying to gather my thoughts before I answered. "I feel very honoured that you should be asking me, Greg. The fact is I have been off the scene for so long that I really have no say in it. It's quite obvious the two of you are very happy together, so I have no problems in giving you my blessing."

"Thanks, Ed, I appreciate that. I just felt it was the right thing to do," he said with a smile.

"No worries, mate, just look after her will you. She's my pride and joy."

"That I will, Ed," he said and we shook hands.

After we had finished our coffee, Greg stood up tapped his glass with a fork and the restaurant went silent.

"Eighteen months ago, this beautiful lady seated beside me came into my life. She is a woman of style, grace and beauty and I could think of no one else I would rather spend the rest of my life with. So with that in mind, I ask you, Michelle Erin Costigan, if you would you do me the honour and accept my hand in marriage?"

A hushed silence fell over the restaurant.

"Yes... yes, I accept!" Michelle gushed as she jumped up and kissed Greg on the lips.

With that, Greg produced a little blue box which contained a beautiful diamond ring and after fitting the ring to Michelle's finger, she held her hand up so the whole restaurant could see.

The gathered diners broke out in spontaneous applause and the staff produced a bottle of champagne on the house. I then kissed Michelle and shook Greg's hand and wished them the very best for the future.

For me it was a wonderful occasion and it only furthered my appreciation for my daughter returning to my life. As I sat back in my chair, savouring the moment, I contemplated how life had become worth living again. After losing Karen, I thought I would never lift myself out of the pit of despair I found myself in. Slowly, I had got myself back up again, in no small part to Michelle coming back into my life.

As the October long weekend of 2005 approached, Anne and Fiona suggested that we organise a party on the Saturday night in celebration of Karen's life. The Saturday night coincided with the anniversary of Karen and I first meeting eighteen years before on the October long weekend in 1987.

At first I was a bit hesitant about holding the party, as I thought I might revisit too many sad memories, but when the two of them insisted I put on a party I agreed. In the end, I was glad for as much as it was a great night it was also a celebration of Karen's life.

Sophie and Felicity Monaghan had some beautiful photographs of Karen blown up and placed them on the internal walls of *Shiloh*. There was one in particular which really captured my imagination and that was of Karen sitting back in *Bella Donna* with her hands outstretched while it was moored on the pontoon. For many of us gathered that night it was a chance to share our stories about her, and it came to be a very cathartic experience.

I invited Mum and all of my family, the Maroubra mob, Michelle and Greg, the Monaghans, the Rowes, and many of our friends. There were other whose lives had been touched by Karen who attended that night including Frank Casey, Sean O'Grady, Schooner Rooney, and many of Karen's work colleagues from St Vincent's Hospital, and her relatives and friends.

About halfway through the evening I gave a heartfelt speech to the guests. It was a speech that was not only a celebration of Karen's life, but it was a thank you to many of my friends and relatives who had seen me through such a difficult period of my life.

"Those who know me well, and that's most of the people who are gathered here tonight, you'll know that my path through life has been at times a precarious one," I began. "After miraculously escaping Vietnam with my life, I proceeded to slowly kill myself through drinking huge amounts of booze. In amongst all the carnage of those years, a great tragedy occurred that still casts a long shadow over my life today. I didn't think I could ever lift myself out of the pit of despair, but a number of people stuck fats during those years. They stopped me from going insane. Those people are here tonight. They include my good mate Bob Rowe who I served with in Vietnam, my cousin Sean O'Grady, and my beautiful sister, Anne Kennedy. I was lucky enough to meet an incredible man who passed a message of hope onto me that not only saved my life, but ultimately gave it back to me. That man is Fr Frank Casey who is also with us tonight.

"It was a message that at first seemed like a flimsy rope that I hung onto, expecting it to break at any moment. I hung onto it with blind faith and got on with my new-found life of sobriety, unsure and fearful of what was in store for me down the track. Then, out of the blue, through some act of serendipity, a beautiful woman came into my life. The photos of this wonderful lady, which her sisters have so beautifully prepared, adorn the walls of *Shiloh* tonight."

I looked at the crowd. They hung on my every word, and I could see that Anne had tears in her eyes. I smiled at her.

"Karen was the love of my life, my soulmate, my friend, my confidante and my lover." I cleared my throat, trying to keep back the emotion. "I spent the best years of my life with this beautiful woman and she not only helped to knock the rough edges off my character, but she also coloured my life in. We shared a life beyond my wildest dreams. Our entire married life was spent within the walls of *Shiloh,* which Karen turned from a house into a home. Most of you who are gathered here tonight have shared many enjoyable occasions here at *Shiloh* with Karen and I, and were witness to her generosity and humour."

I could see nods of agreement in the audience.

"Karen's passing has been a devastating blow to all of us who loved her. Out of this great tragedy though we can take hope by realising that Karen, if not here in person, is at least here in spirit. This evening is not so much a requiem for her life, but rather a celebration of it." I smiled at my friends and family. "I would like to thank so many of you gathered here tonight for your support during this difficult time. Words cannot adequately express my gratitude to you for how you have helped me during this period of my life. The passing of time is easing the blow of her passing, and she is with me every day in thought or prayer. The severity of her passing has been eased through all of your love, so if you could please be up standing, and charge your glasses. To Karen."

"Karen!" came the cry.

Well, you can imagine that my speech was met with rapturous applause. Rather than being a sad occasion it was one of happiness. Many people commented that they felt a connection with Karen that night, as her spirit shone brightly throughout *Shiloh.*

I had always been close to the Monaghans and my relationship with them after Karen's death become even more stronger. Sunday lunch at their place became a regular part of my weekly calendar and it was often a time when everyone could open up and talk freely about how Karen's loss had affected them. Michelle and Greg accompanied me on a number of occasions for lunch and the Monaghans fell in love with them too.

Karen's death had affected her dad Joe, in particular, for she had always been his pride and joy and he found talking to me very helpful. Joe and I started to spend a lot of time together and often took *Bella Donna* out onto the Port Hacking fishing where we would often share stories of Karen's life.

It was a wonderful night in the end, with the Rowes the final guests to leave as the sun was coming up. I looked out into the distance onto the Port Hacking River as the early morning light glistened on the water. I remembered back to all those beautiful times Karen and I had spent in *Bella Donna* and I was overcome with a great feeling of warmth and love for my beautiful dark-haired woman.

Chapter 18

I GLANCED AT MY watch and saw it was almost 7.00 pm. I had been talking solidly for the best part of five hours, and the inside of the caravan was beginning to look gloomy as the sun had started to go down.

Tim was shaking his head, his face ashen at the intensity of it all, when I suddenly remembered the envelope sitting in the back pocket of my moleskins. That initial shock I felt this morning, the one big unspoken thing that had kept me there all day, beyond my need to help the kid, was begging to be revealed. I felt that now was the time to read the letter to Tim.

I pulled the envelope out of my pocket and placed it on the table. "I received this letter in the mail a couple of days ago and I want to read it to you."

Tim looked from the envelope to me and shrugged. He had no idea what it was.

I took the letter out from the envelope and cleared my throat.

Dear Mr Costigan,

There was a time when writing this letter would have seemed inconceivable for me, but a lot has happened in the ensuing years and I have been able to view the events of that tragic day in a more objective light.

When you ran into our car, seriously injuring me and killing my daughter Alison in your truck in Dubbo, all those years ago, I felt as though my whole life had been taken from me. In fact, I hated you so much that I had planned to kill you when you were released from jail. I had the whole thing meticulously organised.

It was my daughter who convinced me that there is no sense in the philosophy of 'an eye for an eye', and it would only turn me into a common murderer and what value would I be to my family if I was serving a life sentence?

It was another set of tragic circumstances which led me to my current state of consciousness and ultimately, to my ability to forgive you for your actions all those years ago.

My mother was a patient at St Vincent's Hospice in Darlinghurst. Her name was Nancy Finnegan. It was your late wife Karen who nursed her through the worst days of her breast cancer. I used to regularly visit my mother in the palliative care unit and when I found out that Karen was your wife, I bitterly resented her.

Karen never disclosed to you my mother's true identity and in the last days of her life, Karen confided in me that she would take that secret to her grave as she thought it might upset you too much.

Karen was a truly unique person though and as much as I resented her at first, it was impossible for me to sustain these feelings of ill will towards her. Karen had one of the most beautiful natures I have ever come across. In time I grew to like her and ultimately love her, and my mum absolutely adored her.

It was Karen's loving attention to my mother that made her last days on this earth so much more bearable and our family will always be in her debt. I know that Mum's death affected Karen greatly and this has prompted me to write this letter.

It was through Karen's help that I was able to come to terms with Alison's death and I was able to find out more about you.

Karen told me about your Vietnam experiences and the horror you went through and your subsequent treatment when you arrived home. My brother was also a Vietnam veteran and we were very close growing up, but he came home from Vietnam a shattered man and never talked about the war. He soon took to the bottle and after we had a huge argument one night over his drinking we became estranged and were never reconciled, as he was killed in a motor car accident near Wee Waa when he was drunk. Karen helped me come to terms with the fact that you were not so much a bad person but a sick person, and that you did not intentionally set out to harm Alison. In saying this, it was a shocking mistake on your part to behind the wheel of a truck in the alcohol-induced state you were in.

I came to believe that a beautiful woman like Karen would not have decided to spend the rest of her life with a man who was all bad, and that she must have made a wise choice in choosing you as her husband.

Karen's death was a devastating blow to me as I regularly kept in contact with her, and when I was in Sydney we would often catch up for a coffee.

Ultimately, it was her death that helped me come to believe that hatred only kills those who hate, and that I had spent many years in a state of resentment towards you which had cost me my own peace of mind.

Ed, I wish to sincerely convey my condolences, as do my family, over Karen's passing. I would also like to say that I forgive you for the past as I know you have suffered enough.

You were an extremely lucky man to have been married to such a beautiful woman and we are all the poorer for her passing.

I wish you the best for the future.

Yours sincerely,

Jenny Mitchell

There was a long silence. Tim had a wild look about him. He was beginning to understand.

"You can imagine how shocked I was when I read the contents of this letter," I told him. "I had planned to read it to Rowy this afternoon, but as fate should have it I ran into you. I never knew, not even for a second, that old Nancy, Karen's favourite patient, that her last name was 'Finnegan'."

Tim was ashen-faced.

"It was only then, only when I got this letter that I realised that Nancy was Finno's mum."

Tim said faintly, "My mum once told me that Dad had a sister named Jenny who lived in Dubbo, but I never knew her as Dad and her didn't talk." He looked up at me in astonishment.

"Well, I figure that you've obviously solved this puzzle, because if the man killed at Wee Waa was your father, then that makes Jenny your aunty. Nancy Finnegan was then your..." I prompted.

"Grandmother!" Tim blurted out. He went white like he had just seen a ghost.

I gave him a reassuring smile. "Absolutely, Tim. That lady my beautiful wife nursed in her dying days was your grandmother."

Tim was lost for words. All the wind had been taken out of his sails.

I sighed heavily. "That also makes Alison Mitchell your first cousin."

Tim looked away and ran his hand across his face in disbelief. It was a lot for him to take in.

"What did Stumpy use to say to me?" I ventured. "There are too many coincidences to be coincidences in this life. Looks like you and I are connected more than we could have ever imagined, Tim."

The young man said nothing, so I went in for the knockout punch.

"Look, Tim, if you want to stuff your life up that's your business, but take this lesson to heart. There has been enough grief in both yours and my family over the years," I told him gently. "To add the catastrophe of your life to the equation is more than most families can handle. How about you wise up, for all our sakes? Get fairdinkum and sort yourself out."

Just then, I noticed a message on my mobile phone, so I

excused myself and went outside the caravan to retrieve it. It was Michelle, reminding me that we had planned to meet up for dinner that night so I quickly rang her back and organised to meet her down at South Cronulla at 8.00 pm.

When I returned, Tim had not moved. He still looked ashen-faced, but it was time for me to go.

"I'm off, mate, dinner with the daughter. I'll be here to pick you up at 6.30 am sharp on Monday morning."

Tim look confused. "What?"

I grinned. "Don't you remember, sunshine? You've got some work to do before you get out of debt. See you then."

I walked out the door of the caravan and was 20 metres away when I heard Tim's voice.

"Hey, Ed!"

"Yeah?" I said, walking back towards him.

"Karen," he said seriously.

"What about her?" I said.

"You're a lucky man to have had such a beautiful lady in your life. I can only hope that I get to meet somebody like that one day," he confessed.

I walked back towards the caravan and smiled. "She was a rare diamond scattered in among a cluster of rocks."

Tim smiled back at me, stuck his hand out and I shook it firmly. "From little things, big things grow."

I smiled at him and said, "If you're serious, I'll help you get your life back on track," I told him. "For your family—and in memory of your dad, the man who saved my life—but mostly, for you. You're worth it, mate."

***

I drove to South Cronulla and parked my car in Roker Street

where Michelle was already waiting for me at Greg's unit. She raced over to me and gave me a big hug.

"Great to see you, Dad! How's your day been?"

"Very interesting, Michelle, very interesting to say the least," I told her, drawing her in close.

"That's great, Dad, you can tell me all about it later. Now, let me tell you all about my wedding dress. Mum's been to Sydney and we've picked out this beautiful gown that is an absolute treat," she said in an excited voice.

I wrapped my arm around Michelle's waist and kissed her on the top of the head as we walked down Elizabeth Place, leading onto the Promenade and Cronulla Point.

"You're a treat, Michelle," I said with a grin as big as a Cheshire cat.

"Oh, Dad, you'll just die when you see this wedding gown Mum and I have picked. It's perfect."

When we reached Cronulla Point, Michelle was still going on about the wedding plans. "Greg and I aren't sure if we'll invite 150 guests or 140. Whatever the case, it's going to a great occasion. Party of the year."

As Michelle chatted away, I was preoccupied with the view over Bate Bay to the north where I could see the area known as Greenhills. The last of the sun was going down as Michelle looked at me and said, "Are you listening, Dad?"

"Yeah, I'm still listening, sweetie," I told her, as I drifted off into my own thoughts. Tim wandered back into my mind. I had a feeling that good things were going to come from him.

There was a lovely light nor-easter breeze blowing and I was overcome with a great sense of gratitude about all the good things that had happened in my life.

"I'll make sure I look after your boy for you, Finno, if it's the last thing I do," I said to myself, as I walked arm in arm with my daughter.

***

The Maoris were sorted early in the morning. They shook their heads in disbelief that I should be wasting my time on what they perceived to be a total loser.

Tim started the long haul working off his debt that Monday morning by washing the Mack tow truck. Over the next week I had him doing a multitude of things around the workshop which kept him busy. I soon figured out that Tim was a pretty handy sort of bloke to have around and that he had a few smarts about him. Coming from the bush, he'd been knocking around machinery most of his life and had a natural aptitude towards things of a mechanical nature.

Within a week I'd moved him out of the caravan park and set him up in the little self-contained room I had at the back of the workshop. It was no Buckingham Palace, but it got him out of that pigsty caravan he was living in, and more importantly it was a fresh start.

I started taking him to regular AA meetings with me where I introduced him to Frank. He was a bit wary of Frank at first, being a priest and whatnot, but soon warmed up to him after he realised he wasn't going to push the bible down his throat.

Within four months he had paid off his debt and I put him on as a casual where he soon became an invaluable member of the team. He saved enough money to buy a good digital camera and set up a dark room off to the side of the workshop to work with film. He told me that what he really wanted to do was to work as a freelance photographer and I told him he could work for me while he got himself established.

He'd come down to *Shiloh* once a week for a feed where I introduced him to both Rowy and Julie. He took to Rowy straight away like most people did and Julie mothered him incessantly.

Although Tim battled in those early days with the temptation to drink he remained sober that first year and became a regular at AA meetings. He realised very early in the piece that he was a shot duck if he thought he could handle his sobriety by himself. He did have a couple of blowouts on the pokies though and I once found him in a club up at Sutherland shoving coins into the machine like it was going out of fashion. I knew he had been travelling a bit rough and followed him to the club one afternoon from work.

He got the shock of his life when I walked up behind him and whispered in his ear, "Swapping the witch for the bitch are you, Tim?"

He nearly shit himself when he spun around in his seat and saw me standing behind him.

"What are you doing here?" he demanded.

"Keeping an eye on you, sunshine."

Tim glared at me and it was a look I hadn't seen from him since that first fateful day when we had met some eight months previous.

"It's a dead end street that will lead you nowhere, Tim," I told him, and I saw him fold. We went to a meeting that very night and he never gambled after that day. In fact, he has remained free of the grog and the punt right up to the present.

There hasn't been a day go by that I haven't thought about Karen and although I miss her I eventually got over the worst of my bereavement. My natural optimistic attitude kicked in after a while and I started to live life to the full once again. I knew Karen would not of expected anything less from me, and besides, like she said, she was only a conversation away whenever I needed to make contact with her. Some may think that's strange but it works for me and that's all that counts.

Anyway, in time Tim started to kick his own goals and it became one of the most enjoyable experiences of my life to see him grow as human being. From the angry young man I first encountered that day in the caravan, he became to a well-rounded human being with a healthy perspective on life.

I had the pleasure of walking my beautiful daughter down the aisle in the autumn of 2006 and over the next few years she presented me with two beautiful grandchildren who have become the apple of my eye and call me 'Granddaddy'. I felt very blessed that this beautiful young woman had come back into my life and given me so much joy.

Greg and I soon became good mates and we used to regularly take *Bella Donna* out fishing, and like so many friendships, it was cemented with a rod in one's hand while sitting in a boat.

Tim moved into his own unit at Caringbah after twelve months and then cupid's arrow struck about twelve months after that. The Rowes were having their Christmas party in early December of 2007. The Monaghans were all there alongside a cast of other friends, and Anne had brought a nurse from St Vincent's with her. Her name was Clare, she was in her mid-twenties and was a beautiful girl with dark hair and gorgeous eyes. Clare hailed from Gundagai originally, and as fate would have it, Tim and her fell in love.

Eight months down the track they got married and over the next few years a couple of kids followed and they also call me Granddaddy. Tim insisted I be their surrogate grandfather as Finno was gone. Our relationship had developed to such an extent that I finally felt like I had the son I always wanted.

When not working for me, Tim travelled to remote areas taking photographs for 4WD and adventure magazines. In late 2010, he hit the jackpot. The Australian War Memorial offered him the position as official war artist for Australian personnel serving in a number of key provinces in Afghanistan. Tim spent four months attached to a number of Australian military units photographing their experiences. It was a landmark piece of work and although Tim missed Clare and the kids while he was away, the experience was a watershed moment in his life that was to have a profound experience on him.

Tim arrived back in Australia and his photographs were displayed in the Australian War Memorial in Canberra to an overwhelming response from the public. He was awarded the prestigious Bayeux War Correspondence Prize and began to get international recognition for his work.

Tim and Clare bought a house in Caringbah and he set up his own photography studio at home. He now divides his time between working at home and long-term assignments in the field, which has also included spending time in remote indigenous communities in Arnhem land. This also led him to exploring new artistic mediums and making a documentary on the one of Australia's last great wilderness areas—the Buccaneer Archipelago off the Kimberley Coast in Western Australia.

I did get to meet up with Kim just before Greg and Michelle's marriage, and although it was difficult, I was able to make my amends to her. What happened after that is best told at another time, for the outcome was totally unexpected.

As for me, following my success with Tim, I've spent a

considerable amount of time doing volunteer work for Frank's organisation by helping disadvantaged youth find employment.

My life has been a heavy load at times, but it has made me who I am today. I have learnt that it can be easier to share the burden rather than bear it alone. Karen, Tim, Stumpy, Annie, Mum, Rowy, Julie, Fiona, Luke, Kim, and even Nana O'Grady and Aunty to name a few—those souls have made me what I am now. They gave me life so I could help give it back to others. And I *will* give back until the day I die.

After all, it's what Fr Frank Casey has often said to me over the years…

"You have to give in this life to receive."

Author's Note

While I've tried to be as accurate as possible with the details—I used some of my personal experiences to bring Ed to life and researched the rest—please just be aware that this book is a work of fiction. I love a ripping yarn, and even though they say that 'truth is stranger than fiction', sometimes fiction is just so much more satisfying.

Case in point; if you're wondering about the magnificent 'Droving into the Light' by Hans Heysen, you'll actually find it in the Art Gallery of Western Australia at the time of publication.

Acknowledgements

Thank you to those who helped me with this book. Your time, information and assistance was invaluable, as was your encouragement and support.

Lyndsay Moynham (2 RAR/NZ), Ray Day (2RAR), Lenny Howell (1RAR), Doug English (3 RAR) The Vietnam Veterans Federation of Australia (Granville), John Mackenzie (Eumungerie), Kurt Johannsen, Warren Buntine, Rod Pilon (Rod Pilon Transport Dubbo), Donny Smith, Leon Cooper, Karl Gye, Jack Shields, Garry Byrnes, Sharon Wiley – St Vincent's Hospital (Sydney), Jenny Baynham – St Vincent's Hospital (Sydney), Van Wallace, Brad Wallace, Don Munro, Bill Hession, Northern Rivers Writers Centre, Lisa Hanrahan – Rockpool Publishing.

And a very special thank you to Rebecca Wylie from Sage Written Word. Without her mentorship, guidance and faith in me, the writing of this novel would not have been possible. To you, my dear lady, I owe a great debt of gratitude.

About the Author

S.E. Nethery was born in Sydney, the seventh child of a seventh child of a seventh child. He has written numerous newspaper articles on his travel experiences and has a love of war history and rural travel. He's been to many remote destinations, including Kokoda, and was in Gallipoli for the 100 year Anzac Day anniversary. *Heavy Load* is his first fiction novel, with more to come.

S.E. Nethery lives in the Northern Rivers region of New South Wales, Australia.

Feedback

If you enjoyed *Heavy Load* please consider leaving a review. Your support and encouragement is what helps authors to continue creating their art, and gives other readers an idea of what to expect from the story.

Also, feel free to drop me a line or find me on social media.

Facebook: S.E. Nethery - Author

Website: www.senethery.com

Email: stephen.nethery@bigpond.com

Thank you!